THE AVENGER
A MEDIEVAL ROMANCE

BY KATHRYN LE VEQUE

THE BLACKCHURCH GUILD:
SHADOW KNIGHTS SERIES

England's most elite training guild.
Knights of the highest order.
Numquam dedite. Never surrender.

THE HISTORY OF THE BLACKCHURCH GUILD

St. Giles de Bottreaux was a knight who had been disgraced for using unconventional tactics. Having served the Duke of Normandy, he was present at the Battle of Hastings. Unfortunately, he caught wind of a Norman lord who was about to betray the duke, and he tortured the lord to gain valuable information about the Saxon resistance.

He was vilified for it.

St. Giles was released from the duke's service because the rebel Norman was both a rich man and a distant cousin of the duke's. With no means of income, St. Giles and his brother, St. Lyon, wandered England, unable to find a suitable position. In desperation, they were forced to become part of a Saxon pirate group out of Watermouth, Devon.

Realizing that piracy was lucrative and putting their knightly skills to good use, the brothers quickly rose in the ranks and ended up commanding their own ships. St. Giles eventually formed his own pirate crew with the help of his brother, men known as Triton's Hellions. Their ships were the *Argos*, the *Mt. Pelion*, the *Pagasa*, and the *Athena*. St. Giles' specialty was in recruiting disgraced knights and giving them a new and rich career. Those knights began training other knights for a life of piracy at an abandoned church on the shores of Lake Cocytus in the Exmoor Forest. The place was called "Blackchurch" because it was a black, burned-out shell of a former sanctuary.

But such a place, hidden from the world, was a perfect staging ground for a warriors' guild.

More trained men meant more ships and more wealth. The pirate ships sailed the known world, bringing back men as well as treasure. As the years passed, those same ships brought diverse warriors from all over the world to the shores of Devon. While St. Giles settled in to manage their growing empire in the Exmoor Forest, St. Lyon assumed the pirate enterprise. All of the trained warriors he brought to Blackchurch combined with other elite trainers to create the most complex and comprehensive battle-training system in the world.

England, who had always dismissed Blackchurch as a pirate training ground, gradually became aware of the quality of those who had completed the course. They were the best-educated warriors in the world. The Earl of Wessex was the first to come to St. Giles and ask him for some of the fine men he'd trained. Soon, fully trained knights with good reputations began asking for admission to the training grounds to learn the "Blackchurch way" of life and warfare. It became lucrative and prestigious. St. Giles' grandson, St. Andrew de Bottreaux, was granted the title Earl of Exmoor by Henry I because St. Andrew gifted the king with an elite group of specialized knights who saved the king on more than one occasion. Soon, the Crown got behind this extraordinary training ground.

Blackchurch's reputation was cemented.

These days, Blackchurch is far less about piracy and far more about training the most coveted and skilled warriors the world has ever seen. Men and women are accepted as long as they are qualified and can pass the entrance test. Every trainer has a specialty—new classes of recruits are formed monthly from qualified applicants from all over the world, and each group of recruits spends at least six months with every trainer. To pay for their training, they either pay the fee once they pass the entrance test or they pledge a portion of their salary once they graduate and find a position. Training is harsh and intense. It is expected that even out of the vetted recruits, most will fail. Those few who succeed become forever known as Shadow Knights, a coveted title denoting their superior status.

As graduates say, you simply don't survive Blackchurch.

You *become* Blackchurch.

THE FAMILY TREE OF DE BOTTREAUX AND THE TRAINERS OF BLACKCHURCH

De Bottreaux tree (Lords of Exmoor, who run Blackchurch):

St. Giles b. 1040 – was part of the conquest of 1066, died 1100. Brother, St. Lyon, served with him as a pirate, and it is St. Lyon's descendants who continue to run the pirate conglomerate known as Triton's Hellions. Now run by St. Abelard de Bottreaux.

St. Simon b. 1070 – d. 1135

St. Andrew b. 1094 – d. 1160

St. Paul b. 1119 – d. 1195

St. Denis b. 1147

St. Denis has two sons—St. Gerard (died 1212) and St. Sebastian, a.k.a. "Sebo," b. 1171 and 1173 respectively. Both trained at Kenilworth and Warwick Castle. Veterans of the Third Crusade.

Note: When informally addressing or using the given name in conversation (i.e., "St. Denis" or "St. Paul"), the "Saint" is dropped and the given name is simply used (Denis or Paul).

Current list of primary trainers (moniker is listed after ancestry):

Tay Munro (Scottish/Greek) – The Leviathan – Teaches endurance, physical fitness, structure, and discipline. He's the boot camp, the gateway to the rest of the training.

Sinclair "Sin" de Reyne (Norman) – The Swordsman – Sword training, warfare, military history, how to command an army, etc.

Fox de Merest (Norman/Saxon) – The Protector – Teaches men how to defend and kill using daggers and other weapons. He's the "MacGyver" of Blackchurch. His class is about defense and thinking outside of the box.

Payne Matheson (Scottish) – The Tempest – Teaches offense. Instructs men on how to size up enemies and figure out their weaknesses. How to fight battles from the ground up.

Kristian Heldane (Dane) – The Viking – He is seabound. Everything he does is on water—fighting on water, instruction on boats, etc.

Creston de Royans (Norman) – The Avenger – Interrogation, treatment of the enemy, anything underhanded. How to handle torture and difficult conditions. (Sometimes works in tandem with The Conquistador)

Aamir ibn Rashid (Egyptian) – The North Star – Military history (global) and tactics from other armies. Understanding different cultures and how that dictates their fighting techniques.

Cruz Mediana de Aragón (Spanish) – The Conquistador – Conquest and diplomacy, politics, and the art of negotiation. Bribes, coercion, and leverage. (Sometimes works in tandem with The Avenger)

Ming Tang – (Chinese) – The Dragon – Former Shaolin monk.

Name means "bright water." Fighting kung fu, using hands, feet, and staff only. Fighting with the mind and not a weapon. Meditation for a warrior to calm the mind and the spirit.

Bowen de Bermingham (Norman/Irish) – The Titan – Warrior etiquette and responsibilities, discipline, hand-to-hand combat, using the landscape/land to one's advantage, living off the land, concealment, stealth. Sometimes works in tandem with The Leviathan and The Tempest.

Assistants (second-level trainers assisting the first level):

Axton Summerlin (*The Protector* and *The Swordsman*) A trainer eventually known as **The Medusa**.

Anteaus de Bourne (*The Swordsman* and *The Tempest*) A trainer eventually known as **The Eagle**. Promoted to full trainer in *The Avenger*, assisting Creston de Royans/The Avenger with his classes because of the earldom Creston inherited. Creston has property to manage and splits the classes with Anteaus.

Rhodes St. James (*The Avenger*) A trainer eventually known as **The Centurion**.

Therron and Torr de Allington (*The Leviathan*) Brothers who trained at Kenilworth, moved into assistant trainer positions for The Leviathan when Bowen moved to a full-time trainer.

Pirate Factions (mostly centered around Cornwall and Devon coastlines, or the Irish Sea):

Triton's Hellions: Led by St. Abelard de Bottreaux, based in Minehead, control most of the northern Cornwall and the Devon coast.

Demons of the Sea: Led by Santiago de Fernandez, based at Fremington, Cornwall and also at Lastres, Castilian coast.

Medusa's Disciples: Led by "Bloody Maude" Kilkenny Matheson of Coll Island in *The Tempest*, now merged with Demons of the Sea.

Kraken's Horde: Irish faction mentioned in *The Swordsman* out of Dublin.

The Sea God/Titans of the Deep: Aragon pirates with bases in Tarragona, Palma, Ibiza.

The usual schedule/order of training for a dreg/recruit through Blackchurch's 5-year course and a recap of what they are taught:

Tay – Teaches endurance, physical fitness, structure, and discipline. He's the boot camp, the gateway to the rest of the training.

Bowen – Warrior etiquette and responsibilities, discipline, hand-to-hand combat, using the landscape/land to one's advantage, living off the land, concealment, stealth. Sometimes works in tandem with The Leviathan and The Tempest.

Sinclair – Sword training, warfare, military history, how to command an army, etc.

Fox – Teaches men how to defend and kill using daggers and other weapons. He's the "MacGyver" of Blackchurch. His class is about defense and thinking outside of the box.

Payne – Teaches offense. Instructs men on how to size up enemies and figure out their weaknesses. How to fight battles from the ground up.

Kristian – He is seabound. Everything he does is on water— fighting on water, instruction on boats, etc.

Aamir – The North Star – Military history (global) and tactics from other armies. Understanding different cultures and how that dictates their fighting techniques.

Cruz – The Conquistador – Conquest and diplomacy, politics, and the art of negotiation. Bribes, coercion, and leverage. (Sometimes works in tandem with The Avenger and The North Star)

Creston – Interrogation, treatment of the enemy, anything underhanded. How to handle torture and difficult conditions. (Sometimes works in tandem with The Conquistador)

Ming Tang – Former Shaolin monk. Name means "bright water." Fighting kung fu, using hands, feet, and staff only. Fighting with the mind and not a weapon. Meditation for a warrior to calm the mind and the spirit.

Location Map for The Blackchurch Guild
Exmoor Forest, Devon, England

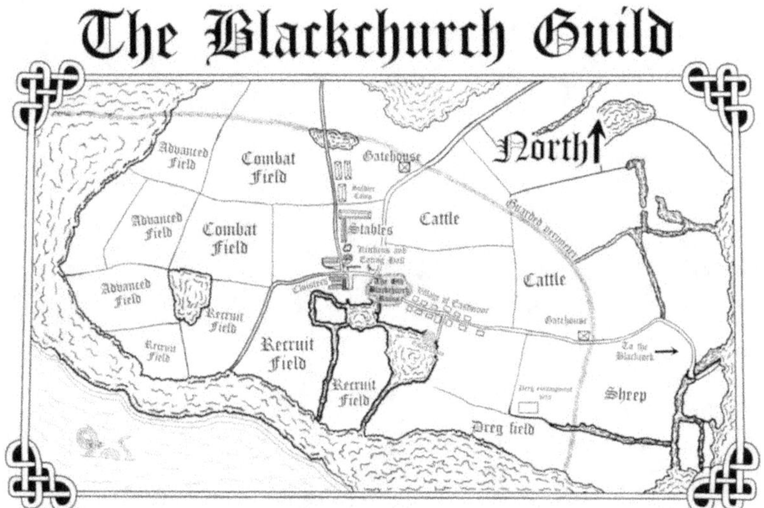

AUTHOR'S NOTE

And we're off on another Blackchurch adventure!

I will admit that Blackchurch has become one of my new favorite series, mostly because it's based on a very different premise. These guys aren't related by blood, but by camaraderie and loyalty to the institution they serve. They are also the most diverse group I write about, with each man from a very different background for the most part. I've discussed characters like Ming Tang in other books because readers ask "Is it really possible to have a Shaolin monk in England?" The answer is ABSOLUTELY!

Shaolin is Buddhism, and it has been around for well over a thousand years. The first temple was built around 495 A.D., so it predates the High Middle Ages by centuries. Is it possible that a monk found his way along the Silk Road to the Middle East, Europe, and beyond? Of course it is. There are warriors at Blackchurch from China, Egypt, Spain, and beyond. I think that makes it so much more "universal" in its teachings. As the saying goes, you can't make a soup with one ingredient. And you can't make a warrior with one point of view.

In this novel, we're focused on a de Royans, one of my favorite families. Creston de Royans is our Avenger. As noted in The History of Blackchurch page, he's responsible for teaching recruits interrogation tactics, treatment of the enemy, and anything underhanded. He's the "sly dog" of the group. He's also a de Royans, which means he's big and blond and looks like an archangel.

But packages can be deceiving.

We don't know much about Creston's background from other books, but we're going to find out here. How he came to Blackchurch and all. Honestly? He starts out as kind of a hot mess, and that's not usual with our heroes, but we discover he's really got a backstory that kind of messed him up a little.

Something else to note with the Blackchurch series—it runs concurrently to the Executioner Knights and also the Sons of de Lohr. They're all kind of happening around the same time. De Lohr takes up the first part of the thirteenth century, while the de Wolfe Pack starts around 1230 and takes up the rest of it—but there are other series running later in the century, too, like the Lords of Thunder. It seems that I'm very fond of the thirteenth century, which means I can do a lot of crossovers, as we're going to see with this book. Blackchurch and the Executioner Knights come together, which is very exciting!

The usual pronunciation guide:

I don't think I've ever made this clear, but St. Denis' name is not the Anglicized pronunciation—"Den-ISS." It's the French pronunciation—"Den-EE." St. Denis would actually be pronounced San Den-EE (and the French speakers know this one). Native English speakers/readers immediately go to the phonetic English pronunciation of "Saint Dennis"—but not in Medieval England!

Well, that was a short pronunciation guide. So, without further ado, get ready to meet The Avenger!

Happy Reading!

PROLOGUE

Year of Our Lord 1224
St. John the Baptist's Church
Symondsbury, Dorset, England

"H E'S NOT COMING."
She'd heard him.

Words coming forth from a cold man, colder still by the expression on his frozen face as he gazed steadily at her grandfather. He wouldn't even look at her mother or at the bride herself. That icy, calculating gaze was fixed upon Lord Oscar de Bulverton, Earl of Sidbury, as if willing the man into accepting his truth.

The truth that this marriage would never happen.

Even as Oscar looked at the man in disbelief, Randa, Lady de Camville, wasn't quite so controlled or so silent. She exploded out of her seat.

"What do you mean he's not coming?" she said. "He *must* come, Lord de Bosque. He has a bride awaiting him!"

Edward de Bosque looked at Lady de Camville, his gaze finally moving to her daughter. The young woman was dressed in pale green that brought out the green in her eyes, a delicate shade to indicate purity. She was a beautiful girl by anyone's standards, accomplished and articulate. Perhaps a bit too headstrong sometimes, but that was to be expected. She was a de Camville and everyone knew they had big mouths and a bold manner. Her father certainly had possessed those traits, and they had contributed to his unfortunate death. In fact, the family seemed to have very little good fortune as a whole.

Today was just another example of that.

The Curse of the de Camvilles.

"I realize he has a bride awaiting him," Edward said steadily. "You state the obvious, Lady de Camville. But I am here to tell you that my son is not coming. He departed for Glastonbury this morning from what I was told."

Randa's expression was twisted with incredulity. "You were *told*?" she said. "You do not know when your own son departed his home?"

Edward shook his head. "Nay, my lady," he said, eyeing de Bulverton as if wondering just when the man was going to let loose with a fist to his head. "I had my own duties this morning. I was informed by his manservant that he had departed for Glastonbury Abbey. Lady de Camville, it is no secret that a monastic life was his destination before he met your daughter. In the past year, I have watched him wrestle with it terribly. He wanted to serve God. But your daughter provided a… diversion. Clearly, it was not permanent."

Standing a few feet from his daughter in stunned silence, Oscar had had enough. He whirled on his daughter, pointing fingers at her. "I *told* you this was a mistake," he hissed. "I told you that this marriage was a folly, but you would not listen. You insisted it was for Lia's own good. Now look what you have done."

Randa was aghast. "What *I* have done?" she cried. "I've done nothing! This is not my fault!"

"It is your fault," Oscar snapped. "It is your fault for listening to your daughter and letting her dictate her future, and it is de Bosque's fault for forcing his son to do something he did not wish to do!"

Now, Edward was being attacked as well, which was what he had expected—and he was prepared. "Cecil is my heir," he said as calmly as he could. "I wanted what any father would want, what it is our right to want."

"A marriage your son did not want!"

"A marriage to continue our family legacy," Edward said, trying not to raise his voice. "Cecil understood this. He understood his role."

Oscar threw up his hands, and given that he was a big man with a big voice, that was saying something. He was intimidating in his anger. "He may have told you that he understood, but here we are," he said, throwing a finger in the direction of his granddaughter. "She is to be shamed now. Shamed by *your* son. What about Lia? Or do you not care about anyone other than your son?"

Somehow, the only person at the church who wasn't up in arms was, in fact, the bride. Lady Ophelia de Camville, known as Lia since infancy, watched her grandfather rage, her mother fall apart, and Edward de Bosque try to defend that which was indefensible.

A son who had left her standing at the altar.

On their wedding day.

But somehow… she wasn't surprised. As Ophelia watched the scene before her, strangely, she wasn't surprised in the least.

If there was anyone at fault, it was her.

Cecil de Bosque was a handsome man, one she'd known for many years. He'd fostered with her at Okehampton Castle, a strapping young knight who had been particularly pious. Not a day or minute or second went by that Cecil hadn't been praying one way or the other. He was more devoted to God than to the knighthood, though he was a decent knight. He was brave and bright. Ophelia had focused her attentions on him, flirted with him, and finally received the response she'd been hoping for even though rumor had it that Cecil was destined for the cloth. He made a yearly pilgrimage to Glastonbury, but Ophelia refused to believe that he was truly destined for the priesthood.

Not when he had her to be his willing life companion.

The Great Beauty of Dorset.

That was what Ophelia was referred to as. At Okehampton, they'd simply taken to calling her Beauty, something she detested, but it also gave her a lot of attention. Sometimes it was unwanted, but other times it was welcome, as it was with Cecil. Ophelia had started showing him some interest first and it wasn't until his fellow knights encouraged him that Cecil responded. Ophelia couldn't help but feel that he'd been pushed into it, something she'd vacated from her mind because it didn't do her pride any good to imagine the man she was fond of had to be forced into reciprocation.

But he had.

Ophelia knew it.

As her mother, father, and Edward argued over whose fault it was that Cecil had run from marriage, Ophelia simply sat down in the nearest chair. Everyone at the church was arguing or hissing or getting excited about the situation, and she knew the rumors would start flying quickly until her grandfather boomed to the people in attendance that if word got out, he would personally punish every one of them. Those in attendance were friends and relatives, on both sides, and even Ophelia knew that something of this magnitude couldn't be kept secret for long. Nor could the secret she carried in her belly.

The last-ditch effort to force Cecil de Bosque into matrimony.

That had been a folly.

"Come, Lia." Her mother was suddenly by her side, grasping her by the arm and pulling her from the chair. "We are leaving."

Ophelia did as she was told. She let her mother pull her out into the morning of a fresh new day, out to the waiting horses that were gaily bedecked with flowers. It was July, after all, and the land was awash with blooms. One of her mother's men helped her onto her white palfrey, but before she could get away, Edward stopped her.

"My lady," he said softly. "Truly, I am sorry for this. Cecil should not have done this to you."

Ophelia had come to know Edward de Bosque as a truly kind man. She smiled weakly at him.

"You are not responsible for his actions," she said. "But I must tell you that I am not surprised by any of this. He was destined for the church when I met him. I was but a slight delay."

Edward sighed heavily. "He should have been honest with you from the start," he said. "Cecil has wanted to be a priest his entire life. He should not have entered into an agreement with you, knowing that. I suppose I am to blame for pushing him into… Well, it does not matter. He has made his decision. We shall simply have to accept it."

"*You* can accept it," Oscar said, having just exited the

church. "Know that this insult will not stand, de Bosque. I will make sure the priests at Glastonbury know what your son has done. Let us see, then, if they accept him into their commune. No one will want a man who breaks his promises."

Edward knew he had no defense for his son. "Please," he begged quietly. "Do not punish him for what were my actions. I forced this on him, I swear it. I will give you money as compensation for the loss. I have several fine horses I will give you also. But please… do not make trouble for my son. He is tortured as it is."

Ophelia was off her horse, coming to Edward's rescue by putting her hands on her grandfather's arm, pulling him away. "He is right," she said. "If anyone should be upset about this, it should be me, but I even I understand that Cecil loved the church before he ever loved me. You cannot fault a man for making a choice that is best suited for him."

Oscar looked at her incredulously. "You defend him?"

"I understand him."

"And you are not troubled by this situation?"

Ophelia tried not to let her emotions show, as was usual with her. Emotions only showed her weaknesses. "Of course I am," she said. "I am very troubled by it. But I love Cecil enough that I want him to be happy. I thought I could make him happy, but it seems it is not to be. I tried. God knows, I tried. But even I cannot compete with a lifelong dream, Grandpapa."

Oscar wasn't the least bit moved by her speech. "So you simply intend to accept what he has done to you?"

"Is there a choice?" Ophelia said, rather strongly. "I cannot compete with the lure of the church and you cannot fight them, so we are at an end. Cecil has made his decision and it is not me."

Oscar didn't have an argument for that. Truth be told, he was angry at the humiliation, but not the act itself. He was actually quite relieved, but he wasn't going to let on. Edward owed him something for this debacle and he was going to collect.

"Our family's dishonor is worth something," he said, looking to Cecil's resigned father. "Lia's dowry was to be eighty gold crowns. I want that from you to compensate us for this... this horror, and I will not go to the church and tell them what I think of a man who very much wants to be a priest. Do you understand?"

Edward did. He nodded wearily and turned away, heading back into the crowd of flabbergasted guests and trying to calm everyone down and convince them to return to his home, where food and drink would be waiting. He wanted to get away from Oscar as fast as he could lest the man come up with something more as a penalty for his son's behavior.

But Oscar let him go. He was looking at his daughter, who was distraught over the entire situation, and he couldn't hold back the anger.

"I told you not to agree to this," he said again. "You let your daughter dictate her life, and do you see what it has cost you?"

Randa was verging on tears. "What do you want me to do?" she snapped quietly. "What do you want me to say?"

"Nothing!" Oscar boomed, but quickly lowered his voice. "There is nothing for you to do or say, but I will tell you this— Lia's future is now in my handsand I will handle it the way I want. You and your foolish daughter will have no say in my decision, so I suggest you prepare for what is coming."

There was nothing Randa could say to that. She knew she was beaten. She'd let her daughter choose her own husband, something that was unheard of, and it had blown up in her face.

But there was something else that was going to blow up in their faces if they weren't careful.

"Whatever it is, make it happen quickly," she muttered. "You know that we cannot wait."

Oscar frowned as his level of displeasure was taken to a new level. He closed his eyes for a moment, struggling not to erupt in fury. When he finally opened them, he had to take a deep breath to fortify his composure.

For surely, it was in danger of breaking.

"*That*," he said. "God's Bones, now we must deal with *that*. Everything would have been fine had Cecil gone through with the marriage. No one would have been the wiser."

"Nay," Randa said, eyeing her daughter, who was hanging her head. "No one would have been. So whoever you find as her husband, you had better do it soon. Otherwise, we may not be able to convince him that his firstborn is actually his child."

There it was. Out in the open now. That secret they'd been trying to hide. Randa had never been able to get a straight answer out of her daughter, whether Cecil had forced himself on her or whether she'd been a willing participant. Whatever the case, Ophelia was with child. Nearly six weeks now, by her estimation. Another few weeks and she would begin to show it. But right now, they had a window of opportunity. She still didn't look pregnant even if her breasts were filling out, but that seemed to be the only symptom so far.

Thankfully.

But they didn't have much time.

Ophelia needed a husband or the de Bulverton family would be the source of rumors for years to come.

"*Why*, girl?" Oscar finally grunted. "Why did you do it?"

Ophelia kept her head down, unable to look at her grandfather. "I told you why."

She had. Oscar growled angrily. "Because you're a whore," he said. "I never thought a grandchild of mine, my *heiress*, would be a whore, but here we are. You are with child and you have no husband. Now I must rush to find you a husband, and even then, he may not believe the child is his. I will have to promise him my earldom to keep him silent, I am certain, but that is what I must do to preserve you and our family honor. Damn you for this. Damn you, *damn you*."

With that, he walked off, leaving Ophelia in tears and Randa trying to comfort her.

But he didn't care. He had a plan and had since before his foolish daughter listened to *her* foolish daughter and this foolery had infected his entire life. A plan he'd been formulating for years, something that would turn his granddaughter into the catalyst for something much greater than she deserved. Thank God that Cecil de Bosque had broken the betrothal, because now, Oscar's dreams were going to come true.

He was taking over his granddaughter's future.

Never mind the fact that Ophelia would be a pawn. As long as Oscar got what he wanted, that was all that mattered. The fact that she was carrying de Bosque's child might complicate things, but in the end, he would have his way.

He would put that plan in action.

PART ONE

CHAPTER ONE

The Blackchurch Guild
Devon
Two Months Later

"I HAVE NOT seen you in three years and you come to tell me that I am to *marry*?"

The words of incredulity came from a man who normally didn't give credence to that kind of emotion. He was a Blackchurch trainer, one of the toughest, most experienced men on earth, and emotions didn't play into the demeanor that his elite status dictated. He was usually calm in all situations, calmer still in the face of danger, because that was what it took to be a Blackchurch trainer, to teach the most qualified and experienced warriors in the world.

Blackchurch trainers didn't break.

They didn't react.

But he was sure reacting now.

"Creston, listen to me," Royston de Royans said to his younger brother. "Do you not understand, lad? This is a great position for you, not to mention the fact that you would outrank me. I am only a warlord, a mere baron, but you... *you* would be an earl. An earl!"

Sir Creston de Royans was listening to his brother with his mouth hanging open. He was simply having difficulty fathoming what he was hearing. His eyes narrowed as he tried to make sense of it.

"You have come all the way from Yorkshire to tell me that I have a bride," he said, repeating what his brother had just told him so they were both clear on what had been said. "She is the heiress to the Earldom of Sidbury and that includes a hereditary position in the Septem Ports Alliance, a collection of lords whose properties include ports all along the coasts of Devon and Cornwall."

"Aye, that is what it includes."

Creston closed his gaping mouth and shook his head in disbelief. "Kent and Sussex have the Cinque ports and those are trouble enough," he said, waving a hand around in agitation. "The Septem ports are even worse—they are riddled with pirates and the battles there are frequent and brutal."

"I am aware."

"How can you be aware?" Creston demanded. "You sit at Tottingham Castle up in the north and have nothing to do with the ports. How are you aware of what trouble they are?"

"Because Lord Sidbury explained everything to me," Royston said evenly. "I've just come from his home, Creston. He told me all about the Septem ports and their battles against the pirates. That is why he needs someone strong to command the earldom when he passes on."

Creston threw up his hands. "Of all the ridiculous nonsense," he said, turning his back on his brother as he began to pace. "Royston, you *do* realize that I am a Blackchurch trainer."

"Of course I do."

"And you further realize that Blackchurch is related—by blood—to Triton's Hellions, the most fearsome band of pirates in Devon?" Creston stopped pacing and glared at him. "You *do* realize that, don't you?"

Royston nodded. "I am aware."

Creston rolled his eyes. "Clearly, you do not, or you would not be asking this of me," he said. "St. Denis de Bottreaux, the Earl of Exmoor and the Lord of Blackchurch, is a cousin to Abelard de Bottreaux, leader of Triton's Hellions. They are close. Abelard is at Blackchurch frequently. We all know the man and share a relationship with him to varying degrees."

"And?"

Creston's eyes widened with disbelief. "*And* what am I supposed to do when Triton's Hellions come to the port at Sidmouth and want to weigh anchor?" he said. "Bulverton probably has a thousand archers aimed at the shoreline to repel any such thing, and if I marry that man's granddaughter, I cannot supersede any of his commands. If he says launch against Triton's Hellions, he will launch, and if I am part of his family, I will be expected to repel them also."

Royston sighed heavily. "You are making too much of this," he said. "No one ever said you must go into service for Bulverton. You are simply marrying his granddaughter and will someday inherit the earldom from him. At that point, what you decide to do if Triton's Hellions come knocking at your door is your business."

That wasn't the answer Creston was looking for. He shook his head and turned away.

"You are trying to put me in an extremely difficult situation," he said. "Moreover, what right do you have to do this? You are my brother, not my father, and I am a grown man. I've not spoken to you for years, Royston. You like to forget you have a brother at Blackchurch."

Tempers were cooling because, at that point, they both turned and walked away from one another.

Just like they had when they were children.

The dynamic between them had been both brotherly and combative. Royston was the eldest by fourteen months, but Creston was the shining star. The warrior, the assassin, the brilliant one. Purely by birth order in the family, however, he was forced to follow when he was a natural leader.

That had never sat well with him.

At the moment, the brothers were in Creston's cottage on the outskirts of the small village within the perimeter walls of Blackchurch, at noon on a bright day. The village was mostly empty at this time of day except for a few wives of the trainers and their children, and those children were usually out in the village square, playing or eating or getting some much-needed sunshine as the mothers went about their chores. But in Creston's sparsely furnished dwelling, there were no children or wives. Only two men shouting at one another, muffled by the stone walls. Royston wiped his hands wearily over his face and found the nearest chair, sitting heavily as his brother began to lob personal insults.

"That's not fair," he finally said, his tone quiet. "You are my only brother. Of course I do not forget that I have one. If I had forgotten, I would not be here. This is a good opportunity for you, Creston. Can you not see that?"

Creston sighed heavily and found another chair to sit on. He was twice the size his brother was, a muscular man with enormous arms and shoulders from the constant training he was involved in, days and days of swinging swords, or other physical activities, that had given him great strength and stamina. As he sat, the chair creaked under his weight and he half expected it to break.

That would have been in line with the luck he'd had this morning.

Sprawling on the floor like an idiot would not help his cause.

"I do see that it is a good opportunity," he admitted. "And I am grateful that you are looking out for my interests. But my life is here, at Blackchurch. I *have* a life here, and a good one. Did you ever stop to think of that?"

Royston looked at him. "Nay," he said frankly. "What man does not want to be an earl?"

"Me!" Creston insisted. "*I* do not want to be an earl!"

Royston shook his head. "So you want to be a trainer for the rest of your life?" he said. "Training other men to go on and do great things? What about *you* doing great things, Creston? Coming here to Blackchurch broke Papa's heart, you know. He expected you to be the greatest knight England had ever seen, but instead… instead, you came here and wasted your talent. Papa never got over it."

The old family hurt was surfacing. Creston had wondered how long it would take Royston to bring that up. Early in his career, Creston had served the Crown with distinction. He'd served King John and he'd been proud of it, no matter how badly the king had been viewed by many. He was still the king and Creston had done what he felt was his duty. John had even noticed the serious young knight built like a bull and beg to use him for more dangerous work.

Even if it hadn't exactly been noble.

Creston began to understand that after a while, but he still completed his orders as assigned. He never questioned, never complained. He was a knight serving the king and he simply did as he was told. But the results of that loyalty put him in a situation where he was denied what he wanted most.

His loyalty to the Crown had cost him everything.

That was when his service to the king came to a halt.

Racked with grief, Creston had walked away. Weeks of hiding out from John's soldiers, who were looking for him, had led him to a seedy tavern near the Thames called The Pox. He'd been drinking himself into oblivion when he met St. Gerard de Bottreaux, the heir to the Blackchurch empire. St. Gerard had been passing through London and the meeting with Creston had been purely by coincidence, but a good coincidence when Creston saved St. Gerard's life from a drunkard with a big knife. One thing had led to another and, in gratitude, St. Gerard offered Creston a position at Blackchurch.

It was the best decision Creston had ever made, even if his father hadn't thought so.

But that didn't matter now.

"I'm not going to have that discussion with you," Creston said after a moment. "Blackchurch has been lucrative. It has been rewarding."

"You are nothing more than a tutor of men."

"It was my *salvation*."

They stared at each other, having quickly reached an impasse in their conversation. However, Royston wasn't finished. He well remembered his stubborn little brother and knew that all of the arguing in the world wouldn't sway him.

He had to go to a higher power.

"I'll see what St. Denis thinks about this offer," he said. "He's your liege, is he not? If he thinks this is a good idea, you'll have to obey him."

Creston frowned. "Leave him out of this."

Royston shook his head. "I won't," he said. "Creston, you do not seem to understand. I am the head of the family. That means you must obey me. Any court in the land will side with me if you refuse to obey my wishes. Worst still, if your beloved liege knows about it and you refuse him, too, then I suspect you will no longer be a Blackchurch trainer. Men like you do not disobey orders from St. Denis de Bottreaux and still remain in your position."

By the time he was finished, Creston's fair face was red with rage. "*Why* would you do that?"

"Because you are being ridiculous when I am trying to do something good for you."

Creston wanted to throttle the man. He really did. But he also knew that he had no leverage in the situation because everything Royston said was correct—he was at his brother's mercy, with Royston as the head of the family. He was a subject of St. Denis de Bottreaux and if the man thought he should marry and become an earl, then there would be no argument. He would do as he was told.

As upsetting as that was.

"When is this all supposed to happen?" he muttered angrily. "The marriage, I mean. Have you planned my life out to the very last minute?"

Royston held his ground at his brother's baiting. "She is already on her way here," he said. "She should arrive very soon. The marriage will take place as soon as she arrives."

Creston was about to explode. He rolled his eyes and hung his head, staring at the ground as clenched fists rested on his slender hips. He was trying to decide if he should kill his brother where he stood, but wisely decided against it. It wouldn't solve anything.

His betrothed was still coming.

"I have a class to instruct," he finally said, pushing past his brother.

Royston watched him go. "I will be at The Black Cock Inn," he called after him. "Come and see me tonight and we shall finalize the details. If you do not come, I shall go straight to St. Denis!"

Creston paused at the door, gearing up for a sharp retort, but he thought better of it. More insults wouldn't force Royston to change his mind. Therefore, without a word, he simply yanked open the door and stepped through.

Royston followed his brother's path to the doorway, watching the man storm off across the quiet compound. He knew his brother was angry, but he also knew, as Creston knew, that he had no choice. Creston would marry de Bulverton's granddaughter and that would be the end of it. Considering the woman was already on her way to Blackchurch, Royston needed his brother's agreement sooner rather than later.

Or things might become a little… difficult.

CHAPTER TWO

"THE EARL OF Sidbury? *You?*"

Seated in the luxurious solar of Exmoor Castle's keep, a structure in the heart of the Blackchurch compound, Creston nodded his head to the man standing before him.

"Aye, my lord," he said. "I have a feeling my brother is going to try to use you as leverage to force me into this marriage, so I came to tell you before he did."

St. Denis de Bottreaux couldn't help but appear both surprised and dubious. He was a short man, with graying, curly hair that hung to his shoulders and a better-than-average talent for swinging a sword. His true strengths lay in his judgment and wisdom, and in his unerring ability to command a battle. He was brilliant in that respect and he, more than any of his ancestors, had built Blackchurch into what it was today. When he had inherited the guild from his father, it was half the size, but he'd built it into something grand and powerful.

The man seated before him had helped him achieve that, and he didn't like what he was hearing from him.

"My God," St. Denis said, awed by what he'd just been told. "Your brother managed to broker a betrothal between you and

Sidbury's granddaughter? How astonishing."

"He has," Creston said. "And he is determined that I should accept it, but I wanted you to know about this, my lord. It is a… complicated situation."

St. Denis grunted. "To say the least," he said. "You explained to your brother that Sidbury is a great enemy of Triton's Hellions?"

"I did, my lord."

"And he is still insisting?"

"He is, my lord."

St. Denis shook his head sadly. "Then I do not know what to say," he said. "I know this will be a great opportunity for you, Creston, and—"

Creston cut him off quietly. "God's Bones, not you, too."

St. Denis held up a hand to quiet him. "Let me finish," he said. "What I was going to say is that sometimes even the best opportunity is not without its battles. Of course, selfishly, I do not want to lose you as a Blackchurch trainer. You are one of our very best. But as the Earl of Sidbury, you will be in a position of great power. We could use that to our advantage."

Creston could hear the hope in St. Denis' voice. "But what if I want to remain a simple trainer with a simple life?" he said. "What if I do not want to become a man of great power?"

There was angst in his tone. A man facing a great decision usually had that kind of torment in his heart and St. Denis wasn't oblivious to it. But he simply didn't think this was the horrible situation that Creston thought it was. He went over to an elaborately carved oak table and picked up the pitcher of wine, pouring some into two cups.

"Let's think about this a little, shall we?" he said, setting the pitcher down and picking up the cups. "Start from the beginning. How does your brother know Sidbury? How did this come about?"

Creston accepted the offered cup of wine gratefully. "Sidbury is a distant cousin to my father," he said before taking a gulp of the ruby-red liquid. "My father and Sidbury shared the same great-grandfather, I think. In any case, he is kin and an ally. He and my father were raised together. He recently sent word to my brother, asking if I were married and suggesting a marriage between me and his granddaughter to strengthen the family alliance."

"That makes sense," St. Denis said. "Do you know the man personally?"

Creston nodded. "Years ago," he said. "He was a follower of King John and we would see each other from time to time, but we did not have a relationship to speak of. He knew when I came to Blackchurch, however."

"How did he know that?"

"My father told him," he said. "You know that my father was not particularly thrilled that I left the king's service to serve at Blackchurch, and he complained to anyone who would listen. I think half of England knew I came to Blackchurch those years ago."

St. Denis shrugged. "Sidbury must not have thought it was shameful if he sought you out as a husband for his granddaughter," he said. "Have you never met the girl?"

"Never."

St. Denis fell silent for a moment, sipping his wine and contemplating the situation. "Is there any reason that you should be opposed to a marriage, Creston?" he asked. "Do you have your eye on someone else as a wife?"

Creston shook his head. "Nay," he said. "There is no one

else. There hasn't been since my time with John."

St. Denis looked at him then. "You had a lady you were fond of, then?"

Creston sighed heavily. "Aye," he said, averting his gaze. "Long ago."

"What happened?"

Creston snorted, a bitter sound. "It is not something I like to speak of," he said. "I haven't spoken of it in years, I don't think."

"Please. I'd like to know."

Creston was staring at his cup. "Very well," he said after a moment. "Her father was an ally of my father's. Mary St. Albans was young and beautiful and her mother was stupid enough to bring her to London, to court, in fact. She did not escape the king's notice, and rather than have his daughter deflowered by a monarch, her father sent Mary to France, into hiding. The last I heard, she had married a warlord and had several children."

St. Denis waggled his eyebrows in understanding. "I see," he said. "But given how John was, I am certain it was for the best. You could not have protected her had you married her, Creston. He would have demanded your wife."

Creston looked at him. "Why do you think I came to Blackchurch?"

St. Denis' brow furrowed. "What do you mean?"

Creston regarded his wine for a moment. "Did your son never tell you how he brought me to Blackchurch?"

St. Denis shrugged. "Only that you saved his life in London," he said. "Why? Is there more to it?"

"A little," Creston admitted. Then he sighed heavily. "Fourteen years ago. It seems like forever."

"What happened?"

"Gerard found me in the seediest tavern in London, drowning my sorrows in a pitcher of the strongest wine I could buy."

"Why?"

Creston shrugged. "Because I knew Mary's father intended to send her to France to escape the king, only I thought I knew better," he said, his expression dull with the painful memory. "I convinced Mary to run away with me. We were going to be married and I planned to serve somewhere in France or Aragon. I had enough friends that I could find a position, but Mary's mother found out about our plans and told her father. When I went to collect Mary, her father was waiting for me to tell me that she was already gone. Worse still, he threatened to tell John if I ever spoke a word of the situation, so my hands were tied. But I ended up walking away as it was. I could not serve a king who had ruined my chance at happiness."

St. Denis understood now. Truthfully, Creston had never struck him as a man with any secrets, but perhaps every man was entitled to at least one.

"I'm sorry, lad," he said quietly. "That is an unhappy tale."

Creston simply nodded, still looking at his wine. "I always thought I would marry a woman I was fond of," he said. "Marriage, to me, is something very special and sacred. I've seen other men fall in love with their wives and I'd always hoped to do the same, but I want to do it with a woman of my choosing. Not of my brother's choosing."

St. Denis couldn't disagree with him. "It is always better for us to marry women of our choosing," he said. "But you waited too long for yours. Your brother has the right to command you to marry, especially in the case of an alliance. You cannot refuse if he presses his rights."

That only depressed Creston. "And he will," he said. "He

seems to think this is a brilliant match, although how he could know that, I do not know. He does not know the woman, either."

St. Denis took a drink of his wine. "I am certain he is thinking about the earldom you will inherit," he said. "He's not wrong in that respect, Creston. It *is* a great match. You will reap enormous benefits from this."

Creston just sat there, looking at his cup, pondering an aspect of his life that he'd never liked to ponder. Not since the day Mary had been sent away.

"There's something else," he muttered.

"What?"

Creston sighed faintly. "Mary was pregnant when her father sent her away," he said. "That is why I was so determined to marry her. I do not know what happened to my child, if her husband accepted him or if he was sent away somewhere. That haunts me, my lord, more than you can imagine."

St. Denis lifted his eyebrows in sympathy. "Having sons of my own, I can most definitely imagine," he said quietly. "When I lost Gerard, something inside me died. Your children take a piece of you when they go, even if you've never met the child. Somewhere, there is a piece of you out in the world, a lad, or a lass, you do not know. You can only hope they are happy and healthy, but you do not know for certain. I can understand how that must haunt you."

Creston could only nod. St. Gerard was killed a few years earlier, something that had affected them all. Now, he was so incredibly depressed that all he wanted to do was get drunk somewhere. Not at The Black Cock, the tavern in the village just outside of Blackchurch, but maybe back at his cottage, where he knew he had stashes of wine all over the house. He had a bit of a problem drinking too much, something he kept hidden from his friends.

But in drink, there was solace.

He needed it.

"Well," he finally said, "now you know everything. I came to tell you what my brother has done, so I suppose I have little choice but to accept the betrothal."

"I would agree with that."

"I also want to tell you that I have no intention of leaving Blackchurch."

St. Denis was relieved to hear that. "Will you bring your bride back here?" he said. "There are other wives who would make her feel welcome."

Creston frowned. "*I* am not even sure I want to make her feel welcome," he said, but realized how cruel that sounded and he eased a little. "I simply do not know, my lord. If she wants to return with me, she may. But if she wishes to remain wherever she happens to be living now, I will not argue with her. She can do what she likes."

It still sounded cruel, but it couldn't be helped. St. Denis stood up and put his cup aside, followed by Creston, who left his empty cup on a nearby table.

"Creston, I must say that I am very glad to hear you will inherit the Earldom of Sidbury," he said. "Abelard will be glad, too. I assume you will be kinder to him than de Bulverton is?"

Creston smiled weakly. "He may have free rein over my port," he said. "But there will be rules."

"Such as?"

"No burning my town," Creston said, his blue eyes twinkling dully. "No robbing people in the streets. No rampaging or pillaging. I have standards. Not many, but some."

St. Denis started laughing. "We must maintain some dignity, I suppose," he said. "What of Santiago? He keeps his ships in Fremington, you know. He will be thrilled if Sidmouth becomes a friendly port."

He was referring to Santiago de Fernandez, leader of an Aragon pirate faction called Demons of the Sea. He also happened to be a cousin to another Blackchurch trainer through marriage, Sinclair de Reyne. Sinclair and Santiago had had some wild adventures in the past, and Santiago considered himself a strong ally of Blackchurch and Triton's Hellions. At least, he had last month.

There was no telling how he felt this month.

Creston snorted at St. Denis' statement.

"I would not dare refuse Santiago," he said. "He's been very good to Sin, you know. Since the man is a cousin to Sin's wife, of course, he's family. He can use the port with my compliments."

St. Denis clapped Creston on the shoulder as they headed for the solar door. "You are already making two pirate factions very happy," he said. "You see? This may not be as terrible as you think, after all."

Creston paused at the door, his smile fading. "But I still must marry in order to inherit."

"That is true. You must."

Creston just shook his head and departed the chamber, leaving St. Denis to watch him go. The Blackchurch trainers, and commanders, were such a tightly knit group that St. Denis knew, before the evening was out, that every trainer would know of Creston's dilemma. That was how the group operated. One man's problem was every man's problem. St. Denis was fairly certain this wasn't the last he was going to hear of this.

It *was* a good opportunity for Creston. He believed that. He only hoped Creston did.

CHAPTER THREE

Outside of Exebridge, Devon

S HE VERY MUCH wished her grandfather hadn't decided to come.

He always made a situation so much more difficult when he was present. His manner was brusque and demanding, and she knew he'd only come to ensure everything was done to his liking and specifications.

That this marriage happened the way he wanted it to happen.

Living with the man over the past two months had been hell.

He never let her forget about the child in her belly and how she was a whore for conceiving a child with a man she was intended to marry. The man hadn't been in her life for years, instead living in the port city of Sidmouth and managing it like his own personal kingdom, because Ophelia and her mother had been living with Ophelia's father, a frail man who had died right before Ophelia's betrothal. He'd had a hand in it, mostly because Ophelia wanted to marry Cecil and her father permitted it. She'd been grateful.

But Oscar de Bulverton had taken charge.

They'd been living with him at Axen Castle, seat of the Earl of Sidbury, and essentially been living like prisoners. More than that, in order to keep the child in her belly from growing too large, Oscar had restricted his granddaughter's food to the point where she had lost weight. Servants, and even her own mother, would sneak her food, but Oscar needed her to appear unpregnant until she married.

After that, she would be her husband's problem.

But he had to get her married.

The result of the restricted food was that Ophelia didn't feel well. All day, every day. She was pale and thin, which pleased her grandfather. Randa hated seeing her daughter looking so unwell, but she could not go against her father. He had control now that her husband was dead, so she had no choice but to obey him. As she sat next to her daughter in the iron carriage that had brought them from Sidmouth to north Devon, she had the same wish that her father had, marrying her daughter off quickly—because, surely, her new husband would not try to starve her simply for appearances' sake.

It was a horrific situation.

"Here," Randa whispered, making sure that her father was out of range. "I brought you something. You'll need your strength when you meet your betrothed."

She dug into the voluminous folds of her brocade gown and came forth with a pair of small meat pies. They'd had several when they broke their fast at an inn that morning, or at least Randa and Oscar had, but Ophelia had been restricted to one little pie and boiled milk. Oscar had been clear about that. But Randa handed the pies over to her daughter, who promptly shoved a whole one into her mouth. She was starving.

"Careful," Randa said quietly. "You do not want it coming back up again. Swallow slowly."

Ophelia slowed down, but she was so hungry that it was difficult. The tears came as well, and she chewed and wiped tears from her face, finally swallowing what was in her mouth. Everything in her life was such a struggle now. Even eating. She was slower with the second pie as Randa put an arm around her slender shoulders.

"It will all be over soon," she murmured. "You will be the wife of a de Royans and you can eat all you wish. Those will be good days, my dearest. Very good days."

Ophelia's mouth was full of pie. "I will never forgive you for allowing him to do this to me," she hissed. "You let him starve your child."

Randa dropped her arm from her daughter's shoulders. "You do not understand."

"Nay, I do not," Ophelia snapped. "How could you let him do this to me? *How?*"

Randa averted her gaze, looking out the window of the carriage. "He is only doing what he feels is best," she said, offering a weak excuse. "You are to be married, Lia. No man wants to marry a woman who is carrying another man's child."

"I was supposed to marry that man."

"Yet you did not," Randa said. "You cannot go to your new betrothed with a rounded belly. He will reject you, you will then give birth to a bastard, and you will grow old a disgraced spinster. Is that what you want?"

Ophelia finished with the pie, licking her fingers of the crumbs. "What I want cannot be," she said. "Now you are hoping to cheat another man into believing I am bearing his child. I am three months pregnant, Mother. He will not believe the child is his."

"It is your duty to convince him that he is wrong."

Ophelia sighed heavily and turned away from her mother. She was feeling a little better with food in her stomach now, and she put her hand on her belly, which was slightly rounded and nothing more. She was wearing a garment that had been specially commissioned by her grandfather, a voluminous lavender-and-blue gown of silk. It had a high waistline, so her stomach was concealed, but it really wasn't necessary—her stomach couldn't be seen anyway.

Oscar had seen to that.

The road they'd taken from Sidmouth had wandered through the gentle hills and dales of Devon, but now they were in flatter, more heavily wooded lands. She inhaled deeply, smelling trees and woods and foliage. When they passed by a lake, it was a lovely bit of glistening water in the midst of the wilds. Truthfully, it hadn't been a terrible journey. Just a long one.

She was looking forward to it being over.

There wasn't much she knew about her betrothed other than he served at the Blackchurch Guild, whatever that was. She'd never heard of it until her grandfather told her that it was a training school for the finest knights in the world and that her husband-to-be was an instructor. He was from the House of de Royans, a powerful family in Yorkshire, and his brother was a baron. Other than that, she knew nothing. She didn't know how old he was, or what kind of character he had, or if he was a fair and moral man. For all she knew, he was Lucifer himself. Did it concern her? Not particularly.

She had plans of her own where her marriage was concerned.

The Sidbury contingent finally hit the outskirts of a town named Exebridge and she heard the men around the carriage saying that it was their destination. Her grandfather had brought one hundred heavily armed men with him, one hundred men who were part of her dowry. Oscar intended to turn them over to her betrothed the moment the marriage mass was complete. He'd also brought a chest with one hundred gold marks and another document giving her new husband a landed title. Upon the marriage, her husband would immediately become Lord Yettington, which was the courtesy title for the heir apparent to the Earldom of Sidbury.

Therefore, the man would be gaining a good deal upon the marriage, but that was by design. He was getting a pregnant wife and Oscar was trying to pull the wool over the man's eyes, hoping that even if he figured out his wife's child was not from his loins, he would look at all of the gifts he'd received for her dowry and simply accept the situation for what it was.

That was the hope, anyway.

But not if Ophelia had anything to say about it.

"Randa!" Oscar pulled his fat, dappled horse alongside the carriage. "My men tell me that there is only one tavern in town worth visiting and it is called The Black Cock. We will be settling there and I will send word to Blackchurch that we have arrived. Make sure Lia is put in a chamber and kept there. I do not want her wandering around."

"I will," Randa said, shielding her eyes from the sun as she looked up at her father. "How far is Blackchurch from here?"

Oscar gestured toward the north. "Not far, I'm told," he said. "It should not take long. Make sure your daughter is presentable. We do not want to give the man reason to reject the contract."

Make sure your daughter is presentable.

He meant *make sure her stomach isn't visible.* Ophelia thought it was all terribly ridiculous because she hardly had a stomach at all. Oscar had made sure of it. She couldn't even look at her grandfather, a man she'd genuinely grown to hate, any longer. As they came into the outskirts of the town, she could see a dark stone steeple rising above the tree line.

A church, she thought.

When she told the de Royans knight she wasn't going to marry him, she had to have a place to go.

Now, she did.

Her grandfather thought he was going to have the last word about her life, but Ophelia had other ideas.

Oscar de Bulverton was in for a rude awakening.

CHAPTER FOUR

The Blackchurch Guild
Two Days Later

"**A** MISSIVE FOR you, my lord."

The wind was starting to pick up on this bright and sunny day, a brisk wind that was scattering leaves and blowing through hair. A soldier from Blackchurch's formidable gatehouse, one that anchored the formidable perimeter wall, had brought the missive as Creston was teaching a group of recruits outside today. Sometimes he taught them in the old barn that was near the eating hall because about half of what he instructed was mental. How to tolerate torture, and how to give it, and things of that nature.

Part of his course was to put recruits through hardship to see if they could mentally and physically withstand it, and that part of his course was coming up. He would order his recruits outside the walls of Blackchurch, into the woods, where they would spend two weeks living off the land and foraging for sustenance, enduring surprise attacks to unsettle them, and other methods to train them to keep their focus no matter the circumstances.

Today, however, they were learning about treatment of the enemy as it related to the art of politics, which had been their lesson for the past four weeks. Creston usually had the same recruit class for about a year because of the brutality of some of the things he had to teach them. One of those things was how to withstand interrogation, and recruits were put through actual interrogation between Creston and another trainer he worked closely with quite frequently. That other trainer was here today because his purview was world politics and that was what they were discussing at the moment. Cruz Mediana de Aragón taught conquest and diplomacy, among other things.

He also happened to be Creston's best friend.

They were closer than brothers. Cruz was a tall, dark-haired man who was muscular and well built, and he was the night sky to Creston's daylight. By appearance, they were opposites, but at heart, they were the same. They shared the same likes, dislikes, sense of humor, and powerful dedication to duty. Cruz was also a prince of Aragon through his grandfather, father to the current king, and he was a member of the Holy Order of Santiago. They didn't come any more royal, educated, or formally trained than Cruz, and he and Creston had been inseparable for about thirteen years, ever since Cruz arrived at Blackchurch.

Now, he was looking at Creston with some interest as the soldier who had brought the missive headed back to the gatehouse and left Creston standing there with the vellum in his hand. He hadn't made a move to open it. As he remained rooted to the spot, racked with indecision, more men began to approach, men who had heard about Creston's betrothal. It wasn't like it was a secret, even though Creston hadn't told anyone except Cruz, and that was only in passing. But, as he'd quickly discovered, St. Denis had told everyone. Blackchurch was a brotherhood, with men who would kill or die for one another, and with training mostly over for the day, most of those men had seen the messenger approach the recruit field where Creston was teaching and come to support their brother in the midst of what was, by St. Denis' account, an unhappy situation.

Tay Munro was the first one to appear, along with Sinclair de Reyne. Since every trainer at Blackchurch had a nickname, something that best represented them, these two were known as The Leviathan and The Swordsman. In Tay's case, he had been a trainer at least ten years, if not more, and Sinclair was about the same, which gave them seniority in the trainer group, along with Creston. They'd been there the longest. But Tay, because of his natural leadership ability, was the unofficial leader of the Blackchurch trainers and greatly respected by all.

Following Tay and Sinclair were Fox de Merest, Payne Matheson, and Kristian Heldane. Fox, a man known as The Protector, was a former royal knight, much as Creston was, only they worked in completely different units for the Crown. Payne, a fiery Scotsman known as The Tempest, was the most fearless one of the group. Kristian was the tall, blond god of a man known as The Viking because, as St. Denis once put it, the man looked as if he'd come to slay them all to honor Odin. He did, in fact, train men on water warfare, using highly advanced cogs that were put to the water on the vast lake in the middle of the Blackchurch dominion known as Lake Cocytus. The shipboard training was, perhaps, the toughest part of Black-church, or second only to what Creston taught.

His classes could drum out recruits faster than anyone else's.

Bringing up the rear of the approaching group were two of St. Denis' most trusted advisors, men whose breadth and scope reached beyond England's borders and stretched to the reaches of the known world. Aamir ibn Rashid was the son of a great Egyptian pasha who had permitted his son to journey to England years ago as a guest of St. Denis de Bottreaux. Amir had been young back then, but he had lived a lifetime as his father's military general. He brought a greater view of the world to Blackchurch, something he educated the recruits on so they had a broader sense of the world in general as they went forth after their training.

The last one rounding out the collection of trainers was a former Shaolin monk named Ming Tang. His name meant "bring water" in his language and he brought morality and a sense of restraint to the group. His class taught recruits how to fight using only hands and feet and mind, something that was most challenging for men and women who had been taught to use weapons. He also taught them how to calm their minds before battle, during battle, and after battle, and how emotion was the pathway to disorder. The entire group relied on Ming Tang's advice, each man for his own reasons, and Ming Tang had a bond with each one of them. He'd come to this land to teach as well as to learn.

His counsel would be most welcome now.

Creston could see his friends as they gathered several feet away, waiting for him to be finished with his recruits for the day. Unable to concentrate with the missive in his hand, Creston dismissed his class of eight men early so they could enjoy some rest.

That was something rare in the annals of Blackchurch, as recruits were pushed to their limits on a daily basis, by every trainer there. New recruits, called dregs, would start with Tay and he would weed out the unworthy. Those who passed his class were considered genuine recruits and moved on to Fox or Sinclair. Then another group would come in and the process would start all over again, so there were at least as many groups as there were trainers at any given time, and classes lasted from six months to a year, depending on the module. Since Blackchurch-trained warriors were the most elite warriors in the world, princes and kings and wildly wealthy warlords were willing to pay a royal ransom for each man or woman. And they did train women. Many had graduated.

But many had failed.

Such was the life of a Blackchurch recruit, regardless of sex.

As Creston's recruits walked away, heading back to the dormitory where all recruits were housed, Creston broke the seal on the missive just delivered to him.

"I assume you're all here to see what's in this missive," he said, unfolding it. "It's probably from my brother, demanding I make my way to The Black Cock and meet my betrothed. Well, mayhap I do not want to. Mayhap I want to run away to Araby and become a horse trader."

He spoke the last few words with some bitterness. The last act of resistance from a man who knew he had no choice, but he was going to go down kicking and screaming. The Black Cock was the tavern in town where the Blackchurch trainers gathered, the only tavern for miles around, and that was where Royston had gone. There were several rooms to rent and a larger, dormitory-style chamber for men who wanted a bed but couldn't pay for a private room. The food there was good, and the wenches joyful, so the trainers had made it a second home.

The Black Cock was legendary.

But it was also far from Araby, and Cruz grinned at Creston's declaration. "Is that your plan if you fail as a Blackchurch trainer?"

Creston started laughing. "Nay," he said. "If that happened, I thought you and I were going to overthrow Abelard and steal his pirate ships?"

That had Cruz snorting. "If you wish," he said. "But we would have to do battle against Payne's wife, since she is the mighty female pirate known as the Sea God, and we'd also have to do battle against Payne's brother, Pope Francis the Pirate. I'm not entirely sure we could come up with more fearsome names ourselves, which means our pirate careers would be finished. No one would be afraid of 'only' Creston and Cruz."

Creston threw his head back, laughing, as the group of trainers walked up. Now that the class was gone, they were approaching Creston, who seemed to be in a good mood. Shielding his eyes from the sun as he watched Creston and Cruz share some humor, Tay spoke first.

"What is so hilarious?" he demanded. "Are the contents of the missive entertaining, then?"

Creston shook his head. "I would not know," he said. "I've not even read it. Cruz and I were simply talking about what we will do after we leave Blackchurch. I suggested piracy, but he does not think our names are fearsome enough."

Payne, whose wife had actually been a pirate and still controlled a Portuguese faction, laughed the loudest. "God love ye, lads," he said. "Ye must have a name that strikes fear intae the heart of men, and I'm afraid Cruz is right—ye canna be a pirate and be simply 'Creston.'"

"It is the only name I have," Creston said. "I suppose I could go by Creston the Bold."

Payne shook his head. "Not even in yer dreams, lad," he said. "A pirate name must be something fearsome, not noble. Ye can call yerself Creston the Nightmare or even Cruz the Slug. That might make the seafarers take notice."

Everyone laughed at Cruz's expense with such an unglamorous name, but Cruz waved his hand to quiet everyone. "Need I remind you that *my* blood is royal," he said. "The Sea King has a good ring to it."

Payne cocked a disapproving eyebrow. "I'll tell my wife that ye'll be ready tae challenge her supremacy at some point," he said, but his focus shifted to Creston. "We came tae see what the missive said, Cres. Is yer brother summoning ye for a marriage?"

Creston lost his humor. With a heavy sigh, he finally looked at the missive in his hand, reading the short but concise message. After a moment, he nodded.

"Aye," he said. "My betrothed has evidently arrived at The Black Cock. He wants me to come."

"You are a grown man," Cruz said, frowning. "Why does he think he can control your life like this?"

"Because he can," Fox said quietly. Much like Creston, he came from a fine noble family and had grown up in that atmosphere. He knew what Creston knew. "He is the head of the family and he can marry off whom he wishes. To create alliances, to create peace... it does not matter. Creston has no choice."

"How are you feeling about this?" Sinclair asked with concern. "We heard about the dictum. Denis said you were... reluctant."

Creston was staring at the missive, trying to articulate his thoughts. "Did he tell you that by marrying her, I will become the heir to the Earldom of Sidbury?" he said, looking up at the group, who was nodding. "When her grandfather dies, I become the earl. The port of Sidmouth will belong to me, as will a seat in the Septem Ports Alliance. If I marry her, power becomes mine. Royston said this is an incredible opportunity for me, and he is not wrong. I'm just not so sure I want it. Or that I'm ready."

There wasn't one man there who didn't understand that. It was an enormous burden for someone who hadn't grown up being prepared for it. As the trainers considered his predicament, Ming Tang stepped forward.

He was the wise man of the group, someone whose advice could always be counted on. Creston saw him coming and there was some relief in his expression, but also some angst. He was looking for answers that his own heart couldn't provide at the moment.

Perhaps someone else could.

"Let me ask you something, Cres," Ming Tang said in his slightly accented speech that made him sound so incredibly brilliant. "Did you never plan to marry?"

Creston shrugged. "I'd not thought on it, really," he said, eyeing the men around him. Then he sighed heavily. "The truth is that something from my past has prevented me from thinking about my future when it comes to marriage. We've all known each other long enough, and we know something of our pasts, but I would be willing to believe every man here has a secret. Men such as us, with experience and education, do not reach this point in our lives without having something in our past we do not speak of. Mine is the fact that I tried to run off with the woman I love when her father denied us, but our plans were discovered and she was taken from me. That was fourteen years ago and I've never forgotten the pain. I'm not sure I ever will."

Ming Tang nodded pensively, understanding his point but not particularly shocked by the confession. As Creston said, most men their age had something in their past to hide or to ignore.

Sometimes those secrets took on a life of their own.

"And you let that dictate your future?" he said. "Did you assume you were only good for one attempt at marriage and no more?"

Creston looked at him. "This one was different," he said. "She was pregnant with my child."

That brought a few raised eyebrows. "What happened?" Sinclair said. "Why didn't her father give you permission to marry her?"

"Because he did not want a knight who worked so closely with John," Creston said, looking at the group. "I was a royal knight, much like Fox, only I served the king directly. If John commanded me to intimidate an enemy, then I did. If he told me to eliminate a threat against him, I did. I do not think many of you knew that about me. I was one of his attack dogs."

It seemed like an odd time for a confession like that, but on the other hand, this was an important moment in Creston's life, and sometimes men felt the need to confide in their friends. Perhaps he'd not done it before for fear of his colleagues viewing him differently, but the truth was that there were no politics at Blackchurch. There never had been. Blackchurch was a guild that provided one thing—training for warriors. They were educated in politics, but on a wider scope. There were no political leanings and Blackchurch never took a side in any conflicts. It was strictly forbidden.

But a man couldn't change his past.

Even if he did serve a hated king.

"I do not think there is one man here who hasn't done something he regretted, Cres," Tay said quietly. "There is no shame in doing your duty, as you were ordered to do it."

Creston shrugged. "Mayhap," he said. "But Mary's father saw me as a vicious brute. He sent her away and I've not seen her since. I do not know what became of her or the child, although I heard she had married a French warlord. But who really knows?"

It was a rather tragic tale, one of lost love and despair. Creston always presented such a strong, even-tempered front, but it seemed he'd been hiding a heartache.

There wasn't one man there that didn't feel some pity for him.

"Creston, I am going to point something out for you to think on," Ming Tang said after a moment. "While I realize you have had a great disappointment in the past when it came to marriage, sometimes things like that are simply not meant to be. If you believe in God, then you must believe that God has a plan for you in mind. Mayhap something greater than marrying a young woman who carried your child. What I am saying is that we all have a destiny, Cres. It is clear that Mary was not yours. But mayhap this earl's granddaughter is."

Creston was listening to him, some angst in his heart from having dredged up the incident with Mary even though it was so long ago. He'd spoken of it twice in a very short amount of time, something he'd not done in years, and it was difficult to fight off the dull ache of the familiar disappointment.

Even after all this time.

"Gerard brought me to Blackchurch at the lowest point of my life," Creston said. "In many ways, Blackchurch was my salvation. It gave me something to focus on other than my grief of losing Mary and our child. I always thought I would simply remain here as a trainer for the rest of my life, and I was content with that. 'Tis a noble thing we do here, training the most elite warriors in the world. It is something I can be proud of, and I can honestly say that it is the first position where I can say that. I am proud to be here. I do not want to leave."

"You do not have to leave," Tay said. "I married, Fox married, and so did Sin and Payne. But we are still here. There is nothing that says you have to leave."

"What about when the earl dies and I assume his title?"

Tay shrugged. "Then mayhap we'll all join you," he said. "We'll make it our next big adventure at the port town of Sidmouth, fighting off pirates."

Creston smiled weakly. "I think Denis would have something to say about that."

Tay waggled his eyebrows in agreement. "In any case, I think you need to look at the situation this way," he said. "If you are concerned that you do not know the woman you are betrothed to, keep in mind that I did not know my wife for very long before we married, either. Neither did Sin, nor Payne. We found ourselves involved in marriages with women we hardly knew, and I can honestly say it was the best thing I ever did. Sometimes in the unknown, we find where we are meant to be. And *whom* we are meant to be with."

Between Ming Tang and Tay, Creston was feeling some courage at the situation. Perhaps his life wasn't going to change as much as he feared. He was a man who liked familiarity, so that was more than likely at the root of his resistance as well.

"I always hoped I would marry a woman I had affection for," he said, his voice growing soft with reflection. "My parents had it, so I had hoped to. And when Mary went away… Well, it sounds foolish to say it broke my heart because I am a grown man and we do not have broken hearts, but I think it did. It hurt. Mayhap I've avoided marrying because I did not want to be hurt again. The heart remembers. And it protects itself."

Those who were married understood that. And perhaps even those who weren't married understood to a lesser degree. There wasn't one man there, except for Ming Tang, who hadn't experienced some kind of heartache when it came to a woman.

But that didn't change what Creston was facing.

"No one is saying you have to fall in love with this woman," Sinclair said as he went to Creston and put his hand on the man's shoulder. "But you must go and meet her. She's probably being forced into this as much as you are, so do not judge her until you discover more of this situation. It's possible she's as reluctant as you, so you should probably not make it worse. If you are to marry her, you do not want to start off by insulting the woman and behaving like an arse."

Creston couldn't disagree with him. "I suppose," he said. Then he sighed heavily. "I should get this over with."

"We'll go," Tay said. "You cannot walk into this situation alone, Cres. It is you against your brother and the woman and her family, so we will be there for support and advice should you need it."

Creston didn't think he needed an entourage, but the thought of his friends being there should he need encouragement was comforting.

"Very well," he said. "But I will do the talking."

"Of course," Tay said, making faces behind Creston's back when the man walked past him. "What could possibly go wrong?"

That was a very good question. What could possibly go wrong, indeed?

Creston was about to find out.

He was wishing more and more that he could just run off to Araby and never look back.

CHAPTER FIVE

"Y E'RE MARRYING A Blackchurch trainer? God love ye, lass!"

The congratulations came from a wench who served at The Black Cock, a busty woman with frizzy hair she tried to tame by tying it up with a kerchief. She smiled a good deal with her yellowed teeth and had been kind to Ophelia after her mother settled her in a small, rented chamber and ordered her a bath. Randa wanted her daughter to wash off the dust of the road and be clean when she met her future husband, so the wench, a woman who went by the name of Greenie, had brought hot water and a copper tub with a stool in it so Ophelia could sit whilst she bathed.

So far, it had been a vigorous affair.

"Aye, I'm marrying a Blackchurch trainer," Ophelia said as Greenie scrubbed her neck rather strongly with a rag and a bar of lumpy soap that smelled of rosemary. "Did my mother tell you that?"

Greenie took her bathing duties seriously as she scrubbed Ophelia's shoulders. "Aye," she said. "She told me that I'm to shine ye up like a new gold piece. She wants ye clean and smelling sweet."

Ophelia was rather embarrassed that her mother had told the woman why she was here. A servant she didn't even know was now aware of her private business. It was bad enough that she was being forced to bathe with an attendant, something she didn't normally do, but now she was to be trotted out like a prized mare.

She was starting to feel sick again.

"What did my mother select for me to wear?" she asked. "Or did she tell you?"

Greenie looked behind her, at the bed where some garments were strewn across the mattress. "There's a brown silk on the bed, I think," she said. "And a shift."

Ophelia sighed. "That's what she wants me to wear," she said. "She says the brown matches my eyes."

Greenie came around to the front of her, studying her face. "Ye have a fine face, m'lady," she said. "I know the Blackchurch lads. They like pretty women. Which one are ye to marry?"

What a lovely thought, Ophelia pondered morosely. *Men who like pretty girls. More than one? Or a different one every night? Is Blackchurch nothing but a stable of oversexed men?*

"De Royans," she said glumly. "Creston is his name, I think."

Greenie stopped and looked at her, evidently with some surprise. "Sir Creston?" she repeated. "Have ye never met him, lass?"

"Never."

Greenie resumed her scrubbing. "Then ye'll not be disappointed," she said. "He's one of the more comely lads of the group. *Quite* comely, I'd say."

That didn't create more interest for Ophelia than she already had. If anything, it might have made it worse.

"Comely," she muttered. "I would assume he knows it?"

Greenie shrugged as she lifted Ophelia's arm and began to wash it. "No more than any other man," she said. "He deserves a pretty wife and ye'll do fine. He'll be pleased."

Ophelia didn't really care if the man was pleased or not. They were both being forced into this, so it didn't matter what they felt. Duty came first. But she was starting to feel sicker, and a little shaky as well, so her thoughts shifted from Creston de Royans to her stomach.

She needed food.

"Greenie, if I asked you to help me, would you?" she said.

Greenie paused, looking at her. "Of course, lass," she said. "What do ye need?"

Ophelia was careful in how she proceeded. "My grandfather," she said. "He… he believes a woman should be frail and pale in appearance and he has not given me much food to eat."

Greenie frowned. "What do ye mean?"

Ophelia sighed heavily. "I mean that he wants me to be frail and pale when I meet my betrothed," she said. "My grandfather believes that is what makes a woman beautiful. The weaker, the better. But the truth is that he has starved me."

Now Greenie was starting to understand. "He did that?" she said, aghast. "Ridiculous!"

Ophelia could see she had support. Reaching out, she grasped the woman's wrist. "Greenie, I'm so very hungry," she said softly. "Could you bring me some food and not tell my grandfather or my mother? She lets him starve me, so she mustn't know. I have a little money. I will pay for the food, but could you bring me some and not let anyone see?"

Greenie dropped the rag into the copper pot. "Of course, I

will," she said, clearly outraged. "I'll get ye something myself. Stay here and I'll return."

Ophelia felt more hope and relief than she had since this entire nightmare had started. Since the day that Cecil had decided to leave her at the altar and her life was turned upside down, nothing had gone her way. No sympathy, no kindness, no love. None at all. Now, one kind person's agreeing to help her, bringing her something as simple as food, was enough to drive her to tears. As Greenie fled the chamber and shut the door, Ophelia climbed out of the tub and bolted the door behind her.

She didn't want anyone coming in, surprising her.

She'd had bathed in her shift, refusing to strip naked in front of someone she didn't know, so now that Greenie was out of the chamber, she pulled off the shift and sat down in the copper tub, finishing what Greenie had started. Using the soap she'd brought, she scrubbed the rest of her body, her face, and behind her ears. Greenie had washed her hair the very first thing, rinsing it with stale ale and then winding it on top of her head and pinning it with big iron pins. When every inch of her body was washed, feet included, she quickly climbed out of the tub and dried off with a long piece of linen that was embroidered around the edges. She and her mother shared it because it was a valuable piece, but it dried her quickly and she pulled a clean shift over her head just as someone knocked on the door.

"Who comes?" she demanded.

"Me, m'lady!"

Quickly, Ophelia rushed to the door and admitted Greenie, who had a small tray in her hands, covered with a cloth. Ophelia followed her like a loyal dog, eagerly, as the servant took the tray over to the small table in the chamber and then uncovered it to reveal a bowl of stew and a hunk of bread. There was also a small bowl of stewed apples with cinnamon and a cup of wine. Ophelia could smell everything. Starving, she sat down and began to stuff her mouth with the mutton stew as Greenie pulled the pins out of her hair and let the damp strands fall.

"I saw yer mother out in the common room," Greenie said. "I don't know if she'll be coming to see ye any time soon, so ye'd better hurry and eat."

Ophelia was eating as fast as she could without it coming back up again. Greenie went back over to the chamber door and threw the bolt so there would be no unexpected visitors.

"You have my undying gratitude," Ophelia said, mouth full. "I will not forget this, I swear it."

Greenie found a comb in Ophelia's smaller satchel and began to comb through her hair. It was long and soft, with a slight wave to it, drying quickly in the warmth of the chamber.

"Not to worry, m'lady," Greenie said. "I cannot believe yer grandfather would starve ye simply for presentation. He expects ye to look like death on your wedding day?"

Ophelia gulped down the small cup of wine. "He thinks women should be fragile creatures, seen and not heard," she said, which was sort of the truth. He didn't like a woman with an opinion, but the part about fragility wasn't exactly true. Her grandfather simply didn't want her to gain weight and look as if she were pregnant. "He is a man of strong views when it comes to women. He makes it difficult sometimes."

She plowed back into the stew as Greenie continued to brush her hair, fluffing it, drying it. The servant couldn't help but think that in spite of the young woman's wealth—and it was clear, from the fine slippers she wore to the milled soap used for her bath, that she came from money—she seemed to lead a rather unpleasant existence. Greenie couldn't even fathom a man starving a woman simply so she'd look thin and frail.

She knew for a fact that Creston de Royans wasn't going to like that.

She knew Creston better than she let on. He frequented The Black Cock with his close friend, Cruz, probably more than the other trainers did. For Creston, it seemed to be a release of sorts—he would drink and play card games with Cruz or the owner of The Black Cock, Hobbes, and sometimes he even played with Hobbes' wife, Margit. They were an older couple who had taken ownership of the tavern from Hobbes' father long ago, and they were childless, so the Blackchurch trainers filled a void for them. They treated the men like family, fed them at no cost, mostly let them drink at no cost—though the trainers insisted on paying—and, in turn for the kindness, the trainers were the security for the tavern. In the wilds of Devon, a place like The Black Cock could attract all kinds of dangerous men, and the Blackchurch trainers were always there to ensure the tavern was a safe place for all. Creston always seemed to be at the forefront of any action in defense of the tavern.

That was how Greenie knew he wasn't going to like someone trying to starve a lady.

He was a chivalrous man.

However, Greenie had never seen Creston with a single, special woman, and there had been plenty of opportunity for it. Serving wenches passing in and out of the tavern, as well as travelers and villagers who haunted the place. Greenie had seen Creston and the other trainers sup with women and even dance with them on occasion, if there happened to be music, but none of the trainers were the predatory type. They seemed quite focused on their duties for Blackchurch and distractions like women weren't really needed or wanted. Of course, a few of the trainers had married, and Greenie knew their wives, kind and upstanding women, but whoring for the trainers was nonexistent. They were married to their duties.

But now, one more would be taking a wife.

Greenie had to admit that she felt rather sorry for the young woman.

"Where did ye come from, lass?" she asked quietly. "Has yer journey been long?"

Ophelia had finished the stew and was now starting on the fruit. "Not really," she said. "I am from South Devon. Along the sea."

"What village?"

"Sidmouth," Ophelia said, mouth full of apples. "That is where my grandfather lives. He is the Earl of Sidbury, which is the area around Sidmouth. Sometimes people call the town Sidbury, too. In any case, my mother and I live elsewhere, but we have been staying with Grandfather recently."

"Do ye like it along the sea?"

Ophelia nodded. "I do," she said. "I like the fresh air, the sand. I grew up in a village that was not near the sea. We would visit my grandfather on occasion and I always loved being near the ocean. There is peace in something that has been here since the beginning of the world and will be here until the end of it. The sea has seen much."

Greenie was fluffing the back of her hair to encourage it to dry faster. "Ye sound as if ye miss it."

"I do," Ophelia said, finishing with the fruit. She set the bowl down and wiped her mouth with the cloth that covered the food. "But here we are, in the wilds of Devon's north coast. I hear there are beasts in these woods."

Greenie continued to fuss with her hair. "No more than usual," she said. "I've lived here all my life and I will admit that sometimes, ye hear sounds from the trees that don't sound like a man or an animal, but I've never seen anything unusual."

"What do you think it is, then?"

"Only God knows, lass," Greenie said, deciding the hair was dry enough as she started to heavily comb through it. "Do ye plan to live here with Sir Creston?"

"I do not know," Ophelia admitted. "I will live wherever he wishes me to live. He may not even want me here. I do not blame him, though. He was forced into this marriage and I am certain he is unhappy about it."

"Forced?"

"Aye," Ophelia said. "My grandfather forced us both."

Greenie didn't reply to that. The young woman seemed uncertain enough, even depressed, so there was no eagerness on her part for this marriage. If Greenie hadn't known better, she would have sworn that the lass was behaving as if she were going to her own funeral.

The uncertainty in the air was palpable.

"I'm going to say something to ye, m'lady," she said as she stopped combing and came around front so she could look the young woman in the eye. "If ye've never met Creston, let me tell you what I know about him. He's a kind and moral man. We've never had any trouble from him here. He's very loyal to his friends and, I'd be willing to wager, he'll be very loyal to his wife. He's a good man, m'lady. He deserves to have someone who recognizes that and treats him with kindness, too. Can ye do that?"

Ophelia was listening to the woman intently. When the

words sank in, her eyes filled with tears. "Damnation," she muttered, looking away. "I was hoping for someone… someone I would not like."

Greenie thought it was a strange thing to say. "But why?"

Ophelia blinked rapidly, trying to chase the tears away. "I don't know," she said. "I suppose because… because my heart belongs to someone else. Someone I wanted to marry. I was hoping that Sir Creston would give me a reason to be indifferent and not feel any remorse over it."

Greenie understood now. "Lass, I'm sorry for ye," she said sincerely. "I cannot imagine not marrying the man I love. But I'll give ye a word of advice—don't take out yer sorrow on Sir Creston. He's done nothing to deserve it."

Ophelia took a deep breath as she wiped at her eyes. "I know," she said. "I will not be unkind. I am expected to be a dutiful wife and that is what I will be."

"Good," Greenie said gently. "And he'll be a dutiful husband. Ye must keep that in mind when ye meet him. Any man would be honored to marry ye."

Ophelia simply hung her head, resigned. "Thank you," she murmured. "Your words are appreciated."

Greenie patted her on the shoulder and went back to combing her hair. Truthfully, Ophelia was a lovely woman, but she was a lovely woman with a heavy heart. In Greenie's opinion, she was too young for such a burden. Although she knew Creston, she didn't know him well enough to be able to predict just how he'd react to a sensitive young wife whose heart belonged to someone else.

That was going to be tricky.

For them both.

A knock on the door jolted her from her thoughts, and the

first thing she did was rush to the tray of empty dishes and shove them far under the bed before answering. Ophelia was so frightened that she ended up burping, loudly, something Greenie had to cover for because the person at the door was none other than the lady's mother.

My grandfather starved me and my mother let him.

Nay, Greenie couldn't let the woman know that her starving daughter had been fed.

The subject never came up, thankfully, because the mother had come to announce that Sir Creston had arrived, so Ophelia was hastened into the garments on the bed and the jewel case was brought forth. Her mother, a flighty thing, seemed most concerned with the fit of a dress that was loose and voluminous to begin with. Greenie didn't understand it, but it wasn't any of her business, anyway. Once the young lady was dressed and her hair properly combed and adorned, the mother practically dragged her out of the chamber and into the common room beyond.

Greenie couldn't help but hope for the best for both Creston and the lady.

Difficult situation, indeed.

CHAPTER SIX

"CRESTON, MEET LADY Ophelia de Camville, granddaughter of the Earl of Sidbury," Royston said. "My lady, this is your betrothed, and my brother, Sir Creston de Royans."

Creston wasn't expecting the vision before him.

He was damn sorry he hadn't cleaned up before coming to The Black Cock.

Before him stood a vision that he couldn't have imagined in his wildest dreams. Ophelia de Camville was an exquisite beauty, every inch a nobleman's daughter, with light brown hair that had copper and gold flecks in it and eyes that were nearly the same color as her hair. Her face was oval, with wide cheekbones, and lips that were full and pink. Clad in an exquisite silk garment with gold embroidery, and with gold jewelry around her neck, she looked like something that had just stepped through a window from heaven.

Creston was genuinely astonished.

"My lady," he managed to say. "It is an honor to meet you. I hope your journey to Blackchurch was pleasant."

Ophelia forced a smile. "It was pleasant, indeed, my lord," she said. "The roads were good, fortunately."

Creston nodded. "The weather has been dry this far north," he said. "How has your weather been in the south?"

"Dry," Ophelia said. "But everything is much greener here in the north. I've never seen so many trees. Is the hunting good?"

It seemed, to Creston, that she was verging on nervous chatter. Not that he blamed her, because nervous chatter was better than heavy silence. He'd only brought up the weather simply to keep the conversation going, and she'd taken the bait. It gave him a chance to watch her mouth as she spoke, and he had to admit that he was pleasantly surprised. She was well spoken, with a soft but clear voice, and he could have looked at that face all day. There was something about her eyes that was both warm and mysterious, something that he found quite enchanting.

A most unexpected reaction.

"It is quite good, I hear," Creston said. "The Earl of Exmoor's lands surround Blackchurch and we are permitted to hunt when we have time, which is rare. Do you like to hunt, then?"

Ophelia shook her head. "I admit that I do not," she said, a genuine smile tugging at her lips. "Other than wild boar, I think animals in the forest are quite majestic. I cannot bear to kill them."

Creston grinned. "Understandable from a woman's point of view," he said. "But I would wager to say that you eat them when put upon your table?"

"It would be wasteful not to do so."

"That is a good answer," he said, scratching his neck as he turned to glance at his friends—all of them—who had commandeered their usual table but were keeping an eye on him. "If you do not like to hunt, what do you like to do?"

Ophelia cocked her head thoughtfully. "Everything a properly bred young woman is expected to do," she said. "I can paint, and draw, and sing."

"Do you sing well?"

"I think so."

"That is good to know," Creston said. Then he looked to his brother and the lady's grandfather, who had been watching the exchange very carefully. "I look forward to discovering that for myself."

"She has had the best education in England," de Bulverton said, having listened to what was bordering on an inane conversation. "She can do everything extremely well. My granddaughter has no defects."

That was a rather cold observation coming from a grandfather. Royston watched his brother as his brother watched the lady, and he swore he could see some interest in Creston's face.

"I'm very glad that you wrote to me, my lord," Royston said, turning to de Bulverton. "I have been married for several years and have three sons. It has been a rewarding institution for me and I hope it will be for my brother as well."

"Of course, it will," de Bulverton said, his gaze on his granddaughter. "I am certain they will have many children together. Every man needs a legacy, and Ophelia brings noble blood to the House of de Royans."

Creston finally tore his eyes away from Ophelia and glanced at Oscar de Bulverton. The man spoke so coldly about a family member he should at least have some warmth toward. But he couldn't see any at all. Ophelia stood there, head lowered demurely, and Creston wondered if it was because she didn't want to meet her grandfather's eye. Already, he could sense the weight of the man's stare, something harsh and critical, and he was fairly certain he couldn't have any manner of meaningful conversation with the lady with her gruff grandfather around.

He faced the earl.

"Would it be acceptable if the lady and I were to sit at a table by ourselves, with the two of you observing from a distance?" he asked. "I should like to speak to her and it would be better to establish our relationship now, under supervision, without the two of you as part of the conversation."

Royston thought it was a good idea, but the earl seemed reluctant. "What do you wish to speak of?" he asked.

Creston shrugged. "I will ask the lady about her education," he said. "Mayhap I will ask her if she has ever traveled. You expect us to be married quickly, I assume, and we have only just met. I should like to at least speak with the woman who is to be my wife and come to know her a little before we take our vows."

Royston was supportive of that. If Creston wanted to get to know the woman he'd been strong-armed into marrying, then he had no objections to it. It was better than Creston trying to jump out of the window and embarrassing the entire House of de Royans.

"I think that is reasonable," Royston said, looking at the earl. "My lord? Surely there can be no harm in that. We will sit a few feet away and watch them. If the lady is uncomfortable, she will signal us and we will join them."

The earl still didn't seem too eager about it. His gaze lingered on Creston, whom he'd not even formally met. The first, and only, introduction had been to Ophelia. Creston met the old earl's gaze, steadily, before the earl finally looked away.

"Very well," he said. "Send for drink, de Royans."

He meant Royston, who was more than happy to comply.

With that, he turned away and went to find a table while Creston indicated a small table over by the windows that overlooked the street beyond.

"My lady?" he said. "Shall we sit?"

Ophelia was demure in her obedience, sitting down primly before he took a seat himself. When a serving wench walked by, he asked for drink. As the woman scurried away, Creston cleared his throat quietly.

"Now," he murmured, "we can speak without my brother and your grandfather hanging over us. I am a forthright man, my lady. I speak what is on my mind. I hope that does not offend you."

Ophelia shook her head. "It does not, my lord," she said. "In fact, I prefer it."

"Good," Creston said. "I assume you have been forced into this marriage, also?"

She nodded. "As you have been."

"Are you opposed to it?"

She shrugged. "It would not matter if I were," she said. "Just like it would not matter if you were. We have an obligation that others have dictated we perform."

Creston could see that she was duty-bound. Even if she were greatly opposed to the marriage, such opposition would do her no good. She was a woman and women did what they were told by the men who controlled their lives.

He could tell that de Bulverton most definitely controlled hers.

"I am not trying to incite a riot, my lady," he said quietly. "I am simply asking you where you stand on the subject of our marriage."

"I have told you," she said, daring to meet his eye. "I am

forced to obey, as you are."

He regarded her a moment, rubbing his chin in thought. "So you were not looking forward to this?" he said. "You did not demand your grandfather find you a husband?"

She looked at him strangely. "Nay, I did not demand my grandfather find me a husband," she said. "My lord, let me be plain, as you are clearly not at all enthused about this contract. I am doing as I am told. I could just as easily commit myself to the cloisters, but my grandfather seems to think that he wants an heir to inherit his earldom. I am the means by which that will be accomplished. I'm nothing more than chattel in this case, a means to an end, so do not think I hold any romantic notions about marriage. It is a chore, like any other chore. Is that enough of an answer for you?"

So she has a spine, Creston thought. He rather liked that she spoke plainly, if not strongly, to him. He knew he'd pushed her a little and she'd reacted in kind.

"It's a good answer," he said. "Thank you for your honesty."

"You are welcome."

"You should know that I don't have any romantic notions about marriage, either."

"Then we understand one another."

"I think we are coming to."

"Then you can tell me what you expect out of this marriage and I will do my best to comply," she said, somewhat stiffly. "After we are married, do you wish for me to return with my grandfather and live in Sidmouth? Or shall I live with you?"

"If you are my wife, you should probably live with me."

"I will not impede your life in any way," she said. "You can continue your life as if you are not married."

"What does that mean?"

"It means that I do not wish to interfere with your life and the way you live it," she said. "You must be unhappy enough being forced into this. I will make it as easy as possible for you."

He still wasn't sure what she meant. "What do you think I do that you would be impeding?"

She shrugged. "I do not know, really," she said. "I do not know you at all, or what you do, or even what a Blackchurch is. I simply want you to know that I will be agreeable with whatever you wish to do and the life you wish to lead."

He sat back in his chair, studying her. He couldn't get a good feel for her, whether she was kind and warm, or stiff and unfeeling. It would be a pity for a woman of such beauty to be cold.

Nay, that wasn't what he wanted.

Perhaps he needed to try another tactic.

"I do not lead an exciting life," he told her. "But I lead a fulfilling one. Has no one told you what the Blackchurch Guild is?"

She lifted her slender shoulders. "I was told that you train warriors," she said. "But I do not know more than that."

The serving wench brought a pitcher of wine and two cups. She set them on the table and Creston poured a cup for Ophelia first and then one for himself. As he took a sip, she took her cup and gulped it down. He was coming to think he might have upset her with his pressing questions.

"It is a training guild for the most elite warriors in the world," he told her, his voice a little softer, a little kinder. "It has been for well over one hundred years. It is owned and operated by the Earls of Exmoor."

"And that's whom you serve?"

"Aye," he said. "I have been a trainer for close to fifteen

years. There are ten of us, all highly skilled knights ourselves. We each teach a different aspect of warfare, something we are particularly knowledgeable about."

"What is it you teach?"

He sat back, cup in hand. "Interrogation tactics," he said. "Treatment of an enemy, spying, covert operations. I also teach a man how to deal with torture and survive it."

For the first time since their meeting, she seemed to show some interest in what he was saying. "That sounds terribly difficult," she said. "Where did you learn such things?"

He smiled faintly. "I trained with the master knights of Kenilworth Castle," he said. "I also trained at Dover Castle and in France at Château de Beynac. I've also traveled to many place and have learned many things from warriors of specific regions. My background is solid and varied, enough so that after my education, I returned to England and became a royal knight."

"Oh?" she said, showing more interest. "Did you serve the king?"

"I did."

"Directly?"

"I was answerable only to him."

He thought he saw a hint of a smile. "He is very young," she said. "I've often wondered what Henry is like. He was so young when he took the throne, but he must be a young man now."

"I served his father, John."

Any shadow of a smile was now gone from her face. "I see," she said. "And… and you enjoyed serving him?"

"I did."

"It must have been dangerous."

"It was."

She simply nodded, but he could see that she wanted to say

more. Perhaps she was determining just what to say given the fact that John was widely hated, still, and he hadn't exactly elaborated on his answers. She surely must have noticed that.

He was expecting the conversation to become difficult now.

John had ruined another relationship for him, too.

"Forgive me," she finally said. "I do not mean to pry, but you do not look old enough to have served John."

That wasn't what he'd expected. No condemnation? No criticism? Her comment made him smile.

It was also a relief.

"How old do you think I am?" he asked.

She flushed, fighting off a smile because he was grinning. "Truthfully, I do not know," she said. "I just meant that you seem ageless."

He chuckled. "That is a kind thing to say," he said. "But I will tell you that I am, indeed, old enough to have served John. I came into his service when I was twenty years old and remained with him for about five years. I left his service before he died, about fourteen years ago."

He could see the thoughts flickering behind those golden eyes. "If you came into his service at twenty years, and remained for five years before leaving fourteen years ago, then you must have come into his service in the Year of Our Lord 1205."

His expression turned appreciative. "You can do sums in your head."

She nodded, modest. "I have always been able to."

"Then given the years and time spans I have given you, how old am I?"

"Thirty years and nine."

He pounded the table softly. "Well done, my lady," he said.

"You are very bright."

She grinned, displaying enormous dimples in both cheeks that he found absolutely enchanting. "As I told you," she said, "I am quite educated. I can read and write, also."

"Good," he said. "If you can read, then I shall have you read to me. I've always loved listening to a beautiful woman with a beautiful voice read aloud."

Her smile faded and she looked at him with a rather shocked expression. "B-beautiful?"

He could see that the gentle compliment had disarmed her. "You are quite beautiful," he said. "I hope that I am not too difficult on your eyes, either."

Ophelia shook her head before she could stop herself. "Not at all," she said. "You are… you are… acceptable."

He snorted. "Acceptable, am I?" he said. "Well, mayhap someday you'll feel comfortable enough to tell me that I am the most handsome man you've ever seen."

"Would that please you?"

"Only if it were the truth."

Ophelia wasn't sure what to say to that. The man had completely disarmed her. Truthfully, this conversation had been most enlightening and nothing she had expected. In fact, Creston de Royans was nothing she had expected. He was indeed the most handsome man she'd ever seen, with wonderfully big muscles and blond hair that hung over those high cheekbones in a most glorious way. When she'd first seen him, she'd had to do a double take because she could hardly believe that he was the man meant to be her husband. *Her!* Somehow, it made the whole situation worse and worse still as she came to know him a little. He was humorous and honest, and she liked that. The man wasn't afraid to talk. It would have been so much easier to go along with her grandfather's scheme if her husband had been a nasty-looking troll who was easy to hate.

But Creston…

Already, she could see that he deserved better.

Greenie had been right.

"I would not say it if it were not the truth," she said after a moment. "May I ask a question?"

"Of course," he said before sipping at the wine in his cup. "You need not ask permission for a question. It does not annoy me if you are curious."

She waggled her eyebrows. "It annoys my grandfather," she said. "It is a habit to ask permission."

"Not with me," he said. "What is your question?"

"I was wondering when they expect this marriage to take place," she said. "Do you know?"

He shook his head. "I do not," he said. "But I suspect my brother and your grandfather are plotting that as we speak. Given the circumstances, I cannot imagine they would wait longer than necessary to see us married. Less chance of one of us running off to Araby and training horses for the rest of our life."

He was smiling as he said it, like it was a joke, but she wasn't so sure there was humor in this situation. Still, she didn't want to appear contrary.

"Is that where you were planning to go to escape this marriage?" she asked, lifting her cup to her lips. "You should have left sooner."

He laughed softly. "I considered it," he said. "But I had a class to instruct."

"Are men easier to train than horses, I wonder?"

"Probably not," he said. "I've trained both, and men are *not* easier."

"Have you been to Araby, then?"

He poured her more wine in her half-empty cup. "I've not had the pleasure," he said. "Why? Do you want to go there?"

She took a sip. "I've never left England," she said. "My grandfather's home overlooks the sea and the sand of Sidmouth and I see the ships come in. They linger in the cove, bobbing gently upon the undulating waters, and I wonder where they have been. Sometimes I imagine they have come from faraway lands that have streets made of marble and buildings made of gold. I heard that about Rome, once. That the streets were made of marble. It almost sounds like heaven."

He was watching her as she spoke, her eyes taking a far-off glow as she thought of golden buildings and stone streets. Most people he knew were older and had been to the places they wished to visit, with very little room left for dreaming. He admired someone who had that quality—

To dream.

He'd lost that ability long ago.

"I have been to Rome," he said. "It is magnificent."

Her features showed the first real excitement he'd seen from her. "Truly?" she said. "You have been so fortunate?"

He nodded. "I have," he said. "It is a very ancient city, more ancient than London. There is a big, circular building in the middle of it that has no roof. They used to have ancient events there."

She was quickly becoming entranced with his tale. "Was the floor of it marble?"

"Nay," he said, smiling at her. "It was dirt. It is crumbling, too. A tribute to the ancient gods who used to watch their ancient games, I suppose."

"But how did you get there?"

"When I was in France," he said. "The lord I was serving had a brother or cousin in the Kingdom of Italy, so we traveled there because he was having trouble with a neighbor. The nights were warm, the days were warmer, and I have never eaten so much good food in my life. I enjoyed it."

As he spoke, Ophelia nearly drained half of her cup, bewitched by his tale. "What did you eat?"

He thought on it. "Pork pies," he said. "Sausages, veal tarts and the like. And they love eggs. Everything has eggs in it."

"I love eggs, too," she said, feeling her stomach rumble. Even though Greenie had given her food, she was still quite hungry. She thought of a way to get around her grandfather's no-food policy. "And speaking of food, may I buy you a meal? I have a little money. It would be polite for me to offer to feed you."

Ophelia was quite pleased with herself. How could her grandfather refuse to let her eat if she was providing food for her betrothed? He would look like an inhospitable cad if he voiced any opposition. But Creston immediately called to the nearest servant.

"Forgive me," he said to Ophelia as he waved the wench over to their table. "I should have offered you a meal the moment we sat down. That was very impolite of me."

That wasn't what Ophelia had expected, but the end was just the same. A servant came over and Creston ordered a meal for them both, a *grand* meal, as he told the wench, and she went scurrying off to the kitchens. When the woman left, Creston looked at Ophelia.

"I should have asked you if you were hungry," he said, genuinely contrite. "I hope you are not too uncomfortable."

"Nay," she said. "I will eat if you wish to eat. But you

needn't go out of your way just to accommodate me."

"It is not going out of my way to offer a lady a meal," he said. "It is my pleasure to do so."

Ophelia wasn't used to someone being so nice to her. In fact, everything Greenie had said about Creston de Royans was, so far, coming true right before her eyes. He *was* kind. He *was* considerate. He didn't even know her, yet he was concerned for her.

God… was there really a world where such men existed?

"Did you order food?"

The earl was suddenly standing next to their table, asking the question, and Creston stood up to face him.

"I did, my lord," he said. "I was very rude and neglected to offer the lady a meal after her long journey. Forgive me for my oversight."

De Bulverton frowned. "She does not need to eat," he said. "If there is no further conversation between you two, I will send her to rest. You and I have much to discuss, de Royans."

It was a rather rude demand when Creston was only being kind. Furthermore, it was clear that Creston wasn't pleased by the man's response. "We may have our discussion after the lady and I finish our meal," he said steadily. "There is no hurry."

De Bulverton did what he probably shouldn't have done. With Creston unwilling to bend to his will, he went to Ophelia and very nearly yanked her out of her chair. "She does not need to eat," he repeated, looking at her when he spoke. "Return to your chamber, Ophelia. I will send for you when I want you."

"Hold," Creston said in a deep, deadly tone. "Remove your hand from her arm."

De Bulverton looked at him, startled, and removed his hand simply because the tone coming from Creston was a command.

He knew a command when he heard one. But he didn't like being questioned, and that had his dander up.

"I may do as I please with my granddaughter, Sir Creston," he said. "She will return to her chamber now. You've spoken with her enough."

There was tension in the air now, prickly and uncomfortable. Creston was coming not to like de Bulverton because of the man's bullying attitude and, even if he *was* an earl, Creston was not afraid of him. Not even slightly. He held the size and weight advantage by a mile. In response, he lifted an eyebrow.

"Has the betrothal contract that was offered been signed?" he asked.

De Bulverton was trying to figure out why Creston asked the question. "Why?" he said. "If it is not, do you think to break it?"

"Answer my question, my lord."

"I will not."

"It is valid," Royston said. He didn't like what he was seeing between his brother and de Bulverton and hoped to stave off any confrontation. "When Lord Sidbury made the offer, it came signed. That is legally binding. You cannot break the betrothal, Creston."

There wasn't much room to move, so Creston shifted the table back. It was a very heavy piece of furniture, but he moved it like it meant nothing. That cleared a path between him and Ophelia, who was watching the situation with concern. He reached out and took her gently by the arm, pulling her to sit down in the chair her grandfather had yanked her out of.

"I do not intend to break anything," he said, effectively putting himself between Ophelia and her grandfather. "If the offer is signed, and I have accepted, then by law and by God, she is already my wife. She belongs to me. And you will never again touch my wife in the manner I just saw. Is that clear?"

De Bulverton had to step back because Creston was close enough to throw a punch if provoked. Still, he looked at Creston in outrage. "How *dare* you speak to me that way," he said. "She is not your wife until I say she is."

Creston didn't back down. "Then we will be married immediately," he said, looking at his brother. "Send word to the Church of St. Andrew. It is at the end of the village. Tell the priest that he is to perform a wedding mass at dawn. I will marry the lady and we will answer this question once and for all. If you refuse, Lord Sidbury, then I will take this to the local magistrate and you will lose."

De Bulverton was furious. He looked at Ophelia, who was gazing back at him with some fear, before returning his attention to Creston. The knight was pompous and rude, and as Oscar looked at the man, he began to think of the absolutely delicious secret his granddaughter was hiding. So de Royans wanted to marry her immediately, did he? All the better for Oscar if he did. The arrogant arse deserved everything he was going to get.

It was all Oscar could do not to smile at the thought.

"If that is what you want, then you shall have it," he said. "You'll have everything in life that is coming for you, de Royans. Mark my words."

With that, he turned and headed toward the kitchens, shouting for Hobbes and demanding to be shown his chamber. His daughter, who had been lingering at the rear of the common room, watching the entire situation unfold, went running after him. That left Ophelia sitting at the table, feeling sick at her grandfather's behavior.

She was horribly ashamed.

"I am sorry," Creston said softly, interrupting her thoughts. "I did not mean to create a scene, but I cannot tolerate a tyrant. I did not like the way he grabbed you."

Ophelia was trying hard not to weep. "It is… his way."

"I suspect this is not the first time he has done this to you."

She shook her head, hanging it. "Nay," she whispered.

Creston watched her lowered head for a moment. "No more," he told her. "That will happen no more. Tomorrow, we wed, and he'll never touch you again. Now, I want you to retreat to your chamber and remain there tonight. I will make sure arrangements are made for a wedding mass at dawn. And I will have the meal sent to your chamber, so you can eat and rest. We will speak more tomorrow."

With that, he extended a hand to her. Ophelia had no idea what he wanted until she realized he wanted her hand. She was so used to being grabbed or forcibly escorted that it was a completely foreign concept to her that a man should be so considerate. Timidly, she put her hand in his enormous one and he gently pulled her to stand. For a moment, they simply gazed into one another's eyes—his were warm; hers were anxious.

He smiled gently.

"Go, now," he told her quietly. "I will see you on the morrow."

Ophelia simply nodded and headed off toward her small, rented chamber. She didn't dare look at anyone around her, afraid that everyone had seen the confrontation. She was unsettled enough as it was. But she did dare to look back over her shoulder, just once, to see Creston in conversation with his brother, who didn't seem too pleased.

Upsetting the bride's grandfather was never cause for celebration.

Bride.

As Ophelia made her way to her chamber, disappearing inside and bolting the door, she knew one thing for certain. Nothing in her life had ever been so clear. Creston de Royans thought he was marrying a pure, innocent woman who was being bullied by her grandfather, but that wasn't the case. He was marrying an impure, pregnant woman, and if he did, her grandfather would have victory over Creston. The insulting scene out in the common room would be avenged.

By Oscar.

But Ophelia couldn't allow that to happen.

She was going to have to save Creston de Royans.

CHAPTER SEVEN

"**I** AM NOT entirely sure how well that meeting just went," Cruz muttered. "It looks as if Cres and that old man nearly came to blows."

He was seated at the table that the trainers regularly used when relaxing at The Black Cock, a heavy, long table situated in an alcove that could be sectioned off with pieces of paneled wood if they needed privacy, but it was raised above the rest of the common room and had a view of the entry door, making it perfect for men who were almost always on their guard.

It had been a prime spot to see Creston's introduction to the woman he was going to marry and then the subsequent events, including what looked to be a confrontation between Creston and an old man with dirty hair and a bulbous nose. Creston's brother, whom none of them had met, was also part of the situation, but he'd been standoffish rather than actively in the middle of it. When the old man stormed off, Creston had sent the young woman to her chamber before he and his brother seemed to have further heated words.

All was not going well with Creston's betrothal.

"It is clear that he does not want this," Tay said, his gaze on

Creston, who was over near the entry door with his brother. "I cannot say that I was eager to wed, either, but meeting my wife changed my mind."

Those who were married, Fox and Sinclair and Payne, nodded, while the unmarried trainers didn't seem to have much of an opinion.

"The right woman can change a man's mind," Sinclair said. "His betrothed is a beautiful woman."

That seemed to be the predominant opinion, as more heads began to bob up and down in agreement. "She's lovely," Fox agreed. He kept moving his head around, trying to catch sight of Creston, because Amir's head was in the way. "I wonder if she has some manner of flaw that we cannot see?"

"Like what?" Tay asked.

Fox shrugged. "Mayhap she has made it clear that she is immoral or unkind," he said. "Or mayhap she smells of compost. Who can say? Clearly, we do not know, but Creston sent her away. There has to be a reason."

"We should not speculate," Ming Tang, across the table, said. "There could be ten different reasons why Creston sent the young lady away. We'll only know if he decides to tell us."

"Here he comes," Payne spat. "Shut up, all of ye. Dunna let him know we've been gossiping like fishwives."

Tay grinned. "I think he knows."

"Then speak of something else, quickly," Payne said. Then he swiftly changed the subject. "Where is Bowen? Why did ye not invite him and the assistant trainers tae sit with us tonight?"

He was looking mostly at Tay, who shrugged. "Bowen may be a fully fledged trainer now, but he still has work to do," he said. "And the assistant trainers were not invited because this is something just for us, as the senior trainers. We have known

Creston the longest. He requires our support at this time and, from experience, I can tell you that it is a very personal time. Marriage always is."

"Unless you marry a woman with an enormous family," Sinclair said, snorting. "Elisiana has more kin than I can count on my fingers and toes. There is always someone new she is speaking of. Do you know that she had an aunt who wanted to send her troubled son to live with us? She thought that because I'm a Blackchurch trainer, I could scare the son into submission."

Laughter rippled around the table just as Creston appeared. Cruz pushed a chair out for him and Creston sat heavily, accepting a cup of wine from Cruz.

"What are you laughing about?" he said. "Tell me so that I may laugh, too, or else I shall tear a few heads off around here before my anger is fully satisfied."

That gave them all a clue as to how the meeting with his betrothed had gone. Sinclair eyed Tay before answering.

"I was saying that my wife has an unruly cousin whose mother wanted me to frighten into behaving," he said. Then he cast Creston a long look. "Speaking of wives, we saw your betrothed. She is a beautiful woman."

Creston took a long drink of his wine before answering. "She is," he said. "Very beautiful. But her grandfather is a despicable creature. I do not like the man."

"The earl?" Kristian said. He'd been largely quiet until now. "Was that the old man you were speaking with?"

Creston nodded. "Aye," he said. "Would you like to hear what that animal has done? I've been told that he has been starving my betrothed so that she would appear slim and delicate to me in the hopes that it would make her more attractive. What kind of man does that to a woman?"

There was no more laughter or humor around the table at that point as the group began to understand the reasons behind Creston's anger.

"Is she well, Cres?" Ming Tang, on his other side, asked with concern. "Will you send for a physic?"

Creston shook his head. "She seems well enough," he said. "She also seems kind and bright, and has a sense of humor. That is a good thing. Beyond that, I cannot tell you much, only that I have decided to go forward with the marriage."

Those at the table nodded in approval. "Congratulations," Tay said. "Lads, we are in the presence of the next Earl of Sidbury. That's a very proud thing, Creston. You deserve it."

Cups were raised in salute, and in spite of his anger with de Bulverton—and subsequently his brother, who'd lectured him on his behavior toward the old man—Creston broke out in a weak smile. Being with his friends always grounded him, and he could feel himself calming. As the men around the table broke off into small conversation groups, Ming Tang turned to Creston.

"It seems you are to join the ranks of husbands," he said, his dark eyes glimmering with warmth. "I am happy for you, truly, if this is what you want."

Creston leaned back in his chair, cup in hand. "It does not matter what I want, does it?" he said. "It is what my brother has demanded. When he first came to tell me, I will be honest in my reaction—I was resentful. I still am. I have always been the achiever in the family, the ambitious one. I can run circles around my brother, mentally and physically, yet it is he who holds sway over my future. I've never quite overcome that bitterness."

"Made worse when he told you about your betrothal?" Cruz said. On Creston's right side, he had been listening to the conversation. "I think you've only mentioned your brother a few times since I've known you. You are not close."

"Nay, we are not," Creston said, shaking his head. "But he will remind me every chance he gets that *he* is the elder brother. Baron Tottington, a legacy inherited through our mother. She was an heiress. I have a sister, too. Did I ever tell you that?"

"Nay," Cruz said, looking at him in surprise. "Why have you never told me that?"

Creston shrugged. "Because she was barely seventeen years of age when Royston found her a husband," he said. "She was absorbed into the House of Summerlin years ago. About twelve years ago, in fact. I was in France at the time and I came home to a sister who had been married for three years already. She had two children and a husband who seemed to be kind to her, but the husband did not want me around, given the fact he was not an ally of the Crown. I've not seen Helen in years."

He seemed somewhat depressed by that. As Cruz knew, Creston wasn't close to any of his family and never had been.

It was a lonely existence sometimes.

"I'm sure she is well," Cruz said. "You would have heard otherwise."

"Mayhap," Creston said. "It's strange… Helen and I were much closer than Royston and I ever were. She was a trouble-maker, however, and I was the one constantly getting her out of trouble."

Cruz chuckled. "That does not sound like a de Royans," he said. "You and your kind are not known to be trouble."

Creston grinned. "Not according to my brother," he said. "According to him, I just created a great deal of trouble for him with de Bulverton."

Cruz grunted. "You do not become confrontational by nature," he said. "You are a master interrogator, Cres. The earl must have said something you did not like."

Creston thought back to the conversation, how he felt when he saw the earl grab Ophelia's arm cruelly. "He *did* something I did not like," he said. "Lady Ophelia weighs as much as my right leg, yet her grandfather did not seem to feel the need to be careful with her. He grabbed her by the arm and pulled her out of her chair, and the way he did it was… cruel."

Ming Tang was listening to the conversation carefully. "Cres," he said slowly, "did you agree to marry this woman so quickly because you feel a need to protect her? You are a defender by nature. Do you feel the need to defend her from her own grandfather?"

Creston looked at him a moment before averting his gaze as he thought on the question. His eyes, so very blue, took on a distant cast as he pondered many things—a frail lady, a cruel grandfather, and the situation that she'd found herself in. A terrible situation that he was about to become part of. *Did* he feel the need to defend her?

Or was there more to it?

"Not defend," he finally said, his voice quiet. "I'm not sure what I'm feeling, but it's not a need to defend her. It's something more."

"How can you know after just having met her?"

Creston shook his head. "I am not certain," he said. "But all I know is that she is a lady who seems to need… something. Mayhap she needs me."

Ming Tang didn't say anything more. As Creston stared off into the room, thinking about the situation, Ming Tang caught

Cruz's eye. They didn't voice what they were thinking—that Creston, unable to get out of the betrothal, was now creating reasons to accept it. In the end, that would only do him, and the lady, harm when he realized he'd failed to accept the situation more than he was finding reasons that the marriage should happen.

She needed him.

She was abused.

It wasn't simply that they were to marry and accepted the situation as it was.

It would have been better if Creston weren't creating phantoms to fight in the lady's name.

Finally, Ming Tang couldn't remain silent.

"Creston," he muttered, "mayhap I should not say this, but I am going to point out a very obvious possibility."

Creston looked at him then. "What?"

"You do not know the lady or her grandfather," he said. "You do not know their character. Is it possible that they staged that little display of cruelty simply so your chivalrous, knightly training would take precedence and you would feel the need to protect the lady? It would be rather coercive of them if they did. All I am saying is, do not think the lady too helpless. She may not be helpless at all."

"Be on your guard, Cres," Cruz said, his voice low. "That entire scene might have been for your benefit."

Creston had to admit that what they were saying had not occurred to him. Was it possible that what he'd just seen was all for show? To make him feel protective toward her? If that were the case, there wasn't much he could do about it except be on his guard.

And he would be if his friends were seeing something he wasn't.

"Time will tell," he said after a moment. "It always does."

Talk of his betrothal was done for the night.

CHAPTER EIGHT

LATER THAT NIGHT, Creston's head had just hit his pillow when there was a knock at his cottage door. Wearily, he lifted himself out of bed, struck a taper, and trudged down the stairs, unbolting the door and yanking it open.

A gatehouse guard was standing in the darkness.

"I am sorry to trouble you, Sir Creston," the man said, "but you have a visitor who was most desperate to see you. She would not leave until she did, so I hope we did right by admitting her."

Creston was annoyed until the guard mentioned that the visitor was a female. Then he became curious.

"Who?"

"Me."

Ophelia suddenly appeared behind the gate guard. With her wrapped in a heavy cloak against the damp night air, all he could see was her face. That angelic face. Startled, he stood aside and indicated for her to enter.

"Please," he said. "Come in."

She swept in as Creston continued to stand in the doorway, realizing there was no one accompanying her. "Are you alone?"

he asked, surprised.

"Aye," she said. "Tell your guard that if anyone comes looking for me, he has not seen me. Please. It is important."

The guard heard her. With a nod of understanding, he headed back for the gatehouse as Creston stood there with the door still open. He wasn't at all comfortable having her in his home without a chaperone.

"Why are you alone?" he asked. "You know that you should not be here without an escort."

She nodded her head. "I know," she said. "But I cannot have my grandfather or mother hear what I am about to tell you. Please, Sir Creston. It is very important."

Be on your guard, Cres.

That was the advice from Ming Tang.

He fully intended to take it, now more than ever.

"I do not understand," he said. "How did you come here without your mother or grandfather knowing?"

Ophelia had a sense of urgency about her. "Because I waited until they were asleep and climbed from the window," she said. "But I share a chamber with my mother, so if she awakens and finds me missing, she will come straight to you. We must hurry."

"I think you need to leave."

There was panic in her expression. "Nay," she begged softly. "*Please.* This will only take a minute, but what I tell you will change the course of your life, I swear it."

She seemed sincere, but he was very hesitant. If this was another situation that had been manipulated by her grandfather, he wanted no part of it. Perhaps the old man wanted for her to be discovered, alone, with her betrothed. He could impose all sorts of demands on him and on Royston for compromising the lady before they were married. He hated to be so suspicious, but Ming Tang and Cruz had him thinking of self-protection.

He left the entry door open.

"Very well," he said. "Why are you here?"

"I have come with a message and a request."

"Who is the message from? And who is the request from?"

"Both from me," she said. "Sir Creston, I simply cannot let my grandfather do this to you."

"Do what to me?"

Ophelia took a deep breath, and he could see that she was blinking back tears. "First, may I ask a question?" she said.

"I told you that you do not need my permission. What is it?"

"Is there a nunnery nearby?"

He wasn't sure why she was asking. "There are a couple," he said. "St. Katherine's is about a day's ride to the east. Why do you ask?"

"Because I would like to know if you will take me there," she said. "I cannot marry you."

He didn't say anything. Either she was being completely honest, or she was a master at her craft. He wasn't sure which. Even if he hadn't had the conversation earlier with Ming Tang and Cruz, he still would have been guarded in this situation. Creston had made it his life's work to study, and combat, psychological torture and other things involving coercion and manipulation, so he had learned to be cautious in any critical situation.

Like this one.

However... her request seemed real. He wasn't sensing any feigned emotion or practiced panic. Everything seemed genuine. After finally closing the entry door, he went into the area at the rear of the cottage where meals were eaten and brought out two chairs. He put them in front of the dark hearth as he set the taper on the mantel.

"Here," he said. "Sit down. Explain why you cannot marry me."

Ophelia sat down, watching him anxiously as he took the other chair a couple of feet away. He simply looked at her, a silent invitation to continue.

She took the hint.

"In order to explain this, I must start from the beginning," she said, her voice trembling. "This is something my grandfather would never tell you. I was told not to tell you either. However, after meeting you today, I find that I cannot let him cheat you out of a happy and noble life. That is what he is trying to do, just so he can have an heir for his earldom."

"How is he trying to cheat me? I do not understand."

She took a deep breath. "Two months ago, I was to be married to the man I loved," she said. "He was from a good family and I had been planning our life together for years. I'd known him for as long. But the day of our wedding, he failed to show up at the church. Instead, his father came to tell me that his son had fled to an abbey. He was to become a priest and there would be no marriage."

Creston nodded in understanding. "Ah," he said. "I am sorry for you. Something like that is never easy."

"It was not," Ophelia said. "I loved Cecil. He was the only man I wanted to marry."

"And now you are going to break our betrothal and commit yourself to a nunnery because you do not wish to marry me?" he said. "Because I am the second choice?"

She sighed, heavily, running a shaking hand across her forehead. "It has nothing to do with that," she said. "My lord, there is no easy way to say this, so I will come out with it. I am pregnant with Cecil's child and my grandfather is panicking. Cecil walked out on me and my grandfather was desperate to find me a suitable husband, and somehow, he found you. Now he is trying to trick you into believing this child I carry is yours. As I said, I was willing to obey him until I met you, and now… now, I cannot let him do it. He wants to lie to you about my condition and I refuse to go along with it any longer. Now that you know, I was hoping you would escort me to the nunnery. Once I commit myself, our betrothal is broken. You will be set free."

Creston was dumbfounded. "You're *pregnant*?"

"I am."

He hissed as the information was confirmed. He wasn't a man easily shocked, but at the moment, he was. "My brother must not know about the pregnancy," he said. "He would never have agreed to this."

Ophelia shook her head. "He did not know," she said. "But I told you once I am an honest woman. I cannot, in good conscience, let you assume this terrible circumstance. I would rather spend my life in a nunnery than see a good man shamed."

Creston stood up. He had to. He had to get some air. He walked away from Ophelia, his mind whirling with what she had told him. The predominant emotion, at the moment, was disappointment. *Great* disappointment, if he were to admit it. That beautiful woman had given herself over to another and now, she was compromised.

Pregnant!

The entire marriage offer had been a ruse.

Ming Tang had been right to a certain extent—he *had* been manipulated, but not by Ophelia.

By her grandfather.

"I do not have to take you to the nunnery to break the betrothal," he said after a moment. "You have given me a legal reason for breaking it. All I have to do is tell him that I know you are pregnant with another man's child, and there is no magistrate in England that will force me to honor the contract."

"I realize that," she said. "But I do not have the same choice. My grandfather will find a man to marry me who is willing to overlook the pregnancy with the promise of an earldom, and that kind of man would not be someone I would wish to be married to."

"Nay," Creston said as he thought of such an opportunist. "That would not be a good situation for you."

"Will you help me, then?"

He looked at her. *Really* looked at her. He found his gaze drifting over that pale face, those lovely eyes, and thinking that this entire situation was something horrific.

Horrific and sad.

"You do not look pregnant," he said. "I would have never known."

His observation brought her to tears. They poured down her face faster than she could wipe them away. "That is because my grandfather has been starving me for the past two months," she whispered tightly. "He thought if I looked thin and frail enough, the pregnancy would not be noticeable. He's hardly fed me at all."

Creston scowled. "God's Bones," he spat. "Are you serious?"

She nodded. Then she stood up and removed the cloak,

throwing it over the chair before pulling back the neckline of her garment to reveal prominent collarbones. Then she rolled up her sleeves so he could see how thin her arms were.

"He did not wish for me to grow plump," she said, still sniffling. "His answer was to withhold food. I've hardly eaten in two months, so you would not see any signs of the pregnancy."

Creston stared at her birdlike arms, her protruding collarbone, and the reality of her situation made him feel sick. He wasn't the one who had been manipulated by the old earl—it had been Ophelia. She'd been manipulated and abused. That beautiful, bright woman had been in a living hell.

It was appalling.

"My God," he finally breathed. "I've never heard of anything so vile."

Ophelia put her cloak back on, tying it around her neck. "Will you *please* take me to the nunnery?" she asked, sniffling. "Or the nearest church so that I may request sanctuary. If it is too much trouble, you can simply tell me where the church is and I shall find it."

Creston could see the desperation in everything about her. But the one thing that stood out, above all else, was the fact that she had confessed the scheme. She hadn't needed to do it. She could have very well married him under false pretenses and told him the child was his. Once they were married, there was nothing he could do even if he figured out the offspring didn't belong to him. She could have trapped him.

But she hadn't.

The woman had sacrificed her future, so he didn't have to sacrifice his.

It was one of the bravest things he'd ever seen.

"Hold," he said, reaching out to grasp her arms carefully.

"Just… hold a moment, lady. Sit down. We must speak of this situation."

Ophelia was confused as he directed her into the chair. "What more is there to say?" she said. "You know the truth now. You cannot marry me."

He was looking at her seriously. "You're like your grandfather," he said. "You are trying to tell me what to do. *Stop* telling me what to do."

She looked as if he'd struck her with his words. She immediately lowered her head and seemed to shrink down. "My apologies, my lord," she said. "That was not my intention, believe me."

He pulled his chair close to hers and sat down so that their shins were practically rubbing against one another. He leaned forward, elbows resting on his knees. He was looking at her most intently and, after a moment, he reached up and pulled her hood gently off her head, revealing that glorious hair. Her features came into the weak light.

She seemed to grow more beautiful by the hour.

"I have something to say about all of this," he said. "Did you think I would not?"

She shook her head. "It is your right to speak, of course," she said. "But I have told you everything. There is nothing more to tell."

He nodded. "I understand," he said. "And I believe I am justified in saying that your news is most shocking. It is also infuriating. If what you've said is true, your grandfather is trying to trick me into this marriage, and I will tell you now that no man makes a fool of me, least of all the Earl of Sidbury. What he's done, to me, is the same as if he had declared war on the House of de Royans. Do you understand me so far?"

Ophelia nodded fearfully. "Please know that I did not support what he was doing," she said. "But I am in a difficult position. If I did not obey him, he would punish me more than he already has."

Creston shook his head with regret. "And that's another thing," he said. "Did the man truly starve you?"

"He did."

"Then we add cruelty to his already horrific behavior," Creston said. "Is your grandfather always like that?"

Ophelia nodded. "Since I can recall," she said. "He has never forgiven my mother for having been born a woman, nor has he ever forgiven me for the same reason. He never liked Cecil, and he was terribly upset at my mother for agreeing to the betrothal, but when Cecil walked out, he saw his chance to take control of my situation and get what he wanted out of it."

"Like a good strategist," Creston muttered. "Why did he not like Cecil?"

"Because he did not choose him."

"He had no part in it?"

"Nay," she said. "My mother and I live at Symondsbury, which is where I was born. Grandfather lives in Sidmouth. When my father died, my grandfather showed no real interest in my mother or me, so we remained in Symondsbury. When my grandfather came to the mass where I was supposed to marry Cecil, it was the first time I'd seen him in years. Then, suddenly, he took control of everything, including my betrothal to you."

Creston grunted. "More than likely because he saw an opportunity to marry you to someone of his choosing," he said. "All the better for him to create an alliance. But I still cannot understand why Cecil would leave you before your wedding.

That is unfathomable. Did he know you were carrying his child?"

She nodded. "He knew," she said. "I met Cecil when we fostered together at Okehampton Castle. He was handsome, and quite pious, but I decided he was not meant for God but for me. No one rejects the Great Beauty of Dorset—at least, I *thought* no one would reject me. I was wrong."

Creston's eyebrows lifted. "The Great Beauty of Dorset?"

She smiled weakly. "That is what those at Okehampton called me," she said. "I think it was more of a jest than a serious title, but Cecil struggled between wanting to be with me and wanting to devote his life to God. I thought I could force him into marriage with a child on the way, but I was wrong. In that respect, I am no better than my grandfather. I tried to control Cecil. But God was stronger than I am, and He took Cecil for His own. 'Tis I who was left ashamed and remorseful. I suppose I knew better all along. Cecil was quite devoted to God, but I thought I could change him."

It was a brutally honest and intimate confession. Creston listened seriously, seeing that situation for what it was—she'd tried to force something because she wanted it badly enough and it had slipped through her fingers.

That wasn't too far off from what had happened to Creston those years ago.

Thoughts of Mary began to fill his head.

"Sometimes we learn lessons the hard way," he said. "No matter how badly we want something, God has a way of showing us that we are never fully in control."

"That is the truth," Ophelia said sincerely. "I learned my lesson with Cecil. I will never do something so unscrupulous again. It was wrong. Now that I see how my grandfather has tried to control you, I can see just how terrible I was. I do not blame Cecil for running. I never did. It was my fault."

Creston was listening to her with some sympathy. "And confessing your grandfather's scheme to me is penitence?"

She looked at him with a guilty expression. "Aye," she said truthfully. "I have already tried to control one man. I could not let the same thing happen to you."

Creston pondered that statement for a moment. "You do realize that you have risked a great station in life by telling me everything," he said. "If you'd just kept your mouth shut, we would have married and quite possibly have been happy. You would have been well respected and the mother of my children. It would have been a good life for any woman."

She nodded steadily. "I know," she said. "But I could not have lived with such a secret. Eventually, it would have come out, and you would have hated me for it."

"I doubt I could ever hate you," he said softly. "But it would have made things difficult."

Ophelia was well aware of that. "Thankfully, now it does not have to be so," she said. "May… may I tell you something?"

"Anything."

"Today, when I arrived at The Black Cock, a servant named Greenie helped me bathe," she said. "Greenie was very kind. She asked why I had come to Exebridge and I told her. She proceeded to tell me what a good man you were and that you deserved someone worthy. I realize now how unworthy I am, so I hope you will not think too unkindly about me in the years to come. In the end, I did what was right for you and for me, so I hope you do remember that."

He cocked his head. "Lady, the sheer fact that you confessed the scheme makes you quite worthy, indeed," he said. "You have risked your entire future to preserve mine. How can I just walk away from that?"

"Because you were lied to," she insisted. "How can you forgive *that*?"

"I am willing to forgive you because you confessed," he said. "You told me that you were honest when I first met you, and you have demonstrated that. But the next question is the one that will decide our fate."

"What fate?"

"Whether or not we will go through with the marriage."

She looked at him in disbelief. "After everything I've told you, you are *still* willing to go through with this?" she said. "That's madness!"

He grinned. "Probably," he said. "But I have found a woman with impeccable honesty and I am not so easily going to let her go. That is why I must ask this question."

"What question?"

"Are you still willing to marry me?"

She looked at him as if he'd lost his mind. "I… I do not even know how to answer that," she said. "You know that another man has touched me."

"I do. A man you believed you would marry."

"And it is his child in my belly."

"When I marry you, the child in your belly becomes mine. He will have no claim."

Now Ophelia was dumbfounded. "Are you serious?"

He nodded. "Quite serious," he said. "Since you have made a confession to me, I will make one to you."

"Go ahead."

He sat back, scratching his head, trying to summarize that terrible time in his life. She didn't need to know all of the details, but she did need to know her situation wasn't so different than one he'd been in once, too.

"Years ago, there was a woman I wanted to marry," he said. "I knew her father did not approve of me, so I coerced her into my bed, and she became pregnant with my child."

Ophelia studied him for a moment as their common situations began to become apparent, and the light of realization struck her. "You did it to force her father to approve of your marriage," she said softly.

He nodded. "I did," he said. "I loved her and she loved me, and I thought my perfect life was planned. But her father still did not approve, so Mary and I made plans to run away together. Her father found out about it and sent her away before that could happen. So, you see, my lady, that somewhere in this world, a man married the woman I loved and is raising my child. I do not know if he was tricked into it like your grandfather tried to trick me, but regardless, another man is raising my child. Mayhap by raising yours, I am accepting him as I hope Mary's husband has accepted my child. You asked how I can forgive what you've done? That is how."

Ophelia was astonished. "I find the fact that you have had a similar experience to mine to be wholly remarkable," she said. "You understand what it is like to lose someone you intended to marry."

"I do, indeed," he said. "If that is not a sign that you and I are destined to marry, I do not know what is."

He had a point. Ophelia sat there, gazing at him, realizing this might not be a horrible ending for her after all. He was willing to overlook the pregnancy, and she could have never imagined that in a thousand years.

"Are you certain?" she whispered.

He nodded. "I am," he said. "Are you?"

"I am."

"A better alternative than the cloister?"

She smiled faintly. "I think so," she said. "I hope so."

Creston smiled in return. "I hope so, too," he said. "But you will not tell your grandfather about this conversation. Do you understand? That is something I will do when the time is right."

She nodded solemnly. "As you wish," she said. "The less said to him, the better. And to my mother—she never protected me through this entire thing. She simply let Grandfather do as he wished."

Creston hadn't even met her mother, but already, he was displeased with the woman. "I understand that it is difficult to take a stand against one's father," he said. "But where a child is concerned, I should hope for better from a parent. In any case, I will take you back to the tavern and you will stay there until I come for you in the morning. Understood?"

Ophelia nodded. "Aye, my lord."

His eyes took on a hint of warmth. "I am to be your husband," he said. "You may call me Creston."

"Thank you, my lo—I mean, thank you, Creston."

He grinned. "Do you go by Ophelia?" he said. "Or do you have another name you would prefer me to use?"

"I am called Ophelia by most," she said. "Though my mother and grandfather sometimes call me Lia."

"Lia," he repeated softly. "I like that. May I call you that?"

"Of course."

That pleased him. He stood up and extended a hand to her, which she took more quickly than she had the last time he'd offered it. She understood what he wanted the second time around. As Creston gazed at her, he began to feel the beginnings of a connection. The advice of Ming Tang was fading quickly because he just couldn't imagine that she would tell him such a catastrophic secret as part of some elaborate lie to manipulate him somehow. It wasn't like *he* was the earl, being trapped into marriage. He was a simple knight with no property, no title, simply an abundance of talent and a prestigious position, so he had nothing of value that the Earl of Sidbury or even his granddaughter should want. Moreover, he'd seen a lot of liars in his time, but she wasn't one of them. He simply didn't think so.

And he was willing to stake everything on it.

"It is time for you to return, Lia," he said softly, watching her flush as he spoke so informally to her. "We shall go back the way you came and I will take you back to the tavern."

She balked. "You must not," she said. "If anyone were to see you and tell my grandfather, I would have a good deal of explaining to do."

"But—"

"Nay," she insisted softly, interrupting him. "We are not yet married, and until we are, there is still a chance he could stop us or delay us if he becomes unhappy with me. Or you. He still has that power."

That was true, but Creston wasn't bending. "I cannot let you go alone."

"I was alone when I came here."

He grunted unhappily, eyeing her, before finally nodding his head. "Very well," he said. "But I will take you to the gate and watch you on the road all the way back into town."

He was already starting to direct her toward the door. "You can see that far?"

"I have the eyes of a hawk."

"At night?"

"At night," he said. Then he came to a halt and quickly went to collect the taper on the mantel. He handed it to her. "Take this and I will be able to see that point of light as you walk."

"What if it goes out?"

"Then I will come for you, so you'd better hope it does not go out."

She waggled her eyebrows, unsure if she could keep a flame from blowing out, but she was willing to give it a try. The road from Blackchurch into the village was straight and the village could be easily seen from the gatehouse of the guild. She didn't need the man running after her down that road because whatever the gatehouse could see, the village could mostly see also. And that would include her grandfather if he were out looking for her.

It was going to be a dicey situation.

True to his word, Creston escorted her to the gatehouse and then went to the wall to watch her walk all the way back down the road and into the village. As he would tell her later, he was reasonably certain she would be safe because outlaws had all but been purged from the forests around Blackchurch. St. Denis didn't want them around, so the trainers and their recruits would happily go out on a regular basis and ride through the groves, hunting down any outlaws that might be lingering. Almost every brigand in Devon and Cornwall knew that after all of these years, so their woods were some of the safest around. Therefore, Ophelia made it back to The Black Cock, snuck in through the rear door used to access the alleyway and the livery behind, and climbed back into her bed without her mother ever knowing she'd been gone.

Unable to sleep, Creston remained on the wall for the rest

of the night, his gaze on the sleeping village in the distance and a certain young woman with beguiling hazel eyes.

And he wasn't the least bit sorry about it.

CHAPTER NINE

*T*HIS IS GOING *to work out better than I hoped.*

Oscar was, if nothing else, a bright man.

As leader of the Septum Port Alliance, he'd learned to deal with every kind of man—the plotters, the brutes, the liars, and everything in between. Men who dropped their anchor in his inlet or on his beaches always had to deal with him directly. They had to pay a toll or, sometimes, they would barter with goods. Oscar had accumulated so much merchandise over the years that he actually had a merchant stall in town where he sold it. The business was quite lucrative. He was a man who was all about opportunity.

And this was a big one.

It had all started last year.

Given that he had a port on the south side of England, and a very busy one, he had anywhere from ten to twenty ships a day coming in or going out. He had an entire group of men who managed the ships for him, and that included the safety of the port itself. Although there was a small inlet, it was only big enough for five ships, depending on the size of them, which meant any other ships that entered his area had to drop anchor on the beach, and that could leave them vulnerable to the many pirate groups that marauded in the area.

One of those groups was Triton's Hellions.

Oscar had had a few run-ins with Abelard de Bottreaux, the commander of that particular pirate faction. Triton's Hellions mostly stayed in Bristol Bay, but they also roamed the Irish Sea. Even though they tended to stay to the north, there had been occasions when they came south, including last year.

That had been a particularly disruptive visit.

They'd closed in on the beaches of Sidmouth and immediately cornered four cogs that had been clustered on the west side of Sidmouth's beach. Three of those ships had come from Malta and points east, while the fourth ship had come from somewhere along the African coast. Fortunately, they had managed to offload most of the goods before the pirates came in and ordered their vessels, but when they refused to cooperate with Abelard and his men, Abelard ordered the ships torched.

All four vessels had gone up in flames, and due to the wind blowing from the south, embers had been transported upon the breeze like flotsam upon the ocean, to the homes and businesses along the beach. Most of the roofs were sod, but some were thatched, and those roofs caught fire. A large portion of those who lived that close to the water ended up homeless because of the fire that spread very quickly.

Oscar had been helpless to watch a chunk of his town burn even as he sent his army down to fight the fire. Axen Castle, his hereditary homestead, sat back on a hill overlooking both the lands to the north and the sea to the south, a position of maximum strategy, and given the castle was built of stone, there was very little chance of it burning. It did, however, have flammable things in the bailey, including the stables, so the roof of the stable was wetted down and the hay, which was sitting outside because of the warm and dry weather as of late, had been moved into the armories and any other outbuilding that didn't have a flammable roof.

But that seemed to be the least of his troubles.

As the fire was going on, Abelard and his Hellions took that as an invitation to raid the village. They used the chaos of the fire to their advantage and proceeded to confiscate valuables or anything else they wanted as the villagers fled in terror. How Abelard managed to keep his three vessels away from the fire that was burning brightly was anybody's guess, but he'd managed to do so. He stole horses and coin and many other things, taking his booty into his vessels and then setting sail, leaving devastation in his wake. It wasn't until three days later when the fire was completely out and people were returning to what was left of their homes that stories of the pirates' thievery began to trickle back to Oscar.

In the end, Triton's Hellions had greatly damaged Sidmouth and her occupants.

And that had given Oscar an idea.

With Sidmouth badly damaged, Oscar was concerned with the perception of the other members of the Septum Port Alliance. It made him look like a weakling, and, as the leader of their alliance, that did not sit well with him. He'd been dealing with the fallout of that horrific fire when he received word that his granddaughter was to be married, something that enraged him because he'd had no part in her betrothal. Not that he paid a lot of attention to her or his daughter, but as the head of the family, he felt strongly that he should have been the one to find Ophelia a husband. She was, after all, his heiress. Thankfully, her foolish betrothed had hightailed it off to the priesthood, where he could live a pious and celibate life, which gave Oscar the opportunity to find his granddaughter a husband who would benefit him.

And he had someone in mind.

He'd heard, long ago, that a distant cousin was a Blackchurch Guild trainer. Some relative on his wife's side of the family. He knew that the Blackchurch Guild and Triton's Hellions were allied through familial bloodlines. Everyone in western England knew that. But it had taken him a solid week to remember just which cousin served Blackchurch, and when he did, he did the intelligent thing by writing a letter to the older brother of the cousin who was a trainer. In any patriarchal structure, the eldest male was always in charge of the family, which meant the younger brother at Blackchurch was not in charge of his destiny so long as his brother had something to say about it.

That was exactly what Oscar was hoping for.

Therefore, he sent a missive to a Royston de Royans and very politely inquired as to whether or not the man's brother was married. In a stroke of amazing fortune, he was told that not only was Creston not married, but he was far too old to still be unmarried and Royston was very interested in Oscar's suggestion of a marriage between his granddaughter and Royston's younger brother.

And here they were.

That was why Oscar had put up with Creston's arrogance. That was why he'd let the man talk to him the way he had, with a rude tone and an even ruder manner. Oh, but he was so very wise to bite his tongue and let Creston threaten and intimidate him, because it was all part of his master plan. He was so close to marrying his granddaughter into Blackchurch, where he could force her to do his bidding once she was rooted. That was the plan, anyway. But what he intended was beyond destruction of Blackchurch and its pirate kin.

He intended total annihilation.

Once Oscar achieved his goal, the rest of the port alliance lords would once again look up to him and realize how intelligent and infallible he was. Make no mistake—this was all about pride and ego to Oscar, but it was also about vengeance. Any man who got the upper hand on a major pirate faction and a warrior training guild would be a hero to many.

Oscar was determined to be that hero.

But he had to get his granddaughter married first.

As the sun began to rise on the day of the marriage, Oscar finally breathed a sigh of relief. He was closer to his end goals as the seconds of the day ticked away. A half-hour after dawn, as the priest said the final blessing over Creston and Ophelia, Oscar shed a tear. But not for the reason anyone thought.

His tears of joy were about something else entirely.

Now, his plan could go forward.

CHAPTER TEN

I T HAD ALL happened so… fast.

Suddenly, Ophelia was a married woman, the wife of a man she didn't know. There was a distinct feeling of shock in that realization. However, she kept looking at Creston as he engaged in conversation with his friends, and there was more of a distinct shock that she was married to him. Not Cecil, but *him*—a blond god of a man who was, by her own admission, perhaps the most beautiful man she'd ever seen.

Her husband.

God's Bones, but it was astonishing.

They were in The Black Cock following a morning wedding mass at the nearby church. The mass itself had been at the door of the church, in the cold light of morning, and the smell of damp earth and incense was enough to cause her to sneeze several times, much to the concern of her new husband and much to the displeasure of her grandfather. Ophelia had sneezed her head off.

But the blessing was finished, mass was said, and Ophelia and Creston returned to The Black Cock as husband and wife. When they arrived, they could see that Hobbes and Margit had closed the tavern to everyone but Blackchurch people, and a lavish feast had been prepared to celebrate the occasion.

Paid for by St. Denis.

Creston had been incredibly touched by the gesture, insisting that St. Denis have a place next to him at the table. With Ophelia on his right and St. Denis on his left, everyone else simply found their seats around the table that had been positioned in the middle of the tavern by putting together smaller tables, like a puzzle. Food and drink was brought out, and the dishes included several types of baked eggs or egg dishes, which Ophelia loved. Given she'd been forced to starve for the past couple of months, she was more than eager to dig into the delicious-smelling food, and Creston helped her dish spoonfuls of the stuff onto her trencher. He was lovely and attentive, and Ophelia truly felt special.

Until her mother took a seat on her right.

Down the table, Oscar had seated himself next to St. Denis.

"You mustn't eat too much," Randa said quietly. "You do not wish to grow plump too soon."

Ophelia didn't want to sit with her mother. She didn't want to be anywhere near the woman, but here they were. She took comfort in the fact that Creston was now the only one she needed to take orders from. Gone were the days of being under her mother's thumb.

Thank God for small mercies.

"I will eat as much as I please," she told her mother as she spooned some baked egg and cheese into her mouth. "You needn't worry about me any longer, Mother. Go back to Axen, or wherever you choose to go, and know that I will do quite well without you."

Randa looked at her daughter. "Why do you say such things?"

"Because you left me vulnerable to Grandfather's whims," Ophelia snapped. "You never tried to protect me. You never even said to him that, mayhap, he shouldn't starve me. You enabled his cruelty and I cannot forgive you for that."

Randa knew she didn't have an argument for that. "But he was simply trying to—"

"I know what he was trying to do," Ophelia cut her off quietly. "You simply let him do it. But thank you for teaching me a lesson, Mother. When my children are born, I will defend them against anyone and everyone until my last breath. I've learned that I do not want to be a mother like you."

Randa looked terribly hurt by that statement. Without anything to say in defense of herself, she simply turned back to her food and Ophelia felt as if a weight had been lifted from her shoulders. She'd wanted to say such things for the past two months, ever since Oscar had taken charge of his granddaughter's future, and it felt good to tell her mother what she thought without fear of reprisal. Although she didn't know Creston well yet, she knew that he wouldn't let anyone punish or hurt her.

That much was certain.

She was embarking on a whole new life.

At some point, Randa left the table. Ophelia didn't know where her mother went and she didn't care. She and Creston enjoyed the wonderful feast that The Black Cock had prepared, and, at one point, she even saw Greenie as the woman served them fresh bread. Greenie grinned and winked at her as if she knew how right she'd been about Creston all along, and Ophelia felt some joy simply seeing the woman again. A woman who had shown her such kindness when she'd needed it most.

"Lady de Royans? My lady?"

It took Ophelia a moment to realize the words had come

from Creston. She looked at him as if surprised to hear her new title, breaking down into soft laughter at her own reaction. That had Creston grinning at her.

"Sounds strange, does it?" he asked.

Ophelia shook her head. "Not strange," she said. "Unfamiliar. But I shall become accustomed to it quickly."

"Good," Creston said. "Are you enjoying yourself?"

"I am, very much."

"I am glad," he said. "Have you had enough to eat?"

She nodded, looking at the empty trencher. "For now," she said. "But only for the moment. They keep bringing out dishes, and I want to try them all."

"And you shall," he said. "But I was hoping you would be gracious enough to allow me to introduce you to my friends."

He indicated the table across from them, another long table, which was packed with men and women, all having a wonderful time. Ophelia nodded eagerly.

"Of course," she said. "I would be honored."

With a smile, he stood up and took her hand, gently helping her out of her seat. She was clad in the same silk dress her mother had commissioned for her marriage to Cecil, and although she hadn't been keen to wear it because of the memories associated with it, the garment was expensive and beautiful, and her mother had insisted. The beautiful green fabric shimmered when she walked, and upon her neck she wore a stunning gold necklace set with pale green stones that had been mined in a faraway land. It belonged to her mother, who had intimated she would give it to her daughter upon her marriage, but after the exchange they'd just had, Ophelia fully expected her mother to take the necklace back. Not that she cared.

Frankly, she was feeling too much hope to care.

With her hands looped around Creston's elbow, he took her over to the table that held the Blackchurch trainers and their wives. When they saw the newly married couple approach, every man at the table stood up to greet them.

"This sounds odd to say, but I would like for you all to meet my wife," Creston said, grinning because it was slightly awkward. "I have the pleasure of introducing you to Ophelia de Camville de Royans. I will fully admit that I never really planned on introducing her to all of you because I wasn't sure I wanted to. But I've had the opportunity to spend time with the new Lady de Royans and I will confess that I'm no longer opposed to this marriage. I believe you will find her as charming and kind as I have."

That brought some chuckles from the men around the table. "God's Bones, Cres," Tay said. He was the closest and shook his head at Creston's introduction. "That was one of the most inelegant, insulting speeches I have ever heard. If Lady de Royans does not run out on you this moment, I will be surprised."

Ophelia started laughing. "My lord, I assure you, I echo his sentiment," she said. "This entire situation is somewhat… strange."

"My lady?" The lovely woman at Tay's side reached out to take Ophelia's hand. "Since my husband cannot seem to properly greet you and *your* husband speaks so awkwardly, let me salvage the situation. I am Athdara, Tay's wife. We are so pleased to meet you. Welcome to Blackchurch."

"Thank you," Ophelia said sincerely. "I am honored to know you."

Athdara was a tall, elegant woman with lovely features. She

didn't let go of Ophelia's hand, instead pulling her away from Creston and introducing her to the other women who were seated with their husbands nearby.

"This is Lady de Merest, Fox's wife," she said, indicating a pretty brunette. "Her name is Gisele and a kinder woman you will never meet. And that lady on the other side of the blond knight is Elisiana, Lady de Reyne. Her family is from Aragon."

Ophelia was making the rounds, greeting these lovely women, feeling their warmth and curiosity even though she'd only just met them. Women could be such pack animals, but she didn't feel that from them at all. Only genuine interest.

"My lady," she said to Gisele before moving to Elisiana. "And, Lady de Reyne, I am very honored to meet you."

As Elisiana smiled and grasped her free hand kindly, Athdara led her to the last lady down the table. "And this lovely woman is Astria, Lady Matheson," Athdara finished. "She is a member of the Portuguese royal family. Ask her about her adventures at sea. She is the teller of exciting tales, I assure you."

Ophelia greeted the lovely, dark-haired woman sitting next to an enormous man with auburn hair. "A pleasure, my lady," she said, dipping into a curtsy because of Astria's royal blood. "I am greatly honored."

Astria stood up. "Please," she said, "there is no need for formality. Mayhap we should leave the men alone to drink and celebrate? Come and sit with us. Let us come to know one another. Blackchurch is a small world, and we are more like a family, and we would very much like to welcome you."

Ophelia let herself be pulled along by Athdara and Astria, toward a small table near the front window of the tavern. Gisele and Elisiana followed, with Elisiana sending one of the serving women for food and drink. Together, the five of them sat down while the trainers at the other table collected their cups to toast the new groom.

"Let the men have their time together," Athdara said, smiling at the women around the table. "They are closer than brothers, so this moment is special to them."

Ophelia looked over her shoulder to where Creston was grinning as his friends congratulated him. "They seem to have a bond, that is true," she said. Then she looked at the women around her. "Truthfully, I'd never even heard of Blackchurch until the betrothal. I do not know much about it."

"You will learn quickly," Gisele said in a soft, sweet voice. "The Blackchurch Guild is the most prestigious training ground for warriors in the world, and those men you see, your husband included, are the master knights who train the best of the best. They are legend."

The serving woman brought them five cups and put a pitcher of wine on the table in front of them. Ophelia felt the woman touch her on the shoulder and looked up to see Greenie.

"I've brought the best for ye, my lady," she said, giving her a wink. "Ye are a beautiful bride."

Ophelia smiled brightly at the sight of the helpful servant. "My thanks, Greenie," she said. "You've been so kind."

Greenie winked at her and headed off. As Ophelia turned to the table, she could see curious expressions and hastened to explain.

"When I first arrived, she helped me," she said. "She was the one who told me about Sir Creston. I knew nothing about him until she spoke well of him."

Athdara chuckled. "You need not call your own husband *Sir* Creston," she said. "But it is difficult, I know. These men demand respect simply from their accomplishments and their manner. It was doubly difficult for me to transition from formality to informality with Tay."

Ophelia looked at the woman. "Why is that?"

"Because she was one of his recruits," Gisele said, her dark eyes twinkling at Athdara. "Blackchurch accepts both male and female recruits. As long as they pass the entry tests, they are permitted to train, and Tay was her first trainer. I heard they nearly killed one another at first."

Athdara laughed softly. "He was my first trainer and it was his duty to try to cause me to fail," she said. "I clubbed him right between the legs and that nearly ended everything. Fortunately, he was forgiving."

Ophelia was listening with interest. "He must have been if he married you," she said, smiling. Then she looked around the table again. "Do you all have such exciting stories of introduction to your husbands?"

The women began laughing. "Not all," Astria said. "In my case, I was a spoil of war. My husband and I were pushed together by circumstance. Fortunately, we liked one another."

"And Fox and I have known one another since we were very young," Gisele said. "I've never loved anyone but him, but I suppose that is rare. Where do you hail from, Lady de Royans?"

"Please, call me Ophelia. I will also answer to Lia. If we are to be friends, we must feel like friends, don't you think?" As the heads around her bobbed, Ophelia continued. "I am from Dorset. I fostered at Okehampton Castle, but I was born in Symondsbury."

"Where is that?" Astria asked.

"South," Ophelia said. "Toward Sidmouth on the south side of England. My grandfather is the Earl of Sidbury and I spent a good deal of time at his home of Axen Castle when I was young. It is by the sea, and I do love the sea."

"Good lass," Astria said, her eyes lighting up. "I love the sea, also."

The other wives glanced at one another, smirking, until Athdara spoke up. "You should know that Lady Matheson likes to sail upon the ocean," she said. "Truthfully, that is putting it mildly. Astria, tell Lady Royans what it is you have done in the past."

Astria cocked an eyebrow because she didn't exactly want to confess to a woman she'd only just met that she was, in fact, a lady pirate by trade, and a ruthless one at that. "Must we make all confessions now?" she said. "Lady de Royans will run screaming if we tell her everything. Better to let her come to know us first before we tell her of our tumultuous pasts."

There were giggles around the table because the truth was that not one of them had had a smooth, uneventful past. Ophelia looked around and figured she had nothing to lose by telling them what she'd recently experienced. She was fairly certain Creston would tell their husbands at some point, and they would tell their wives.

Better it come from the horse's mouth.

"If you wish to talk past experiences, I've got one that might be considered scandalous," she said, watching all eyes turn to her. "When I was at Okehampton, I met a knight whom I fell in love with. I was certain we were going to spend our lives together. Our wedding was to be two months ago, when he left me standing in the church as he surrendered himself to an abbey to become a priest. He decided that becoming God's servant was a better use of his life than becoming my husband."

The humor that had so recently been around the table fled

and the women appeared properly horrified.

"I am so sorry, my lady," Athdara said with sincerity. "He simply… left?"

Ophelia nodded. "He did," she said. "As I waited for him at the church, his father came to tell me that he would not be marrying me. But the truth is that he was a very pious man. I'd known him a long time and he'd spoken of the priesthood before, but I thought a life with me was more attractive. I was wrong. How can I compete with God?"

There was a good deal of unhappy judgment toward Cecil around that table. "Then he did not deserve you," Gisele said. "Let God have a man who would be so cruel toward a woman. He has much penitence to do for shaming you so."

Ophelia shrugged. "There is a part of me that blames myself," she said. "He spoke of serving God and I knew he had wanted to be a priest before he met me. But I thought I could change him."

Gisele shook her head. "Men like that are weak," she said. "If he truly wished to serve God, he would have made that decision from the beginning and not given you false hope. You are not to blame."

"I am assuming Creston knows?" Astria said. "If he does not, he will not hear it from us."

Ophelia thought that was a honorable declaration coming from women she did not even know. She wasn't exactly sure if she believed it, but she didn't say so. Information like that was fodder for gossip. But she took Astria at her word.

For now.

"He knows," she said. "I told him. I could not go into this marriage withholding a truth like that."

"That was brave," Athdara said. Then she eyed the other

women at the table before continuing. "Speaking of brave, mayhap you would like to hear from the rest of us about our stories before marrying our husbands. I think you'll find you're in good company with adversity and difficult situations. I do not think there is one married Blackchurch trainer that has had an easy path to marriage."

Ophelia nodded eagerly. "If you are willing to speak of it, I would like to hear."

One by one, the women told her.

CB

"GOOD," ST. DENIS muttered to his son. "The wives have taken her under their wing. That will make this easier all the way around."

St. Sebastian de Bottreaux was sitting next to his father, watching the women at the other end of the chamber. A tall and sinewy man, he was the manager of Blackchurch these days, as his father had retired to teach the many children of the trainers, something he loved doing. Sometimes it was more difficult than managing Blackchurch, as he'd told his son, but he preferred it. He was old and St. Sebastian was young, and keeping Blackchurch strong was a young man's game.

St. Sebastian had run Blackchurch for the last several years, brilliantly.

"Y-you thought otherwise?" he said to his father, his slight stammer evident. "It is a decent group of women."

"I know," St. Denis said. "I did not mean it the way it sounded. It is simply that one never knows how a situation like this will go, adding a new person into our group. We have such a tight-knit family that one disruptive personality can cause... problems."

St. Sebastian, or Sebo as he was sometimes called, found his gaze lingering on the women on the other side of the common room.

"It's ironic," he muttered.

St. Denis looked at him. "What is?"

St. Sebastian gestured toward the women. "I-I can remember in years past that whenever a trainer married, he surrendered his post," he said. "I remember Grandfather forcing them to choose between marriage and life as a Blackchurch trainer. But you never did. Why not?"

St. Denis shrugged. "Because it did not seem right to do so," he said. "My father had his reasons, and his father before him, but I would rather keep a seasoned, proven trainer than dismiss him simply because he married. Then I have to find a new trainer and start all over again. There is no logic in that."

St. Sebastian agreed with him. "This is the fifth trainer that has married," he said. "C-can you imagine losing Tay? Fox? Sin? And now Creston?"

"You left out Payne."

"That is because he is a thorn in my side."

St. Denis chuckled, knowing very well that his son and Payne were very good friends. "And mine," he said. "But there is no one better at what he does. And no one better than Creston at what he does, so I am glad to see the women getting on. That means Creston will not want to leave because his wife is happy here."

"He will not stay forever."

The statement came from the man next to St. Denis, who happened to be Oscar. He'd been sitting silently since they'd entered the tavern, almost invisible to what was going on around them. When St. Denis and St. Sebastian turned to the man, he seemed to have an expression of distinct displeasure on his face.

He would be invisible no longer.

The Earl of Sidbury had managed to keep silent through the wedding mass, too, but that seemed to be changing. Though he'd been introduced to St. Denis, he'd hardly had a word for the man. Even seated next to him throughout the entire meal, he hadn't spoken. He'd simply sat and drunk away the excellent wine St. Denis had provided. But now, he had something to say.

"Did you enjoy your meal, my lord?" St. Denis asked with forced politeness. "Is there anything else you require?"

Oscar looked at him with eyes that were hard. "Nay," he said. "There is nothing else. But I was addressing your comment. My granddaughter's husband will not be here at Blackchurch indefinitely. He is gaining an earldom out of this marriage. He must learn of this earldom at some point, which means he must come and live in Sidmouth. That is the only way he will learn what is expected of him."

There was something about the man that was icy. "I understand that, and I am certain he does, too," St. Denis said. "But I do not think he has any plans to leave Blackchurch right away. You look healthy enough. I doubt you will be dying anytime soon."

Oscar's left eyebrow lifted, another hint at his displeasure. "Possibly not," he said. "Unless your cousin returns to Sidmouth and finishes what he started those months ago. Abelard, is it? He burned half of my town to the ground, you know. Mayhap he intends to return and burn the other half. Pirates are despicable cowards."

St. Denis could see this conversation wasn't going to go well in the least. "I would be willing to wager there is far more to that story than simply burning," he said. "Abelard does have some scruples, but whatever happened between you and my cousin remains between you and my cousin. I do not want it discussed here, with me, for I have no control over him and, better still, I do not care."

Oscar smiled thinly. "Triton's Hellions and Blackchurch are one and the same," he said. "Everyone knows that."

"Th-that is most assuredly *not* true," St. Sebastian spoke up. He wasn't going to let his father be bullied. "The Blackchurch Guild is not an alliance of pirates, but a training ground for warriors. I thought you would have known that. And if I were you, I would not throw stones at Triton's Hellions. I've not heard flattering things about the Septum Port Alliance. From what I've been told, it's a group of men who intimidate those who do not bend to their will, steal from their own ports, and conduct business that the king would not be happy with if he knew the details. Do you deny this?"

Very quickly, Oscar was on the defensive. "Who are you to make such accusations?" he demanded.

"I *am* Blackchurch," St. Sebastian said, rage in his tone. "M-my name is St. Sebastian de Bottreaux, and when you attack Blackchurch with baseless allegations, you attack me. I have a right to defend myself."

St. Denis was trying to calm his son down, but Oscar's sense of offense was growing. "Then if you find insult with baseless accusations, you should not be making them yourself," he said. "The Septum Port Alliance is beyond contestation. It is a solid alliance of men who protect the ports in Devon and Cornwall, and that includes protecting them from your pirate cousin. The man is a thief and a murderer."

"A-and I've heard the same about *you*."

Oscar stood up so fast that his chair toppled. That had St. Denis standing up, and St. Sebastian next to him. Because the men were on their feet and furniture was falling over, the noise caught the attention of the trainers, who turned to see what looked to be St. Denis and Oscar facing off against one another. Sinclair, the master swordsman, leapt over two tables to get in between Oscar and St. Denis, while Creston and Cruz, the other men who were known to be experts with swords, followed him. It was Creston who put himself in front of St. Denis as Sinclair very nearly shoved Oscar backward.

"Knowing that Lord Exmoor is not a confrontational man by nature, I can only assume that you are, my lord," Sinclair said in a low voice. "I've been watching you since the wedding and it is clear you are unhappy. If it is the marriage you are unhappy with, it is done. But if it is anything else, now is not the time to discuss it, and most certainly not with Lord Exmoor. With respect, my lord, you are not to disrupt Creston's wedding day."

His voice was like a razor sheathed in velvet. Smooth but sharp. St. Denis knew it was a deadly tone, like a viper before it strikes, so he reached around Creston to grasp Sinclair by the shoulder.

"Ease back, Sin," he said softly, assuring Creston that it was safe for him to step aside. "Lord Sidbury and Sebo were simply having a lively discussion. Sometimes passions run hot when subjects are close to the heart."

Oscar was mostly glaring at St. Sebastian, but he was well aware that there were several very large men standing nearby, ready to pounce on him if he made a move against anyone. Not wanting to end up a cripple, or worse, he backed away, finally turning and storming off toward the rear of the tavern, where his rented room was located.

Quickly, the common room was vacated by all that remained of Ophelia's family.

Creston was rather sorry. He hadn't wanted this day to go badly, of course. He hadn't wanted the entire situation to go badly, but more than ever, he was starting to see what a bully his wife's grandfather was. That was going to make it difficult for him in the long run, since he was to inherit the man's earldom. It would have been much easier had they gotten along.

Perhaps that simply wasn't meant to be.

"You have made a mess of this, Creston." Royston, who had been seated at the end of the main table, walked up on his brother. He'd seen everything, from start to finish, and was convinced his brother was to blame. "What were you thinking? Sending your cohorts to rough up an earl? The very man you are set to inherit from?"

"This situation was not of Creston's doing," Cruz growled. He would not be silent when his friend was being attacked. "I've watched you try to intimidate and berate the man since your arrival at The Black Cock. Do not deny it, for we all saw it. He has done what you wanted him to do—he married a woman he did not know and did not want. Her grandfather is a tyrant, or have you not noticed that?"

Creston tried to pull Cruz away from what could potentially be a fistfight, trying to force him to turn away and cool off, but Cruz wasn't going to do it. He and Creston were too close for that, and in his mind, the man needed defending from his own brother.

But Royston didn't see it that way.

"This is none of your concern," he said hotly. "I do not know who you are and I do not care, but go back to your seat and stay there. This is a conversation between my brother and me."

Cruz smiled, but it was a deadly smile. Creston had seen that expression before and knew his brother wasn't long for this earth if he didn't remove Cruz from the potentially deadly situation immediately. Putting both hands on the man's shoulders, he had to struggle to turn him around, straight into Tay and Fox, who pulled Cruz away before any blood was spilled. Creston watched him go, to ensure that he *did* go, but before he could return to his brother, Ming Tang took position where Cruz once stood.

"My lord," he said, addressing Royston politely but firmly, "you must understand that the trainers from Blackchurch are a brotherhood. Like all men who have faced life and death together, or work hard for a common cause, there is very much a bond here that cannot be broken. These men will leap to the defense of each other without question, so do not be offended by it. Your brother is well respected and well loved."

Royston looked at the man with the dark eyes and slightly accented speech. He had a calm way about him, which helped defuse the situation a little. Royston was angry, but he wasn't a fool. He wasn't going to shout at a man who was trying to ease the tension. But his brother was simply looking at him, displeased, and the rest of the men standing around had the same expression.

There would be no winning this situation.

Frustrated, Royston turned away, marching off in the direction that Oscar had gone. When he disappeared from view, St. Sebastian put his hand on Creston's shoulder.

"My apologies," he said quietly. "I did not mean to stir up trouble on your wedding day."

Creston turned to him. "You did not," he said. "My brother did when he forced me into this marriage. He thinks I should surrender completely to Sidbury's manner and demands, but I will not. The man has done terrible things to my wife, and I will not tolerate him."

St. Denis, standing next to his son, heard him. His brow furrowed with concern. "What has he done to her, Cres?"

Creston grunted in disgust. "Starve her," he said. "Evidently, the earl feels that a woman should be pale and slender and weak so that it will arouse a man's natural sense of protection. He wanted to make her appealing to me."

It wasn't exactly the truth, but close. It was a broader picture of de Bulverton's cruelty, and the men who had heard his explanation were clearly revolted.

"Vile," St. Denis muttered. "Is she well enough? She has suffered no lasting damage?"

Creston looked over to the table where the women were sitting, only they were no longer sitting there. They had heard the commotion and were now standing behind the men. Creston caught sight of Ophelia's face, seeing the shame and despair that her grandfather had caused a scene.

He felt tremendously sorry for her.

"Probably not," he said softly. "But I should tend to her. Will you forgive me for retreating with her to my cottage?"

"Of course not," St. Denis said, waving at the trainers to get out of the way so Creston could get to his wife. "Take her now. She needs a tender hand, lad. Be kind to her."

The trainers parted, revealing the women, but Athdara saw him coming. She was almost as tall as a man, so she had seen more of what was going on with Oscar and Royston than the other women had. When Creston came near, she put up a hand.

"Creston, wait," she said. "The other ladies and I were going to prepare your cottage for you. We thought you would be feasting all day and we would have more time. Will you at least give us an hour? We want to make your place lovely for your new bride."

Creston smiled at the women he'd genuinely come to like—Athdara was strong and noble, Gisele was cultured and kind, Elisiana was fiery and fun, and Astria was gracious and generous. They were all gathered around Ophelia in what Creston thought was a rather protective way. He felt it was very sweet of them. He looked to Ophelia to answer their question.

"My lady?" he said gently. "An hour?"

Before Ophelia could answer, Gisele slid her arm through Ophelia's. "She's coming with us," she said. "We will help her prepare for you. You stay here with the men, Creston. We won't be long."

Ophelia didn't even get a chance to answer. She was pulled along by Gisele and Elisiana, the women closing ranks around her and shuffling her out the door, leaving Creston standing there, scratching his head.

"What just happened?" he demanded to anyone who could answer.

Tay snorted, putting his hands on Creston's shoulders and turning him for the table. "My wife happened," he said. "She is the daughter of a duke and the sister of a duke. She is demanding and bold and knows how to get things done. Sit down, Cres. We have an hour before your wife is ready for you."

Creston let Tay push him down onto a bench while Cruz, now sufficiently calm, poured him a drink. Even though it was midmorning by this point, they all settled down with more wine to wait out the hour while the women prepared the cottage of the new Lord and Lady de Royans.

Perhaps the wedding day wasn't ruined after all.

Creston could only hope.

CHAPTER ELEVEN

"**A**RE YOU GOING to let your brother show you such disrespect?"

Royston was out in the livery yard, taking a piss against the wall, when he heard a voice behind him. Still pissing, he turned to see Oscar standing several feet away with something smoking in his right hand.

"I do not know what you mean," he said, turning around to finish his business. "My brother and I have been at each other since I told him about the marriage. Even before that, we were never close. It is the way of things."

Oscar pondered that statement as he lifted a smoking stick in his hand and inhaled the trails of blue smoke that were curling out of it. He inhaled deeply and held it in his lungs for a moment before exhaling.

"He is arrogant," he said simply. "Men like that think they can rule over men like you and me. You are a baron, a titled nobleman. I am an earl. *We* rule this land, de Royans. Not men like your brother or even men like Exmoor. They are insulated in their own little world. They do not know the trouble men like you and I see."

Royston sighed heavily. "Creston used to serve the king, as you know," he said. "Our father was quite proud of him."

"You did not tell me why he left royal service, only that he did."

Royston thought back to that time. He remembered his father's agitation, his rage at the missives Creston had sent him, missives that detailed the dishonor John had put him through and the results when it came to the woman he loved. He remembered his father's distress over the missives he then received from King John, looking for Creston and telling Quinton de Royans to send his son back to London immediately. Even if Quinton had known where Creston was, which he hadn't for quite some time, he knew Creston wouldn't have gone. His mind was made up and royal service was no longer an option.

It had been a difficult time for them all.

"Why else?" Royston finally said. "A woman was the reason that part of his career ended."

Oscar looked at him for a moment, surprise registering in his expression, but only for a flash. "Is that it?" he muttered. "I suppose that is to be expected. Your brother is much more handsome than you are. Women are likely to notice that."

Royston cocked an eyebrow at the insulting comment. "It was *one* woman," he said. "He wanted to marry her, but the woman's father had other ideas. It destroyed Creston, enough so that he left John's service. He blamed the king for the entire thing."

"Why?"

"Because he was the king's muscle," Royston said. "He did anything dirty or underhanded that John wanted him to do. That's what he teaches here at Blackchurch, in fact. Things he learned under John's tutelage."

Oscar grunted. "That must be a great deal."

"I imagine that it is."

"Even so, Blackchurch is not the sort of place a man would be proud to have his son serve," Oscar said. "Blackchurch has endured a less-than-noble reputation for decades. Mercenaries who take money to train men to kill, yet take no side themselves. That makes them manipulators and brutes. Does it not shame you that your brother serves here?"

Royston nodded. "Aye," he said. "But Creston is a grown man. A highly educated, highly intelligent grown man. All I can hope is that he'll grow weary of it and allow you to take him under your wing. The lure of being the next Earl of Sidbury is why I agreed to this betrothal. He will make an excellent earl, but we need to get the Blackchurch stench off him."

Oscar inhaled more of that pungent blue smoke. Royston had finished pissing by this time and was simply standing there, watching a stable servant feed the horses in a small corral across the alleyway. When Oscar spoke next, it was quietly.

"You know that Blackchurch is allied with an infamous band of pirates known as Triton's Hellions, do you not?" he asked.

Royston nodded. "I have heard."

"They burned half of my town last year," Oscar said. "Pillaged, looted, and burned. People were killed. By the time I mustered my army and sent them into town, they were already out to sea and the fires were blazing. It took us two days to get them out. I swore vengeance upon those bastards at the time, and now that I've met St. Denis, I can see that Blackchurch isn't much better. Both Triton's Hellions and Blackchurch are stains upon the green fields of England. They are an abomination to this land."

Royston was looking at him by then. "I am sorry to hear that," he said. "It must be very difficult for you to be here, knowing the relationship between Blackchurch and the pirates."

"It is," Oscar said. He paused before continuing. "You know, de Royans, if Blackchurch did not exist, you would have no reason to be ashamed of your brother. And surely you would avenge your father's disappointment if he no longer served here."

Royston snorted. "If Creston no longer served at Blackchurch, my father would rise from his grave and dance a jig," he said. "But that day is far off."

"Is it?"

Royston's brow furrowed. "What do you mean?"

Oscar inhaled his smoke again, pensively, then exhaled once more. "I mean that I have an idea," he said. "My reason to see Blackchurch fall is because of what their pirate brethren did to my town. I do not have the ships or men to destroy pirates, but I know how I can destroy Blackchurch. If you are willing to help me, we can do this together. I get what I want, your brother is no longer shaming you, and the world will be a better place without this horrific guild of criminals."

He had Royston's full attention now. "What did you have in mind?"

Oscar looked around to ensure there was no one within earshot before answering. "The Blackchurch Guild has a neutral reputation," he said. "They train warriors, but they never take sides. That way, they have no guilt or responsibility for any of the killing their men do."

"I am aware."

"But what if they did?"

"Did what?"

"Take sides."

"How?"

The blue smoke that Oscar had been inhaling, from burning hemp that he inhaled on a regular basis, gave him great clarity of thought. He seemed very pleased with what he was about to say.

"Henry and Louis, the French king, have been fighting over Gascony," he said. "Are you aware of this?"

Royston nodded. "I am," he said. "I was sent a royal request for men, in fact."

"Did you send any?"

"About one hundred, what I could spare."

Oscar moved closer to him. "Have they returned yet from France?"

"Some."

"Then listen to me," Oscar said, lowering his voice. "What if Louis sent a dispatch to St. Denis, thanking him and Blackchurch for providing men and money for him to take Gascony from Henry? Only it would be a forged dispatch and I would send it to London, straight into the hands of the king, with the news that I intercepted it from a French messenger bound for Blackchurch. I could say that I happened to be at Blackchurch because my granddaughter married a trainer, which is not a lie. My presence, and my connection to Blackchurch, gives a forged missive validity. I can say that I saw Blackchurch's support of Louis for myself. And if you were to confirm my information because your brother is a Blackchurch trainer, then…"

Royston caught on quickly. "It would be two affirmations of Blackchurch's loyalty to France."

"Exactly."

Royston could see precisely what the man was planning. "The fact that Blackchurch is neutral in any conflict would be destroyed," he said. "Henry would send his army to Blackchurch and wipe it from the earth."

"Of course, he would," Oscar said. "Blackchurch does not have royal permission to train knights. They do not even have a license. Anyone training knights, for profit, must have one of those things, and Blackchurch has neither because it was started so long ago, back in the days when William of Normandy was battling the Saxons upon these lands. Because of this, the Crown of England has long overlooked the fact that Blackchurch does not have license or permission, but the only reason it does is that Blackchurch, itself, remains neutral in all things. Imagine if they were not only no longer neutral, but siding with the French? Henry would destroy it, indeed."

Royston could see that consequence as clear as day. He could also see his family's honor restored once his brother ceased to be a Blackchurch trainer and assumed his rightful role as the next Earl of Sidbury.

Restoration, indeed.

"Very well," he finally said. "What do you want me to do?"

"For now, nothing," Oscar said, pleased that he had a cohort in crime. He inhaled the last of his blue smoke as the embers in his fingers nearly burned away. "I know a cleric in Sidmouth who is from France. The man will do anything for coin and I will have him draft a dispatch from Louis to St. Denis."

"Is that not complicated?" Royston asked. "What about a royal seal?"

Oscar waved him off. "I have a royal dispatch addressed to the Septum Port Alliance from Louis requesting permission for

French ships to trade in our ports," Oscar said. "Believe me, the writing, and seal, can be replicated based on that royal dispatch, and once the missive is drafted, I will send it to London and let nature take its course. But you must be prepared to say that you, too, witnessed St. Denis' loyalty to France. Mayhap through something your brother said."

"But he's said nothing."

"And there is no missive from Louis. It is all a lie. You must learn to *lie*."

Royston understood. God help him, he did, and he actually felt good about it.

"As you wish," he said. "Then I'll return home and wait to hear from you."

"Good," Oscar said, putting an uncharacteristically friendly hand on Royston's shoulder. "Vengeance for your family's honor. Vengeance for my town. And in the end, Creston and my granddaughter will come to live with me, and I will ensure he is most worthy of being the next Earl of Sidbury."

With that, he patted Royston on the shoulder and headed back into the tavern where he would sleep for the rest of the day. The blue smoke always made him sleepy. Royston simply remained in the yard of the tavern, mulling over their conversation, wondering how he went from pledging his brother to an earl's granddaughter to plotting the fall of Blackchurch.

Now, he was part of it.

But he didn't feel any remorse. What Oscar had said was true—if Blackchurch no longer existed, then Creston would no longer be an embarrassment to his family. Quinton de Royans' spirit might even rest in piece thanks to his heir. Perhaps it *was* up to Royston to bring Creston back into the fold and forget about the stain of Blackchurch.

The situation, he was certain, was about to become very interesting.

The situation, he was certain, was about to become very interesting.

CHAPTER TWELVE

O PHELIA REMEMBERED THIS cottage.

It was the same cottage where she had confessed her pregnancy to Creston, where he'd made the decision to marry her anyway. It was such a cold, dirty cave of a hovel, but it was his, and it had a special memory for her, life-changing as it had been.

Now she was standing there with five women she didn't know, but five women who were quite serious about helping her prepare the cottage for her newlywed life. Standing at the rear door of the cottage, they evidently already had a small army of servants waiting to help, because Elisiana opened the door, and people with buckets and brushes, chairs and fabric began to pour through. As Ophelia stood by the hearth, rather flabbergasted, the gang went to work.

Under Elisiana's supervision, floors and walls were scrubbed and dusted of cobwebs. Astria was in charge of furniture, so she was standing by the back door, calling to servants to bring things in or take things out. Gisele had charge of what were to be curtains on the windows, while Athdara was in charge of the second floor. She made sure beds were assembled and mattresses were stuffed. There was even a small alcove on that level for dressing or bathing, so she had basins put in that small room as well as a dented copper pot that could be used for bathing. It wasn't exactly a tub, but one could sit in it, legs folded, and bathe.

It was more than Ophelia could have asked for.

"I feel rather useless," she said as she stood in the master chamber, watching Athdara direct servants to stuff the mattress with straw and moss, which made it very soft. "You all are doing so much for my home. Is there something I can do to help?"

Athdara smiled. "You are not supposed to help, Lady de Royans," she said. "This is our wedding gift to you. You are supposed to stand by and enjoy it."

Ophelia grinned, looking around to see that her bags from The Black Cock had somehow made it to Creston's cottage. She went over to them and knelt down, unstrapping the satchel and opening the mouth of it to get to the items inside. She looked around for a wardrobe, but didn't see one in the chamber.

"I can leave my clothing in these bags, but is there a chest I should use for them?" she said. "I have not seen one, but this has been quite a day. I may have simply missed it somehow."

Athdara held up a hand, begging for patience, as she scooted over to the bedroom door and shouted down the stairwell.

"Are you bringing the wardrobe?" she called.

There was a muffled reply that Ophelia couldn't quite hear, but after a few moments, she could hear movement on the stairs. Athdara stood back, and male servants carrying an enormous wardrobe appeared. She directed them to put it against one of the walls, and as the servants left to grab the next piece of furniture, Ophelia went to the wardrobe and ran her hand over it in awe.

"It is beautiful," she said. "But I am not certain I can allow you to give me such an expensive piece. You are so kind to do it, but…"

Athdara came up beside her with a damp rag and began running it over the wood. It was old, but serviceable, and elaborately carved. A very expensive piece, as Ophelia had noted. But Athdara simply shook her head as she wiped it off.

"I did not buy it," she said. "It was in a barn we use to store things like this."

Ophelia's brow furrowed. "Furniture?"

"And other things," Athdara said. "You see, this village, long ago, housed people who were not from Blackchurch. It was back during the time when the first Lord Exmoor took possession of Exford Castle. Have you seen it yet?"

Ophelia shook her head. "Nay," she said. "I've not been anywhere on the grounds other than the gatehouse and this cottage."

Athdara stopped dusting and gestured toward the window, to what lay beyond it. "It is a vast place," she said. "Exford Castle keep is in the middle of it, near the old, burned-out church ruins. The blackened church, hence the name 'Black-church.' But as I was saying, the village the trainers live in used to be a village of farmers and merchants, but over the years, Blackchurch simply took it over to house their own people. Items were left behind in the cottages, like wardrobes and chairs and things like that, and they are all kept stored in an old barn. Therefore, I did not buy this wardrobe—I simply had it brought over, along with everything else, to furnish your home. If you do not like it, that is well and good, but it will serve a purpose until you can purchase something else."

That explained a great deal about Blackchurch and the way the trainers lived. Ophelia ran her hand over the carved door.

"I will keep it, if I may," she said. "It is very beautiful. And you have done so much for me. I am very grateful."

Athdara smiled as she returned to her cleaning. "We want to make your life here a good one," she said. "All of us, the wives, know how difficult it is to become part of the Blackchurch brotherhood. It is a very tight community of men who would kill or die for any of us. They are honorable, worthy men, your husband included. We want you to feel welcome."

It was a kind thing to say. Athdara and the other women were going out of their way to make Ophelia feel accepted, but in the back of her mind, she was starting to view them like she viewed Creston—people she didn't know, but people she wanted to know. She wanted to have friends here. She wanted to be accepted. But right now, her relationship with them was built on a lie. They knew about her failed marriage from a couple of months earlier. She'd been honest about that.

But they didn't know everything.

Perhaps if they did, they'd simply walk out and leave her to do the rest of the preparation for her cottage. They were helping her make it a livable home, but that was based on what they presumed—that she was an innocent woman who did not come into the marriage by deception.

But they were wrong. If there was any hope of having a true friendship with them, it couldn't be built on a misconception.

"Wait," she finally said, putting her hand over Athdara's as the woman dusted off the base of the wardrobe. "Would… it be possible to speak with you before you continue?"

Athdara looked at her curiously. "Of course," she said. "What do you wish to speak about? Of course! You do not like this wardrobe."

"Nay, that is not it at all."

"You want something smaller? This is rather large. I think there are smaller ones."

"Nay, truly," Ophelia insisted. "This wardrobe is lovely. It is something else I must speak of. Would it be too rude of me to ask the other women to join us? I should like to speak with all of you, if I may."

Athdara could see that something was on Ophelia's mind, so she nodded and went to the doorway again. There were servants scrubbing the stairs and she sent one of them to fetch Gisele, Elisiana, and Astria. In little time, the women joined them, entering the big chamber and voicing their approval over such a beautiful wardrobe. They thought that might be the reason they'd been summoned, but Ophelia quietly shut the door before turning to them.

Her manner was timid, but determined.

Truthfully, she'd never felt so anxious in her life.

"Firstly, I wanted to thank you all for being so generous with your time and talent," she said. "I know that you are not finished yet, but I feel that it is important I tell you something before you continue. You may feel differently about helping me once I've told you, so I do not want you to think I've taken advantage of your kindness. I would never do that."

So far, no one seemed concerned by her statement. In fact, they were all smiling to varying degrees.

"What is it?" Athdara asked.

That question only made Ophelia feel more nervous. She was positive they were all going to stop talking to her and walk out, but she had no choice.

"I was honest with you when I told you that I was betrothed

to another man a couple of months ago," she said. "A man I thought I could change. I thought that marriage and a family would make him grateful to be a husband and I would have my perfect life. You see, I loved him and never thought he would abandon me. Or mayhap I did, but I would not entertain the thought. I pretended it was not a possibility. But it was. Since we were betrothed, we behaved as married people do, in every sense of the word. When he abandoned me, he abandoned a pregnant woman. I am with child."

The smiles were gone from the faces of the women around her. She could hardly lift her head to look at them, but she could see enough. She could see that they were looking at her, but she couldn't really interpret their expressions. No one said anything for a moment, which made her feel like vomiting. She'd never been so ashamed, or so anxious, in her life.

"Creston knows," she whispered tightly, feeling tears of shame sting her eyes. "It was my grandfather's idea to marry me to a man very quickly so he might think I carried his child, even if that child was to be born early, but I could not let him do that to Creston. I told him before we were married, to give him time to break the betrothal, but he chose not to."

It was Athdara who spoke first. "I thought this marriage seemed to happen quickly," she said. "Now it makes sense."

The tears were starting to leak from Ophelia's eyes and she wiped them quickly. "Now that you know, I am certain you do not wish to waste your time on me, and I completely understand," she said. "I just thought you should know, so there were no secrets between us if we were to be friends. Moreover, in a month or two, you would figure out that my pregnancy was more advanced than it would have been had I conceived on our wedding night or shortly thereafter. I would not insult you by lying to you about it. I believe in honesty, even if it is destructive. It is better than living a lie."

She still had her head down and couldn't see the wives looking at one another. It was Gisele who finally shrugged.

"This chamber needs a table," she said, gesturing toward the window. "Some place where you can sit with Creston and share a conversation or a morning meal. Athdara, are there any small tables left in that barn?"

The women started talking about tables, and Ophelia's head shot up. She looked at them as if they'd all just lost their minds.

"But… wait," she said, stopping their conversation. "Did you not hear what I said?"

"We heard," Gisele said, her dark eyes glimmering. "You loved a man and were supposed to marry him. You conceived a child. The shame is on him for walking out on you, my lady. You did nothing wrong. Had you not told Creston, I might have something else to say about it, but you did. He knows. I see no issue with this."

Ophelia's eyes were wide. "You don't?"

"Nay," Gisele said as she reached out to grasp Ophelia's hand. "Years ago, I, too, conceived the child of a man I thought I would marry. The child was born out of wedlock because I did not marry my son's father for about ten years, so I am in no position to cast judgment. None of us are. We all have a past, my lady. Yours is no more shameful than anyone else's, so please put your mind at ease. But thank you for telling us. You have given us your trust and we will strive to be worthy of it."

That brought tears again, this time of gratitude. "I do not know how to thank you," Ophelia said. "This has been something I've been punished over, by my grandfather, and I've simply learn to associate it with shame."

"There is no shame with us. We understand."

Impulsively, Ophelia hugged Gisele as she burst into quiet tears. Gisele laughed softly, hugging Ophelia until she could reclaim her composure. When she did, or was at least trying to, Athdara hugged her too, followed by Elisiana and Astria. As Gisele had said, they all had a past to a certain extent. No one was without some shame in their lives. Perhaps Ophelia's had been a sin of some caliber, but no one was going to judge her for it. She'd been honest about it and that was all that mattered.

It was a moment of acceptance for the wives of Blackchurch.

Another lady of honor had come into their fold.

"Come, now," Athdara said. "We must hurry. We told Creston an hour and it has been almost that already, so we must quickly finish everything."

Astria and Elisiana broke for the door. "I am almost finished," Astria said, bashing into Elisiana as they both tried to get through the door at the same time. "Lisi, move!"

They laughed all the way down the stairwell, followed by Gisele. "Athdara?" she said. "Do you want me to send a servant for a table for this chamber? It is big enough. It could use one."

"Aye," Athdara said. "And a trunk or a chest. See if there are any in the old barn."

Gisele winked at Ophelia and fled, leaving the remaining two women to sort out the master chamber before Creston arrived.

"Linens," Athdara suddenly said. "We need linens!"

With that, she rushed out. Ophelia watched her go, thinking of the women who had just left the chamber, women who had surprised her with their acceptance of something most noblewomen would not accept. She hadn't expected that kindness, and it truly touched her.

Perhaps she had found a place where she would, indeed, belong.

The sprout of hope that had started when she married Creston began to grow. In this mysterious guild that men spoke of in hushed tones, it was possible that she would actually find a place where she belonged.

With renewed vigor, she went to hang up her clothing.

CHAPTER THIRTEEN

CRESTON WAS FAIRLY drunk.

He didn't mean to be, but he'd passed the last hour drinking with his friends, and before he realized it, he was tipsy. Probably more than tipsy, but he was good at pretending he wasn't. Now every senior trainer at Blackchurch was walking him back to his cottage, and most of them, especially Payne, were singing bawdy tavern songs.

Loudly.

"There once was a lady fair,
With silver bells in her hair.
I knew her to have,
A luscious kiss… it drove me mad!
But she denied me… and I was so terribly sad.
Lily, my girl,
Your flower, I will unfurl
With my cock and a bit of good luck!
Your kiss divine,
I'll make you mine,

And keep you abed for a fuck!"

There must have been five or six choruses of it, all the way up the road from The Black Cock and then once they entered the gatehouse. They also sang a naughty song called "Tilly Nodden," and another about a whore named Rose, but Lily seemed to be the preferred song. Payne's and Tay's voices were reverberating off the walls and trees and anything else that provided a sound barrier. They were having a grand time of it, finally quieting by the time they entered the trainers' village because there were children around.

Their children.

It looked like any other village with a well in the town square. One would expect to see villagers and merchants, but not here. Everyone who lived in this village served a purpose at Blackchurch. Long ago, it was a thriving village before the Lords of Exmoor claimed it and incorporated it into the Blackchurch world. All of the trainers lived here and had their own cottages, and those who assisted the trainers lived here as well, but it was usually two or three assistants to a cottage in their case—assistant trainers and helpers who, at this moment, were out with the recruits and the dregs while the senior trainers celebrated a marriage. Even if the trainers weren't training today, a very rare thing indeed, instruction at Blackchurch still continued.

"Listen," Payne said, holding on to Kristian as they stumbled up the road toward Creston's cottage. "Do ye hear them?"

"I hear nothing," Ming Tang said. He and Amir were the only ones who weren't drunk, mostly due to their religious convictions. "Once we leave Creston with his new wife, we should find yours. Astria would not want you walking around in this condition."

Payne looked at the man as if he'd been deeply insulted. "I'll walk where I want," he said hotly. "And I *do* hear the children. They're playing up the hill, by the kitchens. Such a lovely sound."

Ming Tang simply nodded his head in agreement, though he was fairly certain there were no sounds of children around. They were more than likely with their nurse, sitting somewhere in the sun. Perhaps they were inspecting the chickens, as they so often liked to do. In any case, he couldn't hear them, and a look at Amir told him that he couldn't hear them either.

"Of course, Payne," Amir said, coming over to walk next to a badly weaving Payne. "I hear them too."

Payne slung a big arm around Amir's shoulders. "Do ye?"

"I do."

"Ha!" Payne guffawed. "Then ye have the hearing of a god, because I canna truly hear them. I just said that."

Amir rolled his eyes as Payne laughed loudly at the man's expense. By this time, they were nearly to Creston's cottage and Creston came to a halt, turning to the men following him. He was in the grip of Cruz, who had his arm around Creston's neck as Creston tried to remove it.

"This is where you stop," he told everyone, unwinding Cruz's arm from his head. "I will go in alone. I appreciate the escort, but no further assistance is necessary."

"Lad," Tay said seriously, "you have never been married before. I will give you some advice."

Creston shook his head firmly, and that nearly toppled him. "I do not need advice," he said. "I know what to do."

"Do you?" Sinclair said, approaching him and trying to wrap him up in a bear hug. "Cres, stop moving. I must tell you something."

Between pushing Cruz away and keeping clear of Sinclair's flailing arms, Creston was starting to back away, trying to get free of his friends.

"Tell me later," he told Sinclair. "I have a new wife waiting for me, and, no offense to any of you, I would rather spend the day with her. And the night. Anyone who bothers me before dawn tomorrow will feel my wrath. And I will not hold back."

That had some of the men looking up at the sky. The sun was straight above, indicating noon, and Payne suddenly turned back the way they'd come.

"It's the nooning hour, lads," he said. "We have some drinking and eating tae do."

"Where are you going?" Tay asked as Payne stumbled past him.

"Back tae The Black Cock!"

"But we just came from there."

Payne pointed toward the village. "And we must go back," he said. "St. Denis has given us one day away from our duties tae celebrate Creston's marriage, and I dunna want tae waste it. Hurry, now. We mustn't be late."

They watched him go until Kristian shrugged his shoulders and began to follow. Fox and Amir fell in behind them. Realizing everyone was heading back to The Black Cock, Sinclair blew exaggerated kisses at Creston and went after them, finally followed by Tay. That left Cruz and Ming Tang standing with Creston.

"Well," Ming Tang said, his eyes twinkling, "I have no advice to give when it comes to marriage and women except to say I wish you well. Truly, Creston. You deserve all of the happiness in the world, my friend."

Creston smiled at the man. "I am grateful," he said. "I know your religion doesn't allow for marriage, but I also know you stopped following it rigidly years ago. Maybe we'll be standing in a similar situation in the years to come and I'll be able to give you some advice. I hope so."

Ming Tang shrugged. "It is of no concern to me," he said. "But I shall take my leave of you and return to The Black Cock to ensure our friends do not get into any trouble."

Creston snorted, shaking his head at the drunk group of revelers, as Ming Tang began to walk quickly toward the group returning to the village. When he disappeared into the gatehouse, following the crowd, Creston turned to Cruz.

For a moment, the two friends simply looked at each other and smiled. This was an important moment for Creston, not lost on either of them. A change in a life that neither one of them had seen coming.

"Do you believe this?" Creston exclaimed softly. "That I actually have a wife now? I would have never imagined this, ever. I did not think I would ever marry, but here I am."

"Here you are," Cruz agreed, his dark eyes glittering with warmth. "Like Ming Tang, I have no experience with marriage other than to say: be the man I know you are. Be kind, be considerate, but most of all, enjoy her. The other wives seem to like her, so I hope that is a good omen. I hope she is good for you."

"So do I," Creston admitted. Then he sighed faintly and put his hand on Cruz's shoulder. "You have been my very best friend for years. I've never had a friend like you, Cruz. Not ever. I was always alone in everything I did, but with you… I am never alone. I will never *be* alone. Nor will you. Though I take a wife, it does not change the bond between us. I hope you know that."

Cruz grinned. "I know," he said. "You and I are strong."

"We are."

"Get inside, now. She's waiting."

Creston nodded. Then he hugged Cruz tightly, an embrace of great friendship, before releasing the man and heading to his front door.

His wife was waiting.

As he opened the door, he heard a lot of whispering and scuffling. His cottage had a back door in the area where food was usually stored and prepared, and just as he stepped inside, that door slammed. He could hear laughing as the women ran away. He grinned, knowing it was the other trainer wives. But then he noticed his cottage.

It didn't look like his cottage at all.

It looked cleaned and tended and cozy. The big common room didn't look the way he'd left it. There was a fire blazing in the hearth, a dozen tapers in iron candlesticks on the mantel, two chairs with cushions, and several hides all over the floor. He took a few steps inside, looking around at the furniture, which included a small table, another chair, and a spinning wheel. For privacy, someone had strung curtains over the front window overlooking the square beyond.

Stunned that his barren cottage now looked like a comfortable home, he ventured farther into the common room and was looking around when movement off to his left caught his attention. He looked up to see Ophelia standing between the kitchen room and the common room, smiling at him.

He smiled in return.

She was clad in a robe of silk brocade and rabbit fur, her lovely hair spilling down her back. She came toward him, her face flushed from the heat of the room, or so he thought.

Perhaps it was simply because she was excited or embarrassed, or maybe even happy to see him. All Creston could see was her lovely face, and he felt his heart do a strange little leap. In fact, he put his hand to his chest because it startled him. He hadn't felt anything like that since he'd been embroiled in his romance with Mary.

But he felt it again with Ophelia.

Astonishing!

"Lady de Royans," he greeted her softly. "You look beautiful."

Her smile broadened. "Thank you."

The sound of her voice made his heart leap again, and he reached out to take her hand, feeling that warm and soft appendage against his calloused skin. It felt wonderful.

"The cottage," he said, lifting a hand to the walls around them. "Did you have time to do what you needed to do?"

Ophelia nodded. "Aye," she said. "Lady Munro and Lady de Merest had great ideas for the room. They said it looked like a man lived here and they wanted to make it look like a woman lived here. Are you displeased? I can remove anything you do not like."

"Please don't," he said, lifting her hand to his lips for a gentle kiss. He couldn't help himself. "They were right—it did look like a man lived here. *I* live here. But now you live here, too, so you may do whatever you wish with it."

Ophelia wasn't quite over the kiss to her hand. It had been so warm and gentle. The only one who had ever kissed her hand like that had been Cecil, and it hadn't been nearly as exciting. She had trouble concentrating on Creston's words, instead looking at her hand because she was certain his lips had left a brand on her flesh.

She could still feel them there.

"They… they brought the pieces of furniture," she managed to say, gesturing to the chairs. "Lady Matheson had the table brought over. See it over there? And she found four chairs to put with it."

Creston could see the table in the adjoining chamber, complete with a wooden pitcher that had a bunch of wildflowers in it. They grew wild all around Blackchurch but he'd never once thought to bring her any.

He pointed.

"The flowers," he said. "Did you pick those?"

Ophelia turned to look at the blue and yellow flowers. "Nay," she said. "Lady de Merest brought them to me. All of the ladies are lovely and friendly and they were all so determined to help. It was truly touching."

He was still holding her hand. "They are kind women," he said. "I hope you can become friends. It would mean a great deal to me if you did."

She was electrified by their hand-holding. "I wish the same," she said earnestly. "When I fostered at Okehampton, I had many friends, but when I returned home, there really wasn't anyone except my mother and Cecil. I should love to make new friends."

"Good," he said. "You'll find that we really are a family here. We work together, live together, and share life together. We all get along very well, so I am glad you are agreeable to making new friends."

She nodded, but her smile was fading. "My family is small," she said. "It is just my mother and my grandfather. My father died some time ago, as did my grandmother, and I never knew my father's parents."

"No cousins?"

"None," she said. "I suppose I have some distant cousins, somewhere, but none that I really know of. I think that is why my grandfather was so eager for me to marry someone with family ties, like you have to your brother. He wants us to be fruitful and multiply, I fear."

Creston chuckled. "God willing, we will," he said, but his eyes inevitably trailed to her belly, which was concealed by the flowing robe. "I suppose we have already started."

Her smile faded. "I suppose," she murmured. After a moment, she sighed. "Creston, even though I told you everything, I still feel… guilty. Guilty and ashamed that my grandfather thinks he has made a fool of you."

He regarded her a moment. "In keeping with our policy of honesty, I will say this," he said. "No one has ever made a fool out of me. You saw to that when you told me the truth. But I will ask you now and you will be completely honest—you do not have lingering feelings for Cecil, do you? I am not going to wake up one morning to the news that you have returned to him?"

Ophelia was shaking her head before he even finished speaking. "Never," she assured him with soft conviction. "I have had two months to think about this. I thought I loved Cecil. I truly did. I did everything I could to keep him. But when he left me at the church, I realized there was never any true love between us. If there was, I would not be here with you now. It's ironic what you realize in hindsight."

"That is true," he said. "I think we've all had those moments of clarity once a situation is over and wondered whatever drove us to behave in such a way."

She shrugged, her mind wandering to the godly man she'd

been such a fool for. "I *have* wondered," she said flatly. "And clarity did come in the realization that he never once went in pursuit of me. It was me going in pursuit of him. I convinced him what we had was special, but he never once took the initiative with me, and I think the more apathetic he seemed, the harder I tried. Like a challenge, if that makes sense. In the end, I was left trying to save my pride with a man whom I'd never truly been able to forge a strong relationship with. Something like that… it was never meant to be."

Creston grunted softly. "I cannot imagine any man being able to resist you," he said. "Cecil must have been stupid and blind."

She smiled faintly. "And that," she said, pointing at him, "right there. What you just said. Cecil would have never said that about me, not ever. This… all of this… with you has been so simple so far. We talk, we laugh, and we speak honestly. That has helped to open my eyes a great deal about what I thought I had with Cecil. I sacrificed everything for a chance to be with him, and in the end, he still left me. You cannot know how ashamed that makes me feel. The fact that you are so accepting… Creston, you did not have to accept anything, and it makes me realize how incredibly unworthy I am of you, but I hope to change that. I truly do."

He smiled, somewhat modestly. "As I told you yesterday, the sheer fact that you confessed the scheme makes you quite worthy," he said. "I've made my own decisions, Ophelia. I believe they are sound ones. I believe we can make this marriage a success."

"Why do you have such faith?"

"Because our marriage was not built on lies, but truth," Creston said. "Where there is truth, there is hope. Where there is hope, there is happiness. I'm ready to be happy. Aren't you?"

She really didn't have to think about it. "Aye," she murmured. "I am. I truly am."

"Then that is what we think about from now on," he said. "That is what we work toward. You spent your time pursuing a man who did not pursue you in return. Imagine how your life will be if you actually pursue a man who wants you to."

Her smile returned. "It is an astonishing concept," she said. "I'm assuming that you mean yourself?"

He laughed. "I do," he said. "I must not have made that clear."

"Or I am completely dense," she said. "I wonder… will you tell your brother any of this? That his decision to force a marriage upon you was not a terrible thing?"

Creston shrugged. "I do not know," he said. "Mayhap. You should know that I am not close to my brother. Until this betrothal came up, I'd not seen him in a few years."

"You do not get along with him?"

"I do not think he agrees with the choices I have made in life," he said. "My father was quite upset when I left royal service, more upset when I swore fealty to Lord Exmoor and Blackchurch. In case you've not realized it, Blackchurch does not exactly have a spotless reputation."

Ophelia shook her head. "I would not know," she said. "I've never heard anything at all."

"Not even while you were at Okehampton?"

"Not that I can recall."

"Okehampton is not too far from here," Creston said. "Although we do not really have any contact with them. We do not have contact with any local castles other than Dunstan Castle on the coast to the north."

"Why Dunstan?"

"Because long ago, the Lord of Dunster thwarted an attack on Blackchurch by men who came in through their shores," he said. "I do not know the entire story, but Dunster was able to deter them enough to allow Blackchurch to prepare for the attack, which never came. Ever since then, we've given Dunster our allegiance. Probably the only castle we have any allegiance to other than Tiverton."

"Why Tiverton?"

"House of de Long," he said. "They have a Blackchurch-trained son who did very well for himself."

"Does Blackchurch feel an allegiance to every graduate?"

"Aye, because it is so difficult to complete the entire course."

Ophelia didn't have any further questions after that. They were still standing in front of the hearth, holding hands, standing on hides given to them by the Blackchurch wives. But she did have a surprise for him, so she began to pull him over to the new table in the eating chamber.

"Come," she said. "My new friends have brought us food. So much food. Are you hungry?"

He let her tow him over to the table. "If you wish to eat, I will eat with you," he said. "But I will admit that I've had too much to drink this morning, so I will probably pass on any more wine."

She looked at him. "Are you drunk?"

"Do I seem drunk?"

She grinned. "I really do not know," she said. "I only just met you yesterday."

He laughed softly. "Surely you know what a drunk man looks like."

She looked him up and down. "You do seem a little happy."

The smile faded from his face and his hands came up, cupping her face gently between them. For a moment, he simply stared at her, drinking in the sight of her.

"I am," he whispered.

His lips came down on hers, very carefully at first, as if he were testing the waters, seeing how she would react. Seeing if she knew *how* to react. He kissed her once, twice, and then suddenly she was falling against him, her arms going around his neck. Her mouth latched on to his and she pulled him down to her level.

Creston couldn't have pulled away if he'd tried.

He didn't try.

Ophelia knew how to kiss. That was clear. He was torn between greatly enjoying it and being a bit miffed that she knew. She *knew*! But it also occurred to him that the woman was, by her own admission, pregnant, and she didn't get to that state by not knowing how to respond to a touch. He had to admit that he was feeling some disappointment again. Disappointment that he wouldn't be the first to touch her, that he wouldn't be the one to leave his mark on the woman he married. Someone had already marked her. But, then again, maybe it would make the duty today more pleasant, as he wasn't dealing with a fearful virgin. He was dealing with someone who had experience in intimate matters.

In fact, that intrigued him a little.

So did she.

The truth was that she was feeding his senses. It had been a long time since he'd been with a woman, and that inherent need for contact, for mating, roared. He wrapped his arms around her, pulling her close, and she surprised him by tightening her arms around his neck and nearly strangling him.

Clearly, something was roaring with her, too.

It didn't make any sense. He'd only just met her. But nothing about this betrothal or relationship had made sense from the beginning, so he didn't question his reaction to her. He simply accepted it, and as long as she was responding, he saw no reason to stop. They needed to consummate the marriage, anyway, so the fact that there seemed to be some kind of instant lust between them only made it easier.

And far more enjoyable.

At some point, he moved to pick her up and carry her up the stairs, his lips still fused to hers, but in his haste, he ended up tripping, falling forward with his big arms around her, straight into the table. She ended up sitting on the table Astria had been so kind to give them and had her arms around his head, trapping him against her. When she opened her mouth to him, letting him slide his tongue into the honeyed orifice, Creston nearly went out of his mind.

He had to have more.

In fact, Ophelia took on the aggressor role. She had done it when she'd managed to seduce Cecil, a last attempt at trapping the man once and for all. There were four separate times when she had managed to get him into her bed, or she'd slid into his. He'd never resisted her, but he'd let her do all of the work, as if he didn't know what to do. She'd kissed him, touched him, and when it came time to lose her innocence, that was the one move he'd made. He'd thrust into her body, which had been uncomfortable at first but not painful, and he'd moved a little before spilling himself. That was really as far as it had ever gotten. But she'd gone back three more times, and each time he'd impaled himself on her body, moved a little, and spilled his seed.

It had been enough to plant a child in her womb.

Therefore, Ophelia knew enough to arouse Creston, but not much more than that because her encounters with Cecil had been so brief. She wrapped her legs around his waist, her robe and shift coming between them, holding him tightly as she furiously kissed him. But unlike Cecil, Creston was responding.

Now, he was taking control.

Creston's hands were beginning to roam, and he went from holding her tightly to stroking her back and arms. When she didn't stop him, he grew bolder and moved to her buttocks, squeezing them and pulling her body up against his. Her legs were parted and his body was wedged in between them even though they were fully clothed. Creston fervently wished, at that moment, that they were not.

He'd never been more consumed by a woman in his life.

His mouth went to her shoulder, gently suckling her tender skin, and he began to gently pull back the neckline of her robe. It was loose, and he was able to pull it off her left shoulder, baring her skin, and he feasted on her delicious flesh. He could hear her sighing with pleasure, her hands on his head, her face in his hair. He continued to slowly and steadily pull her bodice off her shoulder, exposing the swell of her right breast.

She still didn't stop him.

Creston grew bolder.

Creston's mouth was on her cleavage now, delightful cleavage that he'd never noticed because of the loose dresses she wore. She was thin, that was true, but she was full where it mattered. Her soft, silky body was in his hands and he couldn't get enough. He pulled the robe and shift all the way down, exposing her from the waist up.

Ophelia cried out softly as his mouth clamped over a tender

nipple. Because of the pregnancy, her breasts were full, but they were also very sensitive. She began to pull at his tunic, trying to undress him, and Creston went right along with her. He wanted her as badly as she wanted him, not stopping to think that he should probably move her to the bed upstairs. If she didn't care, he didn't care.

He'd have her right here, on this table.

His clothing was coming off in pieces until he was nude from the waist up. Mouth on her succulent breasts, he pulled the edges of her robe apart and pushed her shift up. Then, in a flash, he pulled loose the ties on his breeches and everything fell to his ankles. Carefully, so he didn't drive splinters into her buttocks, he slid her forward, toward his waiting erection.

Creston positioned himself between her legs, his arousal at her threshold. He was a big man and his male organ was proportionate, and Ophelia's eager hands moved to his enormous erection as she guided him into her. This wasn't anything like Cecil, with his average-sized member and apathetic reaction toward coupling. Creston was big, hot, and powerful, and she wanted to feel that power inside her. Once his body touched hers, feeling that wet heat beckoning, he coiled his buttocks and thrust firmly into her.

Ophelia bit off her cries of pleasure, muffling the noise on his arm. He could feel her teeth against his flesh and it only served to inflame him. She was exquisitely tight and hot, and he thrust again, feeling her legs wrap around him and draw him in deeper. His arms went around her, holding her tightly as he thrust into her again and again, harder each time.

He no longer had a mind of his own.

He was a slave to his body.

And hers.

Ophelia was nearly incoherent in her passion, feeling every move with the greatest of pleasure. He was so big, and thrusting himself so deeply, that the pleasure-pain of it was quickly driving her toward release. Nothing Cecil had done to her had even been close to this, and with every successive thrust, Creston was succeeding in driving Cecil further and further from her mind. He was erasing any touch the man had ever given her, any pleasure she might have felt. Now there was only Creston, and Creston *was* pleasure. He was a spectacular figure of a man and he belonged to her.

All of him.

She never wanted it to end.

Creston's thrusts grew harder, firmer, and he ground his pelvis against her every time he plunged deep. He suckled her neck as he thrust, listening to her groan with pleasure. It was moving and beautiful and overwhelming, and after one particularly deep thrust, he felt her release around him. Her entire body bucked with convulsions and that threw him over the edge. He released himself into her sweet body, feeling such a climax that stars danced before his eyes. Still, he continued to make love to her, moving within her, feeling her head mingling with his. Everything was wet and sloppy, but he didn't care.

He loved it.

With his body still joined to hers, Creston finally opened his eyes to look down at her. Her robe had fallen off, onto the table, and her shift was bunched up around her midsection, but he could see her legs open wide to receive him. He could also see the sheen of his seed glistening on the fluff of dark curls between her legs, as well as on the inside of her thighs. The mere sight of it was enough to cause him to heat up again. Gently, he bent over, kissing her shoulder, the tops of her breasts, before taking a nipple in his mouth again and suckling tenderly.

In his arms, he could feel Ophelia shudder. She was leaning back on the table, arms braced, so her breasts were defenseless against his onslaught. She watched him as he suckled her, studying his long blond lashes and the curve of his face. He had such a gorgeous face. Slowly, she lay back on the table, and he followed her, his mouth never leaving her breasts, and she lay there as he nursed against her. When he shifted, slightly withdrawing from her body, she brought her legs up and trapped him against her.

"Nay," she whispered. "You're not going anywhere. Stay where you belong."

He grinned, a nipple between his teeth, and thrust into her deliberately with his semi-erection. "Like this?" he muttered.

"Like that," she responded. "Do it again."

He did, only harder, causing her to yelp with pleasure. Then he did it again and again until he had a steady rhythm going. He wasn't as hard as he had been, but the woman had him so wildly aroused that his body was ready to go again anyway. It was probably the wine because whenever he had too much wine, he could go all night. At least, he'd been able to when he was younger, but that hadn't happened in years.

Until now.

They made love twice more on that table before Creston finally carried Ophelia up to their bed, laughing with her because that was where they should have been in the first place. Naked, they crawled into bed together, but before he could take her again, she promptly fell asleep on him. Stress, travel, fear, and the overwhelming nature of the change her life had just undergone had pushed her into sheer exhaustion. Now that she was safe and warm, her body had reacted in kind.

No more flight or fight.

Ophelia was home.

And so was Creston.

PART TWO

CHAPTER FOURTEEN

The Pox tavern
London
Three Months Later

I T WAS THE kind of place one's mother warned against.

Situated in the Ropery district near the River Thames, the dangerous establishment known as The Pox was legendary. It had excellent food, excellent wine, and beautiful women who smelled like flowers. Those were the positive aspects. The negative aspects involved the fact that at The Pox, one could wager on anything. *Anything.* There were the usual games of chance, but a man could also wager on things like how far blood would spurt if a man was stabbed in a certain place. Or how much a man could drink and then how far the same man could vomit. There were no rules on wagering at The Pox, and things had been known to get out of hand too many times to count.

It was a paradoxical place—fine food, beautiful women, and then dangerous or immoral surroundings. Great lords would speak disparagingly about the place, yet they would secretly go, not telling their wives, and then sit in a corner and enjoy the best wine from France. Elite knights and drunkards, lowly villeins would sit alongside one another. As long as a man had coin, The Pox wasn't particular. But it could be quite lively.

As it was today.

Two of those elite knights were in The Pox when the smoke and fog hung around London, so thick that it was as if some great, unseen hand had knitted a blanket and decided to throw it over the whole of the city. Sometimes the smoke from all of the fires around London could be choking, sitting heavy, especially in the summer when there were no breezes to blow it away, and today happened to be one of those days even though it wasn't the season for it. The Pox was full of men and women trying to escape the choking air today, and the knights sat in a corner, backs to the wall and facing the door, as they shared a beef knuckle and fine wine between them.

"Where do you go now, Myles?" a man with somewhat dirty, shoulder-length hair said. He was young and handsome, but he had the look of exhaustion about him. "It seems like we have been on this mission so long that I almost don't know what to do with myself now that it's over."

Sir Myles de Lohr, son of the legendary Christopher de Lohr, Earl of Hereford and Worcester, smiled weakly at his companion's assertion.

"It's like this every time we finish with a task," he said. "You feel lost somehow. You've been going at full pace for months on end in a life-or-death situation and, suddenly, it is over. Every Executioner Knight feels like that after a mission. You've been doing this long enough to know that, Brenton."

Sir Brenton de Royans nodded in resignation. "Almost two years," he said. "Ever since your brother came to Bowes Castle and practically forced me into service."

Myles snorted. "Your father had nothing to say about it."

"My father was helping your brother," Brenton said with some animation. "The two of them, taking turns bending my arm behind my back until I cried for mercy and agreed to join the Executioner Knights. You should have seen it!"

Myles was laughing quietly. He wasn't normally the laughing type, but a rather serious personality, but young Brenton's description of Peter de Lohr, Christopher's eldest son and the head of the Executioner Knights network, physically forcing a big, healthy knight into submission was indeed a humorous visual picture.

Not that it wasn't true.

Peter did have that way about him.

"So you joined us," Myles said. "And you have performed flawlessly. My brother will know about that because I will tell him myself."

Brenton smiled, a smug gesture. "I am a de Royans," he said. "We are always flawless."

"And modest."

"*And* modest," Brenton agreed with exaggerated flair. But he quickly settled down. "In all seriousness, I want to go home and see my father. It has been almost a year and he's an old man. I must spend some time with him."

Myles nodded. "You will," he said, eyeing the men at the next table as they began to argue over something undoubtedly stupid. "In fact, if you want to leave immediately after debriefing my brother on your activities for the past few months, I'm certain he will let you go."

"Is he at Farringdon House?"

He was referring to the London townhome, and main headquarters for the Executioner Knights, and Myles nodded. "Aye," he said. "Especially since he knew that most of us were in

Lincolnshire heading off that Flemish spy. God help us if that woman had made her way to London. A beautiful courtesan who is also clever is a dangerous tool, indeed. Especially to a king who has come of age. She might have gotten close to her had we not identified and neutralized her."

Brenton lifted his eyebrows in agreement. "But we did," he said. "At least Henry seems to be easier to protect than his father was, or so I've heard."

"It's true," Myles said. "John was a nightmare."

Brenton grunted. "I had a cousin who served him, you know."

"Who?"

"Creston," he said. "Have you met him?"

Myles shook his head. "I do not think so," he said. "Does he still serve the Crown?"

"Nay," Brenton said. "He was one of John's closest knights. The things John had him do… Well, you can imagine. Creston is a man of honor and integrity, however. When he could take no more, he simply walked out on him. At least, that's what my father said. I know my father approved even if Creston's father did not."

"That is because Juston de Royans has a greater sense of intelligence and morality than most," he said. "He knows what John was capable of. Where is Creston now?"

"Blackchurch," Brenton said. "He is a senior trainer at the Blackchurch Guild."

Myles' eyebrows lifted in surprise. "Truly?" he said. "Black-church, you say?"

"Aye."

"That's quite impressive," Myles said. "He's your cousin, you said? How is he related to you?"

"My father has one brother, Quinton," Brenton said. "Creston is his second son."

"I see," Myles said, picking up the pitcher to pour himself more wine. "A Blackchurch trainer in the family. That's something to be proud of."

"Did none of the de Lohr sons train at Blackchurch?"

Myles shook his head. "Nay," he said. "My father never discouraged us, but we're all very highly trained anyway, and we went straight into service for my father and the Crown. Most Blackchurch warriors are men seeking positions with great lords or kings or princes. Only a few train to return to the place where they started. Frankly, none of us ever saw the need to train with Blackchurch and, to be perfectly honest, the Executioner Knights have been as intense a training field as Blackchurch is, only we've done it on the job. At Blackchurch, when they fail during their training, they simply go home. With the Executioner Knights, if we fail, we die."

That was the truth. The Blackchurch Guild and the Executioner Knights were two different beasts, each with their own merits, each with their own downfalls. Each one was spoken of with awe in every hall in England. Brenton sat back in his chair, holding his cup of wine, thinking of the cousin he'd not seen in a while as he watched the crowded common room. Most men were simply eating and drinking, with the more private chambers in the rear of the establishment housing nobility that had come in to seek respite. A game of chance over near the door that led to the kitchens caught his attention, men rolling a pair of dice, and he was about to point it out to Myles, to see if the man wanted to participate, when something suddenly fell against him.

Brenton's wine went onto the floor.

Startled, he quickly rolled out of his chair because what had hit him was a body—a man falling into him. It was the man at the table next to him where the stupid argument had been going on, only one of them was now collapsed in Brenton's chair as the other man went after him with a dagger.

Swiftly, Brenton grabbed the wrist of the man who held the dagger, twisting and yanking. Bones snapped and the dagger went flying as the man began to scream. Myles was up, and between the two of them, they rushed the screaming man out of the common room and onto the roadway outside. Beyond was the dirty, muddy ribbon of the River Thames, and as the man pulled out another dagger with his good hand and charged them, Myles turned the dagger back on the man, so he ended up stabbing himself. As he collapsed, Myles picked him up, literally, carried him down to the river, and tossed him in.

Both Myles and Brenton stood there as the body, face-down, was surrounded by a dark red stain. Slowly, it floated down the river before finally submerging.

It was just another day in the life of an Executioner Knight.

"Did he nick you?" Brenton asked.

Myles looked down at himself and then to both arms. "Nay," he said. "Pity he had no common sense."

"You're still in the killer mindset, Myles."

Myles turned to look at him. "That is because I've had to be for the past several months," he said. "Kill or be killed."

"By that courtesan."

"Exactly."

Myles was standing ankle-deep in the dirty river and sloshed back onto the shore, following Brenton across the roadway and back into The Pox. They entered, but no one gave them a second glance. Things like that happened at The Pox all the time, so it wasn't anything unusual. By the time they returned to their table in the crowded chamber, however, the man who had fallen into Brenton was waiting.

"My lord," the man said, obviously drunk. "My deepest apologies that you were involved in such a tangle. I do not even know who that man was. He simply wanted to sit at my table and then became irate when I would not pay for his drink."

Myles waved him off. "No harm done," he said. "Except to that man. He won't be attacking anyone else again."

The man realized that his attacker was either dead or disabled by these fine knights. "You have my thanks," he said, weaving around in his inebriated state. "My name is Duddington. Alaric Duddington. I serve the Earl of Sidbury. May… may I sit with you and buy you a drink?"

Myles looked at Brenton, who shrugged. They both reclaimed their seats as Brenton indicated an empty chair at their table.

"Sit," he told Alaric. "We'll take your drink with gratitude."

"Good," Alaric said, waving down a serving woman and telling her to bring the finest wine in the house. "The earl provided me with coinage to pay for food, so he is the one paying for your drink. He has paid for mine all day."

That much was clear as Alaric struggled to stay upright in his chair. Brenton fought off a grin. "Thank him for us," he said.

"I will," Alaric said. "May I have your names, please?"

"Brenton de Royans," Brenton said. "That blond beast next to me is a de Lohr. Myles de Lohr."

Alaric looked at Myles with some awe. He was, indeed, big and blond and handsome, as most of the de Lohr men were. "De Lohr?" he said. "The Earl of Hereford and Worcester?"

"My father."

"Then I am greatly honored," Alaric said. "I had an uncle who served with your father in the Levant, under King Richard. He spoke very highly of him."

Myles nodded his thanks. "My father has told stories about his time in the Levant," he said. "Not a pleasant place, I think. Did your uncle survive?"

"Surprisingly, he did," Alaric said. "He returned home to his wife, who had given birth to a child a few months earlier. Considering he had been gone for three years, it was not a pleasant surprise."

Myles' eyebrows lifted in understanding. "I would imagine not."

Alaric shook his head. "I suppose the betrayal is worse when it is your wife," he said. "With men, it is expected."

The servant returned at that point, bringing a potent wine all the way from Tuscany. She set it down on the table and Alaric picked up the pitcher, sloppily filling the cups. Myles took his, and Brenton followed suit, both of them taking a healthy drink of the delicious wine. Alaric poured himself a cup and held it aloft, in tribute to the men who had saved his life from a stranger with a dagger.

"Lord Sidbury will know of your help to his cause," he said before gulping down about half of his cup. "If I did not complete this mission, a great deal would have been lost. There is much at stake, so your assistance is appreciated."

Brenton sat back in his chair, cup in hand as he put his big, booted feet on the table. "You're on a mission for the earl?" he said. "Where are you going?"

Alaric was so drunk that he didn't think twice before answering. "To Westminster," he said. "I must see the king. I have a message for him from Lord Sidbury."

Myles shook his head. "He is not there," he said. "He's at Winchester at the moment."

Alaric's face fell. "That is terrible news," he said. "This information is of the utmost importance. It must get to the king immediately!"

"Simply go to Winchester, then."

Alaric shook his head. "I wish I'd known," he said miserably. "I passed Winchester on my way here, from Devon. It will take me at least a week or more to reach Winchester now, going back the way I came."

Myles put his feet up like Brenton had. "It should not take more than seven days with a swift horse," he said. "Is your horse swift?"

Alaric nodded. "A Spanish Jennet," he said, indicating a breed that was known for speed. "Still, it will take time. Lord Sidbury will be displeased because the matter is terribly urgent."

"What is so important?" Brenton asked. "Or is it a secret?"

Alaric looked at him. Then he looked at Myles. He took another drink of wine and appeared to be contemplating the question.

"It *is* a secret," he said, but he was looking at Myles. "I will tell you because you should tell your father. He is an important man and he should know who to trust. Everyone knows Hereford serves the king, so mayhap the king will ask him to do something about it."

"Do something about what?"

Alaric leaned forward, lowering his voice. "The king has been betrayed."

"By whom?"

Alaric looked around to make sure no one had heard him before reaching over to the table behind him and grabbing his satchel. He put it on the table and opened it, digging around until he came to a carefully folded vellum envelope. Drunk as he was, he didn't even think to be careful about this. He'd never met Myles or Brenton before. He didn't know what kind of men they were, but he was going on Myles' surname. *De Lohr.* Everyone knew they were honorable, that they served the Crown. Perhaps telling Myles about the missive he carried was as good as telling the king. Word would surely get back to the man. But it never occurred to him that Myles and Brenton could have been lying about everything. He simply took them at their word.

He put the envelope down in front of Myles.

"Look at that," he said. "Look at the seal."

Curious, Myles collected the envelope without taking his feet off the table. He held it up, studying it for a moment, before his brow furrowed. Then his feet came off the table and he sat forward, peering more closely at the seal because the light was better here. Finally, he lifted his gaze to Alaric.

"*Ludovicus VIII, rex Franciae,*" he said. "That is Louis' seal. The King of France."

Alaric nodded. "It is," he said. "Read it."

Now Brenton's feet were off the table, too, and they both looked at the envelope as Myles noted that the seal was broken.

"Who broke this seal?" he asked.

"Lord Sidbury," Alaric whispered loudly. "And it is a good thing he did. We have found a traitor in England, one who would see Henry destroyed."

Myles still wasn't any clearer, but he was starting to become concerned. "Be plain, man," he said. "What is this about?"

Alaric pointed at the envelope. "I am taking that to Henry with an accompanying missive from Lord Sidbury," he said.

"That dispatch is from Louis, thanking The Blackchurch Guild for providing him with men and money to win the battle for Gascony against Henry."

Myles blinked in surprise. Shock, actually. He ended up carefully unfolding the envelope and, with Brenton looking over his shoulder, read the following:

Mon ami de Saint-Denis,

C'est avec la plus grande gratitude que je vous remercie de votre soutien à ma cause gasconne. Sans vos hommes et votre argent, je n'aurais pu vaincre Henri, le grand prétendant. La Gascogne est de nouveau mienne grâce à vous.

Que Dieu vous bénisse pour votre loyauté envers moi et envers la France.

My friend St. Denis,

It is with the utmost gratitude that I thank you for your support of my Gascon cause. Without your men or your coin, I would not have been victorious over Henry, the great pretender. Gascony is now mine again because of you.

God bless you for your loyalty to me and to France.

Myles had to read it three times. Brenton read it four times. Even when Myles was finished, Brenton took the envelope from him and stared at the words. Myles, however, was fixed on Alaric.

"*Where* did Lord Sidbury get this dispatch?" he asked.

Alaric had finished his cup of wine and was pouring himself another. "A French ship dropped anchor at Sidmouth beach, and the dispatch was brought to St. Peter's church," he said. "The messenger was looking for a priest who is a known supporter of Louis, but instead, he mistakenly gave it over to a priest loyal to Lord Sidbury. It was that priest who brought it to Lord Sidbury, and he opened it. When he saw that it was about Blackchurch, he thought Henry should know right away. Henry lost Gascony and now we know it was because of Blackchurch. They reinforced Louis' ranks."

Myles was greatly confused. "But the Blackchurch Guild does not take sides in a conflict," he said. "Almost two hundred years of precedence says that they remain neutral."

Alaric dipped his head at the envelope. "They are not neutral any longer," he said. "Henry must know."

Brenton looked at Myles. The two of them stared at one another, silent words of shock and confusion and concern passing between them. The missive made absolutely no sense because everyone knew that the Blackchurch Guild only trained warriors. It did not supply armies to kings. It did not take sides. That was how it had survived all of these years, free from conflict or wars, even when it had been begged for support. But if this missive was true and it had finally taken sides, enough so that the English king lost his properties in France, then the consequences were unfathomable.

Blackchurch had sounded its death knell.

"I'm going to Westminster," Brenton said. "I know the king personally. I shall put it right in his hand."

Alaric hadn't been expecting that offer and was caught off guard. "But… it is my duty," he said. "Lord Sidbury will be displeased if I let anyone else complete my task."

"I understand," Brenton said patiently. "But I am a knight. I have taken an oath to the Crown. If you are certain you can get past Henry's guards to deliver this missive to him, then you should go. But if there is any doubt that you might not be successful, you must let me take it. I can get past his guards and make sure he reads this personally. Will you let me do this?"

Alaric was hesitant. "I… I do not know if…"

"It is too important to be left to chance. You *know* this."

Alaric looked between Brenton and Myles before finally shaking his head. "Nay," he said. "I cannot. It is my duty. Though I am grateful that you defended me against that madman, the truth is that I do not know either of you. I cannot give this over to you."

Brenton stood up, grasping Alaric by the arm and pulling him to his feet. "Come," he said. "You and I are going to go outside to discuss this where no one can hear us. Come along."

Alaric didn't have a choice. Brenton was a big man, and he was quite strong, and Alaric was pulled out of the tavern as Myles sat there with the dispatch on the table in front of him. He wasn't quite sure what Brenton's game was, but all would be revealed in good time. He knew the man had a reason.

Pouring himself more wine, he waited.

Several minutes later, Brenton returned to the tavern. But he was alone. Myles watched curiously as Brenton returned to the table, collected his half-empty cup, and drained it. Then he poured himself another.

"Where is Alaric?" Myles finally asked.

Brenton wouldn't look at him. "That dispatch is from Louis," he muttered. "It is to St. Denis de Bottreaux, the Earl of Exmoor and the leader of the Blackchurch Guild. Why in the hell would Louis be sending Lord Exmoor a dispatch thanking him for his support?"

"I do not know," Myles said. "But it is a coincidence that we were just speaking of Blackchurch earlier, is it not?"

Brenton took another drink of wine, staring off into the common room as the noise and laughter and stench went on around them.

"Something's not right," he finally said. "*Is* Blackchurch actually betraying England? Have they finally decided to take sides?"

"It is a mystery."

Brenton didn't like that answer. Something inside him was building into a rage. "If they are taking sides, then my cousin is part of it," he said. "If he *is* part of it, all of the House of de Royans will be blamed. My father will be blamed. *I* will be blamed. And I've worked too hard to be branded a traitor by association."

"What are you going to do?"

Brenton looked at him then. "Go to Blackchurch," he said simply. "Talk to my cousin and find out what he knows. Let me find out if that dispatch is authentic before we decide to do anything about it."

"I take it you're not going home to see your father now."

Brenton shook his head. "And I am not going to Farringdon House to see Peter," he said. "I'm going to Devon to get to the bottom of this."

Myles understood completely. "If my opinion matters, I do not think it is legitimate," he said. "Blackchurch is many things, but a traitor is not among them. I would be willing to stake my life on it."

That seemed to bring Brenton some relief. "As would I," he admitted. "But this dispatch in the wrong hands would be devastating. Will you come to Devon with me?"

Myles nodded. "I think I'd better," he said. "I want to see

how right I am about Blackchurch."

"Hopefully, you are completely right."

Myles couldn't disagree with him. "But until we know for sure, you must tread very carefully," he said. "If Blackchurch has turned, and your cousin knows about it, then your life might be in danger for asking questions. They may want to silence you, and we are talking about Blackchurch trainers. They can silence you twenty different ways, and you would never see it coming, so be cautious. Your father does not need a dead son, nor does mine."

That was the truth. The methods that Blackchurch taught would give even Executioner Knights nightmares. "I'll be careful," Brenton said. "But if the dispatch is a forgery, why? Who would do this to discredit Blackchurch?"

Myles shrugged. "Who knows?" he said. "They've accumulated their share of enemies over the years, so it could be anyone. I might start by questioning Lord Sidbury. He's the one who produced the missive, or so Alaric said. Where *is* Alaric, by the way?"

"In the river with the friend who attacked him."

"That was wise. We don't need that foolish man running his mouth off about this."

"My thinking exactly."

After downing the rest of the wine in short order, Myles and Brenton were out of the tavern and heading to the livery. Within the hour, they were on the road to Devon with the alleged royal dispatch from Louis VIII of France safely tucked into Brenton's saddlebag.

He was going to get to the bottom of this.

Or else.

CHAPTER FIFTEEN

Blackchurch Guild

"HERE HE COMES," Athdara said, glancing up from the garment she was sewing. "I can tell you exactly what he's going to say."

Sitting next to her, Gisele kept her head down, focused on her work, but she was biting her lip to keep from laughing.

"*Greetings, ladies,*" she said, imitating a male voice. "*'Tis a lovely day! I hope you are in good health. Have you seen my wife?*"

Athdara snorted, though she was trying very hard not to laugh. "Exactly," she said, sewing furiously and pretending to be busy. "Those are his exact words."

"I've never seen a man so stupidly happy in my life!"

Athdara couldn't help it now. She started laughing, head lowered so no one would see. She almost couldn't speak when Creston walked up, beaming from ear to ear.

"Greetings, ladies," he said, waving. "'Tis a lovely day!"

Athdara had to take a deep breath. "It is," she agreed with perhaps a little too much enthusiasm. "So very lovely."

Creston nodded. "I hope you are both in good health."

"Verily," Gisele said, struggling to keep a straight face. "And you?"

"Excellent health, thank you," he said. "Have you seen my wife?"

Athdara's lips buzzed together as she tried to hold in the laughter, but Gisele wasn't so adept. She started chuckling, shaking her head at Creston and his very predictable conversation. It had been this way ever since he'd married Ophelia, and in spite of their laughter, they thought it was very sweet. He was ridiculously happy and didn't care who knew it. From a man who had reluctantly entered into a forced marriage to a husband who couldn't be away from his wife more than an hour or two without greatly missing her, the progression of Creston de Royans from hardened warrior to sickly-sweet husband was truly astonishing.

"She told me to tell you that she's run off with a pirate," Gisele said. "She's tired of being deliriously happy all of the time and she's tired of you being so kind to her. You chased her away with your joy, Creston."

He fought off a smile. "That is a pity," he said. Then he sighed dramatically. "Well, I did not much like her, anyway. I suppose I'll get over it."

Athdara burst out laughing, loudly this time. "Surely you jest," she said. "Creston, you are the sweetest, stickiest, sappiest man I've ever come across. You make happiness a new art form. Your wife was here a little while ago, but she's gone back to your cottage to make you supper because she knows you will be tired and hungry returning from your recruits."

Creston grinned. "She is rather wonderful that way."

"She is," Athdara agreed. "She's as sickly sweet as you are."

Creston laughed softly. "Good," he said. "Then we shall be

insufferable together."

With that, he left the women, listening to them laugh. It was at his expense, but he didn't care. All he cared about was that lovely woman in the cottage up ahead. The days were longer this time of year, so the sun was sitting low in the afternoon as he approached, noting Sinclair off to his right as he returned to his cottage and his young son greeted him.

That made Creston smile.

Someday, he'd be experiencing the same thing.

Ophelia's pregnancy was in its sixth month and, fortunately, she was feeling fine. But the difference between the woman he'd married three months ago and the woman of today was like night and day. That pale, fragile woman was gone, replaced by a round, robust, and luscious woman he couldn't get enough of. With the proper nutrition, she'd filled out deliciously, and he swore he'd never seen a more beautiful creature. She was happy and she was healthy, and he couldn't have been more grateful.

But she was many other things as well.

He didn't know her when he married her, but his instincts were good. They told him that she was a decent human being, a woman of solid character, and he'd been right. He'd watched the timid, traumatized woman emerge like a butterfly from a cocoon. She had a great sense of humor. She had a sense of devotion to her husband and also to her friends, which she made quickly. About a month after Creston had married her, Athdara's children all became sick. Soon enough, Athdara and Tay became ill, as well as the woman who usually tended their children, and Ophelia had stepped up to tend to Athdara's younger children while Gisele and Astria and Elisiana tended to the older boy, Athdara, the nurse, and even Tay.

It had been quite selfless on Ophelia's part to tend someone else's sick children, but she'd done so without reserve. She'd stayed up all night with them a couple of nights in a row, only relieved by Creston, who had sat with the children in the afternoons while Ophelia slept heavily. He'd been so proud of her, seeing what a good heart she had, and Athdara had never forgotten that kindness. It seemed to draw Ophelia and Athdara closer together, and the women were quite good friends these days.

It was if she had always lived at Blackchurch.

He couldn't imagine his life without her.

Creston wasn't quite sure when he'd fallen in love with his wife. It could have been within the first few days of knowing her, but it could have also been during the time when she tended Athdara's children. It could have even been before that, or after that. He wasn't sure when, and the truth was that he couldn't remember when he hadn't loved her.

That was why Athdara and Gisele were giggling.

He was a fool in love.

Creston and Ophelia lived in their own little world, protected by the walls of Blackchurch as if nothing outside of those walls existed. They hadn't heard from Oscar again after he left after the wedding, nor had they heard from Ophelia's mother. No one had sent word to inquire about Ophelia's life, or well-being, and she never sent her mother or her grandfather any news from Blackchurch. As far as she was concerned, those people didn't exist anymore. The people who had starved her and abused her were no longer in her thoughts. Nor were there any lingering thoughts of Cecil, not even when the child and her belly moved. As far as she was concerned, and as far as Creston was concerned, that child was his.

He'd never thought any differently.

Nor did anyone else.

Ophelia confessed to him that she'd told the other Black-church wives of her condition on the day of their marriage because, as she explained it, they were all women who had given birth, and they would be able to figure out that her pregnancy was more advanced than what was public knowledge. In order to be honest with them as she had been with Creston, she'd told them everything, and they had been more than accepting. That gave Creston the courage to tell his friends one evening as they sat at The Black Cock, at their usual table.

The results had been predictable.

No one seemed to care that the child wasn't of Creston's loins. All they cared about was the fact that another child was to be brought into their brotherhood, and they couldn't have been happier for him. They bought Creston so much wine to celebrate that Tay and Cruz had to drag him home to his wife, who wanted to know why he was so drunk that he could hardly walk. They were honest with her and told her they were celebrating the coming child, and, for a split second, Ophelia was afraid she was going to see judgment in their eyes. Judgment for a woman who did not carry the child of their dear friend, but the child of another man.

But there had been no judgment.

Only celebration.

While there was no suspicion or condemnation from the trainers, there had been a little through the rumor mill, and Blackchurch had a big one. Every castle, every city, had one, and Blackchurch was no different. Soldiers gossiped like fishwives, and Creston would have been surprised if Ophelia's rather large belly *hadn't* been a topic of conversation. He was extremely protective over her, and rightfully so, and that probably had something to do with the rumors being kept very quiet. No one wanted The Avenger to avenge his wife on someone who spoke less than favorably about her. Creston, more than any of them, was a killer.

No one wanted a man like that coming after them.

But Creston wasn't going after anyone, not any time soon. He was living on love these days and nothing else seemed to matter. He was nearly to his cottage now, seeing the light from within and smelling… something. He wasn't sure what it was—and, if he were perfectly honest, Ophelia wasn't a good cook. Managing a kitchen was something all noble young women were taught, but doing actual cooking was frowned upon. Blackchurch had a big kitchen where one could go and collect food to bring back to the cottage, and Ophelia had done so many times, but more recently, she'd had the cooks at Blackchurch teach her how to make simple dishes, and she'd taken great pride in making food for her husband. Creston was greatly touched by her efforts, even if half of the dishes she made weren't edible. Still, he choked them down and praised her because she'd tried so hard.

Love wasn't only blind—it had no sense of taste, either.

Opening the entry door, he stepped into the warm, fragrant cottage. A fat black cat lounged on one of the chairs in front of the hearth while still another cat, this one black and white, was grooming itself on the warm stones. Ophelia had found the strays last month and brought them home, and now Creston not only slept with his wife, but with two cats, one of whom liked to lie on his head. But he wouldn't deny his wife her pets, as she seemed very fond of them, and they of her, and as he headed into the eating area of the cottage, he saw Ophelia bent over the hearth, stirring something in an iron pot that was hanging over the flames.

"Lady de Royans," he greeted Ophelia as he came up behind her. "I've missed you today."

By the time Ophelia stood up, he had wrapped his arms around her torso and was hugging her tightly. She smiled, leaning back against him, craving his warmth.

"I just saw you at the nooning hour," she said, her arms over his as he held her. "But that seems like so long ago, doesn't it?"

He kissed her on the side of the head. "It seems like forever," he said, releasing her. "Something smells good. What are you preparing?"

Ophelia was quite proud of the mystery dish bubbling in the pot. "Pork and beans in a stew," she said. "The cook told me how to make it. It *does* smell good, does it not?"

He nodded, even though it wasn't exactly true. It smelled burned. "Verily," he said. "But before we eat, let me wash my hands and change my tunic. It seems to have blood on it."

Ophelia put her hands on his tunic, seeing the stains around his waistline. "What happened?" she asked.

Creston watched her inspect the stains. He wasn't exactly sure he should tell her all of it because his training consisted these days of torture endurance, and it was every bit as horrific as it sounded. Not one recruit looked forward to this segment of training because it often involved things like beatings and ripping hair out by the root, or battered testicles or torn toenails. Painful, terrible things that stopped short of permanently damaging a man. The point was to make the recruit resistant to such things, because it was a mental game far more than a physical one.

It was also exhausting for Creston, who taught it in conjunction with Ming Tang, whose training module involved mind over matter and relaxation, among other things. However, when it came to Creston's class, Ming Tang also spoke of a torture method called *Ling Chi*, or death by a thousand cuts. It was an ancient torture method that was exactly like it sounded. Creston had never used it on a recruit, but long ago, he had used it on an enemy of John's. It had been called something else, but the result was the same. The king's enemy had slowly bled to death, his crime being protesting the fact that John had bedded his wife.

Those were the days Creston didn't particularly like to think about.

He focused on today, on the lovely woman in his kitchen, a woman that had him walking on air every moment of every day. He was as happy as he'd never been in his life, smitten by the glorious creature he had married. He went to change his tunic and wash his hands, and she followed him with a pitcher of water. There was a basin in their bedchamber, and she poured the water for him while he washed his hands and face. The bloodied tunic went into a pile of clothing to be washed, like aprons and hose, and while he dried his hands and face, Ophelia pulled a fresh tunic out of a trunk and gave it to him.

Together, they went down to supper.

Creston discovered everything about the meal she'd prepared in short order. The bread was good because she'd brought it over from Blackchurch's kitchens, and there was plenty of butter to go with it. The pork and bean stew, however, was a thick pottage with too much salt and rosemary in it. The Blackchurch cook had told her to season it with herbs, so she'd cut too much fresh rosemary from a bush to the rear of the cottage and put all of it in the stew. He was eating rosemary stew and it was a taste he absolutely detested, but he ate two bowls because she had tried so hard. As she was spooning out a third bowl for him, the rear door swung open and Cruz entered.

"I smell food," he said, coming to the table and sitting down. "What is for sup, Lady de Royans?"

Ophelia grinned. She and Cruz had developed a lovely relationship over the past three months, and she genuinely liked him. He thought she was sweet and delightful, like the sister he'd never had, so entering their home unannounced was something he did on a regular basis, just like he always had when Creston lived here alone, and Ophelia didn't mind in the least. She was thrilled to be cooking for two men, so she produced another bowl of the rosemary stew and put it in front of Cruz, who dug into it with gusto.

Soon, they were all sitting at the table, eating the stew, and Cruz kept up a running conversation about the module that he and Creston were preparing to teach together, which involved politics, diplomacy, and dirty coercion tactics. Ophelia listened to the men talk, eating very little of the stew but eating a good deal of the bread. As the men continued to talk, she got up, went to the table that contained the implements and ingredients she used for supper and scraped the remainder of her stew into an old bucket. She tossed in the inedible parts of the carrots she'd put in the stew, the tops and some dirty pieces that weren't for cooking. Lifting the bucket, she went outside to dump it.

Once she was gone, Creston put his hand over Cruz's as the man lifted a spoonful of the stew to his mouth.

"Stop," he hissed. "You do not have to eat this simply to please me."

Cruz looked at him in surprise. "Why not?"

Creston made sure Ophelia wasn't coming back in through the door before answering. "Because it is vile," he whispered. "I have to eat it, but you do not."

Cruz fought off a grin and put the stuff into his mouth, chewing. "Cres, don't you know by now that food made with love is the best food in the world?" he said. "No matter what it tastes like, love makes it delicious."

Creston thought on that, smiling reluctantly. "God bless the woman, she is trying so hard," he murmured. "I do not want to upset her, so I just eat it. But there have been times when it has been most difficult."

Cruz grinned, patting him on the shoulder. "You are a good man," he said. "God will reward you for being so kind to her."

"If I keep eating this slop, I'll meet him sooner than I'd hoped."

Cruz burst into soft laughter as Ophelia came back through the door with the empty bucket. She put it on the table and busied herself with other things as Cruz and Creston finished off what was in their bowls. Ophelia looked over and, seeing that they were finished, went to collect the dirty dishes so she could wash them. Cruz handed his over, but when Creston did, he happened to look up and see her face.

There were tears in her eyes.

"Sweetheart, what is amiss?" he asked gently, grasping her wrist to keep her from walking away from the table. "Why are you upset?"

Ophelia burst into tears. "Because this is awful," she said, holding up the empty, dirty bowl. "It is awful and you eat it anyway. Worse still, you feed it to your friends."

She gestured at Cruz. Terrified that she had heard him

criticize her food, Creston put his arms around her, trying to comfort her.

"It is not awful," he assured her. "I eat it because you are working very hard at trying to make a home for us. I eat it because I am grateful. It does not matter what it tastes like because I can only taste the love."

He thought that was rather clever of him, given his conversation with Cruz, but Ophelia's tears didn't stop. If anything, they grew worse.

"I want so much to make a meal that you will enjoy, but I cannot seem to," she said, wiping at her nose. "I am so sorry. I will not put you through this torture any longer. I will simply bring you what Blackchurch's cook prepares."

Creston pulled her down onto his lap as she wiped her face. "My sweet lass," he murmured, kissing the side of her head. "You can cook for me every night for the rest of my life and I will be a very happy man. Please do not give up. You've only just started."

"Do you think any cook is good when they first start?" Cruz said, feeling sorry for the woman who was trying so hard. "Of course they're not. It takes time. My *abuela* used to make sweet cheese fritters, but do you think they were always delicious? Of course not. She had to practice until she became very adept at it. You must not give up."

Ophelia was looking over her shoulder at him as Creston held her on his lap, his cheek against her back as he looked at Cruz also. Ophelia couldn't see the faint smile on Creston's lips as he silently thanked Cruz for encouraging her. All she could see was Cruz's earnest expression.

"What is an *abuela*?" she asked.

"Grandmother," Cruz said. "The woman had thirteen children, my father being her eldest son and seventh child. The point is that no one is perfect at first. But we must practice to become skilled, so you must not be discouraged."

The tears had faded and Ophelia wiped the last of the moisture from her face. "I suppose," she said. "I know the food I've made isn't very good, but Creston never complains. I thought it was because he surely must like it, but tonight's stew was terrible. I put too much rosemary in it."

"Then you will not do it the next time," Cruz said. "Because you have learned that rosemary is a very strong flavor."

She nodded in agreement. "It is," she said. "But I like it in soap."

"It smells very good in soap," Cruz agreed. "Now, what sweets have you made for us? You always make sweets, my lady. I have learned that about you."

He was changing the subject, away from her failure, and she went along with it. She didn't want to keep discussing her failures either. With a sigh, she stood up from Creston's lap.

"Well…" she said, going over to the table where she prepared food. "I made a bread pudding. It has eggs and honey and cinnamon in it."

"Then bring it over and let us feast."

She did, bringing over something she'd baked earlier in the day. The cook had evidently instructed her on how to make a bread with custard, and she had, but some eggshells were in the pudding, nearly piercing Cruz's cheek, and the custard hadn't baked well in some spots, leaving it runny. Still, Creston and Cruz ate the entire thing and Ophelia's tears were forgotten.

They were good men, indeed.

After the bread pudding was gone, Creston and Cruz moved out to the main living space, where the cats were now sleeping in both chairs. They removed them, though when Creston sat down, it was with the black-and-white cat in his lap. The animal curled up on his thighs as he petted it. It was a quiet moment in a world that didn't have many.

"Does this seem unreal to you?" he asked.

Cruz looked at him curiously. "Does what seem unreal?"

"All of this," Creston said, looking around the cozy chamber. "This room has always been empty. Cold and empty. But now it's warm and comfortable. I have a cat on my lap. I have never had a cat in my life. Today, I ripped out a man's toenail to see how much torture he could take and not give me the information you had given him earlier in the day, a test we give all recruits, and then I come home to my beautiful wife and the meal she cooked and a cat sleeping on my lap as if the violence of my world doesn't exist. As if the darkness that is Blackchurch doesn't exist. Three months ago, if anyone had told me this would be my life, I would have called them mad."

Cruz smiled, leaning back in the chair. "It is simply another aspect of life," he said. "This is the domesticated side, a side that few men see with such happiness as you have experienced. Tay and Fox, Sin and Payne have, and now you. You should consider yourself fortunate."

"I do," Creston said quickly. "I just find it… baffling. Baffling and wonderful."

"Cres?"

Ophelia called to him, coming out of the kitchen area and wiping her hands on her apron. Creston looked over his shoulder at her.

"My love?" he responded.

"What is the largest town around here, within a day's ride?" she asked.

He thought a moment. "Bampton has a market," he said. "Tiverton is much bigger, but it is about a morning's ride away. Why do you ask?"

Ophelia seemed hesitant. "The only things I have to cook with are things others have given me," she said. "I was hoping… hoping I could have something of my own? My own iron pot and tools?"

He smiled. "Of course, you can," he said. "You do not have to ask. Simply tell me what you want and tell me that we are going to buy it."

She shrugged. "I cannot do that," she said. "I do not make demands very well."

"Nay, you do not, but I dream of a wife who makes demands and orders me about."

She giggled. "I can try my best," she said. "But I was also hoping to buy some fabric to make some garments that will accommodate my expanding belly. May I?"

"We can go tomorrow if you wish."

"But you have recruits to teach."

"Cruz can do it for me."

"Cruz is going with you," Cruz said firmly. "Have one of the assistant trainers teach. Rhodes or Anteaus are excellent choices. Rhodes has already been shadowing you when you instruct. He knows what to do."

He was speaking of a man named Rhodes St. James, a powerful knight who used to serve the Earl of Gloucester. The earl had sent him to Blackchurch for training and was prepared to wait the five years it took for a man to become a fully fledged Blackchurch knight, but somewhere in the process, Rhodes became indispensable as an assistant to trainers like Creston and Cruz, and he'd taken to the water module easily, so Kristian preferred to have the man assist him over any other trainer.

But there was also a problem with him.

"He does know what to do," Creston agreed. "But that is an issue—he knows *too* much. He is ambitious. He is waiting for one of us to get kicked in the head or fall in the water and drown so he can take our place. I do not know if I want to leave him alone, instructing my recruits. He might try to take my position out from under me."

Cruz snorted. "He would never succeed," he said. "He does not have your skill or your support. I would let him take tomorrow's instruction and pair him with Anteaus because Anteaus will not let the man get away with anything. He'll keep him in control."

Anteaus de Bourne was another assistant trainer who would probably become a full-fledged trainer within the year. He was from a very old Northumberland family, having come to Blackchurch to train, but he was so skilled and so knowledgeable that he was easily on the same level as the senior trainers. The House of de Bourne was known for its warriors, but Anteaus just happened to have more modesty and control than someone like Rhodes did. That meant that Creston was comfortable with the suggestion.

"Very well," he said. "They will make a good pair."

"I agree," Cruz said. "We will leave at dawn tomorrow and arrive in Bampton by midmorning. There is a smithy there who makes spectacular daggers. You know the one. I want to see what he has."

Creston waggled his eyebrows as he looked at his wife. "It seems that we are leaving on the morrow and visiting a smithy, as well."

Ophelia grinned broadly. "Good," she said. "I am very

grateful. I will clean up quickly and go to bed if we are to leave early."

With that, she was gone, back into the kitchen room. Creston and Cruz could hear her banging around, wiping out the dishes they'd used. Hearing the noise, the black cat wandered in, meowing as he begged for food, and they could hear Ophelia talking to the cat.

"Shall I hunt down the draughts board so we can play a few rounds?" Creston said, yawning. "We have not played that game in a while."

Cruz nodded. "Go ahead," he said. "I think I beat you last time."

"Liar."

"I am going to tell your wife that you are calling me names."

"Who did you complain to before I got married?"

Cruz shrugged. "St. Denis, but he ignored me."

Creston snorted. "So will she," he said, rising wearily from his chair and going to the wardrobe against the wall that served as a cabinet for some of the things he had accumulated over the years, mostly blankets or odd pieces that weren't worn enough to throw out. Creston tended to collect things that way. The wardrobe had been in the cottage when he'd taken possession, and he'd just left it there, a big, heavy piece that was well made. As soon as he opened one of the doors to hunt down the draughts board and the little pieces that went along with it, there was a knock on the front door.

"I will see who it is," Cruz said, getting out of his chair.

"If it is Ming Tang, I won't play him," Creston said, finally locating the board. "He cannot be beaten in a game of draughts, and he crushes my spirit every time."

Cruz smirked as he headed to the door, opening it to see

one of the gate guards standing there.

"Well?" he said. "What is it?"

The man was an older soldier who had served Blackchurch for nearly thirty years. "Good evening, my lord," he said to Cruz. "I am looking for Sir Creston."

Creston heard him. "What is it?"

He was pulling the game board, a solid piece of wood, out of the cabinet as the soldier stuck his head in and addressed him directly.

"Visitors at the gatehouse, my lord," he said.

Creston was inspecting the board for chips, but he glanced up at the man. "Who is it?"

"A man who says he is your cousin," he said. "Brenton de Royans."

Creston stopped inspecting and looked at the soldier in surprise. "Brenton?" he repeated. "A big lad with shoulder-length hair that looks like it needs a good brushing?"

"The same, my lord."

"He's here?"

"He is, my lord," the soldier said. "And he has one of the sons of the Earl of Hereford and Worcester with him. A de Lohr."

That doubly surprised Creston. He set the board down and went to the door. "Where are they?" he asked.

"I kept them at the gatehouse," the soldier said. "Will you come?"

"Absolutely," Creston said. Then he called back to Ophelia, "Sweetheart, I have been summoned to the gatehouse. I'll return shortly."

She acknowledged him, muffled, and he stepped through the door with Cruz behind him. As the panel shut, they headed toward the gatehouse, following the old soldier. Night had descended, and the evening was crisp. Not exactly cold, but damp and chilly with a full moon overhead. Torches lit the trainers' village, and as they passed through it, there were also torches along the path that led from the village to the gatehouse. There was an entire watch at Blackchurch that was responsible for keeping the torches lit and keeping an eye on the village overnight. Creston and Cruz passed two of the watchmen on their way to the gatehouse, which was lit up in the distance.

They closed the distance in short order.

Just as the soldier had said, Brenton de Royans was waiting for Creston in the guard room of the gatehouse. Creston took one look at his cousin and greeted him joyfully.

"My God," he said, giving his cousin a warm hug. "It has been ages since I last saw you, Brenton. What in the hell are you doing here?"

Brenton patted Creston on the face, but it was more like a slap. He beamed at him. "Traveling home from some business and I thought I would see to my favorite cousin," he said. Then he stepped back and indicated the big blond man behind him. "My good friend and associate, Myles de Lohr. His father is Hereford."

Creston greeted Myles cordially. "Welcome to Black-church," he said. "I'm not entirely sure a de Lohr has ever set food on these grounds, so this is quite an occasion."

Myles smiled politely. "Thank you," he said. "I've always wanted to visit, so when Brenton said he was coming, I came along. I hope that is not too bold."

"Not at all," Creston said. He indicated Cruz, next to him. "This is Cruz Mediana de Aragón. He is a prince of his people, so you must show him due respect or all of Aragon will come down on us all."

He was grinning as he said it, indicating a joke, and Brenton and Myles smiled as well. They greeted Cruz amiably with nods.

"You are a trainer like my cousin?" Brenton asked.

Cruz nodded. "I have been here nearly as long as Cres," he said. "We often train recruits together."

"Remarkable," Brenton said, looking between Creston and Cruz. "It is impressive enough to see one Blackchurch trainer, but now I have met two. I am truly honored."

Creston began heading out of the guard room. "Come," he said. "Let us return to my cottage, and you can meet my wife. We have much to catch up on. How is Uncle Juston?"

They followed Creston out into the crisp night, beginning their walk down the path of torches toward the village.

"He is well, considering his age," Brenton said.

"How old is he now?"

"Papa has seen seventy years and six," Brenton said. "Truly astonishing."

"And he's still healthy?"

"Still," Brenton said. "He can take me down in a sword fight should he so choose."

Creston grinned. "He is the consummate knight," he said. "My father was a good knight, but he never managed to achieve Uncle Juston's level of talent."

Brenton shrugged. "We all have our own levels of talent."

"You and I have done fairly well for ourselves."

Brenton snorted. "That may be true, but I do not have the skill to teach at Blackchurch," he said. "However, I have the skill to make an excellent agent."

"Agent?" Cruz said. He was walking behind the cousins with Myles. "What kind of agent?"

"Marshal agents," Brenton said, glancing at Cruz. "At least, William Marshal formed the group many years ago with the help of Christopher de Lohr, so they are formally known as Marshal agents. Spies, killers, assassins… we do it all. Most people call us the Executioner Knights."

Cruz's eyebrows lifted in astonishment. "Cres, you never told me that you had an Executioner Knight for a cousin," he said, but his focus returned to Brenton. "That is an astonishing accomplishment."

"Not as astonishing as a Blackchurch trainer," Brenton said, slapping his cousin on the shoulder. "That's truly an accomplishment, serving under the Lords of Exmoor. There is nothing so unique in England as a military establishment that has remained neutral for almost two hundred years, yet you turn out the finest warriors in the world without ever fighting an actual battle. How do you manage such a thing?"

Creston shrugged. "Hard work," he said. "St. Abelard and his Triton's Hellions take sides from time to time, depending on where the money is. You have heard of them, of course."

"Of course."

"As I said, they will take sides from time to time," Creston said. "But never Blackchurch. There is salvation in that logic."

"Blackchurch has never taken sides in a conflict?" Myles asked, his voice quiet. "Not ever?"

"Nay, never."

"Does that mean Exmoor has no political affiliations?"

"If he does, he never speaks of it or shows it," Creston said. "I know that sounds strange, but it's true."

"What if a Blackchurch trainer or someone who serves here takes sides?"

"Then he is exiled."

It was a rather brutal, definitive answer that left no room for doubt. "Interesting," Myles said thoughtfully. "The Executioner Knights operate entirely differently."

Creston glanced over his shoulder at the man. "You serve politics," he said. "It is not within your scope of operation to remain neutral. If the Crown has an enemy, you eliminate them, correct?"

Myles half shrugged, half nodded. "We are always on the side of the Crown," he said. "If we must fight a war for, or even against, the Crown, with the ultimate goal of protecting whoever sits upon the throne, then we will."

"That is a luxury we do not have," Creston said. "We train men. We do not support a cause, and if we do, it becomes… tricky."

"Has that happened recently?"

Creston nodded. "When one of our trainers married the daughter of the deposed Duke of Toxandria," he said. "Her younger brother was the heir, and he wanted to regain his property and titles. The trainer wanted to fight for his wife, but that would mean taking sides."

"What happened?"

"Another trainer went to Toxandria as an advisor to the young heir," he said. "The stipulation was that he not command men, or plan a battle, or do anything that would directly involve him in the war. He simply advised. At least, that's what he promised. But the man who went is a master swordsman, so I suspect he did not sit by idly while wars went on around him."

"Then no one is fighting wars in France right now?"

Creston looked at Myles curiously. "From Blackchurch? Never," he said. "At least, not a trainer. But we have trained many men who have gone on to fight wars in France."

They were just coming to the village at this point, which was quiet at this hour. Most of the trainers were either in bed or heading there because they were up well before the sun. But just as they entered the village square, with Creston's cottage off to the right, Brenton came to a halt. He looked straight at Myles.

"Well?" he said. "Are you satisfied?"

Myles nodded, though there was some reluctance there. "I suppose," he said. "The answers were not prompted."

Creston frowned at his cousin and at Myles. "What was prompted?"

Brenton looked at him. "Cres, we've got a problem," he said. "A big problem. I have to ask you a question and you must be completely honest with me. Can you do that?"

"I have never lied to you in my life."

Brenton knew that, but he still had to ask. "Then it comes to this," he said, lowering his voice. "Has Lord Exmoor supported Louis in his quest to take Gascony from Henry?"

Both Creston and Cruz looked puzzled, if not a little outraged, by the question. "Not at all," Creston said. "Why? Has someone said otherwise?"

Brenton sighed heavily. "We must go someplace quiet, where no one can hear," he said. "Cres… this is life or death."

"Life or death for whom?"

"Blackchurch."

There was something so ominous in the way he said it. Considering that Brenton and Myles were trained spies, there was no reason to question what Brenton had just said. Creston stared at his cousin for a moment, realizing this visit wasn't on a whim.

It was planned.

Something was happening, something bad enough that the

Executioner Knights were involved.

It must be very bad, indeed.

"Come," Creston muttered. "We'll go to Cruz's cottage. No one will hear us there."

Beneath the full moon, the four of them headed for Cruz's dark, quiet cottage.

That "something" was about to be revealed.

CHAPTER SIXTEEN

Axen Castle
Sidmouth
Devon

"YOU DID *WHAT*?"

The question came from Randa as she sat in her father's solar, one that smelled of dogs because the man kept many. At least twelve in the solar alone and an ever-changing number in the hall because litters of puppies were born constantly. He never did anything about the dogs and simply let them have the run of the place.

Randa had hated living here.

"Father, tell me again," she said when Oscar didn't answer quickly enough. "What did you do?"

Oscar didn't like being questioned and he certainly didn't like Randa's tone. He had a cup of wine in his hand and found himself staring at the dregs on the bottom of the cup through the ruby-red liquid.

"You are here by my good graces," he said. "I would not speak so harshly if I were you."

Randa eyed her father, knowing that he wasn't beyond

lashing out at her, but also knowing that he'd destroyed her relationship with her daughter. It was difficult for her to acknowledge she'd had a role in it also, because as far as Randa was concerned, it was all her father's fault. He demanded, she succumbed, and Ophelia had suffered the consequences.

But what he'd just told her made her blood run cold.

"You just told me that you had a missive forged," she said, trying to keep her voice down. "You said it would destroy Blackchurch. Considering that is where my daughter lives, I am naturally concerned."

Oscar looked at her then. "You should not be," he said. "In the end, everything will work out in my favor. Lia and her husband will come to live here, at Axen, and I will be able to teach him how to continue my legacy as the next Earl of Sidbury. It's really very simple."

Maybe it was, but Randa still wasn't clear. She'd always known her father to be manipulative, and demanding, but what she'd seen from him since Ophelia's marriage at Blackchurch was different.

Darker.

Something was stirring in Oscar that she was afraid of.

"Will you please tell me what you have done that will achieve this?" she asked.

Oscar drained the cup down to the dregs. They were in his small solar in the entry of Axen Castle's keep, the hereditary home of the Earls of Sidbury for over one hundred years. It was a castle built from pale stone that sat atop a rise with the sea to the south and rolling hills to the north. The elevation of the windows in this chamber afforded a brilliant view of the sea, and after pouring himself more wine, he gazed out this window, feeling the salty breeze on his face and watching the gulls ride the drafts overhead.

"Does it really matter?" he said. "All that matters is that, in the end, the situation is as I wish it to be. Nothing less."

"But you sent a missive to the king?" Randa pressed. "What about? How will this end Blackchurch?"

Oscar thought on that question. "Sometimes, we must do things in life that are not entirely truthful in order to establish the greater good," he said. "Do you remember when the pirates came and burned half of the town?"

"Of course I do."

"And you remember the people that died because of it? *My* people?"

"I remember."

"Then you know that action cannot go unanswered."

Randa wasn't exactly sharp. She was having a difficult time trying to figure out what her father meant. "And you had a missive forged to the king?" she said. "What did it say?"

Oscar turned away from the window and poured himself more wine. "It is a dispatch from the French king thanking Blackchurch for supplying him with men and coin in his attempt to regain Gascony," he said. "Henry will read the missive, believe Blackchurch has betrayed him, and sweep in like the hand of God and destroy that place."

Now it was becoming clear, and Randa was increasingly horrified. "But… but those at Blackchurch have done you no harm," she said. "It was the pirates who—"

"Pirates who are kin to Lord Exmoor," he said, interrupting her. "Do you not understand me? I will seek revenge for Triton's Hellions and the damage they caused me by exacting it from St. Abelard de Bottreaux's cousin. Blackchurch is proud of their alliance with pirates? Then let them suffer the punishment. Let that punishment create guilt and hardship for Triton's Hellions to see Blackchurch destroyed."

Randa was at a loss. She'd seen her father rage throughout the years, but not like this. Never like this.

"And you believe Lia will want to return home after what you've done?" she said, finding her voice and her courage. "You have already caused a rift between my daughter and me with your cruelty, but now you intend to destroy her husband's livelihood?"

"He is to be the next Earl of Sidbury. He does not need a livelihood."

"Then you will keep your vengeance secret?"

Oscar shook his head. "Of course not," he said. "Those pirates will know who destroyed Blackchurch and why."

"If the pirates know, then won't the king suspect he has been tricked?" Randa pointed out. "That you lied to him so that he would bring his army to Blackchurch? How do you think King Henry is going to view Sidbury after that? You will not be in the monarch's favor."

Truthfully, that hadn't occurred to Oscar. He was so focused on destroying Blackchurch that he never gave thought to the fact that if he confessed he was behind their destruction simply to punish Triton's Hellions, then surely that would get back to the king. Henry would, mayhap, not be so pleased about being used by an earl to exact revenge.

Nay, he'd not thought that through completely.

But he was now.

Unable to admit the flaw in his plan—that his daughter had pointed out, no less—he downed the wine in his cup and poured himself more, his movements angry and jerky.

"You will not speak of this, Randa," he said, taking a deep

breath to calm his rage. "I told you so that you could prepare to welcome your daughter and her husband home. Mayhap prepare a place for them to live, rooms they may settle into. But if I find you've told anyone why they are coming, you'll not like my reaction. Do you understand?"

Randa knew he was threatening her. He'd done something quite serious and then foolishly confessed it to her. She was sure he'd done it to gloat, but when she'd pointed out the error in his scheme, that darkness she'd sensed before seemed to over-whelm him. Oscar wasn't a man who took defeat lightly, which was why he'd taken over finding a husband for Ophelia when Cecil had run off to the abbey. Randa originally thought it was because he believed he could find his granddaughter a much better husband than the potential one who had left her at the altar, but as she thought on that, something else occurred to her.

There had been a plan behind Oscar's intentions all along.

"You planned this, didn't you?" she said as realization dawned. "When Cecil ran out on Ophelia and you demanded to be the one to select her betrothed, you were already thinking about revenge against those pirates. It was only by chance that Cousin Royston's brother worked for Blackchurch and was not married. You were already planning for this even then."

Oscar looked at her. "You are smarter than you look," he said. "Your husband understood the necessity of strategic marriage even if you do not. Of course, I was planning this, even back then. Marrying Lia to de Royans was not only a stroke of luck, but a stroke of genius. Since she married at Blackchurch, and we were present for the wedding, I am in a perfect position to tell the king that not only did I intercept the dispatch from Louis, but when I was at Blackchurch, I saw evidence supporting the dispatch. As a lord loyal to the king, it was my duty to report it all."

Randa was flabbergasted at his ruthlessness. "The ease with which you lie," she spat. "I never knew that about you until now. And what about Lia in all of this? If her husband is implicated in the support of France, how is he to be the next Earl of Sidbury? If he is part of Blackchurch, Henry will see all of Blackchurch's command staff executed!"

Oscar set his wine cup down and went to her. "You worry overly," he said. "Her husband will be innocent. I will see to that. Or mayhap I will not and let him suffer the sword like the others. Then I'll find yet another husband for Lia who will not be an arrogant Blackchurch whelp. I'll find a man compliant and dutiful and willing to marry a pregnant woman for the cost of an earldom. Truly, Randa, do not worry. All will be well in the end."

He seemed convinced, but Randa wasn't. All she could see was death and destruction, a horrific fate for them all. Oscar was engaging in a game he couldn't possibly win, only he didn't see it that way. He thought he had control of everything.

But he didn't.

God help them all.

CHAPTER SEVENTEEN

The Blackchurch Guild

"LET ME SEE if I understand this correctly," St. Denis said, struggling with his patience. "You are Brenton de Royans, son of Juston de Royans. And you are Myles de Lohr, son of Christopher de Lohr, the Earl of Hereford and Worcester."

Brenton and Myles were lined up in front of St. Denis, being scrutinized as they'd never been scrutinized in their lives. In fact, the entire solar was full of Blackchurch trainers, and bigger and meaner men had never existed. Creston and Cruz were just the beginning. There was a Northman named Kristian, an enormous knight named Fox, and a massively tall beast named Tay. There were others, including a man from Cairo and another from far to the east. *A Shaolin monk,* they'd been told. All of them were looking at Brenton and Myles in both dismay and outrage.

But no one was more outraged than St. Denis.

"Answer me," he snapped when Brenton and Myles didn't answer fast enough. "Do I have that correct?"

"You do, my lord," Brenton said.

St. Denis was pacing a little. Dressed in a fine leather robe, he'd been dragged out of his bed by Creston and Cruz with the most upsetting information. Worse still, they had the proof—a missive that looked like a royal dispatch, thanking St. Denis for supplying Louis of France with men and money for his Gascon campaign.

The entire thing was baffling.

"And you came across this missive, and the man who carried it, at a tavern in London," St. Denis said. "Did I understand that correctly?"

"Aye, my lord," Brenton said.

St. Denis had the dispatch in question in his hand. He held it up again, to the light, and read the words that not only implied, but spelled out, the fact that he'd sided with the French in the war against Henry. After reading the dispatch for the tenth time, he shook his head and handed it over to Amir, who took it over to the light so he could read it also. Amir was an advisor to St. Denis on many matters, including politics, because that was what he taught at Blackchurch. There was no one more adept at deciphering political games than Amir.

And this one was, indeed, a puzzle.

"Creston and Cruz brought this to my attention, so I do not know how much they have questioned you," St. Denis said to Brenton and Myles. "You will forgive me if I am asking questions they have already asked, but I'm sure you understand the seriousness of this situation."

Brenton nodded. "That is why we brought the dispatch here, my lord," he said. "Knowing Blackchurch is historically neutral in any conflict, it seemed like the right thing to do."

"And it is greatly appreciated," St. Denis said. "Please do not misunderstand. As Creston told me, you are Executioner

Knights. You are spies and this is your vocation. You are also from two of the finest families in England, and that alone tells me you must be trustworthy. You did not have to bring that dispatch to me, yet you did. I am grateful. But start from the beginning and tell me how you came across it and who had it."

Brenton glanced at Creston before continuing. They really hadn't gotten far into the story of the mysterious dispatch before Creston was insisting they tell Lord Exmoor, which was probably wise. Creston was just a trainer—Lord Exmoor *was* Blackchurch. They'd awoken the man out of a dead sleep and explained the situation, but he'd been groggy. Now he was far more alert and asking for the tale to be repeated.

Brenton complied.

"We were at The Pox in London when we came upon a man who claimed his liege intercepted a dispatch from Louis meant for you," he said. "We—"

St. Sebastian, who had been thus far listening in the shadows, interrupted him. "*Who* is his liege?" he said. "And did you ask him how he intercepted it?"

Brenton focused on the tall, younger son of St. Denis. "He told us his liege was Lord Sidbury," he said. "He further told us that the dispatch was brought aboard a French ship and was to be given to a French priest at St. Peter's in Sidmouth. Instead, it was given over to a priest loyal to Sidbury, and that is how the man came across it. It was Sidbury who decided to send it straight to Henry, according to the messenger."

The mention of Sidbury had taken the tension of the conversation to an entirely new level. That was not a name that had been expected, but upon their hearing it, confusion reigned. All eyes turned to Creston, who was looking at St. Denis in horror.

"De Bulverton," he spat. "He's behind this!"

St. Denis was clearly shocked, but it was St. Sebastian who spoke. "B-but how?" he said. "More importantly, why? We have no history with Sidbury, so why are we involved with this… this *lie*? To what purpose?"

Creston was genuinely horrified. "I don't know," he said, putting a big hand to his forehead as if to hold in his brains so they wouldn't explode with confusion. "To be honest, I've hardly had any interaction with him at all. I do not like the man, so my contact was minimal. Is he trying to get back at me somehow?"

"You are his heir," Tay pointed out. He'd been grimly listening, standing in the shadows by the door. "Why would he try to jeopardize his heir? That makes no sense."

"My God," St. Denis finally muttered. "I think I may know."

Everyone turned to him. "W-what is it, Papa?" St. Sebastian said. "What do you know?"

St. Denis had to sit down. "I am not certain," he said. "Mayhap it is nothing at all, but when he was here for Creston's wedding, he grew angry over an attack that Abelard and his pirates had instigated on Sidmouth a while back. It was evidently quite serious. Is he possibly trying to punish my cousin by putting Blackchurch at risk?"

No one had an answer for him, but St. Sebastian wasn't satisfied. "I-if he is, then where did he get the dispatch?" he said. "It even has a royal seal. *Where* did it come from?"

"It is clearly a forgery," Creston said. "The man controls a port and there are many ships that go there to conduct business. Mayhap he came across an actual royal dispatch and saw an opportunity to use it somehow. If a man is determined enough, there is no telling what he can do. But to implicate Blackchurch in something as serious as Louis' Gascon campaign… that is a declaration of war against Blackchurch. And Blackchurch has a right to defend itself."

St. Denis was watching him. "We do not fight wars, Cres," he said quietly. "And you are speaking about the man you are to inherit an earldom from."

Creston didn't care about that. "Think on it this way," he said. "My cousin and de Lohr intercepted this dispatch that was on its way to Henry. It will not reach Henry, but sooner or later, de Bulverton is going to realize that the king never received this missive, and he may very well send another. The Executioner Knights did not thwart anything—they only delayed it. There will be another volley in this war and we may not be so lucky if we do not strike decisively."

"This is not taking a side, Papa," St. Sebastian said. "As Creston said, this is defending ourselves. We have that right."

St. Denis stood up. He began to pace again, but this time slowly and more thoughtfully. The situation was, indeed, shocking in nature, and damaging indeed.

Even he could see that.

"If Henry had received this missive, he would have taken it as a threat," he finally said. "He would have sent an army after us and we would not have known anything about it until it was too late. Our walls are strong and we have a sizable army, but against five thousand royal troops, we might not survive. I am well aware of that."

"Th-then what will we do?" St. Sebastian said. "It does not matter how Sidbury produced that missive. We can guess, but we may never truly know. It does not even matter why he did it, but he has. What matters is how we react to it. We cannot do *nothing*, Papa."

St. Denis knew that. His shock over the situation was wearing off, being replaced by a building anger. That arrogant earl was trying to destroy two hundred years of de Bottreaux legacy. But St. Denis was concerned for one very good reason.

"Our army, historically, has only been for defense," he said, turning to look at the group of men behind him. "All of you—my trainers—are greatly skilled men, but the truth is that none of you, with the exception of Sinclair and Payne, have fought in a real battle in years. Everything you do is here at Blackchurch, teaching others to fight battles. I cannot take my army into Sidmouth to raze Sidbury's castle and punish him. That will be seen as an act of aggression and will remove some of the neutrality we have worked so hard to achieve. It is the only thing that keeps us from being pulled into the numerous battles that England's kings seem to wage. Do you understand me so far?"

Heads were nodding, but not all of them.

Creston didn't seem too apt to agree.

"We are *all* warriors," he said as if St. Denis' words had offended him. "I would trust my life in battle to every man in this chamber."

St. Denis held up a hand to ease him. "I know, Cres," he said. "I did not mean to disparage anyone, simply state a fact. While I do not *want* to take my army into Sidmouth, that does not mean I would be *opposed* to sending men into Sidmouth."

"My lord," Brenton said, "that is what the Executioner Knights are trained for. That is what we do—action against enemies. For my cousin's sake, since I have come to learn the Earl of Sidbury is his wife's grandfather, let me make the offer. You have Myles de Lohr and myself to utilize in this instance. Tell us what you want us to do and we shall do it."

Creston stepped forward. "He's right," he said. "A joint

operation between Blackchurch and the Executioner Knights to remove the threat against Blackchurch. No one need ever know about it. Covert operations are something we do best."

St. Denis cocked his head curiously. "Do you have a plan?"

Creston nodded. "Possibly," he said. "It is one of my skills. Anything underhanded. I remember that you told me when you brought me on at Blackchurch that your recruits needed a trainer like me. To teach them about… questionable tactics."

"And so you have," St. Denis said. "But how do you envision punishing Oscar de Bulverton so he will never again be a threat to Blackchurch?"

"I have an idea."

Myles had spoken, and everyone turned to look at the big de Lohr son. He seemed to radiate the same legendary quality that his father had, so he naturally had their attention. When he saw that all eyes were upon him, he cleared his throat softly.

"I have the advantage of not having any emotional attachments to anyone, or anything, that has been discussed," he said. "I fear that someone like Creston, who is deeply involved, may not see the situation entirely clearly—and that is no judgment against him. It is simply human nature."

As Creston stood, stone-faced, and listened, St. Denis encouraged Myles. "Continue, please."

Myles looked at the group, but he was looking at Creston in particular. "When we came to Blackchurch, I knew nothing about Sidbury's relationship to you, or really anything about the situation as a whole, but I've learned quickly by listening," he said. "It seems that Lord Sidbury came into the possession of a missive from Louis of France thanking Lord Exmoor for men and money in his fight to claim Gascony, only it is obvious that the dispatch is a forgery. Either Sidbury is part of a plot against

Blackchurch or he is instigating one. In either case, he is involved and must be stopped. The fact that he may be seeking revenge against a faction of pirates related to Blackchurch for burning his town seems quite logical. It is a reasonable motivation. He is looking to get back at Triton's Hellions through his damage to Blackchurch."

He looked around, seeing that the men were agreeing with him, before carrying on.

"We can see, clearly, that Sidbury must be eliminated," he said. "The man is trying to destroy Blackchurch, and Creston is correct—you have every right to defend yourself, but you cannot go storming into Sidmouth with an army. That would damage Blackchurch's reputation for neutrality. Therefore, we do what Brenton suggested—we embark on a joint mission to protect Blackchurch and eliminate Sidbury."

St. Denis was listening carefully. "You have mentioned eliminating Sidbury more than once," he said. "I am not opposed to that. In fact, it is necessary. But how do you expect to do it?"

Myles glanced at Creston. "Now I hear that you are to inherit Sidbury through your wife," he said. "You must not be part of this. Killing the man you are set to inherit from will only make you the subject of whispers and mistrust from your fellow peers. No one will trust you if they know you killed a man to inherit his title. Do you understand that?"

Creston did. As much as he hated hearing it, he understood all too well. "I do," he said. "But I will be part of this operation and you cannot stop me."

"No one is going to stop you," Myles assured him. "But your role in this is to protect your wife."

Creston frowned. "Protect her?" he said. "Why do you say that?"

"Because she is going to be the bait."

⊗

"BREATHE, MY FRIEND, breathe."

Cruz was trying very hard to keep Creston calm, but Creston wasn't cooperating very well. Cruz and Tay had been forced to physically remove Creston from St. Denis' solar after Myles' declaration, and even now, Myles and St. Denis and the other trainers were going over a plan in St. Denis' solar as Cruz and Tay kept Creston out in the stairwell. He'd lunged for Myles, who was more than a match in size and strength, so they thought it best to just remove him from the solar until he could calm down.

But he wasn't trying very hard.

"That bastard wants to put my wife in danger?" he hissed. "How dare he suggest such a thing? Lia has no business being part of any plan that puts her in harm's way."

"If you are calm enough, you can hear his explanation," Tay said. "But you lunged at him, and unless we wanted blood on the walls of St. Denis' solar, we had to remove you so you could calm yourself. Honestly, Cres, I do not think the man is suggesting we put your wife in mortal danger, but I would like to hear what he has to say."

Creston just stood there, leaning against the wall where Cruz had shoved him. Head down, his mind was whirling with the situation, with his reaction, with everything that had come up this night. He was unbalanced, and that was an unusual state for him. He wasn't sure how to contain or control it.

After a moment, he simply shook his head.

"I do not know what is happening to me," he said. "I am not one given to fits of rage. I never have been. But mention Lia and I am like a madman. What is wrong with me?"

"Nothing," Tay said quietly. "You are a man with a wife you love and a child on the way. Remember when I first met Athdara? Remember when she was so badly injured by the bounty hunter sent by her uncle? My God, Cres, you *do* remember how I behaved. I was out of my mind with grief. Love is the strongest emotion in the world, but it can do strange things to a man's soul sometimes."

Creston sighed heavily. "Like a weakness."

"Nay," Tay said firmly. "It is stronger than anything because it feeds something deep inside of us that can make us move mountains. Your love for Lia will get you through this. Do not diminish it by calling it a weakness."

Creston sighed again, looking up at Tay and Cruz. "She's pregnant, for God's sake," he muttered. "And de Lohr thinks she should be bait to draw out her grandfather?"

Tay smiled faintly. "The only way you will have an answer to that question is if you go back into the solar and listen to what he has to say."

"I do not know if I can and not want to wrap my hands around his throat."

The door to St. Denis' solar creaked open and the three of them looked up to see Ming Tang and Amir coming through.

Ming Tang gestured to Tay and Cruz.

"Leave us for a moment," he said. "Please. We wish to speak with Cres."

Tay and Cruz did as they were asked, heading back into the solar and closing the door behind them. When the corridor was dark and still, Creston lifted a hand to Ming Tang and Amir.

"I know," he said, sounding defeated. "I should not have become so angry, but the idea of putting my wife in danger does not sit well with me."

"Nor should it," Ming Tang said. "Cres, we came out to speak to you about de Lohr's plan. The man is a genius, a spy, but he is not reckless. He did not mean to upset you as much as he did. Will you at least listen to his plan?"

Creston looked at the pair, men who had not been born in England, with ancient blood flowing through their veins. Much more ancient and rich than any Norman blood that Creston carried. Looking at them was like looking at time itself, at history itself. They embodied everything rich and beautiful in the world and he respected them greatly.

But he was still reluctant to hear about a plan that involved his wife.

"I will listen," he said after a moment. "I cannot say I will be glad to hear it, but I will listen."

"That is a start," Amir said quietly. "What de Lohr has proposed is simple, and you will be with your wife the entire time."

Creston pursed his lips. "That makes me feel better," he said. "I think. So, what is it all about?"

Amir went to lean on the wall next to Creston. "St. Denis is sending a missive to St. Abelard as we speak," he muttered. "At this time of year, Triton's Hellions are usually somewhere around Falmouth or Plymouth, waiting to prey upon the ships bringing merchandise from Cherbourg to the west of England and Ireland. It's the time of year when harvests are usually shipped in this direction. St. Denis is informing them of the situation and will ask that they go to Sidmouth and wait."

"Wait for what?"

"A captive by the name of Oscar de Bulverton."

Creston's eyebrows lifted. "He wants the very pirates that Oscar hates to be his jailors?"

"Fitting, don't you think?"

"Definitely," Creston said. "But how does Lia fit into this plan?"

Amir's dark eyes glimmered. "Think about it," he said. "If your wife goes to visit her mother and grandfather, it will not raise any suspicion. You will go with her under the guise of visiting Axen Castle, which will be yours one day. A reasonable pretext, is it not? De Bulverton will not be suspicious in the least."

Creston could see the logic. "Probably not," he said. "Then what?"

"We will travel with you," Ming Tang said. "All of us, your cousin and de Lohr included. We will not be bringing an army. Nothing that will announce we have come. But we will hide on the outskirts of the village while you and your wife gain access to de Bulverton's castle. You will proceed to have a peaceful visit while the rest of us lie in wait for St. Abelard to appear. When he does, it will be your duty to make sure we gain admission to de Bulverton's castle. Once we are in, you will take your wife to safety and we will capture de Bulverton and deliver him to St. Abelard, who will do as he wishes with him. The man is trying to destroy us to punish the Hellions, after all. Let de Bulverton face St. Abelard, as a man would."

Creston sighed sharply. "He is not a man, he is a viper," he said. "But now that I hear of the plan, I understand it better. I suppose I owe de Lohr an apology."

Ming Tang grinned. "I would not worry about it," he said. "He understands why he upset you. But a word indicating you do not hold a grudge would be appreciated, I am sure."

Now that his fits of rage had died down, Creston was feeling weary. Weary and worried, a combination he was not used to. None of this was anything he was used to, and he didn't like it in the least. Scratching his blond head, he pushed himself off the wall.

"I'll do my best," he said. "It would probably be best if I consult with him on the details of this operation. This is what I instruct my recruits on—interrogation, dealing with an enemy, anything underhanded or dark. I can handle any torture, under any conditions, and I do my job well. But involve my wife in a scheme and it's like I forget who I am. But I will remember. Preserving Blackchurch, preserving our home, means we must defend it. And it means this threat *will* be avenged."

Amir smiled faintly. "Spoken like our Avenger," he said softly. "Even if it means the death of your wife's grandfather?"

"Even if it means that," Creston muttered. Then he held up a hand as if to beg forgiveness. "But I want to be clear. *Very* clear. If St. Abelard takes de Bulverton away as his captive, I will not assume the mantle of the Earl of Sidbury. No matter what the man has done, I am not doing this to usurp the man's title. I am doing this to protect Blackchurch. I am doing this to protect the life I am building with the most wonderful woman in England. Damn the man for trying to destroy it just to exact his petty revenge."

No one could disagree with him. Amir put a hand on his shoulder.

"What will you tell your wife?" he asked. "I am all for protecting women, but she must know. For her own safety, she must. And if it were my wife, I might teach her some ways to protect herself against her grandfather. If the man has any hint that you know what he's done, the stakes may turn… deadly."

That was true. If they were about to head into a difficult situation, then Ophelia had to know why simply to protect herself. Sending her in blind would be the worst thing he could do. Creston snorted softly.

"I've trained hundreds of men, and women, over the years," he said. "It never occurred to me that I would be in the position of training my wife to a certain extent. Lia has a level head—she'll be able to take instruction. She's not the fearful type."

"That is wise," Ming Tang said. "You may not be with her every moment of every day, so she will need to know how to handle herself, or the situation, if you are not with her."

Creston nodded, thinking of that petite, lovely woman in his cottage, waiting for him to return home. *Waiting for him.* That was the sweetest thing in the world, but now, with this crisis, he felt the urge to get home to her more strongly than he ever had.

"I know," he said. "Let me speak with de Lohr first and then I will head back to my cottage. Do we have a timeline of when all of this is supposed to happen?"

The three of them turned for the solar door. "It will take at least three days for a missive to reach Plymouth," Amir said. "If St. Abelard is not there, then it will be another two days to Falmouth. If he still cannot be found, then it simply depends on when the messenger can find him. I have suggested to St. Denis to send more than one messenger. That way, any of St. Abelard's known ports can be covered in a short amount of time, rather than one man trying to hunt him down."

"Agreed," Creston said. "It could take days or it could take months."

"Months we do not have," Ming Tang said quietly.

Amir opened the door to the solar, revealing the group

beyond. All eyes turned to them as they entered, most especially to Creston. He locked eyes with Myles, but before he could say anything, Payne was suddenly in his path.

"Do ye know what the man said about the Demons of the Sea?" he nearly shouted at Creston. Then he threw a finger in Myles' direction. "He's said they're a gang of misfits and rogues. Sin is about tae kill the man, so if ye want tae throttle him, we'll help ye!"

Payne was always excitable in any given situation, but in this case, it was justified. Astria, his wife, was a former pirate, although she did return to sea from time to time, and Sinclair's wife, Elisiana, was a cousin to Santiago de Fernandez, the fearsome leader of the pirate group called Demons of the Sea. Blackchurch had a history with them. But Creston wouldn't be riled up, not again, so he grabbed Payne by the neck and pulled the man back as he addressed Myles.

"De Lohr, I'm afraid you've stirred a hornet's nest," he said. "I apologize for my behavior earlier. It's simply that I am, naturally, quite protective of my wife and I do not want to see her put in any danger."

Myles nodded, accepting the apology. "I was clumsy about it," he said. "I am not married and I should have been more sensitive. As for the pirates… I did not realize Triton's Hellions was the only faction Blackchurch was related to."

Creston nodded, eyeing Sinclair, who was standing several feet away and glaring at Myles. "That was the hornet's nest I referred to," he said. "I know you did not mean to upset some of us, but everything you've spoken of has involved the women we are married to. We are, if nothing else, a very loyal bunch when it comes to our wives."

St. Denis intervened, his hand lifted to halt any further

conversation because this entire situation was already out of control and he didn't want it growing worse. "I've told him," he said. "He knows it now, so there will be no more insulting pirates around here if he wants to keep his head."

Creston still had his hand on Payne's neck to prevent the man from running amok. "Payne's mother was none other than Bloody Maude, the Pirate Queen," he said to Myles. "She was the leader of Medusa's Disciples until her death. It is now led by Payne's brother, Pope Francis. Did anyone tell you that?"

Myles shook his head, eyeing the big Scotsman. "Nay, they did not," he said. "We only discussed the Spanish pirates. But I wish they had told me everything. Now I am standing in the middle of the hornet's nest, and I hope I do not have to jump out of the window to escape with my life."

That brought some soft laughter from around the chamber, from everyone but Payne and Sinclair. St. Sebastian, seeing the two brooders were not helping the situation, ushered them both out with the help of Kristian, who was Payne's best friend. With the four of them out of the chamber, the tension eased a little and Creston returned his attention to St. Denis.

"Amir told me that you plan to send a message to Triton's Hellions," he said. "He has explained everything and I believe it is a solid plan. I want you to know that I will do my duty for Blackchurch, and in this mission, I will not fail. But I will also protect my wife, first and foremost. I understand that she is the most logical person not to raise suspicions of her grandfather, but I will be by her side the entire time. I hope you can understand that."

"Of course, I can," St. Denis said. "I would not expect you anywhere else, Creston."

His words eased Creston a little, but there was still the nagging guilt he felt. None of this would have happened had he not married Ophelia. Even though it wasn't his fault, he still felt responsible.

"I am ashamed that I have brought this bad fortune upon Blackchurch," he said. "Without my marriage to Lia, it is possible that this would have never happened. But know that I will do everything in my power to ensure the situation is resolved. Now, it has become personal."

Brenton, who had been standing by the hearth for the entire conversation, including Creston's lunge at Myles, finally came forward to stand with his cousin. Truthfully, he and Creston didn't grow up together. Their fathers weren't that close, so he'd never spent a great deal of time around Creston enough to truly know the man. Moreover, Creston was older than he was by ten or twelve years. Almost a generation. But he knew, from what he'd seen since his arrival at Blackchurch, that he was watching the actions of a noble and decent man who wanted to do right by not only his wife, but his brethren.

That spoke of good character.

And he was very much loved here.

"I know what you teach," he said, his eyes glimmering with mirth. "While you were out in the corridor having a tantrum, Lord Exmoor spoke of the skills you have brought to Blackchurch. How you teach torture and capture, and interrogation and underhanded dealings like assassination and damage to an enemy. I must say that I am deeply impressed, Creston, but I also know that you learned your skills under King John's tutelage. You learned from the best how to do the very worst."

Creston nodded, lifting his head to look at his cousin. "John cost me the woman I loved and the child she carried," he said. "Mayhap that is why I am so rabid about protecting Lia. She is the woman I married, the woman I love, and she carries our child. I will not let anything, not Blackchurch nor the Executioner Knights nor cruel grandfathers, take that away from me. Not again. So you will forgive me if I am overly zealous about my wife's safety. It has taken my entire life, and eons of healing, to come to this point, and I'll not give it up."

Brenton smiled faintly. "Understandable," he said. "I do not think any of us likes the idea of a woman being involved in a mission like this, though the Executioner Knights has had its share of women agents over the years. In fact, Myles' eldest sister was an excellent agent. But I know this—any woman you have married, Creston, must be a strong and intelligent lady, indeed. You clearly love her and respect her, and that tells me she will be more than up to the task of being part of this. I would wager to say that she is very strong."

Creston cracked a smile. "You have never seen such a strong woman."

"Then teach her correctly for this mission, teach her to keep her head, and she'll be fine."

Wise words, indeed. Creston dipped his head in understanding, truly resigning himself to the fact that this was going to be a situation that Ophelia would have to be involved in.

But he was going to make sure she survived it.

"She will," he said after a moment. "If you have no further need of me, I will return to my wife. Brenton, you may sleep in my cottage if you wish. You and de Lohr."

Brenton smiled. "Thank you," he said. "Shall we come with you?"

"If there is no further business."

There wasn't. St. Denis shook his head, waving them on, and Creston headed out with Brenton and Myles on his heels.

One by one, the Blackchurch trainers filtered out, heading back into the night with the burden of a future mission on their minds. That wasn't usual for them. They taught, they trained, they made sure men and women were ready for this kind of thing.

They didn't normally do it themselves.

But that was soon to change.

A storm was on the horizon.

CHAPTER EIGHTEEN

OPHELIA AWOKE TO the news of visitors.

Creston had informed her that his cousin, Brenton, and a companion named Myles de Lohr would be staying with them for a short time. Myles was the son of the legendary Earl of Hereford and Worcester, Christopher de Lohr, and Ophelia was properly impressed. She knew that name and she knew the earl's reputation. The men were already gone when she woke up, however, and the realization that she had unexpected guests threw Ophelia into a frenzy because she very much wanted to be a good hostess. She wanted to do Creston proud. He thought it was all rather sweet until she started talking about what to make them to eat.

Then he tried not to cringe.

Surely they were hungry, Ophelia said, and she had to make sure they ate something, so she quickly headed over to Blackchurch's common kitchen to collect food from the cook. Creston had kindly suggested that she only collect that which had already been prepared, simply to make it easier for her, and he escorted her over to the kitchens, where they ran into Ming Tang, who was gathering bread and meat. As he was talking with Ming Tang about the messengers St. Denis was sending out to track down St. Abelard, Ophelia collected what she needed and they headed back to the cottage.

That was when Creston discovered that she'd only collected ingredients.

She intended to cook.

God help them.

Creston was powerless as she began to beat eggs together. When she went to collect the milk, he quickly stirred through the eggs to find any shells and only managed to find two tiny pieces, which was an improvement from the bread pudding the night before. Ophelia came back with the milk and poured some into the eggs, all the while wondering where their guests had disappeared to. They'd gone out but hadn't come back. Creston wasn't sure himself, so he left her to prepare her meal and went out to find Brenton and Myles.

They weren't difficult to locate.

He found them down by Lake Cocytus, the enormous lake that carved through the heart of Blackchurch because Kristian had commenced an early class for his recruits. The morning had been a bit misty, and there was a gray blanket hanging over the lake, so Kristian decided to use that to his advantage. They could see an outline of a ship through the mist and hear Kristian's voice as he taught his recruits to judge distances in the mist by shouting. Voices would bounce off solid objects, like trees and rocks, and therefore distances to shore could be determined.

The three of them stood there, listening.

"I spoke with one of the other trainers a few minutes ago," Creston said, referring to his encounter with Ming Tang in the kitchens. "He told me that St. Denis has already sent the missives for his cousin. Five riders have been sent to five different port towns in Cornwall and the north Devon coast in search of St. Abelard and Triton's Hellions. If they are anchored somewhere, we should hear back from them within the week."

As Brenton yawned, Myles nodded. "It would be preferable if we are able to contact them sooner rather than later," he said. "The more time passes that Sidbury doesn't hear from Henry, the more he may be inclined to send another missive. That's something we should avoid."

"Agreed," Creston said. "Did Sidbury's messenger tell you how long he'd been traveling with the missive from the time he left the earl's home?"

Myles cocked his head thoughtfully. "It was my impression that it had been about seven or eight days," he said, looking at Brenton. "What do you think?"

Brenton yawned again. "The same," he said. "In all, I do not think that missive had been in transit more than ten days at the most. Surely Sidbury does not expect a swift answer. It could be months."

"Or weeks," Creston said. "If we can contact St. Abelard in the next week or two, that will put this plan into action very quickly. Sidmouth is a day and a half to the south on a swift horse."

They all turned when they heard something hit the water and a good deal of yelling from Kristian. Creston chuckled.

"Clearly, he was unhappy with someone," he said. "I fear a recruit has gone overboard."

"Kristian," Brenton said thoughtfully. "Is that the big lad who looks like a Northman?"

"The same."

"Fearsome."

"You have no idea."

Brenton grinned at the threat of a Viking trainer as Myles looked around the landscape. "There are other classes being taught this morning," he said. "I saw the big trainer from last night yelling at his recruits as they ran through the paths on the hills. Then there is another one teaching swordplay."

Creston nodded. "Instruction begins before the sun rises," he said. "It goes until the sun sets."

"Where is your class?"

Creston gestured toward the west. "I do not normally teach things that require a field," he said. "There is an outbuilding that used to house animals on the other side of the dormitory and that is where I usually instruct my class. I teach what tends to be applicable academics."

"What does that mean?"

"It means I get into their heads and then teach them how to resist me," he said, a smirk tugging at his lips. "I teach the things we all dread to face. Interrogation, torture. Those subjects."

Myles was listening with interest. "Things that the Executioner Knights use on a daily basis."

"More than likely."

"Have you ever considered becoming an Executioner Knight?"

Creston grinned. "Nay," he said. "I like where I am."

"But the skills and experience you must have could surely be put to better use in the service of England."

Creston shrugged. "Mayhap," he said. "But you must remember that I did everything I teach when I served John. I have already used my skills in the service of my country."

"How long did you serve him?

"*Too* long," Creston said, his voice growing quiet. "I was newly knighted out of Kenilworth when I went into royal service. That was in the year twelve hundred and five. I left his service in twelve hundred and ten. That is five years of hell, lads. Five years of serving a man who slept with the devil every night and had no sense of honor or decency."

"Did you serve with Sean de Lara?" Myles asked.

Creston smiled faintly, but it wasn't one of warmth, instead something between a grimace and sorrow. "Aye," he said. "The Lord of the Shadows and I knew one another and worked closely together toward the end of my tenure. I will say that I never suspected he was an Executioner Knight, a spy for William Marshal, because he performed too flawlessly. But there were moments, many of them, when I saw his humanity. I assumed he was in the same situation that I was—sworn to the Crown, trying not to disgrace the family name. You come to the point where you simply do as you are told until you cannot stand one more order, one more horrific command. We both came to that point, but in my case, there was more to it."

"What more?"

Creston thought on his answer briefly. "A woman," he said quietly. "But that is all I will say about that. How *is* Sean, by the way?"

It was clear that he didn't want to discuss his deepest, darkest dealings with John, so Myles didn't push. "He is well," he said. "He is not terribly active any longer. The man has earned his rest, so he spends his time doing more leisurely things."

"He was badly injured in the battle for London, as I recall."

Myles nodded. "He was," he said. "Were you part of that, too?"

"It was my last act of service for John," Creston said. Unwilling to discuss his royal service any longer, he motioned in the direction of his cottage. "Come with me. My wife is preparing food."

That had Myles and Brenton immediately heading in that direction. "Good," Brenton said. "I am hungry. And I am eager to meet this woman you are so fond of."

Creston took up stride beside them. Any mention of Ophelia had him grinning like a fool. "She is… remarkable," he said. "I cannot believe how fortunate I am. There are times when I will just watch her sleep, caught up in something I never thought I would have."

"What's that?"

"A beautiful life."

On the other side of Brenton, Myles spoke up. "Truly, Creston, I am very sorry that I upset you when discussing the plan to neutralize Sidbury," he said. "I know you do not know me, but I would hope your cousin would vouch for my character. I am not a man intent on offending or antagonizing others unless I want to. And I did not want to."

At the mention of his name, Brenton nodded. "He did not mean anything by it," he said. Then he eyed Creston. "You didn't tell your wife yet, did you? She's not off poisoning his food, is she?"

Creston chuckled. "Not intentionally," he said. "But that brings me to a word of caution."

"What about?"

Creston sighed, thinking of that incredible woman he was married to. "There is nothing about Ophelia that is not perfect," he said. "However, she does have one small flaw. She is learning to cook, and she is not very good at it, but she insists. I do apologize if whatever she prepares for you is not edible. If you could not mention it, I will be happy to find you much better food later. It's simply that she wants to welcome you, and I do not want to hurt her feelings."

Brenton held up a hand to quiet him. "Say no more," he said. "We will make sure that Lady de Royans' efforts are complimented."

"I would be grateful."

Nothing more was said about it, and Ophelia was waiting for them when they arrived at the cottage a short time later. She had changed into a lovely day gown made from muslin, a fine garment she'd made herself from fabric that Athdara had given her, and her lovely hair was braided and wrapped into an elegant bun at the nape of her neck. Truly, Creston couldn't have been prouder of her as she greeted Brenton and Myles, lovely and mannerly in every way, and invited them to sit. She already had bread and butter and watered, warmed wine on the table, and as they sat down, she brought forth a big wooden bowl of the eggs that had been beaten with milk and salt, and then cooked with chives that the cook had given her. But he'd also given her something else, as the men were soon to discover. She gave each man a literal pile of the eggs and they dug in with gusto. Creston was pleasantly surprised until he realized that she'd put garlic, which grew plentiful in the gardens around the kitchens, into the eggs. Nice, big chunks of raw garlic.

But he didn't say a word.

Neither did Brenton and Myles. They ate all of the eggs she'd given them and asked for more. She happily gave it to them, including her husband, until there was nothing left in the bowl. Between the three of them, they had eaten about two dozen eggs and at least two loaves of bread. Ophelia made sure their cups were full of the watered wine, and when all was said and done, they'd polished off a big meal and applauded Ophelia for the fine feast. She blushed at their praise, flattered and pleased, and when she collected the bucket and headed out to the well for some water, Creston finally grunted in pain.

"My God," he muttered. "I am going to smell of garlic for the next month. Men will not even have to see me. They will smell me coming from a mile away."

Brenton was grinning. Even Myles had a smirk on his face. "It was not that bad," he said. "I like garlic."

Creston cocked an eyebrow. "That much of it?"

Brenton abruptly waved his hand in front of his face. "Christ, Creston," he said. "I can smell you over here. Your breath smells horrible."

Creston started laughing. He couldn't help it. He put his hands over his face and giggled like a fool as Brenton followed suit. Soon they were all laughing, and the smell of garlic filled the small kitchen from the sheer force of their breath. Even the cats, who were sunning themselves in the window facing east, didn't seem to want to be around it. They both fled out the back door, which only made Creston laugh harder.

"We must stop," he said, wiping tears of laughter from his eyes. "I do not want Lia to return and find us in fits."

Brenton's eyes were watering because the smell of garlic was so strong. He wiped his hands over his face and stood up.

"I must find the privy," he said. "Where is it?"

Creston pointed out the back door. "Out there," he said. "It will be near the stables. There is a small one, but that is for the women in the village and is kept much neater than the other one, so do not use it or the women will know. They sense these things."

Brenton snorted. "I will avoid it, I promise."

Before he could get away, Creston put his hand on his cousin's arm. "Wait a moment," he said quietly. Then he looked at Myles. "De Lohr, will you please go with him? I must speak to my wife about the events of last evening and I would like to do it alone."

Brenton's humor faded. "You've not told her about our discussion yet?"

Creston shook his head. "Nay," he said. "She was asleep when I returned, and I did not feel like it was right to do so when she was so concerned about making a meal for you, so the time must be now, before the day grows any deeper."

"Then do it quickly," Brenton said, patting his cousin on the shoulder as he headed for the back door. "De Lohr, attend me. Let us get a good look at the infamous Blackchurch and see what mischief we can get into."

Myles obediently followed him and the pair reached the rear door just about the time Ophelia was coming through. She was lugging a bucket of water and Brenton immediately grabbed it.

"Let me help you with this, Lady de Royans," he said, carrying it back over to the table where the dirty dishes were. "Your husband should be doing this for you. If I were you, I would give him a good scolding."

Ophelia wiped her hands off on an apron that was lying over a chair. "I may scold him about other things, but not this," she said. "He is a very busy and important man. Did you not know that about him?"

Brenton chuckled as he headed for the door again. "She is the perfect wife, Cres," he said. "She believes everything you tell her."

Creston cocked an eyebrow. "But I *am* a very busy and

important man," he said. "It is time you learned that."

He could hear his cousin laughing as the two men walked away. Ophelia peered at them, watching them head off.

"Where are they going?" she asked.

"To find the privy," Creston said. "Thank you for the meal, sweetheart. It was much appreciated."

She smiled modestly. "I hope it was good," she said. "The cook gave me the chives and the garlic. Did it taste well enough?"

Creston nodded. "Delicious," he said. "But may I make a suggestion?"

"I wish you would. Otherwise, I will not learn."

He tried to be tactful. "Next time, mayhap a little less garlic would truly make the dish delicious," he said. "I seem to remember the cook roasting the garlic once and then adding tiny pieces of it to the bread. Mayhap you can do the same thing with the eggs. Like rosemary, just a little garlic is probably better than too much."

She seemed quite interested in his suggestion. "I will ask the cook how he roasts the garlic," she said. "Mayhap he will have other suggestions where I can use it. In sauce?"

"Verily."

"What about soup or porridge?"

"Soup, I am certain, but have you ever had garlic in porridge?"

She giggled and shook her head. "I have not," she said. "On second thought, it does not sound very good."

Creston shook his head firmly. "Nay, lass," he said. "Nay."

He dragged the last word out, long and low, and her laughter grew. He winked at her as she turned to the bucket of water with the intention of cleaning the bowls they'd used for the eggs. Ophelia's mood was light, her heart was joyful, and she felt as if she were walking on clouds. Creston made everything brighter and sweeter. Even when he told her that she had used too much garlic, it was still sweet. But as she picked up one of the dirty bowls, something occurred to her.

"Why have you not gone to your recruits?" she asked. "The sun is up and the day has begun."

He was sitting at the table, casually, one enormous arm draped over the back of the chair next to him. "I know," he said. "Can a man not sit and watch his wife go about her chores?"

"Of course, you can," she said as she rinsed out the bowl. "But who is with your recruits?"

"Two assistant trainers," he said. "We are doing a few exercises this morning. I'll join them in good time."

She didn't sense anything out of the ordinary with his explanation or the fact he was lingering around the cottage when he should have been teaching. "When do you think we can go into Bampton or another town and purchase some items for me to use in the kitchen?" she said. "We discussed it last night and I thought we would go this morning, but your cousin is here now and we cannot go. Brenton seems very nice. Also, I have just noticed something."

"What?"

"That your name, and your brother's name, and now your cousin's name all end the same," she said. "Bren*ton*, Cres*ton*, Roys*ton*. Is there a reason for that?"

He gave her a half-grin. "It is a tradition among de Royans males," he said. "All of our names end thus. My father's name was Quinton. Brenton's father's name is Juston. It has always been that way."

She looked at him curiously. "Does that mean our sons will

have to have similar names?"

"If I want to hold my head up in public, it does," he said. "Do you mind?"

She chuckled. "Of course not," she said. "But we will have to think of some names in case the child in my belly is a male. Or do you already have a name selected?"

He shook his head. "Nay," he said. "I thought we would discuss it when the time came. Why? Do you?"

She thought a moment. "Not particularly," she said. "But give me time. I will think of something you can be proud of."

"Good lass," Creston said. She turned back to her dishes with a smile on her face and he watched her for a moment, hating to dampen her good mood, but he knew he had to. It was time. "Sweetheart, put the bowl down and come over here for a moment. I wish to speak with you."

Without hesitation, Ophelia set the bowl down and picked up a rag to dry her hands as she came over to her husband. He pulled a chair out for her and she sat, leaning back on the chair and putting her hands on her belly.

"It feels good to sit," she said. "I fear that I am starting to become overwhelmed with this belly. He is becoming larger."

Creston smiled at her, leaning over to kiss her on the temple. "That is good," he said. "That means our son is growing healthy and strong. He will be here soon."

"Not too soon," she said, rubbing her stomach. "Now, what did you wish to speak of?"

The moment had come and Creston reached out, taking her hand and caressing her fingers. "I wish to discuss the reason my cousin and de Lohr are here," he said. "I'm sure you've been wondering."

Ophelia shrugged. "Not particularly," she said. "I was simply glad to meet someone who is part of your family. Why? Has he come for a reason?"

Creston lowered his voice. "He brought news with him," he said. "I wish to discuss it with you because, eventually, you will be involved."

She was curious. "Oh?" she said. "What is it?"

Creston took a deep breath, thinking of where to start. There was so much to tell her, and since the situation implicated her grandfather, he wanted to be gentle about it. The last thing he wanted was to upset her in her condition, but if she became upset, that couldn't be helped.

She had to know.

"First, I must ask you a question," he said after a moment. "Before your betrothal with Cecil fell apart, had you been in much contact with your grandfather?"

Ophelia shook her head. "Not really," she said. "There was never any reason to. We did visit him on occasion when I was small, but not too often."

"Then you do not know that some pirates burned his town a short time ago?"

She had to think on that. "I think I remember hearing of it," she said. Then she nodded firmly. "Aye, I did. I was down on the waterfront and there were several businesses being rebuilt. Someone told me there was a fire, but I did not know that it was because of pirates."

Creston nodded. "Evidently, it was," he said. "Lia, I am going to present this situation to you as it was presented to me, because we do not know anything for certain, but we are fairly convinced in our conclusions. Convinced enough that we must act."

"Act? On what?"

He squeezed her hand gently. "Brenton and Myles were in London last week," he said. "They were in a tavern when they came across a man bearing a missive from Louis of France. The missive, which is in the possession of St. Denis now, contained a message from Louis to St. Denis thanking him for supplying France with men and money for their conquest of Gascony. Do you know anything about the fight for Gascony?"

Ophelia's brow furrowed. "I think I heard something about it," she said. "Cecil spoke of it, once. Louis and Hugh de Lusignan invaded Gascony, and Henry had to send men to fight them."

"That is correct," Creston said. "Only Gascony fell to Louis. Henry lost it."

She was listening carefully. "And St. Denis helped Louis retake Gascony?"

Creston shook his head. "That's just it," he said. "He did not. You see, Blackchurch is simply a training ground. We do not take sides. We are not political. We do not align ourselves with any cause, so the fact that there is a missive thanking St. Denis for doing just that very thing, an act against King Henry of England, makes it an extremely dangerous situation for Blackchurch. If Henry were to find out about this missive, he would lay siege to Blackchurch and probably destroy us. It would mean the end of Blackchurch as we know it."

"God's Bones," she muttered, her hand flying to her mouth in shock. "What a terrible thing."

"It is."

"But if the missive is not true, why would Louis say such a thing?"

Creston sighed faintly. "Because it is a forgery," he said. "Someone is trying to destroy Blackchurch with a forged French dispatch for Henry to see."

"But who would do this?"

He hesitated, but just for a moment. "The messenger that Brenton and Myles encountered was from Axen Castle," he said. "The missive came from the Earl of Sidbury."

Ophelia's eyes flew open wide and her jaw dropped. "My *grandfather*?" she gasped. "Are you certain?"

"As certain as we can be."

"But… but I do not understand why he would do this! And you are *sure*?"

Creston was still holding her hand as she grew agitated. "Aye," he said. "We are sure that it came from him."

Ophelia was dumbfounded. Even as the information slapped her in the face, she was stunned. Nothing he said made any sense to her, but as she sat there and processed the news, she came to the very quick conclusion that she believed him implicitly.

She knew what her grandfather was capable of.

"Dear God," she finally breathed. "But why? Why should he want to do such a thing?"

"In revenge for the pirates that burned Sidmouth," Creston said. "The pirates in question are Triton's Hellions, and their leader is a close cousin of St. Denis. We believe your grandfather is trying to exact revenge on those pirates by destroying Blackchurch, but it could be more than that. He wasn't exactly friendly when he was here for our wedding, and I know that he and St. Denis had words, so he could be trying to gain revenge on the lot of us. We just don't know."

Ophelia stared at him, her expression full of distress. "Oh, Creston," she murmured. "I do not even know what to say."

"Do you think he's capable of it?"

"Without question," she said with no hesitation. "He is undoubtedly capable of it. He is a vindictive, ambitious man. My mother has made mention of how he's treated enemies in the past. She hasn't told me the details, but she has intimated that he has ruined or eliminated more than one adversary. He does not like to be contested or shamed. I am certain that if I were not his only grandchild, he would have had a horrible fate for me because I shamed him. But because I am his only descendant, he instead made an advantageous marriage that would benefit him."

"And tried to fool me by promising me a woman who was already pregnant," Creston said. "He still thinks he has fooled me."

"I am certain that he does."

"The next time I see him, I intend to remedy that."

"I hope you do."

Creston fell silent. Truthfully, she was taking the news much better than he'd thought she would. No screaming or crying or fainting. Quite honestly, her shock had given way to a kind of steely resolve that he was surprised to see.

This was no weak woman he'd married.

He should have given her more credit.

"Now comes the next part of this tale," he said. "You realize that your grandfather poses a lethal threat to Blackchurch with his actions."

"I do," she said. "What are you going to do to punish him?"

"We have a plan," he said. "But I will need your help. I realize this is asking a great deal, as he is your flesh and blood, but..."

Ophelia sat forward, quickly placing her fingers on his lips to silence him. "He is a man who starved me," she murmured.

"He was cruel and brutal. He has never been kind to me or my mother. For the past six months, I have forgotten him. It has been the best time of my life, forgetting that terrible man, but now that I hear he is trying to destroy this place, and these people, that I have come to love, it does not matter if he is my flesh and blood. Tell me what you want me to do and I shall do it, Creston. All you need do is ask."

Creston was struck by her bravery. Perhaps she didn't know what she was getting into, but that didn't matter. She still offered. He pulled her into his embrace, holding her against him as she wrapped her arms around his head and neck. This was their best position, embracing tightly, their bodies pressed against one another. He could feel her big belly against his midsection, and as he held her, he could feel a strong kick from the child. That made him smile, and he released her long enough to put his hands on her stomach.

"He is very strong," he said. "I think he wants to join us in our quest to stop your grandfather."

Ophelia giggled. "He may not be of your blood, but he is of your spirit," she said softly. "He has the fight of a de Royans."

"He does," Creston said, leaning forward to kiss her. "I hope you have it, too, because it will not be easy for you. We plan to abduct your grandfather and force him to face justice, but in order to do that, we must catch him off guard. He will not go willingly and we cannot bring an army to his door, so there will just be a small number of us to complete this objective. That is where you come in."

"What shall I do?"

"Provide the bait," he said quietly. "Your grandfather will not suspect you, in any way. While you distract him, we will capture him. That is as simple as I can put it."

Ophelia nodded. "I can do that," she said. "I *will* do that. Thank you for trusting me. No one has ever trusted me with something so important before."

He reached out, gently cupping her face with his right hand, stroking her cheek with his thumb. "It will not be easy, sweetheart," he said. "You must not let on that something is coming. You must make him think that your visit is completely normal. You can say that you simply want to visit your mother, or you can tell him that you wanted to see him before the child is born. We will come up with an excuse. But you must stick to that excuse no matter what. Never waver from it. Understood?"

She nodded seriously. "I understand," she said. "But may I ask you something?"

"Of course."

"Do you truly believe King Henry would accept the validity of a missive from the King of France to Lord Exmoor?" she said. "Does it not seem far-fetched that a king would communicate with an English training guild?"

Creston shook his head. "Not at all," he said. "Blackchurch is quite prestigious, and a king could easily communicate with us directly. But to be clear, the issue is this—kings and lords over the decades have begged for Blackchurch's support. They have offered us copious amounts of money for it, but the Lords of Exmoor always refuse. Remaining neutral is what we are known for—we train warriors to fight. We do not fight ourselves. That has saved us from the political winds that so often blow through this land—everyone will leave us alone rather than try to engage, knowing that we will always remain neutral. We are not a threat to anyone."

She accepted his explanation. "And Henry would be insulted if he discovered you supported his enemy."

Creston snorted. "Insulted is where he would start," he said. "It would only end when he wiped Blackchurch from the earth and danced on our graves."

Her brow rippled with concern. "Graves?" she repeated. "*Your* grave?"

Creston nodded. "I would be guilty by association," he said. "All of us would be. We would all face the ax, so the threat against Blackchurch is a threat against us all."

Ophelia hadn't thought of it that way. The king's anger with Blackchurch wouldn't be at the institution itself, the walls, the fields, the lake, the castle.

It would be at the individuals.

Now the tides were turning.

Did she truly think her grandfather had done exactly what Creston was speculating? Without question. There wasn't any doubt in her mind that her grandfather had forged that royal dispatch, meaning for Henry to see it. But instead of simply destroying the buildings and cottages of Blackchurch's property, that destruction would bleed into the trainers. The men who taught the warriors, the men who, in a crisis, would command Blackchurch's substantial army.

Tay...

Fox...

Sinclair...

Payne...

Cruz...

Kristian...

Ming Tang...

Amir...

Creston.

They would be murdered because of a lie. Her happiness

would be ended because of a lie, because of a spiteful, malicious old man who didn't care who or what he ruined in his quest to have his wants fulfilled.

My God... What have I done?

This was her fault, all of it. It became her fault when Cecil walked out on her and Oscar betrothed her to a man of his choosing. It became her fault when she married Creston and became a part of this living, breathing community within Blackchurch, the most wonderful community she'd ever been part of. She had friends that she liked and a husband she loved, and it was the most amazing world tucked deep into the Devon countryside. But in becoming part of Blackchurch, she'd brought the malignancy of Oscar de Bulverton with her.

Now he was trying to destroy everything she loved.

She wasn't going to let him do it.

And she wasn't going to let Creston and the others risk their lives because of her.

"I'm sorry, love," Creston said, breaking into her thoughts. "I did not mean to be so blunt. Do you feel well?"

She didn't. She really didn't. Knowing what she had done, and what she had to do, had her feeling sick to her stomach. She looked at him, at his beautiful face, and tried to smile, but the smile wouldn't come. Instead, she broke down in tears.

"I am so sorry," she wept. "I am so sorry he is doing this."

Creston grunted with sympathy, pulling her into his arms again. "It is not your fault," he murmured, trying to be of some comfort. "You cannot control a bitter old man. You did not do anything."

Oh, but I have. I caused this, she wanted to say, but she bit her tongue. He would just argue with her, and she didn't want his comfort, not now. She'd only brought heartache to the man she loved thanks to her grandfather.

But she was going to do something about it.

She had to think!

"I… I want to rest," she said, pulling herself out of his embrace. "I want to lie down for a while, please."

"Of course, sweetheart," he said, gently helping her to stand and putting his arm around her shoulders. "I'll help you upstairs."

"Nay," she said. "Just… let me go. I will be well, I promise. But I want to go alone."

He was hurt by her words, trying not to show it. "If you wish," he said as she walked away. "I truly am sorry to upset you, my love. I did not want to, but you needed to be told."

"I know," she said, still walking. "I am not angry. Just… tired."

Creston was full of sorrow, watching her until she reached the stairs. "I love you, Lia," he said softly. "Always remember that. You are my living, breathing heart."

Ophelia paused, looking at him. "And I love you," she said. "Everything will be all right, Creston. You needn't worry."

He watched her mount the stairs until she disappeared from view, feeling just as bad as he possibly could. He'd made her sad and miserable. Frustrated with himself, he marched from the back door, standing there a moment, watching the sky, then watching some servants as they drew water from a nearby well, and finally watching the cats as they lay upon the grass in the morning sun.

He began to second-guess himself.

Maybe he shouldn't have told her about this. Maybe he should have simply left her out of it like a decent man would have done, protecting his wife. Well, he *hadn't* protected her.

He'd let de Lohr create a plan that involved her, and, like an idiot, he went along with it.

Now Ophelia was miserable.

He was miserable.

Heading out to a small outbuilding behind the cottage, he found a few bottles of wine he'd stashed there. Sitting down on a three-legged stool to watch the cats play, he drained the bottles.

Needless to say, he didn't make it to his training class that day.

CHAPTER NINETEEN

"**S**OMETHING IS HAPPENING. I can feel it."

The comment came from an assistant trainer, a man by the name of Rhodes St. James. A man of average height, but bearing enormous shoulders and arms, he'd been pacing around, eyeing the circular keep of Exford Castle in the distance. He'd been up before dawn, as all of the assistant trainers and servants who helped the trainers had, and he'd seen St. Denis, St. Sebastian, and Ming Tang coming from the keep in deep conversation. Amir was there, too, and whenever Amir was with St. Denis, it meant that the man was giving counsel. That was what St. Denis relied on Amir for. All of those things added up to "something" for Rhodes.

His suspicious nature had the better of him.

"Be careful with your speculation," Bowen de Birmingham, a former assistant trainer, said in a warning tone. "If they want you to know about it, they'll tell you. Otherwise, do your duty and do not ask any questions. You are too curious for your own good, St. James."

Rhodes hardly acknowledged that comment. He thought he knew best, so there was no need for him to verbally spar with

Bowen, a man he secretly envied. Bowen was a full-fledged trainer now, and his duty, aside from instructing his own recruits, was to manage the assistant trainers and give them their assignments. He was good at it and the other trainers didn't have the time, so he was standing outside the outbuilding next to the kitchen, the building where trainers tended to gather and store things to be used in their classes. The outbuilding was full of swords, spears, shields, and any number of other items.

It was one of the hearts of Blackchurch.

"What is it now?" A tall blond knight with big muscles came out of the outbuilding, leaning against the doorjamb as he inspected a well-made sword he'd picked up inside. "Is St. James speculating about the meeting at Exford again?"

Bowen snorted. "You know he is," he said. "Anteaus, you work with him more than any of us. How do you stand it?"

Anteaus de Bourne grinned, watching Rhodes and knowing the man was struggling not to clap back at them. He took a lot of jesting and taunts from the other assistant trainers, mostly because he thought he didn't want to be one of them. He wanted to be a full-fledged trainer and thought he damn well deserved it.

He did, but no one was going to tell him that.

"He's tolerable," Anteaus said. "Unless he goes off on one of his tangents. If he does that, then I have to muzzle him."

"You've never muzzled me in your life, de Bourne," Rhodes said, unable to keep his mouth shut any longer. "You know I'm right about this. Yesterday, de Royans has two visitors, and then shortly thereafter, every Blackchurch trainer is in the keep with St. Denis and Sebo. One of the servants said they were there most of the night. And de Royans did not arrive to teach his class this morning. Anteaus had to do it."

"I would not read too much into it," Anteaus said. "De Royans has a pregnant wife. Mayhap she is ill and he does not want to leave her."

He looked at Bowen, who would have known why Creston did not teach his class because he was the one who had to make sure there was a trainer to carry on in such an instance, but Bowen simply shrugged.

"I do not know," he said. "When he did not come at sunrise and his recruits were standing around, I simply had Anteaus take over."

"Did any other trainers fail to make their class this morning?" Anteaus asked.

Bowen shook his head. "Nay," he said. "Although I did send Axton to assist Tay this morning. He has an unusually large class of dregs, including seven women. I do not think we've ever seen more than two or three at a time."

Axton Summerlin was another assistant trainer who had been at Blackchurch for a few years, an extremely capable trainer, but more of a follower than a leader. He was a big, mean man and not even Rhodes would tangle with him, but that personality made him perfect to work with Tay, who was also a big, mean man.

They were a match made in heaven.

"If Tay does not run off the women, then Axton will," Rhodes said, snorting with mirth. "If anyone survives those two as the very first trainers they meet at Blackchurch, then they deserve to be part of us. I'm not even sure *I* could survive those two."

"Bowen!"

A shout came from the south, and the men turned to see a pair of assistant trainers approaching, both of them carrying loads of clubs on their shoulders. Anteaus and Rhodes went to help them, and between the four of them, they managed to get the practice clubs back into the outbuilding for storage. Bowen stood in the doorway and watched them arrange the clubs by size.

"Is that from Payne's class, Therron?" he asked one of the men who had brought the clubs.

Therron de Allington and his brother, Torr, were knights who had trained at Kenilworth, the ultimate training castle for the upper-class sons of noblemen. They'd made it through Blackchurch training and were offered positions because Tay, who had worked with them the most, liked the way they operated. They were hard workers, savvy and skilled, and they saw their work at Blackchurch as a stepping stone to a trainer position, like the others did. Originally, they had worked with Tay, but they'd gradually transitioned into assisting Fox, Sinclair, and Payne as well.

Today had been a hell of a class with Payne.

"Aye," Therron said, wiping the sweat off his brow. "I am not entirely certain what had Payne in such a mood, but the man was swearing at the recruits in Gaelic and swinging his club like a madman. This was just supposed to be an exercise, but we ended up losing four men. Four good men."

"See?" Rhodes said, looking at Bowen and Anteaus. "Did I not tell you that something is in the air? Something has The Tempest living up to his name."

"He's right," Torr said. He was a year younger than his brother, but they looked so much alike that they could have been twins. "Tay seems tense also. As does Fox. They all seem to be… edgy."

Bowen simply shook his head. "It does not matter if something is happening," he said, looking to the group. "I will tell all of you that it is no concern of ours. We will do our duties, and do them well. If the trainers need help, we will help them. If they need for us to assume their classes, we will. That is our role here. But if something bigger *is* going on and they want us to know, they will tell us. Meanwhile… no speculation. You are trainers, not fishwives. Gossip is unbecoming, so keep your lips shut. Do you understand me, Rhodes?"

Rhodes wasn't very happy at being called out, so he just waved a hand at Bowen and walked away. Therron and Torr went back to their work, organizing clubs, leaving Bowen and Anteaus alone. The pair of them ended up outside of the outbuilding, watching Ming Tang in the distance lecturing a group of recruits that were sitting on the grass, listening intently.

"Do you think something is happening?" Bowen asked quietly. "Have you seen any indication?"

Anteaus shook his head. "Nay," he said. "But Rhodes isn't wrong. Something *is* in the air, Bowen. As you said, they'll tell us if they want us to know."

Bowen grunted. "It makes me nervous," he said. "When something goes on around here, it is never a small matter. It's usually a life-or-death situation. Remember when Payne's mother came to visit? Remember that entire debacle?"

Anteaus snorted. "A hundred pirates and a big battle," he said. "Mayhap we have more pirates coming to visit and no one is happy about it."

"Mayhap," Bowen agreed. "But something tells me that we need to be ready."

Anteaus nodded. There wasn't much more to say to that other than he agreed, and Bowen already knew that.

Some things were better left unsaid.

All they could do was carry on and hope they were wrong.

CHAPTER TWENTY

AFTER THE DISCUSSION with Creston in the morning, Ophelia had gone up to rest as she had told him, but what she was really doing was plotting.

She needed a plan.

Too many men were in jeopardy because of her, because of what her grandfather had done, and the animosity she felt toward Oscar, something she'd managed to forget over the past six months, came roaring back to life. That evil, bitter man was content with ruining everything that was good in her life, and she wasn't going to let him. She'd spent her entire existence being apathetic to him until the time between Cecil abandoning her and Creston marrying her. She'd had to accept the cruelty, the starvation, and the emotional abuse because she had no choice. Not until she married Creston did she have a choice.

And she was going to make the only choice she could.

She was going to stop him.

Short of murder, she wasn't exactly sure what she could do to stop him, however. That was the rub. She'd never killed anything larger than a spider in her life, but as she lay there in bed and felt the child in her belly move around, she was increasingly convinced that Oscar's death was the only thing that would save Blackchurch. She was damn protective over this life she'd built with Creston, and as she'd told her husband, it was worth more to her than flesh and blood.

Damn that old man.

Damn him to hell.

Creston hadn't come back to the cottage the entire day. Ophelia assumed that he'd gone off to teach his recruits, as he did every day, so she simply lay in bed until early afternoon, until her body was aching from lying around so much that she had to get up and stretch. She wasn't at the terribly uncomfortable stage in her pregnancy yet, but she was at a point where her body ached for strange and unknown reasons. It was better to move around. Therefore, she stood up, put her shoes on, and went downstairs.

There were still dishes, unwashed, in the kitchen so she resumed cleaning up after the morning's meal. She had never actually had any of the egg dish that she'd given the men, and when she picked up the bowl to wipe it out, she could smell the garlic. It was so strong that it had bled into the porous wood of the bowl, and no matter how much she wiped it, that garlic smell wouldn't go away.

When she realized how she'd over-garlicked the eggs, it made her love Creston all the more, because she had fed the man a vile creation and his only reaction had been to suggest maybe a little less garlic next time. That was it. No anger, no insults. If the bowl smelled like garlic, then the eggs must have been absolutely flaming with it.

That sweet, sweet man that her grandfather wanted to destroy.

Somehow, murder to protect her husband didn't seem so

outlandish anymore.

Her thoughts, her ideas, grew darker.

When Ophelia finished with the kitchen and opened the rear door to sweep out the floor, she happened to glance at the yard where her cats were playing in the grass. She paused a moment, watching the felines as they chased bugs around, but then she saw one of the cats run to an outbuilding and disappear inside. It was an outbuilding that was never really used for anything, just one of those structures left over from when the village was a bustling center of commerce many years ago, so she didn't think much of it until she saw what she thought was a shoe. Someone had left a shoe right outside the structure—and then the shoe moved. It took her a moment to realize she was looking at a boot, and that boot belonged to her husband.

Puzzled, she went to the outbuilding.

Creston was there, sitting on the floor of the little structure with an empty bottle of wine in his hand and his head against the side of the building. His eyes were closed, his mouth was open, and he just seemed to be sitting there, sleeping peacefully. Ophelia wasn't sure why he had been sitting there, drinking, but she was fairly certain it had something to do with her and the misery she had brought down upon Blackchurch.

The man had been forced to get drunk to deal with it.

And then it hit her.

She knew what she had to do.

Returning to their cottage, Ophelia flew upstairs and yanked open the doors of the wardrobe in the hunt for her traveling clothes. She was going to Sidmouth. She was going to confront that bastard who called himself her grandfather and she was going to confront him on his plans for Blackchurch. If he didn't admit his nefarious scheme and promise to cease all aggression, then she was going to drive a dagger into his belly.

There was no other choice.

She was going to kill him before he killed the man she loved so well.

It had come down to that.

As she pulled forth clothing, all she could see was red. All she could feel was anger. Anger at her grandfather, anger at herself. She couldn't believe what she had done to these people who had been nothing but kind to her, but she was going to rectify it.

She was going to end it.

Unfortunately, due to her pregnancy, the traveling dress wouldn't fit her. Frustrated, she began to hunt for anything that would fit her and would be hardy enough to travel in, but she couldn't find anything that was suitable. That had her digging into her husband's clothing, and she found a tunic and breeches that served her well enough because she could get the breeches up over her belly and the tunic hung down to her knees. She still had the heavy traveling cloak that she could wear, and she had a pair of doeskin boots that Creston had purchased for her a few months ago, so she pulled those sturdy boots on.

She felt as if she were dressing in a frenzy, and perhaps she was. There was a sense of urgency in her heart that she'd never felt before, even more so when she thought of her grandfather's reaction to her accusations. She knew that he would laugh at her, or perhaps he wouldn't even be angry at her. He might even become violent. Therefore, she went to the big chest where Creston kept his possessions and dug around until she found a large and rather nasty-looking dagger.

For a moment, she simply stared at it.

A weapon. Something that could kill. It underscored the

seriousness of what she was about to undertake, but she had to push aside any doubt or fear. She was fully prepared to use the weapon if she were threatened or if her grandfather refused her demands. Even as she thought of that moment, the very moment that she was risking everything for, she knew it was a foolish expectation. Oscar had never surrendered to anyone, least of all a woman, and least of all her.

But she was going to force this.

He was going to listen.

Ophelia had a small satchel in the wardrobe that had a drawstring closure and long cloth handles, something that she could easily put over her shoulders and carry without having to use her hands. Dressed in her husband's oversized clothing, she rushed back down the stairs and peered from the window to make sure he had not moved, and he hadn't. She could still see his booted foot. Quickly, she put the remainder of the bread from the morning's meal and a piece of white cheese from the previous day into the satchel. That was the only food she could find that would be easily transportable, and once she had it stashed away, she went back upstairs and proceeded to carefully put the big dagger into the satchel as well. She also took her coin purse so she could pay for food and lodgings if she needed to.

And with that, she was ready to depart.

The one thing that would work to Ophelia's benefit was the fact that at this time of day, anyone who knew her would be either training recruits or, in the case of the trainer's wives, be tending to their napping children. There wouldn't be anybody to stop her as she made her way out to the stables where Creston had a couple of fine horses and one small palfrey that he had purchased for her a few months ago when they traveled into the village of Minehead. She didn't like riding on the big horses behind him and preferred to ride alone, so he'd bought the little white mare for her to ride whenever she pleased.

Daisy was her name.

Daisy the mare was very fat and happy because Ophelia didn't ride much these days. She was very glad to see her mistress, however, and Ophelia paid a young stable boy to saddle her horse, giving the lad a silver coin and instructing him not to tell anyone he had seen her leave. The coin was to ensure his silence. The boy agreed, saddled her horse, and even escorted her to the smaller east gatehouse. There were soldiers there, but only a couple, and they didn't pay any attention to her as she rode through. After that, it was simply a matter of skirting the eastern wall of Blackchurch's perimeter so she could get on the road that led south through the village, past The Black Cock, and then straight to Sidmouth.

Ophelia remembered the road they'd taken north from Sidmouth when they came to Blackchurch. There was literally only one main road between Sidmouth and Blackchurch, so all she had to do was stay to the road and she'd make Sidmouth in a day and a half if she was fortunate. She would try to make it as far as she could tonight before finding an inn to sleep, but she was determined to do it. She was blinded by it. It didn't really occur to her that this was foolish, and even dangerous, and that she shouldn't be traveling in her condition. All she could think of was confronting her grandfather and demanding he stop his foolishness… or else.

It was that "or else" that had her worried.

But she wasn't worried enough to turn back.

She kicked her mare in the ribs, and the little horse began to lope southward.

CHAPTER TWENTY-ONE

S OMEONE WAS KICKING his foot.

"Creston? Get up."

Creston didn't even realize he'd been asleep. It was nearly pitch dark as he opened his eyes, which meant he really couldn't see where he was.

Someone kicked his foot again.

"Creston?" It was Brenton, as he recognized the voice. "Are you quite well?"

Creston didn't know. He lifted his head and the hammering started. Putting a hand to his swimming brain, he looked up at Brenton and saw that Myles was standing with him. He could barely make them out in the light.

"Christ," he muttered, his mouth pasty. "What time is it?"

"Late," Brenton said. "Have you been here all day?"

Creston had to think about that. *Had* he been here all day? "Since the morning," he muttered as his memory began to return. "Since I had to tell my wife that her grandfather is trying to kill us all. She went to bed and I got drunk."

Hands were reaching down to pull him to his feet. It took some effort, but they finally got him into a standing position as he tried not to vomit.

"God," he groaned, bending over and resting his hands on his knees. "I haven't done that in years."

"Done what?" Brenton asked.

"*That.*" Creston gestured to the shed behind him. "Drunk myself into a stupor. I used to do it all of the time after I left John's service, but I haven't done that since I came to Blackchurch. I will admit that I do not miss it."

"I would imagine not," Brenton said. "Can you walk?"

Creston stood up, weaving a little. "I can," he said. "Christ, Lia must be frantic. I hope she isn't too upset."

They began to walk, slowly, back toward his cottage. "It wasn't as if you went very far," Brenton pointed out. "All she had to do was come into the garden to see your legs sticking out from the shed."

Creston grunted. "I suppose," he said. Then he peered at his cousin. "Where have you been all day?"

Brenton grabbed him as he stepped on a rock and tripped. "After walking the perimeter of Blackchurch, we went over to The Black Cock," he said. "We've been plied with food and drink all day long. There was even a man with a draughts board, so we played for hours. We figured that was enough time for you to speak with your wife about the situation."

Creston took a long, deep breath. "It was long enough," he said. "She was very upset. Because she was upset, I was upset. But I should not have had so much wine. It was a moment of weakness that I regret."

"We all have those moments," Brenton said. "I have had more than my share."

"Not me," Myles said, looking up into the clear night sky. "My mother would beat me if I had a weak moment, so I have never had one."

The de Royans cousins looked over at him. "Your mother sounds terrifying," Brenton said. "Does she have no sympathy, then?"

Myles smiled, but it was without humor. "She is a sweet, decent woman," he said. "But she will also club you when you are not looking if she is mad enough. She could not be married to my father and be weak."

Brenton chuckled, but Creston's head hurt too badly for such a thing. He was barely holding it together as it was.

"Hopefully, my wife has been sleeping all day," he said. "The pregnancy is taxing enough without me telling her horrible stories about betrayal. I can only hope she does not even realize I have been missing all day. Mayhap she thinks I was training."

Brenton gave him a long look. "Only if she is blind and dumb," he said. "You look like you've been trampled by a wagon and you smell like drink, so mayhap you should wash yourself before you see her."

Creston paused and stood tall, or at least as tall as he could, and thought about his cousin's advice. He didn't want Ophelia to think any less of him if she knew he'd been in a drunken stupor all day.

"Mayhap you are right," he said. "I have already upset her once today. I do not want to do it again."

The three of them veered off to the well that was several yards away. Brenton hauled up a bucket of water and poured it over Creston's head about the time Cruz emerged from the rear of his cottage and saw what was happening. He headed over, looking at Creston with concern.

"What happened to you?" he asked.

Creston wiped the water from his eyes and shook his head, spraying droplets everywhere. "It has not been a good day," he muttered. "Who handled my recruits?"

"Anteaus," Cruz said. "When you did not show up by noon, he took over the training for the day. Your cousin told me you were with your wife, but now I am seeing that might not be the case?"

Creston wiped at his face. "I was with her this morning," he said. "I told her about her grandfather's betrayal and our plan to seek justice. She was understandably very upset and took to bed. I went out in the shed and got drunk because upsetting her made me feel like the worst husband in the world."

Cruz knew that Creston tended to like copious amounts of wine on occasion, but he'd not seen the man drunk for quite some time. Creston had told him once that when he served John, he was drunk frequently because it helped him forget about the things he'd been forced to do in the name of royal service. Below that killer exterior was an extremely sensitive man, even more sensitive now that he was married. Creston had a hard time reconciling his emotions with the duties he was expected to perform without any emotion whatsoever, so drink had been a way to cope.

Cruz put a hand on the man's shoulder.

"You are not a terrible husband," he assured him quietly. "You are a very good one. Your wife knows that even if you do not. Go inside and see her. I'll entertain your cousin for a while to give you some time alone, so you can reconcile what needs to be reconciled."

Creston appreciated that. He simply nodded, leaving Cruz with Brenton and Myles as he headed toward the back door of his cottage. It was open, but it was dark inside. No candles or fire were lit. Striking a flint and stone, he lit a taper so he wouldn't trip over anything in the darkness, and made his way upstairs.

It was still and silent on this floor as he headed to the bedchamber door. The panel was cracked open and he stuck his head inside, lifting the taper so he could see a little better without disturbing his wife.

But she wasn't in bed.

He pushed the door open wide and surveyed the entire chamber, seeing that she wasn't anywhere to be found. He noticed that their shared wardrobe was open and he went over to it, seeing that things had been thrown around. There was even clothing on the floor, including the garment that she had been wearing that morning when he last saw her. Puzzled, but not particularly concerned, he walked through the cottage, thinking he might find her dozing in a chair somewhere, but after a complete sweep of the house, he hadn't found her.

He went back out into the garden.

Cruz and Brenton and Myles were still there, chatting quietly by the well, and they saw him coming out of his cottage.

"Cres?" Cruz called to him. "What are you doing back out here?"

"Looking for my wife," Creston said. "She is not in our cottage."

There was no sense of panic as he spoke, simply curiosity as to where she may have gone. Cruz looked at the other cottages, the rear of Tay's, Sinclair's, Fox's, and Payne's. They were all gathered in the same general area.

"Mayhap she is visiting with her friends," Cruz said. "Or mayhap she is out looking for you."

Creston ran his fingers through his damp hair, looking

toward the south where Tay's cottage was. "Possibly," he said. "I will speak with Athdara."

Cruz and Brenton and Myles remained where they were as Creston headed down to Tay's home, hoping to find his wife. She wasn't there, however, so Athdara went with him over to Fox's cottage, but she wasn't there, either. That had Fox and Gisele and Athdara accompanying Creston to Sinclair's home and, finally, Payne's.

Ophelia wasn't in any of those locations.

Now Creston was starting to become worried.

At this point, Payne went to rouse the other trainers from their homes as Cruz, Brenton, and Myles joined the hunt. Blackchurch was a very large property, so they spread out, speaking to soldiers and servants, as Creston and Cruz went to the kitchens. The cook hadn't seen the lady since that morning, when he gave her eggs and chives and garlic, and he dropped what he was doing to help Creston search.

Soon enough, most of Blackchurch was looking for her.

Creston went to the stables to see if his wife's palfrey was still there. When he saw that the little animal was gone, he gathered the stable servants and asked them what they knew. Unfortunately, no one seemed to know, or had seen, anything, which only fed Creston's panic. He had been halfway through interrogating the stable servants when Cruz, figuring that Lady de Royans had to have used one of the gatehouses if she rode a horse from Blackchurch, raced to the east gatehouse, since it was the closest. Creston sent the stable servants out to look for his wife and the horse on the grounds of Blackchurch, just in case she'd gone for a ride and was injured somewhere, as he went to follow Cruz to the gatehouse.

The men on duty at this time weren't the same ones who

had been on duty during the day. There was a day watch and a night watch. Creston summoned the day watch for both gates and, by this time, St. Denis and St. Sebastian were involved in the hunt. The guards for the day watch at the main gatehouse hadn't seen Lady de Royans, but there were two men on the day watch for the eastern gatehouse that had seen someone ride a white horse from the gates. They hadn't paid much attention since the horse and rider were coming out, not going in.

But that told Creston all he needed to know.

Ophelia had left Blackchurch.

Sick with the realization, Creston put his hands over his face and fell back against the gatehouse wall. "My God," he breathed into his hands. "Why would she leave? *Why?*"

The men were passing concerned expressions at each other, though none of them wanted to say what they were thinking. It was Fox who finally spoke.

"You said that you told her about Sidbury's plot," he said. "When did you tell her?"

"This morning," Creston said.

"How did she take the news?"

"She was upset, of course," he said, growing agitated. "She was so upset that she had to lie down. I went out into the shed and got drunk, angry at myself because I was the monster who had upset her with the news. But sometime during the day, she must have… God, I don't even know what to think. She must have run away from me. *I* chased her away. It is my fault."

Fox glanced at Tay, who nodded faintly. They were both thinking the same thing, and it wasn't that the lady had run from her husband. It was something entirely different. Knowing how Creston felt about his wife, how they all felt about her, he hated to even speak what was on his mind.

But it was necessary.

"Creston," Fox said, "please do not think I am being cruel and suspicious, but there is another possibility."

"What possibility?"

"That she has gone to warn him."

Creston's head shot up, his eyes narrowing at a man who was a very dear friend. "Warn him?" he said. "Warn him about what?"

"That we know his plot," Tay said, taking some of the heat off Fox. "Mayhap she has gone to tell him that we know so that he will cease pursuing whatever it is he is pursuing. We're not saying she is betraying you, or any of us, merely suggesting that she was upset enough to warn her grandfather off his plans."

Creston was struggling not to lash out at them but he couldn't quite manage it. "For what purpose?" he demanded. "If you are suggesting she is somehow in on this plot to destroy Blackchurch, then say so. Tell me that to my face."

He was enraged. Cruz put his arm across Creston's chest, knowing the man was angry enough to strike. "Easy, *mi amigo*," he said softly. "No one is suggesting that. No one believes she is part of this plot."

Creston was so angry that he was trembling. "That is not what it sounded like."

"She is *not* part of any plot."

A female voice came behind Tay, and they all turned to see the Blackchurch wives walking up. Athdara had spoken those words in defense of her friend. The women had been out searching for Ophelia but then saw their husbands gathering at the east gatehouse, so they'd hastened to join them. They'd heard enough of the conversation before they came close, and when all eyes turned to them, Athdara wasn't shy about speaking her mind.

She never had been.

"She has no more gone to betray Blackchurch than I would have," she said, looking at the men standing around. "Mayhap you do not know how cruel Sidbury has been to her. I know that we are all aware she came into this marriage pregnant. Mayhap what you do not know is the fact that her grandfather starved her early in her pregnancy so her belly would not grow and give her away to Creston. He was desperate to make that marriage occur and did all he could to ensure that it happened. The man is vile and Lia feels no loyalty to him. She hates him with every breath she takes, so, nay, she did not go to betray us."

Her words had Creston calming somewhat. "Did she say something to you that might give us any idea as to why she went?" he said. "Please, Athdara. Tell me."

"I wish I could," Athdara said. "But I did not see her today. Tay told me about the plot her grandfather has ordained against Blackchurch, and I wanted to speak with her about it, but I have not seen her all day. I assumed she was sleeping and did not wish to disturb her. But knowing Ophelia as I have come to, my guess is that she thinks this is her fault somehow. She is a very sensitive woman, you know. She has gone to Sidmouth to confront her grandfather and condemn him. I know I would."

"Instead of standing around here, you should be on your horses heading south," Astria said, looking at her husband in particular. "I agree with Athdara—Lia is going to try to stop her grandfather single-handedly to protect the lot of you, so if I were you, I'd be riding to help her. She is doing this for *you*."

That had Kristian and Payne already heading into the stable. They didn't hesitate. Creston was still looking at the women, however, as if they might be his salvation in all of this. His despair was growing by the second.

"I have never understood a woman's mind," he admitted. "But, clearly, you do. Why would she do this? I told her we had a plan."

Athdara shook her head. "That is *your* plan," she said. "It is not Lia's plan. Cres, she is incredibly protective of you. What you told her surely must have frightened her. She has gone to do something about it. Don't you understand? Any wife would want to protect her husband, and that is what she is doing. She thinks she can."

"But the danger…"

"Would danger stop you from protecting her?"

Creston felt as if he'd been kicked in the gut. He exhaled heavily, but it was a sound of pain. He knew that Athdara was right—Ophelia was very protective of him. He also knew she was an incredibly brave woman, even if that bravery was reckless. With increasing horror, he looked at Cruz.

"Oh, God," he muttered. "I must go. I must go *now*."

Cruz nodded quickly, moving with Creston as they ran for the stables. Soon enough, everyone except St. Denis and St. Sebastian was moving in that direction. Even Brenton and Myles were gathering their mounts and the women were going inside to help. They could hear, and catch glimpses of, the trainers as they saddled their mounts and gathered belongings. There was a great deal of activity going on in the stable as St. Sebastian turned to his father.

"Y-you're going to let them all go?" he said.

St. Denis looked deliberately at his son. "Do you want to be the one to stop them?"

"G-good point," St. Sebastian said. Then he began to look

around. "I need a messenger to send to the assistant trainers."

"Why?"

"B-because they are going to be temporarily promoted while everyone is out saving Lady de Royans."

St. Denis was watching his team of trainers prepare to save the wife of one of them. They were behaving as if it were one of their own family members in peril, but such was the bond between the men.

He knew that very well.

"It is more than saving Lady de Royans," he said quietly. "They are off to save Blackchurch. They are off to save what our family has taken two hundred years to build, so what they do, they do for us as well. We have the best knights in the world serving us, Sebo. Never forget that."

St. Sebastian turned to look at the stable, which was now lit up with servants holding torches and lamps as the trainers prepared their mounts. He could see Tay arguing with Athdara because she wanted to go, too. That mountain of a man was being berated by his wife and more than likely losing the battle.

That made St. Sebastian smile.

"W-we have the best *people*, Papa," he murmured. "The very best people. *They* are Blackchurch."

"Agreed," St. Denis said. Having seen enough of his trainers and their preparations, he turned his attention toward the replacements. "Have Bowen step in for Tay. He was Tay's assistant for so long that he'll know what to do. No one handles the dregs better than Tay and Bowen. As for the rest, have Anteaus take Sinclair's recruits in the morning and Creston's in the afternoon. Rhodes seems to do well on the water, so he can replace Kristian for now. We'll work out the rest. Summon them to my solar and I shall meet you there."

St. Sebastian nodded and headed off, commandeering a soldier from the gatehouse as he went and sending the man to find the assistant trainers, who were all out hunting for Lady de Royans. But St. Denis lingered behind, watching his trainers become a military unit. As he'd told St. Sebastian, they were the best knights in the world.

Now they were about to prove it. They were going to save Blackchurch and, God help them, a small lady who was trying to do the same thing.

A terrible situation was about to break wide open.

CHAPTER TWENTY-TWO

Axen Castle
Seat of the Earl of Sidbury

F OUR HOURS OF sleep hadn't been enough.

It was early afternoon and Ophelia was struggling. She'd ridden most of the night, until a few hours before dawn, when she had dozed off in the saddle and nearly fallen off the horse. Therefore, she'd come off the road and into a dense collection of trees, where she'd tethered the horse by a small brook and wrapped herself up in her heavy traveling cloak. Lying down on the bed of the forest, she'd slept until the sun rose. The light of the coming morning had startled her awake and she'd sat up, yawned, eaten some bread, and then continued on her journey.

Daisy had been eating grass and leaves and roughage during the time she'd been sleeping, and the horse farted nonstop as they traveled down the road. By some miracle, she reached the big city of Exeter with its tall church and bustling roads, and the road east from Exeter took her directly into Sidmouth.

It had been shockingly uneventful.

Ophelia arrived in the familiar city at midafternoon, but she was exhausted. The ride had taken more out of her than she'd anticipated, and she thought long and hard about facing her grandfather in this condition. The truth was that she was already at a disadvantage being a woman, and a pregnant one at that, and she very much wanted to face her grandfather as strongly as she could.

She knew she had to rest before she confronted him.

Fortunately, she knew Sidmouth fairly well. She knew that there was an inn along the road she was traveling on just before entering the city proper. It was called The Fish and the Fly, and she stopped there with the intention of resting a few hours before heading to Axen Castle. A stable boy, no more than six or seven years of age, took Daisy into a stall to feed her as Ophelia headed into the inn, which was surprisingly empty at this time of day. But it worked in her favor because it meant she had her pick of beds. The innkeeper, a stout man with swollen legs, took her to a small chamber with a big bed that nearly filled up the entire room. Ophelia ordered a meal, which came shortly, a bowl of stewed meat and carrots and a big pitcher of watered wine boiled with quince. She ate, she lay down, and she promptly passed out, exhausted.

When she awoke again, it was dark outside. She had no idea how long she'd slept, but she was determined to get to Axen Castle. However, when she went to look for her possessions, she couldn't find them. In fact, everything was gone except the clothes on her back. She hadn't taken off her cloak, nor had she removed her shoes. Everything was missing, including her satchel with her purse and Creston's expensive dagger.

Rushing out of the chamber, she ended up in the common room, which was full at this time of night. People glanced at her but no one paid her much attention. Disoriented and upset that her things were missing, she found the innkeeper and questioned him, but he knew nothing about anything. No one seemed to.

Realizing that her things had been stolen, probably by the innkeeper himself, she knew that causing a scene wasn't going to help. It might actually get her beaten, or worse. She was a lone woman and had no protection. Ophelia might have been impulsive, but she wasn't stupid. She left without another word to preserve her safety. But heading into the stable, she realized her horse was missing.

Daisy had been stolen as well.

Sick to her stomach, Ophelia began to walk.

Fortunately for her, Axen Castle was less than an hour's walk, but she had to get through the town of Sidmouth to get there. It wasn't a haven for outlaws, but it also wasn't particularly safe at night. No town was. Since she knew the streets, she took roads less traveled and stayed to the shadows. Because she moved slowly, making sure she wasn't followed, it took her far more than an hour to get to the castle. The streets had been dark and frightening. Once she arrived, she shouted to the gatehouse guards, feeling some relief when they recognized her and opened the portcullis.

Slipping in, she headed straight for the great hall.

Axen didn't spread out over a vast amount of real estate, but it was a sturdy, well-designed castle. In addition to the large gatehouse and long, steeply pitched great hall that hugged the eastern wall, it had an enormous keep built on the north side that took up most of the bailey. The bailey itself was rather small, and most of that was committed to the stables and kitchen yard. Ophelia knew the place and recognized it because she had once lived here, but she didn't feel as if she'd come home. She only felt as if she'd come back, back to something that gave her unhappy memories.

There was no joy here.

It only served to emphasize the darkness that was her grandfather.

Once inside the great hall, which was mostly empty at this time of night but for a woman sweeping the floor, Ophelia inquired about her mother and was told that Lady Randa was still at Axen. She hadn't returned to Symondsbury. After sending the servant to fetch her mother, Ophelia went to stand in front of the dying fire of the enormous hearth, peeling back the hood on her cloak and warming her hands.

And she waited.

Randa appeared in a relatively short amount of time. She was still in her bedclothes, though she wore a heavy robe against the cold night air. She entered the hall, looking at her daughter in shock. Ophelia caught sight of her mother, feeling no happiness. Only disappointment. She'd spent over twenty years of her life with the woman, and their relationship had been dutiful but not close, and all she could manage to feel now was the result of how Randa had let Oscar treat her only child.

"Lia?" Randa said with surprise. "Sweet Jesus, lass. What are you doing here? Where is your husband? Your escort?"

"I came alone," Ophelia said. "Mother, I must speak to you."

Surprise now became confusion on Randa's face. "Speak to me…?" she repeated. "Lia, *why* are you here? What is happening?"

"Is Grandfather here?"

"Aye," Randa said hesitantly. "He is probably in his bed, where I was when I was summoned. Why do you ask?"

Ophelia didn't answer her. She didn't think she owed the woman any responses to her question because she'd not come to be interrogated. She was going to ask the questions because she'd come for answers. There was a table nearby, and benches, and she went to sit on one.

"Sit down, Mother," she said. "We must speak."

Randa followed her, increasingly confused. "Lia, did you leave your husband?" she asked. "Is that why you are here alone? Are you seeking safety from his cruelty?"

Ophelia snorted rudely. "If I were, I would not seek it here," she said. "This is the last place I would go."

"Then why have you come?"

Ophelia looked at her mother. It was so difficult to keep the rage at bay, and, in fact, she couldn't quite manage it. Sighing sharply, she averted her gaze.

"I never thought I would see you again," she said. "I was *hoping* I would never see you again, but here we are because I, once again, must confront Grandfather's cruelty. I do not even know why I am speaking with you. He is the one I must speak with."

Randa frowned. "What cruelty do you speak of?"

Ophelia looked at her then. "I am certain you know," she said. "You grew up with him. He is *your* father. You know what he is capable of."

Randa shook her head. "Lia, I genuinely have no idea what you are speaking of," she said. "Can you please tell me?"

Ophelia's gaze lingered on her mother a moment before she answered. "You should know that the best thing you, and Grandfather, could have ever done for me is the betrothal to Creston," she said. "A more wonderful man does not exist. He is kind and attentive, thoughtful and wise. He is everything a man should be but seldom is. I suppose I should thank Grandfather for that, at least."

Randa wasn't any clearer on why her daughter had come to Axen. "Then if he is so wonderful, why have you left him?"

"Because Grandfather is trying to destroy him."

"Destroy who?"

It wasn't Randa who replied, but a male voice coming out of the darkness. Ophelia and Randa turned to see Oscar entering the hall. Their voices, in the emptiness of the great hall, had carried. He'd heard the last few exchanges of their conversation perfectly.

"Father," Randa said quickly, standing up to greet him because that was what he expected of her, always. "Look who has come—Lia is here."

Oscar's dark gaze moved to his granddaughter, who was still sitting. "I've been told," he said. "A servant roused me from my bed to tell me she had come and I thought I would see for myself. Well? Why are you here, Lia?"

That was it, no greeting beyond a demand for answers, and Ophelia felt the familiar fear and hatred of the man creeping into her veins. Suddenly, she wasn't so sure that this had been a good idea. She wasn't entirely confident in her decision to come to Axen. Somehow, Oscar looked taller and bigger than she remembered. More intimidating.

Courage! she told herself.

She was here.

And she was going to face him.

"I've come to tell you that Blackchurch knows about your forged missive from Louis of France," she nearly blurted, coming straight to the point because she didn't have the patience for a drawn-out explanation. "They know you mean to destroy them. I've come to tell you that I will not permit it."

Oscar's smug, suspicious expression shifted into one of disbelief. It was an unusual expression for him, one that suggested he'd genuinely been caught off guard by Ophelia's statement.

"What...?" he sputtered. "What is this nonsense you spout?"

Ophelia had never known her grandfather to be anything other than haughty and calm. It was a distinct pleasure to see that she'd unbalanced him, which made her feel a little braver about the situation.

"It is not nonsense and you know it," she said. "You were sending a missive to Henry that was allegedly from Louis of France, thanking Blackchurch for their help in Louis' Gascon war. You knew what Henry would do when he read such a thing. You knew he would destroy Blackchurch, and that is what you intended."

Oscar was still in a state of shock, struggling with his composure. "This... this is madness," he said. "Where did you hear this?"

He was being defensive, a sure admission of guilt as far as Ophelia was concerned. "St. Denis has the missive," she said. "It was brought to him. The messenger who possessed it said that the missive had come from the Earl of Sidbury. *You* forged a dispatch from the French king in an attempt to discredit Blackchurch. They are certain it has something to do with the pirate attack on Sidmouth, so in some way, you are trying to exact revenge on those pirates by destroying Blackchurch. Do you deny this?"

Oscar was still off guard, still trying to think clearly in the situation. "Did your husband send you here?" he asked, avoiding her question. "Is that why you have come? To ask questions because he is too much of a coward to do so?"

Ophelia shook her head. "He did not tell me to come," she said. "I came of my own accord because I am ashamed. Ashamed I am related to someone as underhanded as you. Tell me something, Oscar—*why* do you think destroying Blackchurch is going to give you a sense of satisfaction against the pirate attack? Is it because you think you are God and you want to show those pirates how badly you can hurt them if you want to? Or is it because you're the spiteful, malicious bastard you've always been and you cannot stand when someone is stronger than you in every way? Which is it?"

Perhaps her last words to him were a little too much. A little too bold. She'd spat them out faster than she could actually think about what she was saying because, for once in her life, she was speaking her mind. She was standing up to him and it felt glorious. But once the words had left her lips, Ophelia could see the expression of disbelief on Oscar's face turn to rage. A storm was brewing behind his dark eyes as he reached out, grabbing Randa by the arm.

"Get out," he spat at her. "Get out now."

Randa nearly tripped over the bench as he yanked on her. As fearful as she was of her father, she was more fearful of his anger being directed toward her daughter at the moment. Ophelia had revealed the reason for her visit with blunt force, and now it was out in the open. Oscar had been hammered with it.

And so had Randa.

Terror swept her.

"Lia," she gasped as she stepped over the bench and tried not to fall. "Go to my chamber, lass, and wait for me. I must speak with your grandfather!"

"Nay," Oscar snapped, yanking Randa so hard that she finally lost her balance and fell to her knees. "I gave you an order, woman. Get out!"

"No one is going anywhere," Ophelia said as she watched Oscar manhandle her mother. "Then it is true, isn't it? If it were not true, you would not have such a reaction. You *are* trying to destroy Blackchurch!"

Oscar was torn between Randa's clumsiness and his grand-daughter's boldness. He wanted Randa out so he could wrap his hands around Ophelia's throat without a witness, but Randa wasn't leaving. She was wallowing on the ground, imagining she was hurt.

The woman always had been a weakling.

"What I do is none of your affair," he growled. "You would do well to shut your mouth this instant or face my wrath."

Ophelia could hear the danger in his voice. Dark, murky, terrifying danger. Stricken with a sense of self-protection, she stood up and moved away from the table, in the direction of the hearth. She no longer had Creston's lovely dagger, so she grabbed the only weapon she could get her hands on. A sharp, heavy fire poker ended up in her grip and she was fully prepared to defend herself with it.

"I will *not* shut my mouth," she said steadily. "I came to tell you that Blackchurch knows of your plot. You have been discovered. I, therefore, have the satisfaction of looking you in the eye and telling you that the people at Blackchurch are my friends and I will not allow you to destroy them. The man you betrothed me to is the most wonderful, loving man I've ever had the good fortune to know. I have a life there, a beautiful world, which is something you did not expect. I am certain that once I was married, you never gave me another thought. I could have been beaten to death by my new husband, or starved, and you would not have cared, but the reality is this—you did me a favor when you married me to Creston de Royans. For that fact alone, I am doing you a favor by telling you the truth. I am giving you the chance to cease your behavior and plead forgiveness. If you do not, then Blackchurch *will* deal with you. And they will kill you."

Oscar stared at her. He still had Randa in his grip, but he shoved her down again just as she was trying to get to her feet. The contempt in his expression as he moved toward Ophelia was blatant.

"The Great Beauty of Dorset has found her courage at last," he said, his voice dripping with sarcasm. "It is a pity that courage is misplaced. You spout threats and accusations and believe you will emerge unscathed, but you have taken this a step too far, Ophelia de Camville. You have threatened me and I have a right to defend myself against threats."

That wasn't the reaction Ophelia was expecting. She had expected some sort of discussion, confession. An argument, even. Anything but the impending disaster she was sensing.

The fire poker went up.

"Come no closer," she said sternly. "I will not hesitate to use this if you do. Kill me and my husband will make sure your death is as painful as possible. He will take great pleasure in it."

Oscar came to a halt, but it was only temporary. He looked her over, top to bottom, ripples of disgust moving across his features.

"Brave, brave Ophelia," he said mockingly. "Ophelia with a bastard in her belly. When the child is born, *if* the child is born, I hope de Royans discovers that it is not his and steps on its head. You deserve nothing less for your shameful behavior."

Ophelia smiled thinly. "He knows the child is not his," she said. "I told him before we were married."

That brought pause to Oscar. "Is that so?" he said, surprised. "And he still married you?"

"He did."

Oscar shook his head. "Then he is a bigger fool than I thought."

"Untrue. He just wants your earldom."

She made it sound like Creston was greedy because she knew that would upset her grandfather. She wanted him to know that he wasn't able to slip something past Creston because, in the end, the earldom was more valuable than anything Oscar could do to trick him.

She wanted him to know that Creston fought dirty, too.

"I see," Oscar said in a tone that suggested her barb had hit its mark. "If that is true, then I feel obligated to tell you that I will simply marry again and have sons. If de Royans married you just for the earldom, he is to be sorely disappointed."

It was becoming like a chess match between them. She would make one move and he would make another, each trying to outsmart the other. But Ophelia wasn't going to let the man gain the upper hand.

"He will not be disappointed," she said. "Even if you marry again, you've proven that you can only produce female children. Moreover, what father is going to allow his daughter to marry you? You are no prize, Oscar, even with the earldom."

It was a gibe at his ego, and it was a direct hit. He stiffened, eyeing her with great hostility. Perhaps he was just a little surprised that his usually obedient granddaughter was taking a stand.

He didn't like it in the least.

"Mayhap," he said casually. "But, then again, neither were you. Let me explain something to you, Ophelia—you may as well know that your betrothal to de Royans was part of the greater plan. If anyone is to blame for what Blackchurch is facing, it should be you. You did this to them."

"And how is that?"

"Because you were the key," he said. "I'd been trying to find a way to seek vengeance on the pirates who attacked Sidmouth for quite some time when I remembered we had a distant relation through your grandmother who served at Blackchurch. At least, I thought I'd heard that, so I wrote to Royston de Royans to inquire about his brother's marital status, and when I was told he was unmarried, the path became clear. *You* were to marry into Blackchurch and be the beginning of their end. And if you are wondering about Royston's role in all of this, he knew about my plan."

Ophelia wasn't particularly surprised to hear about Royston, since he and Creston were never close, but more than that, she was starting to see what Oscar meant about the implementation of his scheme.

That dark, twisted scheme.

"But Blackchurch was not the group who burned your town," she said. "Why would you punish them?"

"Because they are related to those responsible," Oscar said. "You were simply a tool, my dear. A tool to link me to Blackchurch, so that is how you are part of the blame. The royal dispatch was a tool, also. Now that I know Blackchurch is in possession of it, that makes it perfect. I will tell Henry that St. Denis received the missive from Louis and demanded the king investigate. When he finds the dispatch at Blackchurch, my claims will be proven. Truly, this is a great stroke of luck."

Ophelia could see his point, but she wasn't going to concede it. "All St. Denis has to do is burn the dispatch," she said. "Without evidence, it is your word against his."

Oscar smiled faintly, but there was no humor to it. "He will not burn it," he said. "He will keep it as evidence of my so-called wrongdoing. He will try to use it against me as I will try to use it against him. That dispatch is key, Ophelia. If you are trying to play a man's game, then you should understand how they think."

Ophelia sighed heavily. "I do not want to know how they think," she said. "I do not want to know how *you* think. I am here to tell you that this plan, whatever plan you produced those months ago when you married me to Creston, is in ruins. They know and they are going to punish you for it."

"How?"

She shook her head. "I do not know."

"You are lying."

"Not everyone is a liar like you, Oscar."

He cocked his head. "I would be very careful of what you accuse me of," he said. "Mayhap I will tell Henry that your husband sent you to Axen to plead for my cooperation in forgetting I ever saw the dispatch. Your being here will help my case immensely."

"You are becoming desperate," she said. "Do you truly think I would support your claim?"

"You will have no choice when your husband is dead, Blackchurch is destroyed, and you have nowhere else to go."

"I will go to a bloody convent before I ever come to live with you again."

He shrugged. "All the better for me," he said. "I will be too busy with my new wife and sons to bother with you."

Ophelia actually cracked a smile. "And you think it hurts me to hear you say that?" she said. "It *thrills* me. Understand that in the six months I have been married to Creston, I have learned something. I have learned the meaning of love. I have learned the meaning of kindness and friendship and belonging. If you take down Blackchurch, then you take me down as well, but I know that does not concern you. I am glad it does not concern you because, surely, I hate you as much as you hate me. I cannot wait for the day when Blackchurch comes bursting through your gatehouse and destroys you. I cannot wait for your humiliation when you realize that, in the end, you did not win. I will make sure your Septem Port Alliance associates know what a coward you were in the end. I'll make sure your memory is spat upon for the rest of eternity, a legacy any man would be ashamed of. That is the only legacy you are worthy of."

After that speech, Oscar remained silent. He simply stood there, staring at her. Ophelia was hoping that he would at least realize his efforts were futile. She was hoping her words had made some impact. Just a small acknowledgment and she would have been satisfied, but deep down, she knew that Oscar didn't have the capability of admitting guilt or showing any measure of humility. That simply wasn't the way he was made. As she watched him carefully for any reaction, she was caught off guard when he suddenly charged her and ripped the poker from her grip.

After that, the fight was on.

Even if she was pregnant, Ophelia was faster than Oscar, who had one leg with the gout. She dashed away, looking for another weapon, but all she could see was an empty pitcher at the end of the table. She made a run for it, hurling it at Oscar, who easily dodged it. The poker fell away from his hand also, but he didn't stop to pick it up. He continued his pursuit of Ophelia as she tried to evade him.

"Come here," he demanded. "Come and face your punishment, you foolish chit."

"If you harm me, you'll have my husband to answer to," she shouted at him. "The best thing you can do now is go back to your chamber and remain there. Face your enemies like a man because, surely, they will be upon you soon enough."

Oscar picked up a three-legged stool against the wall of the hall and hurled it at her. Ophelia had her back turned to him at the time and she yelped when it clipped her in the hip, but she kept running. She was trying to head for the entry door, but Oscar blocked her path and she ended up over by the servants' alcove.

"Come *here*," he barked. "If you do not and I am forced to catch you, I can promise you that you will regret your disobedience."

Ophelia had no doubt of that. She knew the man beat his servants, his soldiers. He'd never beaten her mother that she knew of, but it was equally possible that Randa had simply never told her. Whatever the case, she knew for certain that if Oscar caught her, he would kill her. Strangely, she only felt braver in the face of certain death. She wasn't going to let the man get his hands on her. She was going to fight and fight some more, fight until the end of all things because, for once in her life, she was *willing* to fight him.

She couldn't let him win.

But that was until he lunged at her and she dashed into the alcove, completely forgetting that, beyond the tables that held food, there was a narrow staircase that led down to a door, and then the door led to the kitchen yard. It was a fairly steep stairwell and, in the darkness of the hall, Ophelia simply didn't see it. She slipped on the first step and tried to catch herself, but she wasn't able to. With a scream, she plunged down the entire stairwell, straight to the bottom, in a heap.

And then… silence.

Oscar was at the top of the stairs, realizing what had happened. He could hardly see anything because of the darkness, but a window above the doorway below let in some light. He could see a motionless figure at the base of the stairs and his strained face suddenly bloomed with surprise and…

Joy.

Oscar was feeling joy.

"She's killed herself!" he hissed excitedly. "Ophelia? Do you hear me? Answer me!"

There was stone-cold silence. Oscar took the first step, holding himself steady on the walls of the stairwell as he looked down upon the crumpled mass below.

"Ophelia?" he said again. "Do you hear me? Are you dead, you little bitch? Are you finally dead and gone and I no longer have to—"

His tirade was cut short when he suddenly grunted, his body jerking. His eyes widened and as he emitted another sound, his body jerked again and he began to groan.

"Nay," he breathed. "Nay, nay! What is… What is…?"

He never finished. He jerked one more time before suddenly lurching as he plunged down the steps, headfirst, and ending up crumpled against the wall near Ophelia. For standing behind him on the stairwell was none other than Randa with that heavy fire poker in her hand.

A poker that was covered with blood.

Her father's blood after she had stabbed him in the back, more than once.

And she was glad for it.

CHAPTER TWENTY-THREE

CRESTON HAD NEVER been to Sidmouth.

Just past the nooning hour, the group from Black-church entered the outskirts of the bustling fishing town. The glistening sea was to the south and fishermen were bringing in their nets after having brought their catch into market. The fish market stretched about a quarter of the length of the long, sandy beach and was still busy at this hour.

But Creston didn't notice any of it.

His eyes were on the castle to the north.

"Cres," Tay said, riding beside him. "Now that we're here, we cannot all rush the gatehouse. It would be less threatening if only one man approached and asked for admittance."

Creston had his eyes on the castle, incapable of looking at anything else. "Then I'll go."

Tay could see the expressions of the men around them, all of them knowing how determined Creston was to get to Ophelia. They'd literally ridden all night and into the day to get here, only stopping once to rest the horses, so they were all edgy and weary.

But that didn't mean they were going to be foolish about this.

Tay had a plan.

"I do not think that is a good idea," he said. "Listen to me, please. Sidbury knows you and so does Lia's mother. If they are both here, and they know you on sight, then they will know why you have come."

Creston tore his gaze away from the castle, looking at Tay with a frown. "Of course, they will know why I have come," he said. "I am here to collect my wife."

"Think," Ming-Tang, on Creston's other side, said. "Creston, if your wife has come here and told Sidbury that we know of his plans, he will be on his guard. He might have an archer shoot you down before you can even get inside. He will recognize you on sight, but he will not recognize the rest of us. Fox, for example. He does not look like you, so he could simply be a random knight asking for admittance. But once inside, he will take care of the gate guards and admit the rest of us. It is much better that way."

Creston almost argued with him but thought better of it. Given the fact that he taught underhanded maneuvers and tactics to recruits, he knew Ming Tang was correct. He understood.

"I have a better idea," he said. "Send the Executioner Knights in first. This is what they do, after all. They are spies and operatives, so this is something they are better suited at. Brenton?"

Brenton was near the rear with Myles, but he heard his name. "Aye, Creston?"

"Will you and Myles go in first and neutralize the gate sentinels?"

Brenton and Myles pushed their way forward, until they were riding in front of Creston. "Aye," Brenton said. "We can do that. We'll open the gate for the rest of you, but I suggest one of you cover the postern gate from the outside in case your wife's grandfather tries to escape."

"I will," Amir said. "Ming Tang will come with me in case it is a two-man job."

"Good," Tay said. "Then it is settled. Let us get a little closer to the castle and get a sense of the way it is constructed before we move."

The men were in agreement.

Once they reached the heart of the city, they split up. There were several smaller roads that led north, toward the castle, and they didn't want to be spotted as a big group by the sentries at Axen's gatehouse. Still, they attracted some attention as they moved through town, finally coming to a juncture on the north side of the village where three of the smaller roads came together. The town of Sidmouth seemed to thin out here, and there were clusters of trees that provided some concealment from the castle. Dismounting, the group led their horses into a particularly dense cluster of trees to the northwest, securing the animals near a small pond with some grass around it.

With the horses properly concealed, and safe, the group moved forward, along the edge of the road while still being concealed by the trees. They hadn't gone far when the trees ended and the road was the only thing between them and Axen Castle. It wasn't a big castle, but the walls were high, and they could see a tall keep sprouting above the walls. Constructed of gray granite, the side that faced the ocean was bleached by the salt and the wind, and it seemed like a quiet place. They didn't see any activity at all. In fact, the closer they looked, the more it appeared as if the gatehouse was simply open. The portcullis was lifted, and they didn't see anyone around the opening or on the walls above.

"Where are the guards?" Fox wondered aloud. "I don't see anyone at all."

"Nor do I," Tay said. "Sin? What are you seeing?"

Sinclair, the master swordsman, was also a skilled scout. He was standing behind a tree, eyes trained on the castle in the near distance, but after a moment, he simply shook his head.

"The entire place seems vacant," he said. "But that may be a trap."

"Especially if they know we are coming after Lia," Creston said. "I still think Brenton and Myles should go first. We will wait for a signal from them if everything is as clear as it appears."

That statement had Brenton and Myles returning to collect their horses. Once mounted, they took off down the road as Amir approached Tay.

"I will find the postern," he said. "If you need me, that is where I'll be."

He motioned to Ming Tang, who quickly followed. They went on foot, dashing across the road and heading for the castle by skirting the line of trees off to the east. That left Creston, Cruz, Tay, Fox, Sinclair, Payne, and Kristian waiting for a signal from Brenton and Myles.

There was nothing more they could do until then.

"He would not hurt her," Cruz muttered to Creston as they watched Brenton and Myles approach the gatehouse. "You must not worry about that."

Creston glanced at his friend. "I hope he will not hurt her," he said. "I've gone back and forth between the terror of the situation and being so angry that I want to spank her until she cannot sit for an entire month. I still cannot believe she left. After everything I told her about this situation, still, she came here."

Cruz didn't say anything for a moment. "You do realize that we are only speculating that she would come here because there is nowhere else she could go," he said. "If she is not here, then where will you look?"

Creston sighed heavily. "I have considered that," he said. "I did not want to, but it is difficult not to. What if she simply ran off? I would not even know where to look. But I can tell you this much—I would look forever."

"And if you never find her?"

The pain in Creston's eyes flickered. "If I cannot be close to her, then I will settle for the ghost of her," he whispered. "I lost one lady, Cruz. I will never lose Lia, not in this life or in the next. If her ghost is the only thing she leaves me, then I will have to be content with that."

Cruz's dark eyes glimmered at the sweet sentiment. "This is the same man who wasn't sure he wanted this marriage?"

"That man was a fool."

"That man is in love."

Creston smiled weakly. Cruz patted him on the shoulder and they turned their attention to the gatehouse in the distance just as Brenton and Myles reached it. With the portcullis open, they entered unopposed. Once they disappeared from view, everyone waited anxiously for the next move.

And waited.

Time passed slowly. *Too* slowly. Creston stopped watching the gatehouse like a hawk and took to pacing around in the trees, looking up at the gatehouse every so often to make sure he didn't miss anything. He didn't even know how much time had passed. He was starting to lose track of it. The afternoon was progressing, the sun moving across the sky, and had he not been so preoccupied with the castle, he would have thought it to be a lovely day. The breeze was gentle from the ocean and he could smell the salt. Growing increasingly edgy, he went to stand next to Tay, both of them watching the gatehouse.

And then it happened.

Myles appeared, waving his big arms frantically.

That was as much signal as anyone needed, and they began to move.

Creston didn't even wait to collect his horse. He just started running. Everyone else, however, returned for their mounts, and Creston was halfway to the castle when Cruz thundered alongside him, leading Creston's horse. Creston did a running mount, leaping on the horse's back and taking off toward the castle. He wasn't the first one in, but he still made it in record time. Once through the gatehouse, he bailed from his horse and began to look around anxiously.

"Cres!" Brenton was standing near the keep, waving at him. "Here! Quickly!"

Creston raced to his cousin's side. Tay, Fox, and Cruz were already there while Payne, Kristian, and Sinclair had spread out of the bailey and onto the grounds, armed. They were looking for resistance, or the enemy, or both, but so far the bailey seemed to be completely empty. It was strange and eerie.

Regardless, Creston was focused on his cousin.

"Well?" he demanded. "Where is my wife? Is she here?"

Brenton put his hands on Creston's upper arms, trying to still the man because he was quite distressed.

"She is here," Brenton said steadily. "But de Bulverton is dead."

Creston's brow furrowed. "Dead?" he repeated. Then his expression washed with horror. "My God… did Lia kill him?"

"Nay," Brenton said. "Creston, stop for a moment. Listen to me, please. You *must* listen."

Creston was trying to push past him to get into the keep, but Brenton and Tay and Fox stopped him. Because Fox and Tay had arrived a minute or so before Creston, they'd only heard part of the story from Brenton. But what they'd heard had been alarming.

Something wicked was afoot at Axen.

"Cres," Tay said, putting his hands on the man's shoulders. "Listen to him. He has something to tell you."

"What?" Creston demanded. "Where is my wife?"

"That is what I am trying to tell you," Brenton said. "She is inside, with her mother. But I got my news from a soldier I came across in the great hall. I am sorry it took so long to wave you in, but this big place is literally deserted. The soldier said they all abandoned the place after de Bulverton was killed. But more importantly, there has been an accident."

"What accident?"

"Your wife, Cres," Brenton said as gently as he could. "She had a confrontation with de Bulverton and had an accident."

That had Creston pausing, his eyes widening in shock. For a moment, he didn't say anything as he digested what he'd been told.

Ophelia. De Bulverton. Accident.

"Brenton, *where* is my wife?" he asked, his voice beginning to tremble. "Is she dying?"

Brenton looked at Tay, unable to tell him more, and it was Tay who made the decision to let Creston move forward.

"She's inside with her mother," he said, pulling Brenton

away so Creston could pass. "Creston, be calm. If you are agitated, it will only further upset the situation. Try to be calm, lad."

Creston wasn't listening. He rushed into the keep and up the stairs, his heart in his throat as Cruz followed on his heels. He came to the first level and feverishly searched the two rooms that were there, only they were empty. He continued on to the next level, where he immediately saw a chamber with an open door. Inside, there was light, and he went right in.

There were people inside.

A woman was sitting next to the bed, and a man and another woman were standing at the end of it in quiet discussion. The noise of boots and men startled them. When the woman sitting next to the bed turned around, Creston immediately saw that it was Randa. He'd barely exchanged two words with her at their wedding, but now he needed answers, and she had them.

"My wife?" he asked her anxiously.

Randa's face was pale, her eyes red-rimmed. She stood up, indicating for Creston to sit in the chair.

"Here," she said. "She is here. Sit with her, my lord. Talk to her. Mayhap she will hear you."

Creston had no idea what she was talking about until he looked at the bed and saw Ophelia there. She looked as if she were sleeping, as white as the linens she lay upon. There was also a compress on her head with bloodstains on it.

Then it began to dawn on him.

An accident.

She'd had an accident.

"Oh… God," he breathed, immediately going to Ophelia's side. "What happened to her?"

Randa watched the very big, very blond knight lean over her

daughter, his features full of grief.

"She came to us earlier," she said, wiping at her tearful eyes. "She wanted to speak with my father. Did you know she was coming?"

Creston was stroking Ophelia's face, lifting an eyelid to see if her pupils were reacting to the light. "Nay," he said. "I did not even know she had left."

"But you know why?"

He sighed heavily, the very air around him infused with pain. "I know," he said. "I know why."

Randa watched him as he touched her daughter. She could see, just in those first few moments, that this was no ordinary relationship.

Something special had happened between them.

"Then you should know that she and my father had words," she said. "Terrible words. She told him that Blackchurch knew of his attempt to betray them to the king. She tried to force him to… stop, I suppose. Retreat. She said that you were her family and that she loved you, and she cursed him for trying to ruin her happiness."

Creston couldn't help it. His eyes filled with tears. "She came to fight him alone," he whispered tightly. "Please tell me she did not physically fight him."

"Nay," Randa said, noting that more men were entering the chamber now. Very big men that she'd seen at her daughter's wedding, men who were part of Blackchurch. "She did not physically fight him, but he tried to capture her. She ran from him and fell down a flight of stairs."

Creston looked at her in horror. "Oh, God," he breathed. "Is that the accident I was told of?"

"It is."

"What of the child?"

"I believe that he is dead, my lord."

The man at the end of the bed spoke up. When he saw Creston looking at him in shock, he stepped forward to explain himself.

"My name is Kerne," he said. "I am the physic in town. Lady de Camville summoned me to tend her daughter and I am sorry to say that I believe the child is dead. I cannot feel any movement and there has been a great deal of blood."

Creston was hit with a wave of grief. "And my wife?" He could barely speak. "Will she die?"

"I do not believe so," he said. "But she is bleeding. Her body is trying to expel the child, so we must let it."

"She is laboring?"

"She is."

Creston had to catch his breath. He closed his eyes tightly and sat heavily on the chair that Randa had been sitting on. Leaning forward on the mattress, he put his face in his hands, struggling not to come apart. Collapsing wouldn't help Ophelia, so he wouldn't do it. He had to be strong for her, for them both, because they were facing something unimaginably awful.

"Has she been awake at all?" he finally asked, his voice hoarse. "Does she know about the child?"

The physic shook his head. "She has not awakened," he said. "She struck her head when she fell, so we must be patient."

"But you do believe she will awaken?"

"I do," the physic said. "Her eyes are normal and her breathing is even, so there is no indication that she has done anything more than knock herself unconscious. But I do believe she has broken her right arm in the fall and mayhap a rib or two."

Creston closed his eyes at the diagnosis. It could have been so much worse, so if Ophelia only had a few broken bones, they would heal. But the loss of a child was something altogether different. Other than Ophelia's death, it was the worst thing he could have imagined.

He was gutted.

Standing up, he turned around to see Tay, Fox, and Cruz behind him, each man with expressions of grief and sympathy. His friends. His dear, dear friends, now witnessing this terrible moment with him.

He was glad they were here.

"Tay," he said, his voice raspy with emotion, "bring Ming Tang here. He has a knowledge of healing. I want him to look at Lia."

Tay nodded and was gone. As they heard his bootsteps fade down the stairs, Creston returned his attention to Randa.

"I was told that my wife did not kill de Bulverton," he said. "Is this true?"

"It is."

"Then who did?"

Randa's eyes were full of tears. "I did," she said. "He was going to kill her. I… I had to do something. I could not stand by and watch him harm her. Not again."

Creston knew what she meant. "You mean the starvation?" he said. "Forcing her to conceal her pregnancy from me?"

Randa nodded, wiping the tears that were now falling. "I could do nothing," she said. "We were at his mercy. My husband is no longer alive, so I had no choice but to obey my father. Lia… She is angry about it, and rightfully so. She was so brave to stand against him today, my lord. You would have been proud of her. But when she fell down the stairs, I found my courage, too. I could not let him hurt her any more than he had."

Creston didn't know if he felt better or worse with that knowledge. "Did he push her?"

Randa shook her head. "Nay," she said. "It was dark and she did not see the stairs as she ran from him. She simply fell."

The whole thing seemed like such a senseless tragedy. Creston grunted in understanding, knowing it was just an accident, as he'd been told. But there was one thing on his mind, something he needed to have clarified.

"Please tell me that what she did was not part of this plot against Blackchurch," he said. "Did she intend to betray us, too?"

"Nay," Randa said firmly. "She knew nothing. That's why she came—to stop him. My lord, I heard what she said to my father. She said that she has a wonderful life at Blackchurch and she loves the people there. She loves you. It seems that you have given her a joyful life, and as her mother, I am very grateful. She wanted to protect that life, and that is why she stood against my father as she did."

That was good enough for Creston. He thanked Randa silently and went back to the chair, sitting down beside Ophelia and trying not to break down. The physic and the woman with him, possibly his wife or a midwife, were lifting the covers up to check on the progress of the labor, and when Fox and Cruz saw this, they went outside and shut the door. That left Creston with Ophelia, holding her hand, while the physic and his wife went to work down below.

But Creston wouldn't look.

He couldn't.

Everything was in God's hands now.

∽

OPHELIA GRADUALLY BECAME aware of the sound of a fire snapping softly in the hearth.

She could smell smoke from the fire and it made her want to cough. She did, a little, but it hurt to move her chest, so she stopped. Struggling to open her eyes, she could see that it was dark in the room. The flames in the hearth created patterns dancing on the walls and she turned her head slightly, trying to orient herself. She had no idea where she was, or why she was lying in bed, but when she tried to move, a big hand stopped her.

"Easy, sweetheart," Creston said. "Are you awake? Can you hear me?"

She grunted softly. "I hear you," she said, though she'd closed her eyes again because the very act of speaking seemed to hurt her chest again. "Creston?"

"Aye, love, I'm here," he murmured. "How do you feel?"

Ophelia didn't answer right away. She was still trying to figure out what had happened. "I do not know," she said, but then she moved her body slightly and darts of pain shot up her torso. "God's Bones. Everything seems to hurt."

Creston was standing over her, his hand gently holding hers. "The physic says you broke some ribs in the fall," he said. "That's what you're feeling."

"Fall?" she said, puzzled. She rolled her head to the right and opened her eyes to look at him. "What fall?"

"Do you know where you are?"

She looked around, but she didn't move her head. She didn't recognize the room right away. "I am not certain," she said. "Where am I?"

"Axen Castle."

It took a moment for that information to sink in, but when it did, her eyes opened wide and she gasped. "My grandfather!" she said. "Where is he?"

Creston was standing by her right side, putting an arm across her torso to prevent her from moving around too much. "You needn't worry about him," he said. "He cannot hurt you anymore."

"But—!"

"Trust me," Creston insisted softly. "You do not need to worry about him any longer."

She was still frightened, but he could see from her expression that she was trying to trust him. "Where is he?" she asked.

"Gone," he said. "Lia, I know why you came here. Your mother says you were very brave."

Ophelia didn't even know why she'd come. It took her a moment before her memory started returning. The ride south, the inn where she was robbed, the confrontation with her grandfather. All of it came flooding back. But as she became more lucid, she also remembered that she had fled Blackchurch without a word to her husband. She'd run off and hadn't told him where she was going.

Surely the man must be angry with her for it.

"Creston, I know you must be furious with me, and I am very sorry to have caused you any distress, but I am the reason Blackchurch is in danger," she said, hoping to explain herself before he berated her. "I brought that trouble with me when we married, and I had to speak to my grandfather and tell him—"

Creston silenced her by bending over and kissing her, very tenderly. "I know," he murmured against her mouth. "I told you that I know why you came and I am not angry with you.

You thought you could save us."

"I did," she said, tears coming to her eyes. "I needed to save you because… because you saved me. In more ways than you will ever know, you and Blackchurch saved me. I had to return the favor."

He kissed her again, wiping the tears that were beginning to fall from her face. "Nothing your grandfather did was your fault," he whispered. "He made his own choices. You had nothing to do with it."

Ophelia's lower lip was trembling, her eyes closed as he continued to sweetly wipe away her tears. "I am sorry for what he's done," she sobbed. "I wanted to stop him. I tried to."

"That is a very courageous thing to do."

"Are you certain you are not angry with me?"

"Of course not," he said. "But please, in the future, do not leave me again. I think I've aged twenty years in the past day or so, worrying over you."

He was smiling as he said it, jesting lightly with her, but she was too emotional to play along. "For that, I am deeply sorry," she said. "I truly am."

He kissed her forehead. "Not to worry," he said. "I will survive. But can you tell me what happened with de Bulverton? Your mother has told me a little, but I would like to hear it from you."

She strained to think about it. "I came to talk to my grandfather, but we argued," she said. "He would not acknowledge what he'd done at first, but the more I pressed him, the more we argued. I remember running from him because he was angry and trying to capture me. But… I do not remember what happened after that. Did he beat me?"

"Nay," Creston said, trying to be very gentle with her. "He

did not beat you. You fell down a flight of stairs and your mother, fearing for your life, killed your grandfather before he could harm you further."

Ophelia gasped in shock. "My *mother* killed him?"

Creston nodded. "Aye," he said. "When I said he was gone, I meant it. You needn't worry about him any longer. None of us will."

Ophelia still wasn't quite over the surprise of her mother having killed for her. "How astonishing," she said. "My mother truly did that for me?"

"She did. She said she could not allow him to hurt you more than he had already."

That statement made Ophelia see her mother in an entirely new light. Though they'd never been close, perhaps her mother cared for her more than she realized. It was heartening.

She was starting to feel a little better about the entire situation.

"That was brave of her," she said. "I am grateful."

"As am I."

"Will I be able to return to Blackchurch soon?" she said. "When I am well?"

He nodded. "When you are well, but you must heal first."

"And the babe? He is well?"

Creston's composure took a hit. He'd known she was going to ask, but he found that he was hardly ready to answer her. Still, he had to.

He took a deep breath.

"He is now an angel to watch over us," he said, a lump in his throat. "He did not survive the fall. He was born sleeping, but I held him so he would not be alone. I have been holding him ever since. I only just put him down when you began to stir."

Ophelia's face crumpled and more tears came. "My God," she sobbed. "My babe is dead?"

Tears came to Creston's eyes, too. He was trying so hard to be brave for her, but the grief was too much. "He is," he murmured soothingly, putting his arms around her as best he could without hurting her. "I know, my love. I know it hurts."

Ophelia cried openly, feeling a pain that a mother hoped she would never feel. "I killed him," she wept. "When I fell, I killed him!"

"Nay, sweetheart, you did not," Creston insisted. "It was an accident. You could not help your fall. It was simply an accident. But he suffered no pain, I promise. And he has only known love since his birth. Even if his spirit is gone, his body has only known comfort. I made sure of it."

Ophelia had her hand over her face, weeping painfully for her dead child. "It was a boy?"

"It was."

"Did you name him?"

Creston blinked and tears streamed down his cheeks. "Not without consulting you," he said. "I did not wish to name him something if you already had a name in mind."

Ophelia's hand came away from her face and she gazed up at him, her eyes overflowing. "Please," she begged. "Let me hold him, please. I want to see him."

Creston had known she was going to ask that at some point. Truthfully, he and Ming Tang and the physic had inspected the child after it was born, and it was obvious from the start what had killed the child. Somehow, when Ophelia fell, she must have fallen directly on her belly, because the infant's head was crushed. The bones of the skull were very soft for infants at birth, in any case, and the child's head simply couldn't withstand the pressure of a falling body.

Death had been instantaneous.

Ming Tang had tightly bound the infant's skull and then swaddled him so that when Ophelia looked at her son, she would not be distressed by his injuries. It had been such a kind thing to do. With a sigh, Creston stood up and went over to a nearby table where the infant was lying in a basket. Gently, he scooped up the baby and brought him over to meet his mother. Very carefully, he helped Ophelia sit up a little so she could take the baby from him. Settled into his mother's arms, the child looked as if he were simply sleeping.

"Oh… Creston," she murmured, looking at that little face. "He is perfect. So perfect."

Creston never knew he could feel such sorrow as he did when he watched Ophelia view their son for the first time. "He is," he said. "He is quite beautiful, like his mother."

Somehow, Ophelia had forgotten her tears as she inspected the pale little face. He looked so peaceful, so it was both easier and more painful to accept the death. Creston had already had time to come to terms with it, but Ophelia hadn't. She touched the little face, tracing her finger over the eyebrows, lovingly touching his lashes, and Creston lost his poise. He had his arms around her, but he had to turn his head away so she wouldn't see the tears that were streaming down his face. Ophelia was so caught up in the vision of her son that she didn't even notice.

All she could see before her was that life that had grown inside of her.

"How long ago was he born?" she asked.

Creston took a deep breath, composing himself. "About six hours ago."

"I did not even feel a thing."

"You were unconscious," he said. "But your body knew what to do."

She fell silent, but just for a moment. "I wish I remembered," she said. "Even if he did not draw breath when he was born, I would have liked to have seen his birth. We've spent every day for the past eight months together, he and I. Mayhap if I had been awake, his spirit would still be lingering and I could tell him how much I loved him. From the moment I knew he was growing in my belly, I loved him. I never felt any differently."

Creston kissed her shoulder, getting his tears on the garment she was wearing. "He knew," he said softly. "You are his mother. He knew he was loved. Would you like to bring him back to Blackchurch for burial? We can bury him at the church where we were married."

Ophelia looked at him then. "You are the Earl of Sidbury now," she said. "Would you not like to bury him here, at Axen? It is your property now that my grandfather is gone."

That fact hadn't occurred to Creston until that very moment. To hear it at this tender moment felt rather jarring. He realized that he didn't want to think about it, or talk about it. There were too many other important things to deal with, not an earldom he felt no connection to.

He was only concerned with his wife and child at the moment.

"We can discuss that later," he said. "It is not relevant to our situation at the moment. Since we do not intend to live here, at least not at the moment, mayhap you would consider burying the baby where we were married. We can visit him often there."

Ophelia nodded, gazing down at the child's face once more. "I would like that," she said. "He needs to have his parents close by."

"I agree."

"You asked me if I had a name for him. I do, but I need your approval."

"You do not need my approval, but what is it?"

"Quinton."

Creston couldn't help it. He drew in a sharp breath and looked at her. "After my father?"

"Does that displease you?"

Tears stung his eyes again. "Nay, of course not," he said. "You… you truly want to name him after my father?"

"Unless you wish to save the name for a living son."

He put a big hand on the top of the infant's head in a tender gesture. "I can think of no greater honor for my father than for our firstborn to carry his name," he said. "Thank you, my love. That is very considerate of you."

She watched his face as he looked at the baby and her mood changed into something timid, yet hopeful. There was so much emotion going on in that room that it was difficult for her to put it into words.

"You know that I came here to confront my grandfather because I thought… I hoped… that I could make a difference," she said, meeting his eyes when he looked up at her. "I wanted to do this because you have made such a difference in my own life, Creston. I do not think you understand just how much of a difference. Before I met you, I was searching for… something. I do not even know what it is, but I was searching so hard that I tried to force poor Cecil to provide it. I did not even stop to realize that he couldn't. It was not his fault what happened, you know. I was blinded in my quest to find something I could be part of, someone I could love, a belonging I needed deep in my heart. I found that—all of that—at a training guild for warriors.

Who knew that was where I would discover the true meaning of joy?"

He smiled. "And who knew I needed you as much as you needed me?"

She met his smile as her tears for her son were forgotten for the moment. "Do you realize how truly fortunate we are?" she said. "So many people speak of love and romance, and there are stories from ages past about great lovers and how they could never be separated. We have that sort of love that people dream of, and I had to protect it at all costs. Even at the risk of a great tragedy."

She meant the child. They both turned to look at the infant with his perfect lips and perfect nose. Creston kissed the child on the forehead before kissing Ophelia on the lips.

"Sometimes happiness does not come without risk," he said. "In our case, you met the danger, at great cost. But your bravery will not be forgotten, nor will Quinton's death be in vain. I promise you that he will continue to be part of our lives, for as long as we live."

"Do you really think so?"

"I do," he said, nodding. "It was because of Quinton that you and I shared our first true test of trust. Remember? You told me of your grandfather's plan and were willing to sacrifice your future just to save me. And just now, you did it again. You were willing to sacrifice yourself to save me and all of Blackchurch. They call me The Avenger because of my dedication to justice in all things, but I think you deserve that name more than I do. I have never met a braver woman in my life and I am incredibly fortunate to call you my wife. You and I, my love, are meant to be."

She smiled at him, adoringly, and he kissed her sweetly. It

was a kiss of love, of trust, and of the beauty of two lives that were so connected that the bond could never be broken. It was also a kiss of appreciation in a situation that had come to a conclusion. Perhaps not one Creston had hoped for, but at least he still had Ophelia. As long as he had her, he was a content men.

If I cannot be close to her, then I will settle for the ghost of her.

He'd once told Cruz that when it came to being with his wife, in this life or in the next, he would take any form of her that he could get. He would love her ghost, love her spirit, love her heart, living or dead. Perhaps they had only been married a short time, but one didn't need a lifetime to know that what they had was special. A relationship that bled into the realm of legend.

For The Avenger and his protector, what they shared would always be powerful.

Legends always are.

EPILOGUE

The Blackchurch Guild
Year of Our Lord 1234

"TOMORROW, WE'LL START the interrogation instruction, so be prepared," Creston was saying. "In order to be prepared for any capture, a warrior must be prepared for the interrogation, and that is never pleasant, so be advised."

It was nearing sunset on what had been a particularly strenuous day. It had been raining, so it was quite muddy, but the sun was starting to peek out from behind the clouds. It glistened off Lake Cocytus, giving the land a rather fresh appeal. But Creston and his assistant, a recent Blackchurch graduate by the name of Tobin du Reims, were trying to stress the intense module that their recruits were about to face. Since Creston's classes were usually at the end of a recruit's five-year cycle through Blackchurch because they could be so brutal, the men—and three women—that they faced seemed ready for what was to come. They'd already proven themselves through the instruction of Tay, Sinclair, Fox, Kristian, Cruz, and Payne, so now they were facing the last of it. They were a tough lot.

But tougher times were to come.

"If there aren't any questions, I suggest you eat and sleep well tonight," Creston continued, looking over the hardened faces around him. "Tomorrow, you descend into hell."

"My lord?" a man from the back spoke up. He was from Athens, a big recruit who had scars all over his body. "Can you tell us what sort of interrogation instruction we will be starting with?"

Creston folded his big arms across his chest. "A fair question," he said. "For the next week, we will be discussing the historical aspects of interrogation and give examples. The Dragon will be part of this discussion, as he has experience in things we do not normally see in the Christian world. But after that, each man and woman here will have to face the practical application of interrogation methods."

"I've heard that you tear off toenails," someone else said. "Is that true, my lord?"

Creston nodded without hesitation. "This will be explained to you tomorrow, but since you have asked, I will go ahead and tell you the truth," he said. "You will be tested with pain. If you break, the pain will be doubled. Meaning if I am tearing off a toenail and you confess the information you have been told not to tell me simply to make the pain stop, I will break a toe. You will be expected to function after that. I will proceed to tear off each toenail and go to work on your fingernails until you can resist the pain and not divulge the information you have been told not to divulge. This is necessary to teach you pain resistance. Your training at Blackchurch until this moment has been a simple thing. Now, the real training begins. Are there any more questions?"

After that, no one had anything more to say, but the recruits were looking at each other anxiously. Seeing that he had the group properly terrified, Creston had Tobin dismissed them. They ran away as if their arses were on fire, leaving Creston and Tobin chuckling.

"How many do you think will return tomorrow?" Tobin asked.

Creston shrugged. "I have been doing this almost twenty-five years," he said. "It is different with every group. Sometimes they all return, sometimes only a few. We shall see tomorrow."

Tobin was still smiling. "I do believe you gave that same speech when I was part of your class," he said. "Fortunately, I only sustained one lost toenail. I held out."

"You did," Creston said. "But, as I recall, you nearly chewed a hole in your tongue."

"True."

"I've had more than one recruit bite half their tongues off."

Tobin grimaced. "Charming," he said with distaste. "Yet you are still here, still torturing recruits."

Creston snorted. "Still here," he said. "I would not miss it."

Tobin hesitated. "My lord, may I ask you a question?"

"Of course."

"You are the Earl of Sidbury," he said. "Why do you not simply retreat to your properties and live as a lord of the realm? Why remain here and teach?"

Creston lifted his eyebrows, a thoughtful gesture. "I only train part time as it is," he said. "Anteaus handles my class sometimes, so I do spend about half my time at Axen."

"Why not all the time?"

Creston smiled faintly. "Because I believe what I do here is important," he said. "I've seen hundreds of men and women come through this guild, and I am proud to say that I had a small hand in training them to be better warriors. It is important to me. Besides—I can bring my sons with me, and they train alongside the very best in the world."

He was referring to his older boys—Garston, Keaton, and Preston. They went everywhere with him, including Black-church when he returned periodically to finish training a class that Anteaus had started. His eldest, Garston—or Gar, as he was called—had seen eight summers, and a brighter, more deter-mined boy had never been born. Creston was wildly proud of the child, who spent most of his time at Blackchurch with St. Denis and St. Sebastian, as the two were essentially his teachers and acted as mentors to the children of their trainers. Even when Creston returned to Axen, Gar would stay behind at Blackchurch. Keaton and Preston, six years and five years, respectively, were still a little too young to be away from their mother, but even they spent all of their time at Blackchurch with St. Denis, the great instructor.

But that was St. Denis' calling these days.

Once the Blackchurch instructors started having children, St. Denis had transitioned to becoming more of a tutor and less of a guild administrator. That role fell to St. Sebastian. But two years ago, St. Denis had suffered an attack of apoplexy that left the right side of his body slightly damaged, so he was slowing a little in his old age. He had an entire gang of boys and girls that he tutored, all of them very attached to him, and he relished his role at Blackchurch these days.

Life, for him, continued on.

And it continued on for Creston de Royans, the Earl of Sidbury.

Before Tobin could reply to Creston's statement, Creston caught sight of an approaching soldier, heading in from the south. Tobin saw that Creston was distracted, so he began to collect the pieces of vellum that had been passed around to the recruits, drawings that depicted some of the methods of interrogation and torture that Creston had been speaking of. Some of the recruits couldn't read, so diagrams were the best when explaining certain things. As he cleaned up the area, the soldier approached Creston.

"My lord," he said, "there is a knight at the gate who is asking to see you. His name is Theo de Betheny."

Creston's brow furrowed. "I do not know that name," he said. "Who does he serve?"

"He did not say, my lord."

"Did he say what his business is with me?"

The soldier shook his head. "Nay, my lord," he said. "He told me to tell you 'Mary.' He said you would understand."

That didn't clear things up for Creston at all. "Mary?" he repeated. "That's odd. As in Saint Mary?"

"I do not know, my lord," the soldier said. "Shall I send him away?"

Creston shook his head. "Nay," he said. "Keep him at the gatehouse. I will be there shortly. And make sure he is unarmed."

"Aye, my lord."

With that, the soldier headed back the way he had come and Creston moved in the direction of the village. Ophelia was at their cottage with the younger children and he wanted to see her before heading to the gatehouse. Even after ten years of marriage, he still missed her when he wasn't with her. He looked forward to the conclusion of his classes so that he could be with his wife again. She fed his heart, his soul, and everything about him, like food to a starving man. Therefore, he would drop in to inform her he had business at the gatehouse before returning for supper.

Thankfully, her cooking had gotten better and he actually didn't mind returning for it.

As he entered the village, he could already hear the voice of his four-year-old daughter, Violet. She was crying about something, which was a regular occurrence with her. His only daughter, his sweetheart, was very sensitive. He could also hear the voice of his two-year-old son, Shepton, and he suspected, correctly, that the two of them were fighting. They usually were. As he entered the cottage, the pair sat on the floor of the main chamber, a toy of some kind being pulled between them.

"Vi?" Creston said as he went to the tussling duo. "Shep? What is amiss? What are you fighting over?"

"The wooden horse." An exhausted voice came from the kitchen area. "That is Vi's horse, but Shep wants it and they fight over it constantly. Honestly, Cres, the way that lad claims everything in this house as his. He is a tyrant."

Creston grinned as he pulled the horse out of Shepton's grip and picked the lad up. "He takes what he wants," he said proudly, wiping the tears from Shepton's face. "There is nothing wrong with that. It shows initiative."

Ophelia stuck her head out of the kitchen. "It shows that he is spoiled," she said, frowning. "You must not indulge him like that. It ruins all of my hard work."

Creston laughed softly as he made his way over to his wife, kissing her sweetly. "Shepton is my conqueror," he said. "He will go on to do great and powerful things."

"He will go on to be a dictator."

Creston poked the boy in his rounded belly, turning his tears to laughter. "Is that what you are going to be?" he asked, teasing him. "A dictator?"

Shepton squealed with delight as his father tickled him. But he eventually wanted to be set on his feet, so Creston put down the boy, who then promptly ran back to his sister and stole her wooden horse.

The fighting started all over again.

"Apologies," Creston said, giving his wife a remorseful look. "Do you want me to break it up?"

Ophelia shook her head wearily. "Nay," she said. "They will eventually give up and move on. But this is constant, Cres. I do not know how I am going to have the time to deal with them once this child is born."

She put her hand on her rather large belly and Creston put his hand over hers, pulling her against him and kissing her somewhat passionately. There was always passion between them—even more so when she was pregnant, because he found nothing more arousing than a woman pregnant with his child.

"Mayhap this babe will be an easy one," he murmured against her mouth, her cheek. "One can always hope."

Ophelia gave in to his warmth, his power. The man she could not live without. "Mayhap," she whispered. "But I was thinking that I should find a nurse to help me. I've done it all on my own with five children, but with one more, I could use the help."

He kissed her cheek one last time and looked at her. "If that is your wish, then we shall find one," he said. "But you will be losing Gar soon. He will be fostering here year-round, so that is one fewer child to manage."

She nodded, turning back to the food she was preparing. "I do not know what Keaton and Preston will do without him," she said. "They want to do what Gar does, all of the time. They will be lost without him."

"True."

Violet suddenly screamed, loudly, and Creston turned for the common room to see what was amiss. Once more, Shepton had the horse and was running around as she chased him. Then she tripped and began to wail.

Creston just shook his head.

"And this has been going on all day?" he asked incredulously.

"Aye," Ophelia said. "For Christ's sake, have another wooden horse made for Shep so we can have some peace around here."

Creston chuckled, but nodded. He went to pick Violet up, comforting her over her beastly little brother. As he cuddled her and soothed her, Ophelia called out from the kitchen.

"Will you help them wash their hands?" she asked. "Supper will be soon."

That comment reminded him about his gatehouse visitor. "I will when I return," he said. "I have business at the gatehouse. I'll return shortly."

"Be quick about it," Ophelia said. "Everything is ready."

He kissed Violet on the cheek and set her to her feet, swiftly heading out of the cottage. He could hear the yelling starting up again and almost turned back, but thought better of it. He'd only be a few minutes, just to see what this visitor wanted of him.

As he was a member of the Septum Port Alliance, it could be anything.

Business for the Earl of Sidbury took many forms. It wasn't just that he was a trainer at Blackchurch. As the leader of the Septum Port Alliance, the hereditary seat for the Earl of Sidbury as a founding member, he'd had to catch up very quickly on port business those years ago. Fortunately, he'd taken to it easily, but it was one of the most difficult group of responsibilities he'd ever encountered, not the least of which had to do with the pirates who liked to ravage the ports.

That was where it became interesting.

Because of his connections to Blackchurch, Triton's Hellions and the Demons of the Sea now gave a wide berth to all of the ports connected with the alliance, but in order to do so, they were paid an annual tribute. All of the port lords had readily agreed to that simply to avoid the raids and destruction that could be so costly. Medusa's Disciples was another group that avoided Sidmouth, but they had been known to harass some of the others.

The biggest problem was a group known as Kraken's Horde, an Irish faction, whom none of the port lords had had any luck in formalizing an agreement with. Creston had been trying for about ten years, but so far, there had been no progress. As a result, he'd doubled the army at Axen Castle and built two stone garrisons down by the beach to ward off any raids.

But he had a secret weapon.

Given that Sidmouth was a port city, it saw its share of ships from all over the known world. About five years ago, he'd been given the opportunity to purchase something called a "sleeve"— it was an iron tube, essentially, that could be mounted to a wall. Using a rare powder from the east called serpentine, or fire medicine, one could ignite the powder and fire a projectile, usually a smooth iron ball, straight into a ship and damage it. Even though it was terribly unpredictable in its accuracy, the truth was that if it hit its mark, it could be very destructive. Creston was the only one in all of England who had such a thing, so ever since he acquired it, any pirate faction had avoided Sidmouth like the plague.

Creston was proud of himself for it.

Naturally, men had been trying to replicate the sleeve or buy it from him ever since. That had him wondering if the visitor in the gatehouse was yet another man attempting to buy what he had, perhaps a knight sent from a rich lord, wanting to know what his price was. The truth was that he had no price and, already, Kristian's cogs on Lake Cocytus carried four sleeves that had been made by Blackchurch smithies. Blackchurch had what so many others wanted, and if it weren't so difficult to make what the serpentine required, they might even have more.

Such was progress in the military world.

Creston's mind was on his valuable sleeve as he entered the gatehouse. The commander in charge pointed him to the guard room, and he entered the large, somewhat comfortable room built into the gatehouse itself. There were a couple of guards there, and a big knight standing near the hearth. The guards pointed to the knight before vacating the area, and Creston approached the man.

"I am de Royans," he said. "You wish to see me?"

The man turned to him. He was young, slightly taller than Creston, with long blond hair and blue eyes. When their gazes met, the knight just stared at him for a moment before breaking down into a weak smile.

"I do," he said. "My name is Theo de Betheny. You would not recognize that name, I do not think, but I serve the Comte d'Anjou."

Creston nodded in understanding. "Louis' youngest son," he said. "You serve in France?"

"I was raised there, my lord."

"Charles is still quite young, as I recall."

De Betheny nodded. "He is, my lord," he said. "He has seen seven years."

Creston grunted. "I have a seven-year-old son," he said. "I cannot imagine a boy that age having such a great responsibility, even with regents."

De Betheny agreed with him. "Much is expected of royal children, I suppose," he said. "My role is in commanding the comte's household. I am in command of his military force and bodyguards. Though it is small, it is important."

Creston couldn't help but feel as if he'd met this young knight before. There was something familiar about him. "I see," he said. "And what, may I ask, have you come to speak with me about? Does this have to do with Sidmouth?"

The knight shook his head. "Nay, my lord."

"Then what is your business?"

"I've not come on business," de Betheny said. "I've come on an errand of a rather personal nature. I told the gate guard why, but I do not suppose you recognize the name?"

"What name?"

"Mary."

"Who is Mary?"

"My mother."

Creston wasn't making the connection at that point. He was about to ask the knight's business yet again when a light went on in his mind. Mary. Of course, he'd known that name from long ago. Very long ago. So long ago he'd buried that memory.

Suddenly, the memory wasn't so buried.

"Mary," he repeated softly. "*Mary…*"

As he looked at the knight, he began to realize why he

looked so familiar. His breathing quickened as memories of lovely Mary from his youth came tumbling down on him—all of the pain and longing that he'd ever felt, the fear, the concern for the child she carried that he would never see.

Realization swept over him like a wave.

Now he knew why the knight had come to see him.

"She was sent away when her father discovered our plans to be married," he finally said. "I am assuming that is the Mary you are referring to."

The knight nodded slowly. "It is, my lord," he said quietly. "Mary St. Albans."

Creston felt as if he'd been physically struck. It was confirmation of his suspicions, something he was wholly unprepared for. He didn't know what to say. He didn't know what the knight expected from him, but as he looked at that tall young man, all he could feel was surprise and gratitude. Great gratitude that his son had been born and was now a man with responsibility in the French court. God, what a prideful thing that was to hear.

His son had survived.

He had also thrived.

Slowly, Creston lowered himself down into the nearest chair.

"If you've come to berate me for not marrying your mother, then you should know that I very much wanted to," he said. "I knew she carried you and I was desperate to marry her. Your grandfather, however, had other plans. After Mary was sent away, I tried to locate her, but I was met with walls at every turn. Someone finally had the decency to tell me that she had married a French lord, so I stopped looking. After that, there was no point. But I will say that her loss drove me out of the

English royal court. Blackchurch found me around that time and I have been here ever since."

Theo found another chair, sitting across from Creston and simply staring at the man. "My mother told me about my origins," he said. "She did not tell me until I came of age and she would not tell me your name at first. She would only say that I was conceived in love with a man who was not her husband, before she ever met my father. And I do call Raul de Betheny my father, because he was. He was a good man."

"I'm glad," Creston said sincerely. "I truly am. You cannot know how I have worried about you, hoping your mother married a man who would accept you. She was in such a difficult position. I prayed that her husband was good to her."

"He was," Theo assured him. "He was good to us both. He was an older man, with daughters, and when I was born, he was overjoyed—and I do mean overjoyed. They never had any more children, so when my father died years ago, I inherited everything. I was his heir, his son, and he was very proud of that."

It did Creston's heart good to hear that news, more than he thought it would. A man in need of a son had found a boy in need of a father. Tears stung his eyes as he smiled at the young knight.

"Thank God," he said hoarsely. "I am so glad to hear that. You cannot know how that eases my heart."

Theo nodded faintly, still studying Creston's face as if he'd never seen another face in his entire life. His curiosity, his scrutiny, was overwhelming.

"I have had a good life," he said. "I just wanted you to know. And… well, I suppose I just wanted to meet you. Now I see where I get my handsome looks."

Creston burst into soft laughter, though there were still tears in his eyes. "I was thinking how much you look like my father," he said. "The resemblance is uncanny."

"And you have other children now? Other sons?"

Creston nodded. "I married my wife about ten years after the debacle with your mother," he said. "We have six young children, though one of them, the eldest, was stillborn. I still include him when I speak of my children because he existed. He is important to us, still."

Theo's eyes glimmered with some warmth. "That is generous," he said. "You are compassionate."

"I love my family."

Theo's smile grew. "You are happy?"

"Never happier," he said. "And you?"

Theo nodded. "Verily," he said. "In fact, there is a young lady I am fond of. I am hoping for a betrothal, though negotiations have been difficult. I have no parents any longer, so it is just me, and I believe her father thinks I am too young."

Creston grinned. "You are *not* too young," he said. "Besides, you have de Royans blood. That means you were a man when you were born. If it would help, I will write to this man and tell him so."

Theo chuckled. "Hopefully, that will not be necessary," he said. "I hope to convince him on my own."

Creston didn't want to overstep his bounds, but it seemed to him that Theo might be lonely, given both his parents were gone. If he were an only child, other than older sisters, it might be a difficult time for him. It might be why he'd come to England, seeking his biological father. Truthfully, Creston couldn't get a good feel off the knight as to why he'd actually come. Perhaps it was nothing more than curiosity.

He wanted to know.

"May I ask you a question, Theo?"

"Please."

"Why *did* you come to see me? Is it more than simply meeting me?"

Theo didn't seem to have a quick answer for that. He shook his head and shrugged, looking at his feet as he tried to come up with an answer.

"I am not sure," he said. "As I said, I did want to meet you, but I loved my parents. They were good to me, so I am not looking for another father or mother, but I suppose every man has a right to know where he came from. *Who* he came from. I wanted to see for myself."

"Are you satisfied, then?"

Theo nodded. "I think so," he said. "But now that I am here… would it be too much if I wanted to come to know you a little better? If you do not want me to, I completely understand."

"I would be honored."

That seemed to ease Theo's mind a little. "And your children… I only have older sisters who are long since gone. I've never had any other siblings."

"How would you like me to introduce you to them?"

"What do you mean?"

"What should I call you when I introduce you?" Creston asked. "Brother Theo? Cousin Theo? Theo from France who has randomly come to visit?"

There was a smile on Theo's lips as he considered the questions. "You would let me meet your children?"

"Is there a reason I should not?"

Theo shook his head. Then he sighed and stood up. He took

a few steps, pacing away from Creston, considering his question. In the end, he snorted with soft irony.

"I always thought my father was a warlord from France," he said. "Raul has a lineage that goes back centuries. I was proud of that. But when he was gone, my mother told me that Raul was not my father by blood, that my real father is a knight from England named Creston de Royans. I never intended to seek you out until I met a knight at court who had trained at the Blackchurch Guild and one of his trainers was a knight named Creston de Royans. That is how I found out that you were a Blackchurch trainer. Surely there could not be two Creston de Royans in this world. So I came."

"And here you are," Creston said. "What is it you wish to know? That I am the Earl of Sidbury? That makes you the son of an earl. And our family? Descended from the Northmen who plundered the area of Roian, France, many centuries ago. Family legend says that we are descended from the leader of that raid, a man named Golden Helgarth. He married a local woman and had twenty children, or so the tale goes. You have a very proud lineage, Theo. It is your blood and you are entitled to know your history."

Theo pondered the information, hearing about his true lineage for the first time. "All the way here, I was wondering if I was somehow betraying Raul by coming to meet you," he said. "My father was a generous man. I do not think he would condemn me for it. I hope not."

Creston stood up, facing the young man who seemed perhaps a bit overwhelmed by the conversation. He thought of what to say to him, hoping it would be of some comfort.

"When I married my wife, she was pregnant with another man's child," he said. "It is no secret, so I am not divulging unknown information. When she told me about the child, I immediately thought of Mary, carrying my child, and I prayed she had married someone who would treat my child well. It seemed that I was in a similar situation, preparing to raise the child of another man, and I had nothing but love and acceptance for the child because that is what I wanted for you—love and acceptance."

Theo was listening closely. "Was he the stillborn you mentioned?"

Creston nodded. "He was," he said. "But the point is this—had Quinton grown to manhood and wanted to seek his father by blood, I would have encouraged him to do so. There is a natural desire for a man to know his lineage, and I understand that. I hope his father would have accepted him, and, to be honest, I would not have been threatened by their relationship purely because I am secure in my love for my son. A man can have two fathers and, I believe, he can be richer for it. I would hope that Raul de Betheny would believe the same thing."

Theo thought on that a moment before smiling timidly. "You are very wise," he said. "I miss that about Raul. You remind me of him a little. Truthfully, given that you are a Blackchurch trainer, I rather imagined you to be a barbarian. Christ, was that an insult? I did not mean it the way it sounded."

Creston started laughing. "You were right," he said. "What we teach can sometimes be barbaric. But we are a collection of the most civilized, educated, and experienced men in the world. I hope it does not shame you that I serve here."

Theo shook his head quickly. "Never," he said. "In fact… part of the reason I am here is because I was hoping to explore the possibility of training here. Everyone knows that Blackchurch knights are the most elite warriors in the world. Imagine what I could take back to Charles' court were I to be Blackchurch trained."

Creston shrugged. "If that is something you would like to discuss, I am happy to do so."

"Would you be training me?"

"There are several different trainers and each one teaches certain skills, but to answer your question, I would teach you a certain segment."

"What segment is that?"

"Are you sure you want to know?"

Theo grinned in a gesture that looked very much like his father. "Why?" he said. "Is it terrifying?"

"It can be."

"Then I am looking forward to it."

Creston could only chuckle at an eager young knight with his entire life ahead of him and with the ignorance of saying he was looking forward to Blackchurch training. That told him that Theo probably didn't know much about Blackchurch other than what he'd heard. That being the case, he was in for an eye-opening experience.

"Would you like to discuss it privately?" Creston finally said. "Or would it be too much if you were to come and share supper with my wife and me?"

Theo's smile faded. "Would it be too much of an imposition?"

Creston shook his head. "We'll take it slowly," he said. "Slowly for us all because, for certain, these are unfamiliar waters for us both. But I do not think one supper would be too much. Do you?"

"Nay, my lord."

"Good," Creston said. "Come with me, then. I want you to meet my wife."

"I would be honored, my lord."

He was a polite, mannerly young man. Creston had only known him all of ten minutes, but already, he was proud of him.

That pride only grew in the days and months to come.

Theo de Betheny did, indeed, endure Blackchurch training. For five years, he was at the top of his class, from Tay's brutal introductory course all the way through Ming Tang's final instruction on the power of the mind in battle. All of the Blackchurch trainers knew that he was Creston's bastard son, but no one treated him any differently. He had de Royans blood and, therefore, was family. He also had the natural ability to excel. Once he graduated, they were all sorry to see him go.

Until St. Sebastian offered him a position as an assistant trainer.

And with that, Theo de Betheny became part of Blackchurch just as his father was, and in the years to come, when the core trainers retired one by one, Theo was there to take over Creston's class for good while Creston retreated to Axen Castle, living his best life alongside his wife as the Earl and Countess of Sidbury.

Life, for them, went on.

Creston never did speak with his brother again, knowing he'd been in on the plot to destroy Blackchurch, but the silence between brothers never bothered him because he had his own family, a big family, that would never betray him. It was all he ever needed. In the end, Creston and Ophelia had nine children, all of them accomplished men and women, all of them educated and happy. All of them married and had their own children, and when Creston lay old and gray in his bed, he had fifty-four grandchildren to carry on the de Royans name. Counting Theo and the young lady from France that he eventually married, the grand total was sixty.

And this was for a man who had been forced into an unwanted marriage.

Not strangely, he wasn't sorry about it.

Once, Creston had told his brother that Blackchurch had been his salvation, but he realized as the years went on that he hadn't known the meaning of that word at the time. True salvation came when he married Ophelia, the most remarkable woman he'd ever known, and in the years following their marriage, he'd discovered true deliverance.

Deliverance into a life, and love, that grew into legend.

That's what it was all about.

If I cannot be close to her, then I will settle for the ghost of her.

That was what he'd told Cruz, once. Luckily for Creston, he'd settled for all that and more.

And so had Ophelia.

Their love, and legend, lived on.

C3 THE END 80

Children of Creston and Ophelia (following the family tradition of all male children being given a name that ends in "ton")

Quinton (stillbirth)

Garston

Keaton

Preston

Violet

Dalton

Shepton

Ruby

Aurora

AFTERWORD

I hope you enjoyed Creston and Ophelia's tale. I so love revisiting Blackchurch for these stories. It's turned out to be one of my favorite series.

I wanted to address something that happened mid-tale, and that was the scene where Oscar is inhaling the smoke from a cluster of burning weeds in his hand. Yes, this is cannabis. There is evidence of cannabis, hemp, and opium smoking in France in the thirteenth century, though it doesn't appear to be widespread until about three hundred years later. Still, hemp was available, as was opium, and people learned that it killed pain and gave them a high, so it stands to reason that there were those addicted to the result of smoking it. Oscar happens to be a weed smoker, for lack of a better term, and he would have access to much of those things, given his property involves a port with ships from around the known world.

Also, I managed to work the Executioner Knights into this series and I love it! If you've read *Lion of Hearts* (and any of the other Sons of de Lohr books), then you recognize Myles de Lohr. This book takes place about nine years before his story in *Lion of Hearts*, so this was back when he was a full-on Executioner Knight. Brenton de Royans is the son of Juston de Royans (*Lord of Winter*), the man who was a mentor to Christopher and David de Lohr. Great tie-ins, so if you haven't read these books, they're a must!

Lastly, what is a "sleeve"? A cannon, of course. Cannons were being used in China around this time, and it was the Chinese who invented gunpowder, so given the fact that ships sailing around the known world often came up with these incredible inventions, it was absolutely plausible that Creston should end up with a cannon. It is a little early in the historical timeline for one, but who knows? Given trade routes of the time, anything is possible.

And with that, we conclude *The Avenger*. Until next time…

With affection,

KATHRYN LE VEQUE NOVELS

Medieval Romance:

De Wolfe Pack Series:
Warwolfe
The Wolfe
Nighthawk
ShadowWolfe
DarkWolfe
A Joyous de Wolfe Christmas
BlackWolfe
Serpent
A Wolfe Among Dragons
Scorpion
StormWolfe
Dark Destroyer
The Lion of the North
Walls of Babylon
The Best Is Yet To Be
BattleWolfe
Castle of Bones

De Wolfe Pack Generations:
WolfeHeart
WolfeStrike
WolfeSword
WolfeBlade
WolfeLord
WolfeShield
Nevermore
WolfeAx
WolfeBorn
WolfeBite
WolfeHound

House of de Norville:
The Best Is Yet To Be
Castle of Bones
Nevermore

The Executioner Knights:
By the Unholy Hand
The Mountain Dark
Starless
A Time of End
Winter of Solace
Lord of the Sky
The Splendid Hour
The Whispering Night
Netherworld
Lord of the Shadows
Of Mortal Fury
'Twas the Executioner Knight
Before Christmas
Crimson Shield
The Black Dragon
God of Vengeance

The de Russe Legacy:
The Falls of Erith
Lord of War: Black Angel
The Iron Knight
Beast
The Dark One: Dark Knight
The White Lord of Wellesbourne
Dark Moon
Dark Steel
A de Russe Christmas Miracle

Dark Warrior

The de Lohr Dynasty:
While Angels Slept
Rise of the Defender
Steelheart
Shadowmoor
Silversword
Spectre of the Sword
Unending Love
Archangel
A Blessed de Lohr Christmas

Sons of de Lohr:
Lion of Twilight
Lion of War
Lion of Hearts
Lion of Steel
Lion of Thunder

The Brothers de Lohr:
The Earl in Winter

Lords of East Anglia:
While Angels Slept
Godspeed
Age of Gods and Mortals

Great Lords of le Bec:
Great Protector

House of de Royans:
Lord of Winter
To the Lady Born
The Centurion

Lords of Eire:
Echoes of Ancient Dreams
Lord of Black Castle
The Darkland

Ancient Kings of Anglecynn:
The Whispering Night
Netherworld

Battle Lords of de Velt:
The Dark Lord
Devil's Dominion
Bay of Fear
The Dark Lord's First Christmas
The Dark Spawn
The Dark Conqueror
The Dark Angel

Reign of the House of de Winter:
Lespada
Swords and Shields

De Reyne Domination:
Guardian of Darkness
The Black Storm
A Cold Wynter's Knight
With Dreams
Master of the Dawn
One Wylde Knight

House of d'Vant:
Tender is the Knight (House of
d'Vant)
The Red Fury (House of d'Vant)

The Dragonblade Series:
Fragments of Grace
Dragonblade
Island of Glass
The Savage Curtain
The Fallen One

Great Marcher Lords of de Lara
Lord of the Shadows
Dragonblade

House of St. Hever
Fragments of Grace
Island of Glass
Queen of Lost Stars

Lords of Pembury:
The Savage Curtain

Lords of Thunder: The de Shera Brotherhood Trilogy
The Thunder Lord
The Thunder Warrior
The Thunder Knight

The Great Knights of de Moray:
Shield of Kronos
The Gorgon

The House of De Nerra:
The Promise
The Falls of Erith
Vestiges of Valor
Realm of Angels

Highland Legion:
Highland Born
Highland Destroyer
Highland Slayer

Highland Warriors of Munro:
The Red Lion
Deep Into Darkness

The House of de Garr:
Lord of Light
Realm of Angels

Saxon Lords of Hage:
The Crusader
Kingdom Come

High Warriors of Rohan:
High Warrior
High King

The House of Ashbourne:
Upon a Midnight Dream

The House of D'Aurilliac:
Valiant Chaos

The House of De Dere:
Of Love and Legend

St. John and de Gare Clans:
The Warrior Poet

The House of de Bretagne:
The Questing

The House of Summerlin:
The Legend

The Kingdom of Hendocia:
Kingdom by the Sea

The BlackChurch Guild: Shadow Knights:
The Leviathan
The Protector
The Swordsman
The Tempest
The Avenger

Guard of Six:
Absolution
Insurrection
Obliteration

Regency Historical Romance:
Sin Like Flynn: A Regency Historical Romance Duet
The Sin Commandments
Georgina and the Red Charger

Gothic Regency Romance:
Emma

Historical Fiction:
The Girl Made Of Stars

Contemporary Romance:

Kathlyn Trent/Marcus Burton Series:
Valley of the Shadow
The Eden Factor
Canyon of the Sphinx

The Eagle Brotherhood (under the pen name Kat Le Veque):
The Sunset Hour

The Killing Hour
The Secret Hour
The Unholy Hour
The Burning Hour
The Ancient Hour
The Devil's Hour

Sons of Poseidon:
The Immortal Sea

Pirates of Britannia Series (with Eliza Knight):
Savage of the Sea by Eliza Knight
Leader of Titans by Kathryn Le Veque
The Sea Devil by Eliza Knight
Sea Wolfe by Kathryn Le Veque

Note: All Kathryn's novels are designed to be read as stand-alones, although many have cross-over characters or cross-over family groups. Novels that are grouped together have related characters or family groups. You will notice that some series have the same books; that is because they are cross-overs. A hero in one book may be the secondary character in another.

There is NO reading order except by chronology, but even in that case, you can still read the books as stand-alones. No novel is connected to another by a cliff hanger, and every book has an HEA.

Series are clearly marked. All series contain the same characters or family groups except the American Heroes Series, which is an anthology with unrelated characters.

For more information, find it in **A Reader's Guide to the Medieval World of Le Veque**.

About Kathryn Le Veque

Bringing the Medieval to Romance

KATHRYN LE VEQUE is a critically acclaimed, multiple USA TODAY Bestselling author, an Indie Reader bestseller, a charter Amazon All-Star author, and a #1 bestselling, award-winning, multi-published author in Medieval Historical Romance with over 100 published novels.

Kathryn is a multiple award nominee and winner, including the winner of Uncaged Book Reviews Magazine 2017 and 2018 "Raven Award" for Favorite Medieval Romance. Kathryn is also a multiple RONE nominee (InD'Tale Magazine), holding a record for the number of nominations. In 2018, her novel WARWOLFE was the winner in the Romance category of the Book Excellence Award and in 2019, her novel A WOLFE AMONG DRAGONS won the prestigious RONE award for best pre-16th century romance.

Kathryn is considered one of the top Indie authors in the world with over 2M copies in circulation, and her novels have been translated into several languages. Kathryn recently signed with Sourcebooks Casablanca for a Medieval Fight Club series, first published in 2020.

In addition to her own published works, Kathryn is also the President/CEO of Dragonblade Publishing, a boutique publishing house specializing in Historical Romance. Dragonblade's success has seen it rise in the ranks to become Amazon's #1 e-book publisher of Historical Romance (K-Lytics report July 2020).

Kathryn loves to hear from her readers. Please find Kathryn on Facebook at Kathryn Le Veque, Author, or join her on Twitter @kathrynleveque. Sign up for Kathryn's blog at www.kathrynleveque.com for the latest news and sales.